King's Walk

MOB

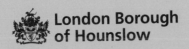

London Borough of Hounslow

Library at Home Service
Community Services
Hounslow Library, CentreSpace
24 Treaty Centre, High Street
Hounslow TW3 1ES

0	1	2	3	4	5	6	7	8	9
	861		9754					3068	
									9689
			3193						

P10-L2061

King's Walk

Jeanne Whitmee

ROBERT HALE · LONDON

© Jeanne Whitmee 2002
First published in Great Britain 2002

ISBN 0 7090 7094 2

Robert Hale Limited
Clerkenwell House
Clerkenwell Green
London EC1R 0HT

2 4 6 8 10 9 7 5 3 1

Typeset in 11/13pt Plantin
by Derek Doyle & Associates, Liverpool.
Printed in Great Britain by
St Edmundsbury Press Ltd, Bury St Edmunds, Suffolk.
Bound by Woolnough Bookbinding Limited.

PROLOGUE

1938

'**G**O ON. I DARE you to!'

'No, Rachel. Let's go.' Cathy pulled at her arm. 'Mrs King is a witch. She might put a spell on us.'

The little group of children stood outside the tall gate that led into the garden of Cedar Lodge. Finding the gate locked, Rachel had been goading thirteen-year-old Peter to climb over the wall and pick some of the rosy apples that dangled just out of reach on the other side.

Rachel laughed. 'Cathy Ladgrove! You don't believe in all that stuff do you?'

Eleven-year-old Cathy blushed. 'She saw me looking through the gate last week and she shouted at me. She's got funny eyes, like bits of coal.'

Peter pushed his unruly ginger hair out of his eyes and wiped his nose on his sleeve. 'Well, I'm not scared of her,' he said bravely. 'I've been over the wall lots of times before. Serves the old cow right if people scrump her apples. She never picks 'em. Just lets 'em go rotten.' He looked at Rachel. 'So – are you gonna give us a leg up then?'

She nodded, grinning gleefully as she began to help him climb the wall. Casting a pitying glance in Cathy's direction she said, 'Don't stand there looking scared. If you don't wanna join in clear off home.'

'I'm not scared,' Cathy protested.

'OK then. If you wanna share the apples go an' keep a look out – see no one's coming.'

Her heart in her mouth, Cathy ran the few yards to the corner and almost collided with a boy coming in the opposite direction. To make matters worse she recognized him as fourteen-year-old John King, the younger of the 'witch's' two sons from Cedar Lodge. She blushed furiously.

'Don't go round there,' she spluttered in her confusion.

'Why not?' He was tall for his age and wore white shorts and an open-necked shirt. He smiled disarmingly at her. 'I'm looking for a ball. We were playing tennis and someone lobbed one over the wall.'

'Oh.' Cathy heard a scuffling noise from round the corner accompanied by smothered giggles. John looked at her.

'What was that? Is someone there?'

'It's only Rachel and Peter,' she told him, still barring his way. 'We were playing and – and . . .'

'Cathy! So there you are!' Cathy's elder sister, Pauline appeared on the other side of the road. She began to cross towards them. 'Mum's been looking for you. Supper's ready. Where've you been?'

'Sorry, I was just coming.' Ever since Cathy could remember her sister had been able to win people over with one of her dazzling blue-eyed smiles. She noticed now that John King had coloured hotly. Clearly he was as susceptible as everyone else to her beauty.

'Has my little sister been up to mischief?' Pauline asked with all the authority of an elder sister.

'No. I was just looking for a ball,' John told her.

'Is this it?' Pauline held out a fluffy white tennis ball. 'I picked it up just now.'

'Thanks.' John took the ball, smiling at her bashfully.

The garden gate opened and a tall fair boy in white flannels and shirt appeared.

'What on earth are you doing? Honestly John, you're too slow to catch a cold! You're holding up the game.' Laurence King's fair hair flopped over his forehead and his handsome face was marred by an irritable scowl, which quickly vanished when he caught sight of Pauline.

'Oh, I see.' His smile was directed at Pauline. 'Who have we here?'

6

'I'm Pauline Ladgrove and this is my sister, Catherine,' Pauline told him haughtily.

'How do you do, Pauline. I'm Laurence King and that horrible child is my brother, John.'

'I know.' Pauline sniffed.

'Do you play tennis?' Laurence asked.

'A little,' she said with studied nonchalance.

'In that case come and play on our court,' Laurence said. 'Come tomorrow after tea if you like.'

'Us too?' Rachel and Peter appeared round the corner, both of them brazenly munching apples. Peter's knees were grazed where he had slid down the wall and Rachel had a streak of grime down one cheek.

Laurence looked somewhat taken aback. 'Do these two belong to you as well?'

'Good heavens no!' Pauline said.

Cathy spoke up for the first time. 'That's Rachel Sands,' she said, pointing. 'And he's Peter Harvey.' She glared a silent warning at them, daring them to cheek the superior being who glowered down at them.

'Where did you get those apples?' Laurence demanded.

'Mind your own business,' Rachel said defiantly through a mouthful of fruit.

'Because if you've been pinching our apples . . .'

Peter started to say something but Rachel kicked his ankle viciously. 'Didn't I just hear you inviting us for tennis?' she asked. 'Do we get tea and chocolate cake an' all?'

'I asked Pauline and her sister, not you,' Laurence said, looking at Peter's crumpled clothes and tousled hair with revulsion. He turned on his heel and began to walk away. 'But maybe it wasn't such a good idea after all.'

John looked embarrassed. 'Take no notice of him,' he said apologetically. 'Come anyway. About half-past five tomorrow. All of you of course,' he added with an apologetic look at Peter and Rachel.

When he'd gone Peter drew another apple out of his pocket and sank his teeth into it noisily. 'Catch me going in there,' he said. 'Stuck-up lot. Think they're everyone, them Kings. My dad says there's gonna be a war. If there is and I get to go an' fight I'm gonna shoot stuck-up twerps like him!'

7

Rachel laughed. 'You're not supposed to shoot English people, stupid! It's the Germans you're supposed to shoot.'

Peter turned away, thrusting his hands in his pockets and kicking at a pebble. 'I know who I'd rather shoot,' he growled.

Pauline sighed impatiently and gave her younger sister a push. 'Come on, Cath. Mum's going to be cross if we let supper get cold.'

Cathy followed Pauline round the corner and crossed the road towards the row of neat semis. 'Are you really going to Cedar Lodge to play tennis tomorrow?' she asked.

Pauline tossed her blonde curls. 'I might,' she said. 'If I feel like it.'

Cathy wished with all her heart that she could be more like her sister. Nothing ever seemed to shake Pauline's confidence. She had passed her school certificate this year and left school. She'd been taking shorthand and typing at night school for almost a year now and next week she was about to start training to be a secretary at Mason and Gregson's the solicitors in the high street. She was all grown-up and could do anything she liked. Cathy sighed. Sometimes it felt as though she would always be a child.

'Was it right, what Peter said?' she asked as they reached the gate of number four. 'Will there really be a war?'

Pauline shrugged. 'Probably.'

'With bombing and shooting and all that?'

Pauline turned to look at her. 'Well they won't be fighting with pillows,' she said scathingly.

'Will it mean Dad will have to go in the army.'

For the first time Pauline hesitated. 'Oh – I shouldn't think so,' she said. 'After all he's thirty-eight.'

'How do you know?'

'I heard Mum tell Mrs Sands the other day. That's really old, isn't it?'

Over supper Pauline complained to their mother about the state of Peter and Rachel.

'Honestly, Mum, you should have seen them,' she said. 'That Peter Harvey was filthy. His trousers were torn and his nose was all runny too. Honestly, I was ashamed to admit that I knew him. And that Rachel Sands. She's so rude.'

Phyllis Ladgrove shook her head as she shared out the shepherd's pie. 'Peter's mother walked out and left him and his father when the boy was only four,' she said. 'You should make allowances for him. I'm sure his poor father does his best.'

'Well, maybe.' Pauline tucked into her shepherd's pie. 'There's no excuse for that Rachel though. She just doesn't care. You'd never think her father was a preacher.'

Phyllis said nothing. *Blood will out* she thought to herself as she took her place at the supper table. Not many people knew that the Sandses' daughter was adopted; born to a single girl who had got herself 'into trouble'. She herself had been told in confidence and she wouldn't dream of letting the cat out of the bag. Goodness only knew what badness there might be in the child's background. No one knew for sure who her real father was. If the Lord had intended the Sandses to have children he'd have given them one of their own. You'd have thought they'd have realized that, what with him being a preacher.

Cathy was silent as she picked at her food. She hoped Pauline wouldn't insist on taking her along to Cedar Lodge to play tennis tomorrow afternoon. John was nice enough but she was terrified of Mrs King. And the big boy, Laurence, was almost as bad with his cutting remarks and insolent stare.

She glanced across at her father sitting opposite, quietly eating his supper, and felt the familiar rush of love for the big, gentle man. Would that man Hitler in Germany really start a war? Was Dad really too old to fight? When she asked questions like this the grown-ups just laughed at her. They thought she didn't understand, but there were pictures in books in the library and at school. Pictures of death and destruction from the last war that made her shudder.

Please God, don't let it happen, she prayed quietly, her fingers crossed under the tablecloth.

CHAPTER ONE

1946

THE JOURNEY HAD BEEN long and tiring. Finding her way from Euston to Waterloo to change trains was something Cathy had been dreading and the reality had been worse than anticipated. Even though Pauline had given her instructions she had found the Underground bewildering. There were so many people rushing about and they all seemed to know exactly where they were going; no one had time to stop and give her directions; she daren't even ask. By the time she had puzzled out the map Pauline had given her and found her way to Waterloo she had missed her connection and been forced to wait half an hour for the next one.

When she had heard that the job she had applied for as waitress at the Marine Bay Hotel, Bournemouth, was hers, she had been both excited and apprehensive. Her mother had been uneasy at the notion of her going so far away from home.

'You're only eighteen, Cath, and you've never been further than Skegness,' she said. 'And that was only for the day!'

Her sister Pauline laughed. 'Mum! This is 1946. Girls of Cathy's age joined up in the war – went all over the world. She's only going to Bournemouth. And she'll be living in at the hotel.'

But Phyllis Ladgrove was not convinced. 'Girls who joined the services weren't wandering round on their own. Anyway,' she added with a disapproving sniff. 'Heaven knows what some of *them* got up to. And she's going to have to *cross London* too!'

Pauline laughed at her mother's scandalized expression.

'Well, I don't suppose the white slavers will exactly be waiting to throw a bag over her head the minute she gets off the train,' she teased.

'And working as a waitress,' Phyllis fretted. 'That's no better than going into service! After passing the scholarship to the grammar school I thought my girls would have a better start in life.'

'I'll be fine, Mum,' Cathy had said with a conviction she didn't feel.

Now here she was with only half an hour to go before she reached Bournemouth and the daunting prospect of her new life. As she watched the Hampshire countryside begin to give way to suburbs her stomach began to churn. She would have given anything to be back at home in the shop, serving Woodbines and evening papers. Better still, she longed to go back ten years to when they were all children, playing without a care in the rambling back garden of number four King's Walk before the cataclysmic war years that had changed everything.

When the war ended in 1945 the weary people of the British Isles heaved a collective sigh of relief. In King's Walk, as in other streets all over the country, the residents had set about the task of picking up the threads of their disrupted lives and facing the future. Cathy's father had returned from the Japanese prisoner-of-war camp a mere shadow of the man his wife and daughters had known. He'd tried to return to the job that had been reserved for him in Sweetings, the men's outfitters in the high street, but the constant nightmares that reduced him to a trembling wreck and the recurring attacks of malaria meant that he was hardly ever fit for work, and three months after his return he was asked for his resignation.

The loss of Robert's job threw the Ladgrove family into crisis. Eventually they had decided to buy the newsagent's shop on the corner, using Robert's war gratuity as a down payment. Tobacco shortages and sweet rationing had run the little business down so they got it at a low price. Phyllis recognized that it would take a lot of hard work to get it up and running again. She also knew that she would be the one getting up at five to take delivery of the papers, she who would be doing most of the work, but she was resigned to it. After all, she told herself, a good many women had lost their husbands in the war. At least she had got hers back. And with time things would surely improve.

That was the point at which Cathy's dream of going to art college crumbled. Ever since she could remember she had dreamed of studying to become a commercial artist. The head-mistress at Queensgrove Grammar School had encouraged her, impressed by her talent, and her art teacher had promised to help when the time came for her to apply for a place at college. Last year Cathy passed her school certificate with flying colours. Then came her father's repatriation and the realization that leaving her parents to cope alone was out of the question.

When she had first suggested staying to help they had been adamant.

'I'm damned if we're going to let him take away your chance after all I've been through,' Robert said, referring to Hitler. 'You're to go to college, Cathy, love. Your mum and I will manage.'

But the following winter Robert had caught pneumonia through struggling to do the paper round when the boy failed to turn up and Cathy knew that her mother could not have managed without her through those weeks when her father lay ill. Later, as Robert slowly recovered, the doctor had told Phyllis that he had developed emphysema and would never be strong enough to work for more than half a day.

In private, alone in her bedroom in the flat above the shop, Cathy mourned the diminishing dream she had cherished since childhood, but she kept her disappointment to herself. Day by day she worked beside her mother in the shop, worrying about her father's health, only too aware that the inadequate profit from the business only just kept their heads above water.

In all of this there was one ray of light for Cathy: her deepening friendship with John King.

John still lived with his mother at Cedar Lodge, the large Victorian house on the corner of King's Walk. He had been away at college until he was eighteen and then in the army, doing his National Service, and it wasn't until he came into the shop one evening to buy a paper that he and Cathy met again.

He'd grown taller and the dark business-suit he wore made him look leaner than she remembered, but Cathy recognized the melting brown eyes and warm smile at once. As she gave him his change she said shyly,

'You're John King, aren't you?'

He looked up in surprise. 'That's right – but . . .'

She smiled. 'You don't remember me, do you.'

He hesitated. 'I heard that the Ladgroves who used to live at number four have bought this shop. Surely you're not . . .' He shook his head, looking doubtful. 'Pauline?'

'Catherine – Cathy,' she said. 'Pauline's married. She lives in Manchester.'

He laughed. 'Little Cathy? I don't believe it.' He took in the oval face and large grey eyes. 'You've changed, but I recognize you now.' He frowned. 'You used to have two little pigtails.'

Cathy laughed and shook her ponytail of long brown hair. 'I finally managed to lose them. How are you, John?'

'Fine.' He sighed. 'I took over the business when my father died last year. You probably heard that my brother Laurence was killed in the war.'

She nodded. 'Yes. I'm sorry.'

'Laurence's death was the finish of Father.'

Cathy nodded. 'It must have been a terrible blow.'

'It left me to take over the factory. I was doing my National Service at the time and as soon as I finished I had to come home. I've been in charge for the past ten months.'

'And your mother?' Cathy enquired. She well remembered the tall imperious woman who was Theresa King. As far as Cathy knew she had never spoken to any of the other residents of King's Walk.

Even during the war when class and snobbery seemed to disappear and people supported one another she kept her distance.

'She's the same as ever,' John said as though he read her thoughts. 'Mother doesn't change.'

Cathy said nothing. She was remembering the time Mrs King had shouted at them when they went to play on the tennis court at Cedar Lodge. She shuddered at the memory of the fierce-looking harridan who had screamed at the four of them to get out of her garden and never come back. Pauline had been so upset and humiliated that she had cried herself to sleep that night.

13

John picked up his paper and smiled at Cathy. 'Look, I've got to rush. I've got a meeting, but could we meet sometime?'

Cathy hesitated, remembering the prejudices of the past. Then she reminded herself that John was a man now and could make friends with whomever he chose.

'I'd love to have a chat about old times,' John said.

Cathy smiled. 'That would be nice. I'd love to, John.'

At the door he turned. 'Tomorrow? I'll pick you up about seven.'

When Cathy told her mother that John King had invited her out Phyllis was sceptical.

'He was always a nice enough lad,' she said. 'But you want to steer clear of his mother. A proper tartar, she is, as you know all too well. Everyone felt sorry for her when she lost her son and then her husband. But did she want our sympathy? Not a bit of it. Shut the door in our faces. Too proud even to accept the flowers we took her.' She looked at her daughter. 'You won't be good enough for her, that's for sure. She still thinks we lower the tone of her neighbourhood. Apparently she's saying that since the war it's gone from bad to worse. Full of a lot of conchies and work-shy layabouts.'

Cathy looked at her mother, aghast. 'She said that?'

'She did! Mrs Sands told me she heard her say it with her own ears in Garland's department store.' Phyllis finished cashing up and slipped the shop takings into the bag for Cathy to take to the night safe. 'You can imagine how upset Mary Sands was. Her husband was no conchy. He couldn't help being unfit for the army, could he? And him a preacher too'

Cathy thought about John's mother's remark as she cut across the park to the bank. When she had been a child she had been terrified of Theresa King. The woman clearly resented the close proximity of working-class families and took every opportunity to let it be known.

The Kings had moved into Cedar Lodge just after the Great War, during which King's Footwear had made a fortune out of making army boots. The house had been surrounded by extensive grounds then, but a few years later, much to Theresa's disapproval, Albert King had decided to sell some of the land for development. Albert had always had a shrewd eye for a good deal and the shortage of building-land after the war meant that the two acres made a

14

good price. His only stipulation, which he made tongue in cheek, was that the new development would be called King's Walk.

Cathy was ready and waiting when John called for her. She wore her blue coat, the one she had bought when she went to stay with Pauline in Manchester last winter. The collar was trimmed with velvet, which framed her face flatteringly. Wearing it always made her feel good. She smiled at her reflection in the mirror as she brushed her hair and pinned it into a chignon.

Pauline had told her it was unfashionable now to have long hair.

'You should let me take you to the hairdresser's,' she'd said on Cathy's last visit. 'Have it cut. It'd suit you.'

But Cathy had drawn the line at cutting her hair.

John had the car waiting at the kerb outside the shop. It was his father's old 1935 Rover, laid up all through the war. After a thorough overhaul it was as good as new and very comfortable with its leather seats and soft new carpets.

'I thought we might take a run out to a little country pub I know,' he said. 'Unless you'd prefer to see a film.'

Cathy was unsure. You couldn't talk in the pictures, yet she was a little apprehensive about going into a pub. She was only just old enough to be allowed in and it would be the first time for her. She found the idea a little intimidating. John was looking at her.

'Maybe there's something else you'd like to do.'

She shook her head, blushing. 'No,' she said brightly. 'A country pub sounds fine.'

As they drove Cathy stole a look at John. He was dressed less formally this evening, in a blazer and grey flannels, a cravat at the neck of his shirt instead of a tie. He wore his hair a little longer than most young men and she thought, romantically, that he had the look of a young poet. He felt her eyes on him and turned, smiling.

'I'm not driving too fast for you?'

'No. Not a bit.'

He laughed. 'Not that this old bus of Father's will go very fast. Built more for comfort than speed. I'd like a sports model, but you can't get new cars these days.'

Buying cars was outside Cathy's experience. Her father had never owned one. He and her mother had always dreamed of it, planning trips to the seaside and weekend picnics. But the war had put paid to all that as it had to so many other dreams.

Cathy found the pub quite homely in the end. Situated on the edge of a village it was called, quaintly, the Hat and Feathers. Outside a colourful sign bearing a flamboyant Cavalier's hat swung in the evening breeze. Inside the low oak beams were blackened with age and smoke and a log fire took the chill off the cool March evening. A couple of locals sat up at the bar talking to a plump woman who stood polishing glasses. She smiled as they came in.

'Good evening. What can I get you?'

John looked at Cathy. 'What would you like?'

She bit her lip, staring at the confusing array of bottles behind the bar. Her only experience of alcoholic drinks was the occasional pint of beer her father enjoyed and the bottle of sherry that the Ladgroves always treated themselves to at Christmas.

'Sherry, please,' she said on impulse.

The landlady looked at her enquiringly. 'Dry, dear?'

'No.' Cathy bit her lip. 'Just the usual – er – wet kind, please.'

The woman grinned and winked at John. Cathy realized with embarrassment that she must have said something foolish. As they sat down she whispered to John, 'What did I say?'

He smiled. 'She meant did you want dry or sweet. It's all right,' he added quickly, seeing her blush. 'I think she thought you were pulling her leg.' He reached out and touched her arm. 'Cathy, if you're not happy we can drink up and leave.'

'Oh no!' She bowed her head to sip her sherry. 'I like it here – really.'

He looked at her. 'So – tell me what you've been doing all this time.'

She shrugged. 'School. Queensgrove Grammar. As you know the war was pretty uneventful here. No bombs to speak of. We did have a couple of evacuees from London, but they didn't stay. What about you?'

'Not very exciting. College, followed by National Service. I'd almost done my two years when Father died and when I came home I had to go straight into King's Footwear.'

Cathy sipped her sherry, secretly wishing there was less of it. 'Were you always going to take over from your father? I'd have thought that as your brother was older . . .'

16

'Laurence was to have studied medicine,' John explained. 'That was always Mother's ambition for him. She had a younger brother who was killed in the first war, you see. Laurence was named after him. He was to have been a doctor too.'

'I see.'

John picked up his glass again. 'It's just as well that I was designated to take up the reins from Father under the circumstances.'

Cathy nodded. 'I suppose so. So now you're in charge at King's.'

'That's right.'

'Do you like it?'

He gave her a wry smile. 'I don't have much choice. But actually I do quite like it. I've got a lot of ideas for the place once our present government contracts have been honoured. I'd like to branch out into fashion footwear.'

Shs smiled. 'That's interesting.'

'It's a long way in the future yet. Tell me about you and your family. Your sister Pauline is married, you say?'

'Yes, to Jack Harris. He was in the air force – stationed out at Blaydon Heath. He was shot down and injured in '43. They invalided him out and he and Pauline got married. They live in Manchester and he works in a bank.'

'I see. Flying a desk as they say.'

'They've got twin boys.'

'Really? I remember Pauline very well. Laurence had a monumental crush on her. Is she still as beautiful?'

'Even more so,' Cathy said wistfully. 'Being a wife and mother seems to have made her bloom. She was always the pretty one.'

'I disagree.' He smiled at her. 'You might have been a funny little kid once but you've blossomed now.'

She shook her head, 'I don't know about that.' She was pleased by the compliment but not sure that she believed it.

'What made your parents take on the shop?'

'Dad spent two years in a Japanese POW camp. It wrecked his health, so he and Mum decided to buy the shop.'

'That's tough. Has he recovered?'

She shook her head. 'He still has bad days.'

'I'm sorry.' He nodded towards her glass. 'Drink up and let me get you another.'

17

She paused, then said, 'To tell you the truth I don't really like it very much.'

He smiled. 'We'll go, then.'

In the car he asked her, 'What are your plans, Cathy? I mean, you're not going to make a career out of working alongside your parents, are you?'

She sighed. 'Like you, I don't have much choice. I was to have gone to college to study art, but with Dad so poorly I couldn't leave Mum to cope alone.'

He frowned. 'You gave up your place?'

She shook her head. 'I hadn't got round to applying.' She smiled. 'We have to stick together and support each other, don't we.'

He'd noticed the wistful look in her eyes. 'I'm sorry, Cathy,' he said. 'It can't be easy for you.' They drove for a while in silence then John suddenly asked, 'What happened to the other two kids?'

'Rachel Sands and Peter Harvey?' she said. 'I don't see much of them, but Rachel works in a dress shop in town and Peter . . .' She broke off, biting her lip.

He looked at her. 'Yes?'

'Maybe I shouldn't say, but Peter has been in trouble with the police. His father was away all through the war and Peter's grandmother rather let him run wild.'

John was smiling. 'I can't say I'm surprised. He was always a little hothead, wasn't he?'

'He was always a bit of a daredevil, but it's a shame. He's a nice boy really.'

When John halted the car outside the shop he turned to Cathy. 'I've really enjoyed this evening, Cathy. Thank you.'

She bit her lip, unable to meet his eyes. 'I'm sorry.'

'Whatever for?'

The surprised tone of his voice made her look at him. 'I'm not used to pubs. That must seem really old-fashioned to you. Pauline's always telling me how unadventurous I am.'

He reached out a finger to touch her cheek. 'You're the Cathy I remember,' he said softly. 'Gentle and sweet and unspoilt. Don't try to change.' He leaned forward and kissed her very softly on the lips. 'The war changed so many things. And not always for the better. Promise me you'll stay just as you are.'

18

Moved, she nodded, her eyes luminous in the dim light of the car. 'I'll try,' she whispered.

'I'd like to see you again, Cathy,' he said. 'If you want to, that is.'

'I'd like that very much,' she said. 'And thank you for a lovely evening.'

He laughed. 'A short drive, a drink you didn't know how to swallow and me firing questions at you? Next time we'll do something you choose.' He looked at her enquiringly. 'We could go out on Sunday if you like – make a day of it.'

She smiled. 'I'd like that.' She looked at her watch, surprised to find that it was ten o'clock. 'I'd better go in now.'

'Of course.' He walked round the corner with her to the door of the flat. 'Goodnight, Cathy.'

'Goodnight, John.'

Later, as she lay in bed, she thought of John and felt a warm glow. He was so nice. Just like he had always been. And he had kissed her. It was odd; she had known John King since childhood and yet, until this evening she had never really known him at all.

After that evening Cathy and John saw each other regularly. That summer they drove to the coast most weekends, picnicking on the beach at Holme-next-the-Sea, swimming and sunbathing. During the week they went to a film or had dinner. Soon Cathy knew that she was in love and she was ecstatic. Her mother however was sceptical.

'He hasn't taken you home to meet his mother yet, has he?'

Cathy shook her head. 'I'm not anxious for that to happen.'

'But it will, you mark my words,' Phyllis told her. 'I wouldn't mind betting she doesn't know it's you her precious son is seeing. And when she finds out. . . !'

'What's wrong with me?' Cathy demanded indignantly.

'You ask *her*, not me,' Phyllis said. 'The woman's a complete snob. She'll want her son to marry a doctor's daughter at the very least. Preferably someone with some cash to put into the business.'

'Who said anything about marrying?' Cathy asked.

Phyllis sniffed. 'The way that lad looks at you, my girl, it won't be long before he asks you.'

And although Cathy protested, she could not deny that it was what she hoped for too. Held in John's arms in the car each time they said goodnight she had begun to be aware of deeper feelings. Kisses were nice, but the beating of her heart and the disturbing sensations deep inside her told of desires as yet unknown.

She and Pauline had talked of sex, as sisters do, after the light was out late at night. Since her marriage, Pauline had told her that there was no ecstasy on earth like making love with someone you loved. Now Cathy could believe her. She sensed that John wanted her too. But she had been brought up to the strict belief that marriage was the only means to fulfilled love. To give oneself to a man without at least some kind of definite promise was to lose his respect, and Cathy could not bear the thought of that.

And so the summer passed into autumn. The trips to the seaside came to a close and still John had said nothing about where their relationship was going. Then one evening after a trip to the cinema he said suddenly,

'I want you to come to tea on Sunday. and meet Mother.'

Cathy's heart skipped a beat. 'Are you sure, John?'

He laughed. 'Sure? What a question.'

She bit her lip, remembering the things her mother had said. 'Your mother wasn't exactly welcoming when we were children.'

He laughed. 'I think she can trust you not to pinch her apples now, can't she?' He lifted her chin and laughed into her worried eyes. 'Or is that all you want me for?'

She laughed in spite of herself. 'It's just . . .'

'Just what?'

'She'll think I'm not good enough.'

His eyes darkened. 'Don't ever let me hear you say that again, Cathy,' he said, 'You're my girl, and if that isn't good enough for Mother then it's just too bad.'

So Cathy had gone to Cedar Lodge the following Sunday. She had perched on the edge of her chair and eaten tiny sandwiches and thin slivers of cake whilst Theresa King, her eyes as mysteriously dark and glittery as ever, had interrogated her about her education and family. It had been an ordeal; one she did not wish to repeat. Afterwards, John had apologized.

'Mother doesn't mean anything,' he said. 'She's just showing an interest. It's so long since she mixed socially that she's lost the knack of making conversation.' He peered anxiously into her eyes.

'You won't let it put you off, will you darling? After all, it's our future that matters.'

But Cathy wasn't so sure. Surely Theresa King could influence her son if she wanted to. He was all she had now and she was a strong woman. She would not reliquish him without a struggle. And certainly not to a girl she deemed unsuitable.

Soon after Christmas another family crisis hit the Ladgrove family. One afternoon in late January the telephone rang. Cathy took the call.

'Hello. Ladgrove's.'

'That you, Cathy?'

'*Pauline!*'

'I know. I'm sorry. I know I haven't been in touch for ages.'

'We didn't even get a Christmas card from you,' Cathy admonished. 'Mum and Dad were worried. Where are you?'

'I'm at the station.'

'The station? You mean here – Queensgrove?'

'Yes. Can I speak to Mum, Cath?'

Pauline sounded close to tears and with a feeling of foreboding Cathy fetched her mother from the stockroom where she had been taking a break. She listened to the one-sided conversation with a sinking heart. When Phyllis rang off and turned to her she saw the disquiet in her mother's tired eyes.

'Pauline and Jack have parted,' she said, sinking on to a chair.

'Parted! But why?'

Phyllis shrugged. 'Seems he's been seeing someone else – says he wants a divorce.'

'Oh Mum! What's she going to do?'

'She's done it. Upped and left. She's here – at the station, asking to come home.'

'With the twins?'

Phyllis nodded. 'Oh Cath, where are we going to put them all? If only she'd stayed on and stuck it out. That other woman will walk in now and she'll never get a penny out of him.'

'Come on, Mum,' Cathy had tried to comfort her mother. 'It can't be as bad as all that. I daresay it'll all blow over. Before you know it Jack will be here to fetch them and they'll be back together again.'

21

But Jack hadn't come to fetch his family. It seemed he was tired of coming home to a wife who was always weary; sick of sleepless nights and the two small demanding tyrants who had changed their life into one of drudgery.

Soon the tiny flat above the shop was full to bursting, Pauline and the two cots crammed into Cathy's tiny bedroom. Baby-washing steamed in front of the living-room fire for most of the day, making Dad's cough worse and the two little boys, Paul and Michael, seemed to be into everything, demanding constant attention.

Apart from the overcrowding it was clear to Cathy that the income from the shop would not support them all any more than the walls would expand to make more room. She racked her brain for a solution.

She was in the town one morning, picking up the weekly supply of stamps from the post office, when she ran into her old art teacher. Jean Tanner was disappointed that Cathy had been unable to follow her ambition to study art and sympathetic about the Ladgroves' problems. The following day she telephoned with a suggestion.

'Listen Cathy. I've had an idea. I don't know whether this will appeal to you or not but I have a cousin in Bournemouth,' she said. 'Martin and his wife Clare manage a large hotel down there. They're engaging staff now for the summer season. You mentioned that you're overcrowded at home and I wondered how you'd fancy a job with them?'

Cathy was puzzled. 'In a hotel?'

Jean laughed. 'I'm sorry, Cathy. My mind is racing ahead of my tongue. What I didn't say was that there's a very good art college down there. If you were working there you could probably fit in a part-time course at the same time. As a matter of fact I've taken the liberty of ringing them and there's a vacancy for a job as a waitress. They'd be happy to have you.'

Cathy promised to think about it and let Jean know within a couple of days. It would certainly be a solution to all their problems. Pauline could take over her job, helping Mum in the shop and it would make more room for them all at the flat. But what about John? Her heart sank at the thought of their parting.

All that day her mind was torn between accepting Jean's offer and taking the chance to study, and giving up the idea so that she could stay near John.

When she told her mother about the offer Phyllis looked doubtful. 'I'd feel as though we'd pushed you out,' she said. 'Besides, Bournemouth's an awful long way away. What if you get homesick?'

'I expect I would just at first,' Cathy admitted. 'But I'd get over it. When I get settled and when Pauline is used to the shop you could bring Dad down for a holiday,' she added optimistically. 'The sea air would do you both good.'

Phyllis could not see that ever happening but she said nothing. 'What does John think about you going all that way away?' she asked.

Cathy sighed. 'He doesn't know yet. It won't be for ever, will it? And he's got the car. He could come down and visit.'

Phyllis shook her head. Privately she hoped that Cathy would forget the idea. She wasn't altogether happy about her seeing so much of John King, but this was worse. It was true they were crowded, but they'd manage somehow, she told herself. She wouldn't let herself think of her younger daughter going away.

When Cathy told John he was appalled. 'Bournemouth? Do you want to go?' he asked.

'I don't know,' Cathy admitted. 'I'm not sure about the job, but it would be a chance to study art.'

'You haven't mentioned leaving me,' he said, looking crestfallen.

She slipped her arms around his neck. 'Obviously that's the worst part,' she told him. 'But it wouldn't be for ever and you could always come down and visit.'

He sighed. 'Bournemouth is a long way and with things getting busier and busier at the factory I can't see myself having many free weekends,' he said. He held her away to look into her eyes. 'Oh, Cathy, I want you to have your chance, but the thought of not seeing you for months on end . . .' He shook his head. 'Look, I was going to wait till your birthday but I might as well say it now. I'd like us to be engaged.'

She looked at him, her eyes full of tears. 'Oh, John, you know I'd love that, but what does your mother think about having me as a future daughter-in-law?'

He shook his head. 'It's got nothing to do with her.'

She searched his eyes. 'You haven't mentioned it to her, have you?'

'Before I'd asked you? Of course I haven't. It doesn't matter anyway.'

'It does. She wants better for you, John,' she said gravely.

'There'll never be anyone better for me.'

'Someone higher up the social scale, I mean. Maybe it would be better to wait for a while; to be really sure.'

'*Sure!*' He ran an exasperated hand through his hair. 'If you felt the way I do, Cathy, you wouldn't use that word so glibly.'

'I *do* feel as you do,' she whispered, hiding her face against his neck.

He kissed her. 'Oh, Cathy, if you're really set on going away, could we go away – have a weekend together? At least we'd have that to remember. I want you so much, Cathy.'

His kisses grew more passionate and he unfastened the buttons of her dress, sliding a hand inside to find the warm roundness of her breast.

Hardly able to breathe for the pounding of her heart, she summoned every ounce of her will power to push him away. '*No!* John, I don't want it to be this way.'

He stared at her. 'You said you felt the same as I do,' he said raggedly.

'I *do!*' She swallowed the tears that gathered in her throat. 'But not like this.'

'How then?' She could see by his face that he was hurt and angry. 'What am I supposed to think when you say things – when you kiss me as though you mean it? Don't you mean it when you say you love me?'

'Of course I do. You know that.'

'I'm not sure that I do!'

'I just don't want some hole in the corner weekend where we'd have to lie – pretend to be married. It would – spoil things,' she said miserably, turning away.

'How could it *spoil* anything? We love each other, Cathy. What could be more natural?'

She shook her head miserably. 'It's different for you.'

'Obviously,' he said bitterly.

She cried herself to sleep that night, stuffing the sheet in her mouth in the hope that Pauline wouldn't hear, but after a while there was a rustle as Pauline turned to her in the darkness.

'What's up, love?' she asked quietly.

'Nothing,' Cathy sniffed.

''Course there is, you've been crying your heart out. Is it John? Doesn't he want you to go?'

Cathy swallowed hard. 'It's not only that. Tonight he suggested that we go away for a weekend together.'

'So why are you crying?' Pauline sat up. 'You didn't turn him down?'

'Yes.'

'What for?'

'I don't want it to be like that, sneaking away – lying.'

'Don't you want to sleep with him, Cath? You're not scared, are you?'

'No!'

'Then why, for God's sake? At least he's prepared to do things nicely and take you away somewhere.' After a pause she said, 'You don't want to lose him, do you?'

'Of *course* I don't! That's why I said no. If I let that happen he'd lose his respect for me.'

'Oh my God!' Pauline laughed. 'You've been reading those magazine agony pages again. You don't believe that old guff, do you? They have to say that to deter girls from having unwanted babies. All you need do is take proper care. John will know all about that.'

'How do you know so much?' Cathy peered at her sister through the dim light. 'Are you saying that you and Jack. . . ?'

'Of course we did! It makes sense, Cath. How else will you know if you're right for each other.' She reached out to pat Cathy's arm. 'Don't worry about it any more. Just say yes. You'll be sorry if you don't when it's too late.'

Pauline quickly fell asleep, but Cathy still lay there in the darkness, wide awake and her mind filled with even more doubts. It was all very well for Pauline to say that she should do as John wanted but she wasn't convinced. Pauline and Jack's marriage hadn't lasted, had it? Perhaps it was partly because they had started off badly.

She couldn't understand why John refused to understand how she felt. She'd always thought that a man wanted the girl he married to keep herself for their wedding night. She wanted everything to be perfect, just as she'd always imagined it.

John didn't get in touch, either next day or the one after and Cathy was bitterly hurt. She'd expected him to come round or ring with an apology Finally she made up her mind to accept the job offer. She telephoned Jean and asked her for the address, then she wrote to the hotel. Two days later the arrangements were under way.

The weeks that followed were hectic with packing, making travel arrangements and writing letters back and forth to the Tanners at the Marine Bay Hotel, negotiating her pay and accommodation.

John maintained his silence, and although Cathy was heartbroken she was too proud to make the first move. It seemed she would have to leave without even saying goodbye.

This morning her father had travelled in the taxi with her to the station leaving Mum and Pauline busy with the papers. In spite of the fact that it made him short of breath he had insisted on carrying her case on to the platform for her. As they stood there waiting for the train the awkwardness of station platforms made them tongue-tied.

'Shall I get you a magazine,' Robert asked.

Cathy shook her head. 'No thanks. I've got a book in my bag.'

He nodded and stood shifting his weight from one foot to the other. At last he said, 'Your mum and I feel awful about this, Cath.'

'Why, Dad? You always wanted me to go to college.'

'Not like this though. We wanted you to go in style, love, with us helping you through. We hate the thought of you working all day and studying at night, you'll wear yourself out.'

She laughed and stood on tiptoe to kiss his cheek. 'No I won't. I love my art. It'll be more like a treat. Anyway, what else would I do in the evenings? Don't worry about me.'

'You're only young once, love,' he said. 'You should be enjoying yourself – getting more out of life. Ever since I came home you've been stuck in that shop.'

'I don't *mind*, Dad, really!'

'And what about young King? Is it all off between you?'

She shrugged. 'Perhaps it's for the best.'

'But if you weren't going so far . . .'

'Dad! I told you, everything's fine.'

But he looked so unhappy that in the end she suggested he make tracks for home.

'Look, don't wait,' she urged. 'The train will be at least another ten minutes and there's a lot to do back at the shop. You go. I'll be fine.'

He sighed. 'You'll ring and let us know as soon as you get there?'

She looked at his anguished face and felt the tears prick her eyelids. 'Of course.'

'You mustn't feel there's no room for you at King's Walk. I daresay our Pauline will marry again before too long – handsome lass like her.' He searched her eyes. 'And you know you can come home if you don't like it there? You mustn't feel you've failed just because you don't like it. This is your home and you'll always be wanted here.'

'Of course I know that, Dad.' She hugged him. 'Now off you go.' She watched his slightly stooped figure as he walked away and felt a lump thicken her throat. She was leaving so much behind, all she had ever known and loved. She only hoped it was going to be worth it.

The train steamed in a few minutes later and she climbed aboard with a heavy heart, heaving her case after her and slamming the door. The guard blew his whistle and she had just settled in her corner seat when she caught sight of a familiar figure dashing through the barrier and running along the platform. Her heart leapt. Standing up she wrenched at the window, but it wouldn't budge. She waved frantically and knocked on the glass as the train began to move.

John saw her and his face lit up. Running along beside the train he mouthed the words, *I love you*. Her throat tightened as she nodded and returned the words, *I love you too*.

As the train gathered speed he mimed writing with one hand on the other. She nodded breathlessly. And then he was left behind, a diminishing figure growing further and further away as he stood on the end of the platform, waving for as long as he could see her.

Cathy sat down at last and it was only then that she noticed that all the other occupants of the carriage were smiling at her.

For once she didn't care.

The train steamed into Bournemouth Central station and passengers began to stand up and gather their luggage together. Cathy did the same, her heart quickening. This was it. She'd arrived. Martin Tanner was supposed to be meeting her and she scanned the faces of people waiting on the platform as the train slowed, wondering which one was him.

Heaving her case down from the luggage rack she reminded herself that when she got off this train a new phase of her life would begin.

CHAPTER TWO

THERESA STOOD LOOKING OUT of one of the long windows of the drawing-room at Cedar Lodge. She'd always loved this room with its heavy mahogany furniture and red velvet swagged curtains. Albert had always thought it pretentious. If he'd had his way he would have lived in the kitchen as his parents had done, in the little terraced house in Myrtle Street that they'd never left in spite of the success of King's Footwear.

It was because she loved the room so much and spent so much time enjoying the splendid view of the gardens that she'd resented Albert's selling a large part of their grounds for development. When the new estate was built the mean little houses of King's Walk had been clearly visible from her drawing-room windows. *King's Walk!* She allowed herself a snort of disapproval. It had been Albert's idea to call it that. As though it were something to be proud of! Happily, since the war the new trees she'd had planted had grown, softening the landscape and mercifully hiding the view. Now, thank goodness, she could almost imagine that the little houses and their common occupants did not exist.

She and Albert had married in 1918, soon after the end of the Great War. When her father had indicated that it was his wish that she should accept the young Albert King's proposal of marriage she had been shocked. After Ian had been killed in 1916 she had resigned herself to remaining single.

Young Doctor Ian Campbell had been her father's partner. He had arrived in Queensgrove to join Doctor Marshall's practice in the autumn of 1913 and Theresa had fallen in love with him at first sight. Later he had confided that he had been smitten in the same

29

way. When he had gone off to join the RAMC soon after the war began she had been sure he would be safe. Surely doctors would not be put in the firing line? But the ambulance Ian was in had been caught in crossfire whilst rescuing casualties from the front line at Gallipoli and he had died later from his wounds. On the day that the news reached the Marshall family Theresa had told herself that her life was over.

Theresa had met Albert King a few times at social occasions where he had always seemed ill at ease and out of his depth. He was good-looking enough, in an earthy kind of way she supposed, but rough and crude with his common accent and big coarse hands. If it hadn't been for his father's success he would certainly never have been invited anywhere. But her father's finances were in a bad way and it seemed that marrying into the town's most prosperous trade family was a way to save him from bankruptcy.

As a last-ditch attempt to save his family from penury and disgrace, Doctor Marshall had offered to invest the last of his capital in King's Footwear, putting his proposal over lunch with Gerald King at the town's Conservative Club.

Gerald, who had made his fortune during the war out of government contracts, was not in need of any financial input, but he was a shrewd businessman and he saw the opportunity he had been waiting for. For some time now his wife, Mabel, had been fretting about their lack of social acceptability. Now Gerald saw a way to put things right. Word had it that the doctor had caught his toe badly with some duff shares. Gerald saw his chance and seized it.

He agreed affably to the doctor's proposal, offering a generous share in the business provided that he could engineer an alliance between his son and Doctor Marshall's only daughter.

'After all, your T'resa must be knockin' on a bit,' Gerald had pointed out over the brandy and cigars. 'What is she – twenty-six, -seven?

Doctor Marshall cleared his throat, trying not to show how affronted he was by the man's brashness. 'Twenty-nine,' he muttered.

Gerald nodded. 'There you are then. She's lost her fiancé too if I've heard right.' He shook his head. 'This bloody war! Damnable waste of young lives. A lot of young women are going to have to face being left on the shelf with so many of our poor lads wiped out.' He regarded the doctor's crestfallen face shrewdly. 'Now – my Albert's a few years younger but that's no matter. She'll not get a better offer, not in this town,' he added. 'If King's hadn't been in the footwear business our Albert might well have gone to France and gone the way of so many others. I reckon your T'resa'd be well advised to snap him up. He's not a bad-lookin' lad, after all, an' he's our only son. He'll be set up for life when I'm gone. King's and everything I've got is left to him.'

He leaned forward, eager to press his point. 'You want to see her settled, don't you? Tell you what I'll do,' he said stabbing the air with his cigar. 'If she'll have him I'll buy them a house. I've got one in mind. Cedar Lodge, on the corner of Wellington Road, opposite the park. What d'you say?'

When her father gently put the idea to her later that night in his study Theresa had been appalled.

'Father, I couldn't!'

Doctor Marshall sighed. 'I wouldn't even suggest it to you under normal circumstances,' he said. 'The truth is, I've been rather unfortunate with my finances since the war began. I'm confiding in you, Theresa. I don't wish to worry your mother, but things are looking very bleak. I worry about letting you both down, and of course there's the future to think of. With Ian gone the thought of you being left without support worries me terribly.'

Thinking it over later, Theresa saw that the truth was that the family's future security rested on her acceptance. She could see no alternative but to agree to her father's wishes.

That had been in the final year of the war. A month later her young brother Laurence was killed and after that Theresa neither knew nor cared what the future held. Her mother and father were as distraught as she was. First her dearly loved Ian had been taken; then came her father's financial defeat and now this terrible blow. If accepting Albert King as her husband would ease her parents' pain and take some of their anxiety away, then so be it. What did her own feelings matter?

The wedding was postponed because of Laurence's death, but it took place the following summer, with Theresa in white satin and tulle and six bridesmaids in pastel silks. The reception was held at the Marshall's elegant home and attended by the élite of Queensgrove. Gerald and Mabel King were delighted.

31

The honeymoon, in Paris, was a disaster. Theresa would not let her new husband near her for almost a week. At first he was patient but eventually he had lost his temper and insisted.

'Damn it, woman, we're wed, aren't we? You're just going to have to get used to it. I've always had a healthy appetite – for food and sex alike, and now it's your duty to see both catered for!'

With fists and teeth clenched and eyes tightly shut, Theresa had endured the indignity of Albert's nightly attentions. Even now the memory of his rough, shovel-like hands on her unwilling flesh, the coarse hairiness of his naked body and his disgusting grunts of satisfaction had the power to make her shudder. She suffered it for five years, until after her two sons had been conceived and safely born. After that she had moved her belongings to a room of her own and firmly closed the door, making it clear that she considered her duty to be more than satisfactorily completed.

Tucked away in her underwear drawer she kept a cherished photograph of Ian, taken when he first joined up, handsome in his uniform, and when Theresa was especially unhappy she would take it out and slip it under her pillow in the hope that they would meet in her dreams.

If Albert's mother had imagined that Theresa would teach her son good manners and etiquette she was mistaken. It wasn't that she didn't try, more that Albert positively despised such things. He took exception to being corrected by his wife as to how to hold his knife and which cutlery to use.

'I'll behave as I please in my own home, missis,' he told her. 'I'm the one that pays the bills and while I do, I'll do as I like. If I want to eat peas with a knife and let the gravy run down my chin, I will – and you'll have to bloody well put up with it!'

And a long-suffering Theresa had no choice but to avert her gaze and comply.

Cedar Lodge compensated a lot for what Theresa had to endure. She loved the graceful house with its high-ceilinged, spacious rooms and extensive grounds. From her room she had views of the park with its green acres, its lake and ancient trees, and the garden was a joy. The drawing-room windows looked out on to colourful borders, the lawn and the tennis court. But Albert could not even permit her that pleasure, selling off much of their grounds in favour of the despised estate, ruining her view and putting an end to their privacy.

But even Albert could not take away her pride in her boys, especially Laurence who had turned out to be the image of her adored young brother. Theresa watched with pride as he grew into a lovely golden boy and then a handsome young man. It was true that at school he was happier on the cricket pitch than in the classroom. It was also true that money seemed to slip through his fingers. But he was only young once, Theresa told herself. And when the time came he would settle down and make her proud when he qualified as a doctor. Only then would her fortunes come full circle.

Then came the gathering clouds of another war, which like the one before it was to twist and distort their lives. King's Footwear flourished again, getting Government contracts to make army boots for which they were renowned. But to Theresa's horror her beloved elder son was called up before he had time to begin his studies, soon to be posted abroad. A sense of foreboding descended on her. Was it really possible for history to repeat itself? In naming her son after her brother could she have tempted providence? Could God be so cruel as to take him too?

When the War Office telegram came early in 1944 to say that Laurence was missing, believed killed, Theresa had fainted clean away on the hall floor, the envelope still in her hand. It was half an hour before she was fully conscious again. The doctor said it was as though she wanted to remain unconscious so as not to face the reality of Laurence's death. And when Albert had died suddenly of a heart attack just three weeks later the loss had hit her harder than she would ever have thought possible. He had done many thoughtless things since their marriage; she strongly suspected that he had done them to mock her gentility. But by far the cruellest blow he had ever dealt her was to die and desert her, right after the loss of her beloved Laurence. But then Albert always was insensitive and inconsiderate.

This morning Theresa had good reason to feel relieved. The *girl* had gone. When John had first taken up with the Ladgrove girl from the corner shop she had been appalled. Unlike her beautiful Laurence, John had always favoured his father in looks and now it seemed that he had the same taste for common women. She could not understand it. Heaven only knew, enough had been spent on his education. One would have thought some of her own good taste would have rubbed off on him. She knew all too well what misery life could be, married to the wrong person.

A girl from King's Walk and a shop-girl into the bargain! He'd even had the effrontery to bring her to tea one Sunday. Theresa had tried her hardest to point out the girl's inadequacies to him, but to little effect. It was as though history was repeating itself. But *she* had been obliged to marry in order to save her father. John had had ample choice. He could have had his pick of any young women in Queensgrove, yet he'd chosen Catherine Ladgrove.

She'd tried to tell John that a young woman like that could never aspire to be an asset and helpmeet to him.

'You could never take her anywhere,' she said. 'And in the end you'd despise her for ruining your life.' But he refused to listen, going on about her being a well-brought-up girl of whom any man could be proud; saying that he loved her. *Love!* Lust more like, if he was anything like his father. Men were so foolishly susceptible to a pretty face. They never saw any further than the ends of their noses and that kind of girl was always free with her favours.

Anyway, now the girl had gone off to some domestic job on the south coast and Theresa could breathe again.

Theresa blinked as the sun suddenly came out from behind a cloud, its brilliance dazzling her. Dust motes danced in the beams and she sighed. It was time for spring-cleaning again. Betty Mason, who had been her 'daily' for the last ten years, was getting past it. She would have to try to find someone a bit younger and more nimble to help her with the heavy work. It was getting increasingly difficult to get domestics nowadays. She blamed the war – working women had risen above themselves, earning ridiculous money in the factories and on the buses. Well, they'd soon have to settle for domesticity again now that the men were home. Someone had suggested a woman from King's Walk. A Mrs Harvey. Theresa wanted no one from that street inside her house, but John had been quite sharp with her when she had said so.

'Don't be such a snob, Mother. I'll call round and ask her if she's free this evening if you won't go.'

Theresa still smarted when she remembered the day soon after

34

Laurence had been posted missing when a deputation of King's Walk women had arrived on her doorstep with a bunch of flowers, offering her sympathy. She'd given them short shrift. How dare they patronize her? What could they know about her suffering? She didn't want their sympathy. They were poles apart and always would be.

John pushed open the gate of number twenty King's Walk and walked up the path. The front garden wasn't as neat as the others in the row. A few scrawny daffodils struggled their way through the uncut grass, and weeds whiskered the cracks in the path. The paintwork was peeling too, but he noticed that the windows sparkled with cleanliness, the net curtains were fresh and crisp and the front step was well scrubbed.

Dennis Harvey had been a foreman at the factory before he signed up for the regular army. John knew that his wife had left him years ago to bring up his young son alone. He remembered Peter Harvey from the days when he used to climb over the wall and steal the apples, a scruffy boy with ragged trousers and a permanent grin of defiance. John had always had a secret desire to know the boy better. There was something about his disregard for authority that the twelve-year-old John – a shy and diffident child, had found magnetically attractive.

When Dennis Harvey had been left alone his widowed mother had moved in to care for young Peter and she had been there ever since, keeping house for them both. It was she whom John had come to see.

He rang the bell and a few moments later the door was opened by a grey-haired woman with sharp blue eyes. She peered at him, wiping her hands on a print overall.

'Yes?' Her face registered recognition. 'Oh, it's Mr John, isn't it?'

'That's right. Are you still taking on domestic work, Mrs Harvey?'

'I am.'

'My mother could do with some help with the spring-cleaning and she wondered if you'd be free to give her a few weeks.'

Mrs Harvey looked doubtful. 'What about Betty Mason? I wouldn't want to put anyone else out of a job.'

'Oh, there's no fear of that. Mother thought she could do with some help, that's all.

'Well . . . When would I be needed?'

'Would next Monday be convenient?'

'Half-eight be all right?'

'I'm sure that would be ideal. Thank you, Mrs Harvey.' He was half-way down the path when she called to him.

'Same pay as Betty, I take it? I mean, if I'm to be doing all the rough, I'd expect the same.'

'Of course.'

'Oh, and by the way, the name's Clarice if you don't mind. I hate being called Mrs Harvey.'

John smiled. 'I'll tell mother. Goodbye then – Clarice. And thanks.'

John closed the rickety gate carefully behind him. It was a beautiful spring evening, mild and still. His thoughts were with Cathy. He'd had just one letter from her since she left Queensgrove. She seemed happy enough but he thought he detected a note of homesickness in her letter. He had missed her unbearably and he ached to see her. They had never really made up their quarrel and he regretted it. She was a good girl and he knew he should appreciate her wholesomeness. But he was only human and very much in love.

As he crossed the road he breathed deeply. The row of tall poplars that fringed the park gave off a sweet fragrance that wrenched at his heart. He didn't feel like going home just yet. Sometimes the atmosphere at Cedar Lodge and his mother's bitter prejudices stifled him. On impulse he decided to take a walk round the park before going in.

He went in through the gates, striking out along the path towards the lake, admiring the gold and crimson of the sunset. The park was almost deserted. At the lake's edge he was surprised to see a young woman, throwing bread to a cluster of ducks that gathered round her feet. She turned as he came up.

'Noisy little devils, aren't they? Just thought I'd give them the rest of my sandwiches. Mum gets cross if I take them home with me.'

With surprise John recognized Rachel Sands from number fourteen King's Walk. She'd grown up a lot since he last saw her;

developed from a long-legged tomboy into a very pretty girl. She wore a light-coloured coat, the belt tightly pulled in to emphasize her slender waist. Her blonde hair was cut in a short curly style, and he couldn't help noticing that the long gangling legs he remembered were now very shapely in their high-heeled shoes. But the face was the same, the hazel eyes as challenging and the wide mouth as audacious as he recalled. It was clear now that she recognized him too.

'Hey! You're John King, aren't you?' she said. 'Been doing your "National", have you?' She continued to throw her sandwiches to the ducks.

He nodded. 'And before that, college. Seems I've missed a few years as far as King's Walk is concerned.'

She pulled a face. 'I shouldn't worry. You haven't missed a thing. It's just as boring as ever.' She tipped out the last of the crumbs and crumpled the bag into a ball, tossing it into a nearby litter bin. 'You in charge now up at King's, then?' she asked.

He nodded. 'What do you do?'

'I work at Glenda's Gowns in the high street.'

'Like it?'

She shrugged. 'It's a job, and I get a bit of discount off my frocks. Not much happens round here though, does it? Every day the same. I'd like to go up to London.'

'You might find it just as boring as here,' he warned.

'You make your own excitement in this world, I reckon,' she said philosophically.

'In that case couldn't you make it exciting here?' John asked with a smile.

She raised an eyebrow at him. 'With parents like mine?' She nodded towards the park gates. 'You going back now?' He nodded and they fell into step. 'Be in by ten, no make-up, no drinking, no fellers, no fags.' She blew out her cheeks. 'I mean, honestly! At *my* age! Not that I take any notice of course. But they go on and on! Sometimes I feel if I don't get away soon I'll suffocate!'

John knew the feeling but he said nothing. If his mother had her way she'd organize his life too. She had inherited everything when his father died, so she was in effect, his boss. He drew a monthly salary like the other management staff, but all the profits went into her bank account. But they both knew that she couldn't manage without him to run the factory and take charge of finances and he'd already made up his mind not to let her get the upper hand.

As they reached the gates Rachel turned to him. 'What do you do with your spare time then, John?'

He was a little taken aback. 'Oh – nothing much. My girlfriend has just left to work down south. Naturally I miss her.'

Her eyes narrowed. 'That'd be Cathy Ladgrove. Oh yeah, I heard she was going out with you. Lucky girl!' She smiled boldly into his eyes. 'Well, if you get lonely just let me know. I always come home across the park about this time so you'll know where to find me. Night, John. Be seeing you – I hope.'

CHAPTER THREE

RACHEL WENT STRAIGHT UPSTAIRS when she got indoors and wiped off every vestige of her make-up. It was ridiculous that she should have to do this, she reflected as she put away the jar of cold cream in her dressing-table drawer. Everyone wore make-up now. Mrs Gifford, the manageress at Glenda's Gowns actually insisted on the girls wearing it. She said it was bad for business not to, but still her parents frowned on it.

Rachel looked around her bedroom. It was nothing like the bedrooms she admired in the films, all thick fluffy carpets and big soft beds with frilled canopies. She hated the linoleum-covered floor with its threadbare rug. She hated the scuffed pine dressing-table with its spotted mirror and the drawers that always stuck. She hated the single bed with its lumpy flock mattress. She'd spent the night once with Cathy Ladgrove when the family had lived at number five. The Ladgroves weren't rich but Cathy had a pretty eiderdown and sprigged curtains.

'The trouble is,' she said to her disgruntled reflection. 'The trouble *is* that Mum and Dad have no style; either that or they just don't care.'

Satisfied that she looked suitably dowdy, she went downstairs to the kitchen where Mary Sands was preparing the evening meal. Mary was only forty-three, but her drooping shoulders, lined face and neglected grey hair made her appear much older. She looked up as Rachel came in.

'Hello, dear. Are you hungry?'

Rachel nodded. 'Ravenous.'

'Did you eat your sandwiches?'

39

'Yes.' Rachel turned away and began to lay the table, but Mary had caught the look on her face.

'You didn't, did you?' she accused. 'Really, Rachel, I don't know why I bother. You're too bad. I put the last of the cheese ration in those sandwiches for you and you know how partial your father is to a bit of cheese after his supper.'

Rachel sighed. 'I wasn't hungry,' she said sullenly. 'I can't *make* myself hungry, can I?'

'So where are they then? If you didn't eat them what did you do with them?'

'I gave them to Sally,' Rachel despised herself for the lie. Why shouldn't she be able to tell her mother that she hated cheese – that she'd given her sandwiches to the ducks on her way home through the park? But she knew that if she did it would only lead to more nagging.

You should be thankful you've got good food to eat.

I never saw such an ungrateful child.

Why can't you appreciate what's done for you?

She'd heard them all a thousand times before. And then again, she wasn't allowed to walk home through the park. It was supposed to be full of rapists or white slavers. She'd been instructed to walk home the long way round, putting another mile at least on the journey. If she complained she'd only be accused of laziness. Rachel had long ago realized that lying was the only way to gain approval in this house.

She turned to her mother. 'Shall I lay the table?'

'Yes, then call your father. He's working on next Sunday's sermon.'

Ten minutes later the Sands family were seated round the table in the dining-room. The furnishings here were as drab as those in Rachel's bedroom. A square of carpet of which most of the colour had faded to an indeterminate beige covered most of the floor. There was a square table and matching chairs, an oak sideboard with a mirrored back and two well-worn fireside chairs. Above the fireplace hung a gloomy print of *The Stag at Bay* which Rachel had always loathed.

Herbert Sands said grace while Rachel and her mother bowed their heads, then Mary dished out the mutton-stew, potatoes and cabbage. As she ate Rachel glanced at her parents. Herbert was about the same age as his wife but he looked even older. His clothes hung on his angular frame. He wore steel-rimmed spectacles and the thinning hair, that had once been fair, was now almost colourless. He looked up at Rachel.

'Did you have a good day, Rachel?'

'Yes thank you, Father.' She looked at the clock as Mary gathered up the empty plates. 'Is it all right if I skip the pudding? I said I'd meet Sally and go to the pictures.' She began to rise from the table but Herbert raised his hand.

'Sit down.'

'But I'll be late . . .'

'I said, sit down,' Herbert repeated. 'Your mother has been good enough to make a rice pudding. The least you can do is to eat it.'

'I don't like rice pudding,' Rachel said defiantly.

Herbert straightened his back and looked at his daughter with gathering brows. 'How dare you! Do as you're told. You'll eat the pudding whether you like it or not.'

'But Sally . . .'

'Sally will wait for you. If she doesn't then you will return home.' He applied himself to his food once more. 'Anyway, you know I do not approve of the cinema. And certainly not on weekday evenings. It would have been polite to have asked me first whether you may go. Please do not make arrangements to go again without asking.'

Rachel sat fuming with rebellion as Mary placed the bowl of thin rice pudding in front of her. She knew better than to argue. Her father was perfectly capable of sending her to her room. He might look mild but when he lost his temper Herbert Sands could be formidable. And he never lost an opportunity to remind her that but for his generosity she would have grown up in an orphanage. She had no wish to hear it again.

With one eye on the clock, Rachel swallowed the gruel-like substance and glanced at her mother.

'Is it all right if I . . . ?'

'Stay where you are!' Herbert thundered. 'I have not finished yet. You do not leave the table until I have.'

Seething with impatience, Rachel watched as her father slowly and carefully spooned the last of his rice pudding into his mouth, scraping the bowl meticulously and then dabbing his mouth with his napkin. Only then did he look at her.

41

'You may be excused now.'

She got up from the tabie hurriedly.

'And please do not be home any later than half past nine,' he ordered as she reached the door.

She glared at the back of his head. 'But the film doesn't finish until a quarter to ten,' she said.

'Then you will need to leave the cinema a little early, won't you?' Herbert said without turning.

The bus shelter was illuminated by a single streetlamp and with the aid of this Rachel applied her lipstick, propping her handbag mirror up on a ledge and bending her knees to see into it. She'd said she was meeting Sally but it wasn't true. She'd seen Peter Harvey at lunch-time when she'd popped out to buy crisps for lunch. He worked at Prinn's Motors in the next street to Glenda's. He'd asked her out and she'd agreed to meet him.

Her parents had never approved of Peter, feeling him to be a bad influence. True, he'd had a few narrow escapes. When they were children they had landed in scrapes together all the time, but they'd been close friends for as long as Rachel could remember. Peter was fun with an exciting hint of danger that Rachel found irresistible.

Her make-up completed, she walked along to the corner. The streetlamps illuminated the main road, throwing the park into darkness. She thought of John King and their talk on the way home. Cathy had gone down to Bournemouth, then? Rachel had heard that her sister Pauline had left her husband and come home with her two kids. Maybe there was no room for Cathy in the flat above the shop any more. She sighed, wishing something similar would happen to her. There was no way she'd ever be allowed to go away to work.

Lately life had become so dull. Now that the Yanks had gone Rachel missed the dances she'd been to at the airbase. Those were the days. Those boys knew how to treat a girl. Of course she'd had to lie through her teeth to get there. And once Dad had found out where she'd been going on Saturday evenings there'd been hell to pay. She hadn't been allowed out for weeks after that. Life at home was like being in prison, with father as a suspicious, narrow-minded gaoler. It was a wonder he didn't lock her in her room at night.

She wondered idly if there was some way she could attract John. It'd be lovely being his girlfriend. He'd got a car and he'd be able to take her to smart places. He wouldn't be afraid to spend either. He must be pretty well off now that he owned the factory. He was quite good-looking too now that he was older. His brother Laurence had been a real smasher of course, but he'd been killed in the war.

She was confident that if she could get John to take her out just once she'd be able to hang on to him. She knew how to do that all right. Cathy Ladgrove would soon find she couldn't just go off and leave her feller to rot! It'd serve her right.

'Wake up! I thought you were going to walk right past me.' Peter grabbed her arm and grinned into her face. 'Proper Dolly Daydream, you are. Penny for 'em?'

Rachel shrugged. 'Not worth it. Right, so where're we going?'

He pulled a face. 'Dunno. Trouble is I've got no cash. I tried to touch Gran for a few bob but she wasn't having any. Said I never paid her back last time.'

'And did you?'

He shook his head. 'S'pose not, come to think of it.'

Rachel sniffed. 'I thought we'd go to the Roxy. They've got *The Wicked Lady* on there. Everyone says it's really good.'

'You're my wicked lady,' Peter said, pulling her arm through his. 'We can still go – if you've got some lolly.'

'Well I haven't!' she said indignantly. 'Not till pay-day. You should know better than to ask a girl out when you've got no money.'

'I wouldn't normally but it's different with you,' Peter said.

'What, you mean I don't deserve to be treated right?' Rachel was feeling let down. John King would never do such a thing, she told herself. Sometimes she wondered why she bothered with Peter. He'd got no right to take her for granted like this. She pulled her arm from his. 'I might as well go home, then,' she said.

He frowned. 'Oh, come on, Rach, don't be like that. It's a nice dry evening. We can go for a walk. And I've got about enough for a couple of shandies. We could finish up in the Crown.'

'Do you have any idea what my dad would say if he knew I'd been in a pub?' she challenged.

He grinned. 'When did that ever stop you doing what you wanted? Oh, come on, Rachie. Stop messing about.'

She paused, weighing up the alternative of going home to a boring evening with her parents, sitting round the wireless, listening to the *Brains Trust*. 'Oh – all right then.'

'Why not the park?' Peter nodded his head towards the gates. 'They don't lock up till ten.'

'I've got to be home by half-nine,' Rachel told him.

Peter blew out his cheeks. 'Christ! Why don't they just get you a collar and chain and be done with it!'

Under cover of the dark shadows of the trees Peter put his arm round her shoulders. 'Let's sit down on that bench over there. It's ages since we had a cuddle.'

'Get off!'

Peter withdrew his arm and they walked in silence for a few minutes, then he said, 'I've got something to tell you.'

'What?'

'I've had my papers. I've got to go and do my National Service.'

She turned to look at him. 'I thought you were allowed to finish your apprenticeship first.'

'Yeah. I have. I finished last week, so now I've got to go.'

Rachel felt her jaw drop. 'When?'

'Next week.' She said nothing and he went on, 'That's why I wanted to see you. Look, Rach, let's go somewhere tomorrow. I can get a car. We'll drive out somewhere and have a meal. What do you say?'

She stared at him. 'Where're you going to get a car from – and the money for a meal?'

'Leave that to me. I can wangle a car from work and Gran'll let me have some cash if I ask her nice.'

She smiled. 'All right then. Oh, Pete, I'm going to miss you. It won't be the same round here without you.'

'I daresay there'll be leave,' he told her. 'And it's only for two years, though most of the lads get off in one and a half. Will you write to me?'

She nodded. 'If you'll answer.'

He grinned. 'You know I'm not much of a one for writing but I'll try.' They reached a bench and he took her hand and pulled her over to it. 'You're a great girl, Rach.' He slipped an arm round her.

'You're like me. You want something better from life and you'll get it – one day. We're two of a kind, you and me. I'm going to have a lot of money one day and when I do you can have anything you want.'

'A lot of money – you?' She looked at him doubtfully. 'How are you going to get a lot of money? Going to have your own garage – is that it?'

He shook his head. 'There's big money to be made out there. Just stick with me, eh, Rach?'

She laughed and nudged him. 'Get off, Pete. We're not the sort to get rich.' She looked at his face, and suddenly her heart softened. 'Come on then. Are we going to have that shandy?'

He pulled her close and kissed her and, as always, her lips parted for him. 'Promise to come out with me tomorrow night?' he said, his mouth against hers. 'It could be the last time for months.'

'Oh, all right then.'

It took every ounce of Rachel's inventiveness to persuade her parents that she needed to go out again the following evening.

'It's overtime – stocktaking at Glenda's,' she said. 'Mrs Gifford says we have to go. I don't want to lose my job, do I?'

'How long will it take?' Herbert asked.

Rachel shrugged. 'I don't know. At least till ten. It depends.'

'In that case I'd better walk down to the High Street and meet you,' he said. 'One can't be too careful. You never know who's about.'

Rachel's heart turned to ice. 'No!' she said, her brain ticking over wildly. 'Mrs Gifford's husband is coming to meet her. She said they'd see me home.' In actual fact Maudie Gifford was divorced, but Herbert seemed to be satisfied.

'Very well,' he conceded. 'But if you're later than ten o'clock I shall have words with Mrs Gifford myself.'

Suitably warned Rachel set out to meet Peter at half past six. She'd had to put her coat on over her best frock. Wouldn't do to be seen going off to do stocktaking in her Sunday best.

He was waiting for her near the park gates, sitting at the wheel of a black Vauxhall saloon, his copper hair neatly brushed and wearing his best suit. He looked pleased with himself. Rachel opened the passenger door and climbed in.

'You got it then,' she said.

'Looks like it.' He started the engine and put the car into gear.

'Did your boss say you could borrow it?'

He grinned. 'Let's just say I took his permission as read.' He reached out to squeeze her knee. 'I thought we'd drive over to Peterborough. I know a grand place there.'

'Are you sure this is OK?' she asked him. 'I wouldn't want you to get into trouble, Pete.'

'What can they do to me, give me the sack?' he asked. 'I'm leaving to serve my King and country, aren't I?'

The pub was called the Ring of Bells. It had a thatched roof and there were coloured lights strung out all round the forecourt. Peter parked the car and they went inside. Sitting on a high stool at the bar, Rachel sipped her port and lemon, but when Peter passed her the menu she looked in horror at the prices.

'You can't afford this,' she whispered to him.

He threw back his shoulders and grinned at her. 'You leave all that to me,' he told her expansively. 'Order what you like.'

She thought of the insipid grey shepherd's pie she had been obliged to consume less than an hour ago and ordered a chicken salad. By the time they reached the coffee stage it was almost nine o'clock. Rachel looked at Peter apologetically.

'I'll have to be in by a quarter past ten,' she told him. 'I'm supposed to be stocktaking at the shop and if I'm late Dad might set out to meet me.'

He laughed. 'Can't have that. OK, I'll pay the bill and we'll go.'

They were half-way home when Peter drew the car into a lay-by and switched off the engine. She looked at him.

'What's up?'

'We've run out of petrol,' he said with a grin.

'Come on Pete, stop messing about.'

He turned to her and put his arms round her, pulling her close. 'We've got time for a cuddle. Could be the last time for ages.'

She allowed herself to relax in his arms, but when he began undoing the buttons of her dress she grasped his hand.

'No, don't.'

He kissed her throat in the way he knew excited her. 'Come on,

Rach. You're not going to be mean to me when I'm going away, are you?'

She swallowed hard, trying to quell the arousal that made her heart race and her stomach churn 'We haven't got time,' she muttered breathlessly.

'Yes, we have. It won't take me long to drive back to Queensgrove. We've got bags of time.' He kissed her, his hand pushing up her skirt to find the gap between stocking-top and suspender-belt, his fingers seductively stroking the warm soft skin of her thigh. 'Come on, Rach. You know you want it too.'

She gasped as she felt his hand creep higher. 'Oh, Pete – are you sure it's all right? Have you got any. . . ?'

He stopped her words with his mouth on hers. 'Everything'll be fine. Just leave it to me. Shall we get in the back?' he asked. 'It'll be more comfy in there.'

In the half-hour that followed Rachel forgot everything; time and place seemed to melt away as she gave herself up to the sheer ecstasy of their lovemaking. Sex was nothing new between them. She and Peter had been experimenting with it since they were fourteen and by now they were ideal partners, each of them knowing what the other liked and how to supply it. At last, sated and slightly dizzy with satisfaction, Rachel rested her head against his chest and sighed.

'I'm going to miss you so much.'

'Me too. There's no one like you, Rach. One of these days we'll get married.'

She said nothing. Peter was fine. He was a good friend and she enjoyed his company, but when she married she'd be looking for something different; a man who would be able to give her the things she wanted; to make her feel secure and comfortable as well as loved. All the same, she knew that she and Peter would never stop being friends. 'What's the time?' she asked him sleepily.

In the dim light he reached out his hand to look at his watch.

'Half past ten,' he said.

Her eyes flew open. 'Oh no! We'd better get going. Dad'll be on the warpath.' She fumbled on the floor of the car for her hastily discarded knickers, frantically pulling them on and almost falling out of the car.

In the driving seat Peter took out a comb and began to comb his hair with the aid of the rear-view mirror.

'Leave that!' she demanded, giving a nudge. 'Get me home – and *quick*!'

CHAPTER FOUR

CATHY'S ROOM AT THE Marine Bay was on the top floor of the hotel. It was small but adequately furnished with a single bed, dressing-table and wardrobe. There was even an armchair where she could curl up with a book in her rare leisure time. If she opened the window she could even smell the salty ozone of the sea.

In the first few days she was there Cathy thought she would die of homesickness. Each morning when she woke she promised herself to stand it for one more day, telling herself that if she knew there was an escape route things would be more bearable. She knew deep inside that in reality she could not return home. The truth was that even with the best will in the world there was no room for her there any more and the business could not afford to support her. One way or another she must make a new life here. She must work and save and try to get herself trained for the job she dreamed of. There was no turning back. But it did not stop her from missing her family, John and all the familiar things that meant home to her.

To help take her mind off the pain of longing she used her free time to explore the town. It was much larger than she'd expected, bigger than any of the east coast seaside towns she was used to and much more sophisticated. The shops were a revelation and she discovered that there were several cinemas and theatres as well as the splendid Pavilion with its grand forecourt and the famous fountain that changed colour after dark.

She walked wide-eyed around the exquisite gardens, admiring the palm trees and tropical plants, the waterfalls and rockeries. The promenade was wide and spacious with its seafront cafés and ice-cream kiosks. The sea was blue and the beach boasted soft yellow sands. Cathy looked forward to some leisure time in the coming summer when she would have a chance to enjoy it.

The Marine Bay was a medium-sized hotel and the Tanners were kind employers. Cathy was on duty in the dining-room for breakfast and lunch, and during the mornings, after laying the tables for lunch she helped another girl with cleaning the bedrooms. But in the evening another waitress would take over so that she could attend her art classes. Her old art teacher, Jean, had made sure that was one of the stipulations of her employment.

On the first opportunity Cathy searched out the college. She found it quite easily just a short walk from the hotel, a large red-brick building.

On the day she went to enrol she was nervous. She'd taken the portfolio of drawings and paintings that Jean Tanner had suggested she assemble, but she hadn't done much artwork since leaving school and she was terribly afraid her work would be considered too simplistic for acceptance.

She was ushered into a small office just off the main hall by a tutor who introduced himself as Paul Samuels. He asked her to sit down and began to look at her work. She held her breath as he turned the pages of the portfolio, looking thoughtfully at her line-and-wash drawings of Queensgrove park; the charcoal studies of Mrs Harvey's tabby cat, asleep on the wall and the delightful watercolour portrait she had painted of Pauline's newborn twins. When he had studied them all he closed the portfolio and looked up at her.

'What branch of art are you interested in pursuing, Catherine?' He smiled. 'I may call you Catherine?'

She nodded, swallowing. 'I'd like to work with fashion design. If I were ever good enough.'

He smiled. 'I think there's a very good chance that you'll be good enough, but had you thought of taking a teaching diploma?'

She shook her head. 'No.'

'It would always be a good stand-by,' he told her. 'The fashion industry is highly competitive, but if you were qualified to teach you need never be out of work.'

She nodded eagerly. 'It sounds wonderful.'

'So you'd like to enrol for a full-time course?' He looked at her enquiringly but she blushed and bit her lip.

'I'm afraid I can't. I have to work in the daytime. I can only manage evening classes.'

He nodded. 'That's a pity, but it can't be helped. Evening classes are better than nothing, and maybe you'll be able to manage some afternoon classes too. The new term begins next week. Can you start then?'

She nodded happily, unable to keep the delighted smile off her face. 'Oh, yes please.'

He rose from behind his desk. 'If you come with me I'll show you where everything is and you can register.'

Later, as he walked with her to the front entrance, Paul Samuels glanced at her elated face. 'It's good to welcome someone as keen as you, Catherine,' he said, holding out his hand. 'I'll look forward to seeing you next week.'

Now Cathy had been in Bournemouth for almost a month. At first she had found it hard, getting up early and doing a day's work and then rushing off to college in the evenings. On Paul Samuels's suggestion she found she could fit in two afternoon classes too. On Mondays and Wednesdays she attended the life class and found drawing the human figure new and exciting.

The Tanners specialized in their cuisine and the Marine Bay was open to non-residents at mealtimes. As Cathy was the only waitress she found it hard going when they were busy at lunch times. But the tips were good and she was allowed to keep them all for herself. They all went towards her fees and art materials.

Once a week she wrote home, but every night before she went to bed, she wrote a few lines to John. She told him about her day; amusing anecdotes about the Marine Bay's clients; about her art classes and the other students and about Paul Samuels, her kindly tutor. She even drew a small caricature of him, with his dark beard and compelling eyes, his crumpled shirt and paint-stained denims. In his turn John wrote back, telling her all the news from Queensgrove. Peter Harvey had been called up for his National Service, He had persuaded his mother to employ Peter's grandmother to helping with the spring-cleaning at Cedar Lodge. The factory was flourishing and he was experimenting with a few fashion designs. He always ended his letters by saying that he loved and missed her. Cathy cherished the letters, keeping them all in a pretty chocolate-box along with her handkerchiefs and reading them over and over in bed each night.

A week after she began her art course Cathy met Harry Flynn. She'd noticed him right from her first class. It was hard not to notice Harry with his shock of fair hair and his exuberant laugh. Everything about him exuded enthusiasm and high spirits. He seemed to attract attention wherever he went. To begin with the naturally shy Cathy gave him a wide birth, but it wasn't long before he made a point of singling her out. One evening during their coffee-break she found herself standing next to him in the queue at the canteen counter.

'Hi! Catherine, isn't it? I'm Harry.'

She smiled. 'Hello.'

'Enjoying the course?'

'Very much.'

'Why haven't I seen you around in the daytime?'

'I only come in the evenings. I have a daytime job.'

He pulled a face. 'It's going to take you ages to get your ATD part-time,' he said. 'I come every day and three evenings a week as well. Mind you,' he pulled a face, 'I've already flunked it once so who am I to talk?'

'I know it'll take me longer.' She shrugged. 'But I don't have any alternative. I have to work to pay my fees.'

'I've seen your work. You've got talent,' he observed.

'I'd like to hope so, or I wouldn't be here.'

'Take it from me, you have,' he said with confidence. They collected their coffees and Harry indicated a free table close by. 'Where do you work then, Catherine?' he asked as he sat down.

'Cathy,' she told him. 'I prefer being called Cathy. I work at the Marine Bay Hotel – as a waitress. I live there too.'

'Right.' He pulled a face, 'Do they keep you in a kennel in the back yard.'

She smiled. 'Not quite.'

'Still, they obviously let you out sometimes. Do you get any time off?'

She laughed. 'I get Sundays off.'

'Great! Come out with me next Sunday, then.'

She felt her cheeks colouring at his direct approach. 'Well –
I . . .'

'I know – come round to our house for lunch,' he said. 'It's
liberty hall at weekends. Everyone welcome.' He laughed at her
expression. 'Don't look so worried. It's open house. Everyone
brings their friends home on Sundays. My parents are musicians
with the local symphony orchestra. Dad plays the French horn
and Mum's a violinist. I'm sure you'll like them. I've got two
brothers too.'

'Are they musicians as well?' she asked.

He shook his head. 'One is. Philip plays the cello. He's a chip off
the old block. And the other, Andrew, is an actor, at least that's
what he *says* he is – when he's working, that is. He lives down at
Christchurch on the river, in a clapped-out old boat with another
crackpot would-be thespian called Finn Costello.' He laughed at
her crestfallen expression. 'I can see you think we're all a bit mad
and you're probably right, but you might as well check us out to
see. I'll meet you outside your hotel at twelve o'clock on Sunday
then. OK?'

And before Cathy had time to reply he was gone.

Cathy was apprehensive when Sunday arrived. Maybe Harry
would have forgotten his invitation. He had a reputation for being
scatterbrained. Anyway, she wasn't sure that she really wanted to
go. His family sounded quite formidable. Cathy was used to
normal, conventional people. And besides, she had homework to
finish. Maybe she could stay for an hour and then come home.

She need not have worried. He was waiting when she emerged
from the hotel; leaning on the rail on the other side of the road,
watching the hotel's front entrance. It was a gloriously warm
sunny morning and Cathy was wearing the first summer dress of
the season, a pale-blue cotton seersucker. Harry saw her crossing
the road towards him and beamed his approval.

'You look wonderful,' he said. 'That colour is terrific on you.
You should wear it all the time. Come on, Dad's car is in the car
park. It's only about five minutes from here but I thought we'd do
it in style.'

The car turned out to be a large white pre-war sports Jaguar.
When Harry switched on the ignition the car roared into life,

trembling alarmingly and snorting like a barely controlled wild animal. He glanced at her.

'It's OK. I passed my test a month ago and I've only had two accidents so far.' He looked at her stricken expression and roared with laughter. '*Joke!*'

She laughed shakily. 'Thank goodness for that.'

'Of course it was. I've only actually had one,' he said with a grin.

The Flynn family lived on the outskirts of the town in Penrith Avenue, quite close to the railway station. Their house was the first in a terrace of three-storey dwellings that Cathy guessed were probably late Georgian. At the front a flight of steps led down into a basement area and, after parking the car at the kerb Harry led Cathy down these steps and through an open door at the bottom. A dim passage led through to the back, opening on to a large living-room. Harry threw out his arms.

'Well, this is it – the hub of the Flynn empire!'

Cathy thought she had never seen such an untidy room. The curtains were of a red-and-white fabric in an incongruous jazzy pattern that jostled uneasily with the furniture which was a mixture of English and Oriental antique. A table in the centre of the room was covered in red chenille and littered with Sunday newspapers and toast-crumbs. In the fireplace the ashes of yesterday's fire spilled copiously on to the hearth and a fine dust covered the mantelpiece.

'My mama isn't exactly what you'd call house-proud,' Harry said dismissively. 'Come and meet everyone. I think it must be lunch-time by the way my stomach's rumbling.'

He led her through a door and up another flight of steps to a large square courtyard at the back. It seemed to be milling with people and Cathy hung back shyly, but Harry took her arm.

'Come and be introduced.'

Harry led Cathy up to a tall slender woman who was dispensing wine.

'This is my dearest mama,' he said. 'Faith – meet Cathy.'

Faith Flynn turned towards them and Cathy saw that she was extremely beautiful with golden skin and bright, intelligent blue eyes. Her fair hair was pulled back from her face and hung down her back in a long plait.

'Hello, Cathy,' she said warmly. 'Do help yourself to something to eat and a glass of wine. Don't wait to be asked. It's every man for himself here on Sundays.

A long trestle-table was laid out with an assortment of salads and cold meats and Harry steered her towards it.

'Get stuck in before the vultures arrive,' he advised. 'By half past one there'll be nothing left but the sun-bleached bones.'

Cathy looked round at the assortment of guests and wondered who they all were.

'Most of this lot are musicians,' Harry told her, biting into a hunk of French bread. 'We're hopelessly out-numbered. That mad-looking one over there with the fair hair is my brother, Andrew, and the shambling wreck beside him is his friend, Finn.'

Cathy followed Harry's gaze to where the two young men stood drinking wine. Andrew didn't look at all mad to her. He was fair and blue-eyed like Harry and his mother. He looked pleasant enough in his jeans and leather jacket, whilst his friend was dark with longish hair and looked more exotic.

'And over there,' Harry went on, 'the handsome swine in the white shirt talking to the pretty dark girl, is Philip. He's the sexpot of the family. I think the girl's name is Gillian something-or-other and she's from the orchestra too. I've an idea she plays the flute or the oboe.' He shrugged. 'All the same to me, philistine that I am.' He pointed. 'See the tall thin old bloke with the glasses? That's my pa – Mike. You'll like him. He's shy, like you.'

Cathy reflected that if anyone could manage to stay shy in a household like this, it must be quite an achievement

'As I said, most of the others are musicians, and I think I've spotted one or two of our lodgers,' Harry said.

'Lodgers?'

Harry nodded. 'We've got six bedrooms. We let off three of them – to students mainly.

Philip Flynn spotted them and came across.

'Well now, is this the girl you've been telling us about, Harry?' He smiled down at Cathy and held out his hand. 'I'm Philip Flynn. Welcome to the madhouse.'

She warmed to him immediately. 'Hello. Nice to meet you.'

'No, good of you to come. A Flynn Sunday must be a bit of an ordeal for a newcomer,' he said. 'But I see that for once my little brother wasn't exaggerating. He's talked of nothing else but the divine Cathy for a week. You should feel honoured. These crushes of his usually only last about three days.' He went off, chuckling to himself, and Cathy was surprised to see that Harry looked embarrassed.

'Trust your bloody nearest and dearest to let you down,' he muttered. He looked at her. 'It's not true. At least the bit about me talking about you is, but the other part . . .'

'You mean your crushes usually last longer than three days?'

He shook his head. 'I haven't had all that many.' He took her empty plate from her. 'Look, don't know about you but I've had enough of this lot. Come and see my room. It's right at the top of the house and there's a wonderful view of the town. I've got an electric kettle up there. We can have a quiet coffee.'

As they climbed the three flights of stairs Harry explained that although the family occupied the same house he and Philip led independent lives.

'We each have our own room and the use of the kitchen, the same as the lodgers,' he told her. 'Faith and Mike have to work such strange hours what with rehearsals and concerts that it's impossible to have a conventional family life, so we all go our own ways, except for Sundays when we all get together. It's their only chance of any kind of social life.' They reached the top landing and he opened a door.

'This is it,' he said, standing aside for her to pass. 'My sacred sanctum. No one enters these portals unless invited. We even do our own cleaning.' He grinned. 'Well, when we get round to it.'

The room was quite large but the sloping ceiling, which came down almost to floor level on two sides, made it seem smaller. On one side was a single bed covered with a plaid rug. The walls held a collection of books on home-made shelves and there were large posters of Picasso reproductions. Harry's easel occupied the space under the window; beside it was a small table covered with tubes of paint, palette and brushes. But when Cathy turned she saw that the wall behind her was covered by a huge abstract mural. She gasped.

'Wow! That's terrific.'

'Glad you like it.' Harry grinned. 'Did it one hot night last summer when I couldn't sleep.'

'Is that your speciality – abstract?'

He shook his head. 'I like it but Paul frowns on abstract – for us sprogs anyway. I like to dabble but I have to do it in my own time.'

By the bed was a record-player and a collection of records was scattered over the floor. Harry selected one at random and put it on.

'Help yourself to the view,' he invited, waving an arm towards the window. 'I'll go and fill the kettle so we can have some coffee.'

As the strains of Mendelssohn's *Italian* symphony filled the air Cathy looked out of the window. Harry had been right; from up here it was as if the whole town was spread out. A fine mist seemed to veil everything in a dancing haze. She could even see the sea sparkling away in the distance and for the first time Cathy was aware of being glad to be here. She loved this house with its easygoing atmosphere and glorious muddle. It felt warm and welcoming and lived-in. To her surprise she realized that she couldn't remember the last time she had felt homesick. She was actually beginning to enjoy herself.

Harry came back with the kettle and plugged it in. He held out his hand to her. 'Come and sit down.'

They sat down side by side on the bed. 'You're a lovely girl, Cathy,' he said. 'I don't think I've ever met anyone quite like you. You're shy, but I get the feeling that there's an awful lot going on behind that hesitant smile.'

'Harry – I think perhaps I should tell you now that there's someone – at home,' she said awkwardly. 'Someone special.'

He stood up. 'Hang on a minute while I make the coffee.' He spooned instant coffee into two mugs and poured on the boiling water. 'Hope you don't mind it black?'

She shook her head. Harry handed her a mug and sat down again. 'So – you were saying. There's some pining swain back home eating his heart out?'

She smiled. 'I don't know about the pining swain bit. His name is John and we grew up in the same road.'

He shook his head. 'I might have guessed. Time you came out of that tight little shell, my angel,' he said, shaking his head. 'It's my guess that a lot of fellers are going to be falling in love with you now that you're launched on the big wide world. How are you going to handle that?'

She shook her head. 'I can't see it happening.'

57

'Oh, it will,' he told her. 'Ever read the story about the princess and the frog? Well I reckon you're going to have to kiss a lot of frogs before you find your prince. But if you don't kiss them how will you ever know?'

She burst out laughing. 'Harry! You really do talk a lot of rubbish.'

He grinned. 'Never mind this John of yours. You and I can still be friends, can't we?' He gave her hand a squeeze. 'You're what the Italians call *simpatico*.'

She laughed. 'Am I? I'm not sure I know what that means.'

'It means you're the kind of girl who doesn't hurt for the sake of it. I like that. So – are we friends?'

She smiled at him. 'Of course we are, Harry. And thanks for asking me here today. I've really enjoyed it.'

'Does that mean that asking you again can't be completely ruled out?'

'I've got some homework to finish this evening, but I'd love to come again.'

'Great! That's settled then. I'll walk back to the Marine Bay with you.' As he held the door open for her he gave her a mischievous wink. 'I meant it about the frogs, though. I'll remind you about it some day.'

CHAPTER FIVE

CLARICE STOOD IN THE doorway and watched, seething as Theresa King ran a finger along the mantelpiece. This was the fourth time she'd caught her doing it this week. She decided enough was enough. It was time to speak her mind. She cleared her throat loudly.

'I haven't done in here yet, Mrs King,' she said stridently, making Theresa jump. 'But if you find my work unsatisfactory I'd be obliged if you'd say so so's I know where I stand.'

Theresa drew herself up to her full height. 'I have a perfect right to check, Mrs Harvey. Betty never objected.'

'More fool her then.' Clarice muttered under her breath. She folded her arms across her print-overalled bosom. 'If you take on an employee you should trust them. If you can't then you should find someone else.'

'There is no need for that.'

'There's plenty of people asking for me,' Clarice said, pressing her point. 'And while we're on the subject, now that Betty's got to have an operation she'll be away for several months. I didn't mind helping out when I thought it was only for a week or two but I can't be expected to keep on doing the work of two people for the wage of one!'

Theresa bridled. No one had ever spoken to her like this before. She longed to show the impudent woman the door but she knew she couldn't. Cleaning women were hard to find nowadays and now that Betty was ill she was lucky to get anyone at all. By and large Clarice Harvey was a thorough worker, but she'd always found in the past that it did no harm to keep them on their toes.

'I have promised Betty that she shall have her job back as soon as she's well again.'

'Yes, but you're not paying her while she's off though, are you?'

'That is really none of your business,' Theresa told her.

'It is when I'm doing her work as well as mine,' Clarice pointed out.

'Are you really expecting me to pay you double?'

'Maybe not double,' Clarice conceded. 'But more'n what I was offered when I started. That'd only be fair considering I'm doing twice the work.'

Theresa sighed. 'I shall consult my son,' she said. 'I will speak to you about it at the end of the week.'

As Theresa swept past her, Clarice added, 'There's another thing while we're talking, Mrs King.'

Theresa sighed. 'Yes?'

Refusing to be put down by Theresa's frosty expression Clarice went on. 'Anywhere else I've ever worked I've had a cup of tea and a biscuit mid-morning. You know – elevenses.'

Theresa's eyes snapped like icicles. 'And who is supposed to make these – elevenses, pray?'

Clarice shrugged. 'The missis usually makes it,' she said casually.

'You are saying that you want *me* to make *you* a cup of tea?'

It was all Clarice could do not to laugh at the outraged expression on the other woman's face.

'Well, why not?' she said. 'With anyone else I've ever cleaned for we've enjoyed a nice sit down together in the kitchen mid-morning and a good old gossip. It makes the morning pass more pleasant like.'

Theresa did not reply. She swept out of the room and closed the door firmly behind her.

Clarice sighed and shook her head. Who did she think she was, for heaven's sake? Too good to make a pot of tea for the likes of her, obviously! But Clarice got to thinking as she started to clean the room. There weren't many women about like Mrs K nowadays. More to be pitied really, poor old cow. She didn't know she was alive, living in this great house, just her and that poor lad of hers. Clinging to the past, that's what she was doing; like a lone survivor clinging to a raft. True, she'd lost her hubby and her elder son, but then so had a good many others. At least she'd got her John left. Not that she seemed to appreciate him.

I could easy have given up when my Reg died, Clarice reminded herself as she polished Theresa's mahogany davenport. She had shut herself away for a long time, just like her ladyship, but the moment she saw that her Dennis and young Peter needed her she pulled herself together again. Best thing that ever happened to her, coming to look after the pair of them, getting back in the swing of things again and living a useful life instead of brooding over what she'd lost.

'All looking back ever did was give you a pain in the neck,' she said aloud to her reflection in the overmantel. Keeping house for her son and grandson had given her a fresh reason for being alive. She nodded wisely to herself. That's what Mrs K needed – a reason for being alive. Maybe she could think of something – though she doubted if it would be appreciated.

It was a quarter past eleven when Theresa King appeared in the doorway of John's bedroom where Clarice was busily hoovering and singing to herself. At the sound of her employer's voice Clarice switched off the machine and looked up enquiringly.

'Did you want me?'

Theresa gave a little cough. 'Your – er – elevenses are in the kitchen, Mrs Harvey.' She turned and walked back downstairs. Somewhat surprised, Clarice straightened her back and followed.

Well! Wonders will never cease, she told herself. And although Theresa vanished into the morning-room and closed the door firmly, leaving Clarice to help herself to the pot of tea that stood brewing on the kitchen table, it was at least a step in the right direction.

John had decided that the factory could manage without him for a long weekend. If he left for Bournemouth on Friday morning and started back early on Monday morning he would only have to be away for a day and a half. His new deputy, Derek Simpson, a young man he had taken on soon after he had taken over from his father, was perfectly able to cope.

He missed Cathy. Being apart like this was ruining their relationship. Letters were a poor substitute and he was terribly afraid that if he didn't see her again soon she might find someone new. He wrote to ask if she could have any time off. She replied that as the summer season was getting under way she really couldn't ask. But she did have Sundays off and as the college was closed for the Whitsun break she was free on Friday as well as on Saturday evening. John seized the opportunity and arranged to leave the following Friday, asking Cathy to book him a room at the Marine Bay.

When he told his mother she made no attempt to hide her disapproval.

'I thought that when that girl left you would come to your senses,' she said. 'I really don't know what you're thinking about, John, consorting with a girl who cleans in some seaside boarding-house. I'm sure there are dozens of nice, well-educated girls who would jump at the chance to be asked out by you. Why don't you join the Young Conservatives or the tennis club? You'd meet young people of your own class there.'

John sighed, trying hard to hang on to his patience. 'Mother, apart from the fact that I really haven't the time, things have changed. The boundaries of *class* as you knew it have shifted. We've had a war, remember. There is absolutely nothing wrong with Cathy's upbringing and she is trying to further her education by doing this work down south. By the way, it's a hotel, not a boarding-house. And she isn't a cleaner.'

'You're just splitting hairs, John. You know perfectly well what I'm saying. You're attracted by her looks, that's all, and they won't last, you know. What can you possibly have in common with a girl like that? In three months you'd be bored with her.'

'We have more in common than you might think.' John got up from the table where he and his mother had been breakfasting. 'Anyway, it's all arranged. I'll be leaving on Friday morning.'

'John! Before you go, there's something I want to talk to you about.'

He sighed. 'I told you, Mother, there's no more to be said.'

'It isn't that. It's about Mrs Harvey.'

'Clarice? What about her?'

'She seems to think she should have more money, with Betty being away ill.'

'I suppose that's only fair. It looks as though Betty will be laid up for some time now so Clarice will be semi-permanent.' He looked at her. 'You're satisfied with her, aren't you?'

Theresa hesitated. 'She's a thorough worker, yes,' she said grudgingly.

John raised an eyebrow. 'Yes – but. . . ?'

'Well, for one thing, she tends to be over familiar,' Theresa said. 'She's always asking me to call her by her Christian name.'

'Nothing wrong with that, is there? You've always called Betty by hers.'

'That's different. Betty treated me with respect. I happen to prefer to keep things on a formal basis where Mrs Harvey is concerned,' Theresa said. 'Before we know it she'll be calling me by mine! And do you know what she asked me to do yesterday?'

John suppressed a smile. 'I can't possibly imagine.'

'She asked me to make her a cup of tea. She even expected me to join her. She suggested we might have what she called a *good old gossip* over our elevenses!'

'And did you?'

'Of course I didn't. I did make her the tea though. Earlier the wretched woman was actually threatening to leave. Really, John, it's quite intolerable. Once these people have the upper hand they think they can demand anything. Before we know it we'll have anarchy on our hands.'

John laughed out loud. '*Anarchy*! Because she asked you to join her for a cup of tea? Really, Mother!'

Theresa reddened. 'I can see it's no use talking to you. Heaven only knows how you allow the workforce at the factory to treat you. In your father's day—'

'Mother!' John's tone was warning. 'I think you can safely leave the running of King's to me. I can tell you now that if I tried to run things with your attitude I'd have a strike on my hands in a week! Give Clarice Harvey twice what you pay her now. She's worth every penny. And for heaven's sake unbend a little. Have a cup of tea and a gossip with her. You might even find you enjoy it.'

John arrived at the Marine Bay Hotel early on Friday afternoon. Cathy had been looking out for him and as soon as she saw him drive into the car park she ran out to meet him. John saw her as he got out of the car. She looked wonderful, her skin tanned a golden colour that made her eyes appear brighter than ever. She'd had her hair cut too. He held out his arms and she ran into them, clinging to him, her face upturned, her mouth soft and expectant and her arms warm around his neck. He held her close, savouring the fresh fragrance of her skin and hair, pressing his cheek against her soft skin. The weeks of missing her and wanting her gathered inside him till he thought he would burst with love.

'I've missed you so much, Cathy,' he said thickly.

'Me too.' She was half-laughing, half-crying as she pulled his head down to kiss him again. 'I've longed so much to see you. And now you're here I can hardly believe it. We're going to have the best weekend ever! I've got the whole of tomorrow off so we can go somewhere for the day.'

'Well, I should hope so!'

She frowned. 'And tomorrow evening I've got a special surprise for you.' She linked her arm through his. 'Come on. I'll take you up to your room. Then, when you've unpacked, we can go out.'

They drove to Weymouth for the afternoon, having tea in the little teashop near the seafront, then lying together on the beach. John told her all that he'd been doing at home, although there wasn't a lot to tell. Work took up so much of his time that there was little left over for a social life. In her turn Cathy told him all about her work at college and the friends she'd made, especially the eccentric Flynn family.

'Faith and Mike Flynn have these marvellous Sunday morning get-togethers,' she told him. 'And their house is the most disorganized, chaotic, *fascinating* place you ever saw. Harry is the youngest son. He's on my course at college – hoping to get his ADT and teach. He has one brother who is a musician and another who's an actor. He lives with a friend on a boat down at Christchurch. Harry took me down there the other Sunday evening and it's lovely.' She laughed. 'Creaky and ramshackle but lovely. We're invited to a party at their house tomorrow night.'

'Oh.' John frowned. 'Do we have to go?'

She looked at him in surprise. 'I've said we will. You'll love them, John. Everyone says their parties are wonderful.'

'I came to see *you*, Cathy. I imagined it'd be just the two of us.' He knew even as he said it that he sounded stuffy.

'But we *are*.' She leaned across and kissed him. 'I can't begin to tell you how terrific it is to have you here. I just thought you'd like to go to a party, that's all. There aren't that many at home in Queensgrove, are there?'

'No. We can't all live like social butterflies.' He bit his tongue hard, horrified to realize that he sounded just like his mother.

'*Butterflies?* Have you any idea how hard I work?' she said, her eyes moist with hurt.

He put his arms round her and pulled her close. 'I'm sorry darling. It's just that I want you all to myself.'

'Do you want me to say we can't go?'

He shook his head. What he wanted her to say was that *she* didn't want to go, that she'd rather be alone with him, but she didn't.

'No. Of course we'll go.' He stood up, brushing the sand from his trousers and holding out a hand to her. 'Come on. Let's go and get something to eat and then how about a film?'

It was late when they got back to the hotel. They went quietly upstairs and as they paused at the door of John's room he took her hand.

'Come in for a while.'

She waited, her heartbeat quickening while he unlocked the door, then she allowed him to take her hand and draw her inside. In the darkness he gathered her close and began to kiss her. The kisses and caresses grew more and more passionate until at last she drew away, breathlessly.

'John – I . . .'

'Stay with me – please, Cathy.' He reached for her hand and in the darkness his eyes were luminous with longing. 'If you only knew how much I want you.' He pulled her to him. 'I thought you felt the same.'

'I do – but . . .' Trembling, she pulled away from him.

'What is it? I promise I won't let anything happen. Look, please, Cathy. I am prepared.'

'Prepared?'

'I brought – you know, protection.'

She backed away from him. 'You mean you took it for granted I'd say yes?'

'I hoped you would. Of course!' He grasped her arm and pulled her almost roughly to him again. 'I love you, Cathy,' he said exasperatedly. 'I thought you loved me too.'

'*I do.*' Her throat was tight with tears. 'I'm sorry if you feel you've had a wasted journey.'

'Oh God! Don't say things like that.'

They stood staring at each other in the dim light of the room. Cathy thought of what Pauline had told her and wondered if there might be something wrong with her. She'd heard of women who were frigid. Was she?

John pulled her close, more gently now. 'Darling, I'm sorry. You're tired. I didn't mean to rush you.'

She felt foolish. This was 1947 and she was supposed to be a modern girl, yet here she was behaving like someone out of a Victorian novel. 'You didn't.' she repeated. 'It's just . . .'

'You're worried about the Tanners – that they might find out?'

'Yes. That's it.' She grasped gratefully at the explanation. It was no use. She just couldn't explain. She knew she loved John. She just – wasn't ready to take things further.

He kissed her. 'Go to bed now. See you in the morning.'

An hour later both were still awake. John lay on his bed, wondering if Cathy could possibly really love him when she found him so repellent. He ached with frustration, torn between love for her and anger with her inhibitions. She wasn't a child. Surely she must know what it did to a man, this thoughtless teasing. Perhaps it would be better if he got up now and just left. If she loved him it would be up to her to write and tell him so. If not . . . He tried to imagine what his mother would make of his sudden return, and how difficult it would be to explain. He was still trying to make up his mind as dawn broke – and sleep finally claimed him.

Up in her own room Cathy cried until she had no more tears. She had looked forward so much to John's visit. Why couldn't she let him make love to her? Why couldn't she just relax and go with her own feelings? The obvious answer that lurked at the back of her mind refused to be acknowledged. In truth it was disappointment she was really afraid of. Her own and John's. Something that would surely ruin everything and end their relationship. Her mother had told her once that sex was overrated – that people made too much of it and that for women it was little more than a duty.

Saturday was a dismal failure. Cathy showed John all the places she had discovered and tried to instil some of her own pleasure into him but he was quiet and unresponsive. By the time evening arrived she felt exhausted with the effort of pretending everything was all right. She was in no mood for a party. They really needed to talk and there was so little time left. She suggested that they call it off. John was adamant.

'It would look rude to refuse at this late stage,' he said.

She tried to explain that everything at the Flynns was informal and that no one would care too much or even notice if they failed to turn up, but John insisted. When he knocked on her door she was dismayed to find that he was dressed in a suit and tie. She should have told him not to dress up but she felt it was too late. Anything she said now would probably be construed as criticism.

The front door of the Flynns' house was wide open and the sounds of merriment that issued from inside indicated that the party was already in full swing. Harry greeted them in the hall. He wore jeans and a bright-red shirt open at the neck.

'Hi there! This must be the famous John,' he said. 'Come and get yourselves a drink. You've got some catching up to do.'

The buffet was laid out in the back yard as for the Sunday morning get-togethers and the whole house seemed to be buzzing with people, all of them casually dressed. Harry escorted them to where drinks were being dispensed.

'Never set eyes on some of these folks,' he said, waving an arm. 'We've all invited our own guests, so with five of us it's no wonder, I suppose. Some of them are what you might call well refreshed as you can tell.' He poured two glasses of wine, eyeing John in his formal dark suit.

'You've got a little gem of a girl here you know,' he said as he handed them each a glass. 'Talk about talent. Not many that can hold a candle to her. Half the blokes on the ATD course are in love with her, you know. I wonder you dare let her out of your sight.' He laughed. 'You wouldn't believe the rush there's been to enrol on the evening classes since she arrived.'

John face darkened. 'Really?'

Undeterred Harry went on, 'So, what do you do for a crust, John? I think Cathy told me once but I've forgotten.'

'We're in footwear. My family own a factory,' John said.

Harry grinned. 'Ah – bloated capitalists, eh? Should have known.' He slipped an arm round Cathy's waist and gave her a squeeze. 'Art is all very well but it's nice to have something soft to fall back on, eh darling?'

Cathy was horrified. Harry's twisted sense of humour would get him into trouble one day. After the tense day she and John had spent together it was about the worst comment he could have made. She felt John stiffen beside her.

'We made our success on the backs of two world wars.' he said. 'So I daresay we could be classed as bloated capitalists, though to our credit, we do employ ex-servicemen.' He turned and put down his untouched glass of wine. 'Cathy, I've just remembered; I've got an important meeting early tomorrow. I think it might be as well if I made a start for home now.'

As he made his way determinedly between the crowds of guests, conspicuous in his dark suit, Cathy pushed her glass into Harry's hands.

'You really are an *idiot*, Harry! Here, take this. I'll see if I can catch him.'

'Sorry. I didn't mean any harm. I . . .' Harry stared after Cathy as she hurried after John. Really! Some people were so bloody touchy!

She caught John as the car was pulling away from the kerb. 'John! Wait!'

He stopped but did not switch off the engine. Cathy opened the passenger door and climbed in beside him. 'You shouldn't take any notice of Harry,' she said. 'He doesn't mean any harm. He just a bit brash and insensitive.'

He didn't look at her but stared straight out through the windscreen, his mouth set in a determined line. 'I think he knew exactly what he was saying. A lot of things are clear to me now.'

She frowned. 'What do you mean?'

'There's someone else, isn't there?' For the first time he turned towards her and the look in his eyes tore at her heart.

'Of *course* there isn't!'

'What was all that about everyone being in love with you? All that attention must be very flattering. And very tempting. It must make people like me seem very dull.'

'*No*! I told you, Harry talks a lot of rubbish. That's just *him*. Anyway, it's not true, John, if you only knew how much I've looked forward to this weekend. And now it's all . . .'

'All what? All spoiled, is that it? *I've* spoiled it, you mean.

Because I tried to make love to you? Because I don't fit in with your arty new friends.'

'That's not true!'

'Isn't it? You couldn't even bear to be away from them for one weekend. I think that says it all, Cathy.'

'Please, John. Don't let our weekend end like this. We can go somewhere else. If you like we can go back to the hotel – to your room. I'll . . .'

'You'll what? Make the *supreme sacrifice*? Don't bother, Cathy.'

Cathy was silent, her heart heavy and her throat aching with the tears that she refused to shed. Neither of them spoke for several seconds, then he turned to her.

'I'd better go. Why don't you get back to your friends? They must be wondering where you are.'

'I can't go back in there now,' she said quietly. 'Would you mind giving me a lift back to the hotel?'

'As you wish.' He put the car into gear.

She hoped the drive would have calmed him down, but as he parked the car and got out outside the Marine Bay he gave no indication that it had. She followed him upstairs to his room. Using his key he opened the door and went inside to throw his things into the grip he had brought. She stood in the doorway.

'Can I do anything?'

He glanced at her. 'I don't think so.'

When his bag was packed he turned and looked at her.

'It's goodbye then.'

She pushed the door shut and stood with her back to it. 'John – *please* don't do this. If you leave like this . . .' She couldn't hold back the tears now. They spilled over and ran down her cheeks as she clamped a hand over her mouth. 'Oh *damn*! I'm sorry,' she choked. 'I didn't mean to let you see . . .'

Suddenly all the heat went out of his anger. He put down his bag and went to her, taking her gently into his arms and holding her until she regained control.

'I'm sorry too, Cathy. I behaved like a boor. It was just the disappointment – the hurt.'

'You'll stay then?' She looked up at him appealingly. But he shook his head.

'It's no use, is it, Cathy?' he said, 'You down here and me at

69

home in Queensgrove. It won't work. We should have realized.'

'But it isn't for ever. Surely what we feel will stand a little time apart.' She looked up at him with brimming eyes. 'And when I get my qualification . . .'

'When you get your qualification you'll be looking for a job,' he said. 'And ten to one it won't be in Queensgrove. We have to face the facts, Cathy.'

'I meant it when I said I loved you, John.'

He sighed. 'I'm sure you thought you meant it. You're young, Cathy,' he said. 'Younger than me. This is your first experience of the outside world. There'll be other men – other loves – opportunities. A whole new life opening up for you. It wouldn't be fair of me to ask you to give it all up. Better face up to that now before we both get hurt too much.'

'It won't make any difference. *You're* what's important to me. I don't care about the rest.'

'But you do.' He shook his head, smiling at her sadly. 'Life changes all of us.'

'It won't change me. I'll prove it.' She looked into his eyes. 'We will keep writing, won't we? Even if you stop, I won't! And I'll be home at the end of the summer season, before the new term starts. We'll see each other then. We *will*, won't we?'

'Yes, of course.' He took her arms from around his neck and held her hands against his chest. 'Don't make it any harder, Cathy. Let me go now.'

'I love you, John,' she whispered miserably. 'I really, *really* do.'

He kissed her gently. 'If you can still say that to me and mean it two years from now, then maybe there might be some hope for us.'

She stood at the kerb, waving until he was out of sight. Up in her room she undressed and got into bed to lie staring numbly at the ceiling. The weekend she had looked forward to so much had all gone wrong and now she was terribly afraid she had lost John; lost him for ever. And all through her own stupidity. Why couldn't she have shown him that she loved him in the one way that would have convinced him?

Driving into the falling darkness John's heart was heavy with regret. He had behaved badly; he knew that. And all because he could see the Cathy he loved growing up and slipping away from

70

him. When she had agreed to this weekend visit he had assumed that she wanted to seal their relationship. He sighed. If only she were a few years older. He sometimes forgot that whereas he had been away to college and in the army, Cathy had never left Queensgrove and the little street where she had grown up until now. He'd been right. It wouldn't be fair to either of them to force her to choose between him and her chosen career.

He drove on through the night, his heart sore with longing. The dark road before him seemed as bleak as his future. In his pocket the tiny box that contained the ring he'd hoped to give her pressed against his side. A reminder of the failure of this weekend.

Theresa had been asleep for some time when the headlights swung across her window, waking her. She lay listening as the front door opened and closed quietly down in the hall and stealthy footsteps padded up the stairs.

Her heart pounding, she sat up and called out. 'Who's there?'

'It's all right, Mother. It's only me.'

She sighed with relief at the sound of John's voice. She switched on her bedside lamp and looked at the time. It was one o'clock.

'Are you all right, John?' she called out.

'I'm fine. Go back to sleep, Mother. I'll see you in the morning.'

Theresa switched off the light and lay down again feeling slightly peeved. No *I'm sorry I disturbed you, Mother*. The young were so thoughtless. Lying in the darkness she began to wonder why he had returned early from his weekend. Had they quarrelled? Had it been a failure? She hoped so. He'd be hurt, but he'd get over it soon enough. As she'd told him, there were plenty of nice suitable girls in Queensgrove. Perhaps now that he'd seen for himself that he and the Ladgrove girl were unsuited to one another he'd settle down. She sighed and turned over.

CHAPTER SIX

RACHEL WAS GOING QUIETLY frantic. Life at home had been even more difficult since that last night she'd gone out with Peter.

When she failed to arrive home at the appointed time her father had gone out to look for her. He'd been standing unseen at the corner of King's Walk when Peter let her out of the borrowed car. That in itself would have been bad enough, but from the shadows he'd watched as she bent down and gave Peter a lingering good-night kiss through the car window. It was to be a long time before she forgot the row that followed.

When he silently stepped out of the shadows and spoke her name he'd frightened the life out of her. Grasping her by the arm he'd frogmarched her in silence down the road and it wasn't until the front door was firmly closed that he'd started his tirade.

'Where were you and who was that man you were with?'

Rachel tried to brazen it out. 'I told you, I was stocktaking at the shop. I had a lift home.'

'Don't lie to me!' he'd thundered. 'I've been down to the High Street. There was no stocktaking going on there tonight. The shop was in darkness. I saw you kissing whoever the lout was who brought you home – brazenly in public; making a disgraceful exhibition of yourself!'

'There was no one to see!' Rachel interrupted. 'Except you and your nasty suspicious mind, spying on me. If it wasn't for your narrow-mindedness I'd feel free to tell the truth. If I lie, it's your fault – *Oh!*' The hand that lashed out and slapped her across the face was hard and bony. Herbert Sands's eyes were like granite behind the steel-rimmed spectacles as he glowered at her.

'How *dare* you speak to me like that! There's bad blood in you, girl. I've always thought so. And badness has to be stamped out before it gets the upper hand. From now on you'll go to your room after supper and stay there till morning. Do you hear?'

'I won't!'

'*Yes you will!*'

'Why? I haven't done anything.'

'You will do it because I say so. *Is that clear?*'

Mary Sands had come out into the hall now. She stood at the foot of the stairs, cowering before her husband's incandescent rage. From the kitchen she had heard the resounding slap and Rachel's cry. Now, seeing the girl's white face with the livid finger marks across one cheek she gave a little gasp of distress, her hand flying to her mouth.

'Do as Father says, Rachel' she said quietly. 'Go upstairs.' She didn't add: *Before he does something worse.* There was no need. With a stifled cry Rachel ran upstairs and shut herself in her room. Throwing herself on the bed she sobbed with a mixture of anger and frustration. She had to get out of here. She just *had* to. Much longer in this house and somebody would get murdered!

That had been almost two months ago and Herbert had kept his word. Every evening when she got home from the shop she ate a silent meal with her parents, then she was sent up to her room where her father would lock her in until he and Mary retired. Nothing had changed – except for one thing.

As the days and weeks passed a suspicion grew into a dread – then a certainty. Rachel was forced to face the fact that she was almost definitely pregnant.

She had plenty of time to think about it, sitting on her bed every evening, counting off the weeks in her diary. What on earth was she going to do? She knew girls who had resorted successfully to various remedies. She'd heard talk of hot baths and gin. But in the Sands household baths were taken once a week, when the Ideal boiler that crouched redundantly in one corner of the kitchen would be lit specially. She knew vaguely of knowledgeable women who performed 'operations' to get girls out of trouble. But that cost money. Quite a lot if what she had heard was true. It brought its own problems too and there was no privacy in this house. She would have little hope of concealing an abortion and its results from her mother.

Since Peter had been in the army she'd had only one letter from him. An ill-spelt, badly expressed letter saying that he was liking the life but that he missed her and Gran. It was little better than the kind of thing people wrote on holiday postcards and it gave her no hope of the kind of future she dreamed of. She was angry with Peter. He'd promised her that everything would be all right that night in the car. It always had been before, so she'd had no reason to worry. She had no intention of being forced to marry him. Fond as she was of Peter he would never be able to give her the life she craved. The likelihood was that even if they did marry she'd be obliged to live on here with her parents until his National Service had been completed. Wouldn't *that* be a bundle of fun! Herbert would be sure to remind her of the burden she was and the shame she had caused him at every possible opportunity.

On the other hand, she thought of what would happen when her father discovered she was about to become an unmarried mother? She shuddered. It had been impressed on her from an early age that she was likely to take after her immoral mother. This would be all Herbert Sands needed to prove he'd been right. She'd be sent away to one of those homes she'd heard of where the baby would be taken away from her at birth. She'd even heard of extreme cases where girls were certified insane and shut away for years. She was chillingly aware that Herbert Sands would have no pity. He would never forgive her.

Every night Rachel cried herself to sleep, terrified of the future and what it would bring. A few moments of pleasure, which Peter had no doubt forgotten all about by now, and her life had been cruelly shattered.

When the idea came to her it was in the small hours of the morning. It hit her so hard that she sat upright in bed. Why hadn't she thought of it before? It would solve everything. And she was pretty confident that she could pull it off.

She got out of bed and went to the window. It was a warm night and she saw the swing of headlights' beam light up the trees as a car turned into the driveway of Cedar Lodge. Could that be John – coming home at this hour? She wondered vaguely where he had been and whether he had thought of her again since the evening they'd met in the park? In spite of her invitation he had made no effort to see her again. She climbed back into bed and planned what she would do.

Rachel was waiting for John the following evening, by the staff entrance of King's factory. The moment she saw his car approaching the gates she made a great show of hopping about on one foot, holding her left shoe in her hand.

He pulled up and wound down the window. 'Hello, Rachel, what's wrong?'

'Heel came off my shoe,' she told him. 'Just back up the road there. I turned my ankle too.'

'Oh dear. Is it painful?'

'It is, a bit.' She gave him a tremulous smile. 'You couldn't do me a favour and give me a lift home, could you?'

'Of course.' He reached across and opened the passenger door for her while she ran round the car gratefully, remembering just in time to limp.

'Thanks,' she said as she settled into the seat. 'Don't know what state my feet would have been in if I'd had to walk all the way home without shoes. 'So – how have you been?' she asked brightly as he began to drive. 'I haven't seen you around lately.'

He shrugged. 'Working mostly.'

She gave a little giggle. 'You know what they say about all work and no play.'

He shook his head. 'I think I'm already pretty dull anyway.'

Rachel pulled a face. 'You sound a bit low to me. Maybe you need cheering up.'

He gave her a wry smile. 'I think you'd be hard put to it to cheer me up, Rachel,' he said. 'I'm a lost cause.'

She paused, glancing at him sideways from under her lashes. 'Don't tell me you've fallen out with Cathy,' she ventured. She held her breath, unable to believe her luck. When he didn't reply she said quickly, 'Oh, listen to me! Take no notice. Just tell me to shove off and mind my own business.'

He looked at her quickly. 'I'm sorry, Rachel. I didn't mean to be rude. I'm just not very good company at the moment.'

'Well, I know how you feel.' She sighed. 'My life is a mess too. My dad's as suspicious and narrow-minded as ever. That's why I was worried about getting home from work late. He doesn't trust me. He's *paralysed*!'

John hid a smile. 'I think you mean paranoid.'

'I expect he's that too,' Rachel agreed. 'Take the other week – we were stocktaking at the shop and I was late because my boss took me for a coffee as a kind of thank you. God only knows what Dad thought I was up to but there was hell to pay when I was late getting home.'

'So you don't get out much?' John said.

Rachel bit her lip. She was overdoing it. If he thought Dad was that bad he'd be nervous about asking her out. And she supposed that if she was really pushed she could always climb out of the bedroom window on to the kitchen roof.

'Oh, I can go out at weekends,' she told him. Her mind was working overtime. If she were to start going steady with John it could not be in secret. People – especially her parents – would need to know about it. When he failed to rise to her bait she glanced at him slyly. 'What do you do at the weekends, John?' They'd just turned into Wellington Road now. A few more yards and he'd be stopping to let her out. She had to make a move now – get him to ask her out or the chance would be lost.

'Weekends?' He gave an odd little laugh. 'Very little, actually.'

'Do you like the sea?' she asked him boldly. 'Looks like the weather's going to be good this weekend too.'

He'd stopped the car now, round the corner into King's Walk in the shelter of the high garden wall. He had no wish to be interrogated again by his mother and if she saw him with a girl in the car she'd be sure to start asking questions.

'So what do you reckon?' Rachel was saying. 'Shall we go down to Hunstanton on Sunday?'

He looked at her and laughed. She really did have the cheek of the devil. Suddenly he felt his spirits lift. He'd been dreading next Sunday, kicking his heels around at home all day, thinking about last weekend and wondering what Cathy was doing.

'All right then, Rachel. Why not? We'll go if that's what you'd like.'

'Really?' Her face lit up like a child's and he couldn't help feeling flattered.

'Yes, really,' he laughed. 'Suppose I pick you up just here – say ten o'clock?'

'Right! Ten o'clock it is, but pick me up in town, by the war memorial.' Suddenly she reached across and gave his cheek a quick peck. 'We'll have a smashing time. Just you wait and see. See you Sunday then.'

She got out of the car and he watched her tripping down King's Walk, her limp quite forgotten. She'd put her shoe back on again and he couldn't see much wrong with that either. Had she made up the story just to get him to drive her home? Again he felt flattered. There was a naïvety about Rachel that he found oddly endearing. Why shouldn't he take her out for the day? It would be nice to spend the day with someone uncomplicated – make up for last weekend's fiasco.

The memorial Theresa had had erected to her son, Second Lieutenant Laurence Henry King of the Royal Engineers took the form of a granite cross on which his name, rank and regiment was engraved. Below were the words:

BELOVED SON OF THERESA AND ALBERT KING.
FELL BRAVELY IN BATTLE JUNE 1944.
SADLY MISSED

It stood on the west side of the churchyard, close to the one her parents had had erected for her brother – and as far away from Albert's grave as was possible. Each week she visited it and took flowers which she arranged tastefully and lovingly in the vase at the foot of the memorial.

She'd noticed the woman before, since she'd changed her day for visiting the churchyard, from Friday to Wednesday. Occasionally she had passed her on her way out of the cemetery. Once or twice she'd had to stand aside to allow her to pass through the lych-gate in front of her.

She was a tall, slender woman some ten years younger than Theresa; upright and well dressed, the touches of grey in her dark hair only adding to her smartness. Theresa was curious enough to follow her one afternoon when she saw the woman enter the churchyard ahead of her carrying a bunch of sweet peas.

This afternoon she stood out of sight in the church porch and watched to see which grave the woman visited. Peering out from her hiding place she watched the woman cut across the churchyard, picking her way between the graves until she reached the far side and stopped at one of the graves Theresa held her breath as she saw the woman take a vase to the stand-pipe, fill it and return to unwrap her flowers. She couldn't be certain from where she was but she could have sworn that the woman was arranging flowers on Albert's grave!

Keeping out of sight she waited till she heard the creak and whine of the lych-gate, then she came out of her hiding-place and crossed the churchyard, carefully following the woman's footsteps.

Albert's grave bore a simple headstone and marble chips with a rail around it. There was no maintenance and Theresa rarely visited it. But someone clearly did. There on the marble chippings close to the headstone was a heavy white vase. In it were the sweet peas Theresa had seen the woman carrying not fifteen minutes ago.

On Sunday morning Rachel got ready for chapel as usual. She'd already made what she thought of as foolproof plans: enlisting the help of her friend Sally at work whom she persuaded to come round to the house on Friday evening to ask permission for Rachel to spend a day at the seaside with her and her family. Herbert could hardly refuse to allow her to go. Sally's father was a respected town councillor.

At ten o'clock she slipped out of her pew at the back of the chapel and hurried towards the war memorial in the centre of the market place. John was already waiting, the car parked nearby. She thought he looked handsome in casual clothes, grey flannels, open-necked shirt and a blazer. She only wished she'd had something more suitable to wear. She had to hand most of her wages over to Mary every Friday evening and there was little left over for clothes.

As she got into the car John smiled at her. 'You look nice,' he said, looking at the demure navy blue two-piece with its white collar and cuffs.

Rachel pulled a face. 'I've come straight from chapel,' she said. 'And I didn't want to waste time going home to change.'

'No need anyway,' he said as he started the car. 'You look very pretty.'

The ride through the Norfolk countryside was pleasant and

when they reached Hunstanton and the car dipped down towards the seafront, Rachel caught the familiar scent of ozone mingling with fish and chips and frying onions. She shivered with delight.

'I love it here,' she told John. 'All the people and the sounds and the smells.'

'What about the sea?' John asked wryly.

'Oh yes, that as well.'

'You wouldn't prefer somewhere quieter, further along the coast?'

Rachel hesitated. 'That might be nice later,' she said.

They walked along the promenade and ate ice-cream. At Rachel's request they went into a fish restaurant where she ate a hearty helping of haddock and chips. She was so hungry lately and Mum's cooking left a lot to be desired. Afterwards they sat on the beach, surrounded by children making sand-castles, mums in deckchairs and dads and older siblings playing beach games. Finally the tide came in and they had to move.

'I know where there's a nice quiet sandy beach,' John told her as he brushed sand off his trousers. 'You could take your shoes off and paddle if you liked, then later we could find a country pub and have a drink.'

Along the coast at Holme-next-the-Sea they parked the car and walked across the golf course to the sand-dunes. It wasn't Rachel's idea of a fun place but for what she had in mind it could be perfect. John had been right about the beach; the sand was soft and golden and the wavelets lapped at its edge invitingly. Rachel took off her shoes and ran into the shallows, pulling up her skirt to reveal dimpled knees and shapely thighs. She splashed in the water, calling out to John to join her.

'Oh I *wish* I had a swim suit with me,' she said. 'If I thought no one would come I'd strip off and go in without.' She looked at John's startled expression and giggled. 'Don't look so shocked.'

He shook his head. 'I'm not. It – sounds like a good idea.'

'Really? You mean it?' She stood still, her heart quickening as she searched his eyes. 'If we went a bit further along, where we wouldn't be seen – we could. . . ?'

He regarded her for a long moment. 'Rachel Sands, I do believe you're challenging me.'

She threw back her head and laughed. 'Time someone did if you

79

ask me.' She picked up her shoes and began to run along the beach. 'Come on – last one in's a cissy!'

Running on ahead of him she found a secluded spot and began to pull off her clothes. John caught up in time to see her running naked into the sea, looking for all the world like a modern-day Aphrodite. He caught his breath. He certainly hadn't expected this when he'd suggested coming here. He'd never met anyone quite so uninhibited before. Her boldness aroused and excited him. He stood watching as the waves swallowed her up and she gave a shriek of delight. As she began to swim, she called:

'Come on! What are you waiting for? It's lovely.'

Hesitantly John began to undress. Leaving his clothes in a neat pile he ran down to the water's edge and hurriedly immersed himself waist high to hide his nakedness. Rachel swam towards him.

'That's right.' Her feet found the sand and she stood up, droplets of water sparkling like diamonds on her full round breasts, the nipples hard and firm as ripe cherries. John gasped as she reached out and encircled his neck with her wet arms.

'Mmm. You know, you should take your clothes off more often,' she told him softly. 'You've got a very nice body.' Her mouth close to his was soft and inviting and when he kissed her, her lips opened eagerly for him. His heart quickened and his arousal turned to urgent need as her body pressed close to his, but as his arms tightened round her she slipped out of his grasp like a mermaid, laughing tantalizingly as she swam away.

'Race you to that breakwater!' she challenged.

She won easily, holding on to the wooden post and laughing as he caught her up. Then just as quickly she slipped under his arm and was off again.

'Now back again!' she called.

As he reached the shallows she was sitting at the water's edge, her arms around her knees. Her hair clung to her head and face in damp tendrils. Her eyes were shining and her face and body were rosy with the exercise. He threw himself down beside her.

'You must be fitter than me,' he said breathlessly. He glanced at her, trying not to stare at the magnolia skin and the tempting, voluptuous curves. 'I suppose we should get dressed. What do we do for towels though?'

She stood up and held out a hand to him, her eyes bold and full of meaning. 'I reckon we'll just have to find another way to get dry.'

In the shelter of the dunes she held out her arms and he caught her to him. Her kisses were warm and uninhibited and John felt his blood race as she pressed herself against him and drew him down on to the dry grass. As he kissed her she moaned with pleasure, her tongue exploring his mouth sensuously as her hand moved down the length of his body to find his arousal, making him gasp with desire. Rolling her on to her back he moved over her, unable to resist any longer.

A hundred thoughts chased through his brain as he gave in to the overwhelming urge to make love to her. *Cathy!* He was being unfaithful to Cathy. But would she even care if she knew? She clearly didn't want him. This girl did. And at this moment he needed her so badly. But as he climaxed he was unaware that it was not Rachel's name he called out but Cathy's.

Rachel was aware of it though, but she didn't mind. She couldn't afford to.

Afterwards they lay in each other's arms without speaking. As Rachel rested her head in the crook of his shoulder she tried to assess his mood. With one finger she traced the line of his jaw.

'You're not sorry, are you? You don't wish it hadn't happened?'

He smiled down at her. 'Of course not. It was wonderful. You?'

'No. It was lovely. I've fancied you for ages, John,' she confessed. 'Ever since we were kids really. I just thought – well, recently anyway, that Cathy was your girl.'

John sighed. 'That's over. She's made a new life for herself. One that doesn't include me.'

'Do you mind very much?'

He shrugged non-committally. 'These things happen. No good minding, is it?' He felt her shiver and sat up. 'You're cold. We should really get dressed. Can't have you catching pneumonia.'

They found a village pub and sat outside in the evening sunshine.

'Your father's very strict with you, isn't he?' John said. 'We'd better be getting back soon.' Rachel put down her glass and dissolved into tears. Shocked, he put an arm around her. 'Rachel! What's wrong? Is it something I said?'

She shook her head. 'No. I've had such a wonderful day. I'm just sad it's coming to an end.'

He was touched. 'We can meet again – if that's what you want.'

She smiled. 'I'd like that. It's Dad though. He hardly ever lets me out. You'd have to . . .' She shook her head. 'No. I can't ask you to do that.'

'Can't ask me to do what?'

'It sounds really old-fashioned but you'd have to ask him first. I'm supposed to be with a girl from work today. It was the only way I could get him to let me out. He *makes* me tell him lies and I hate it. I've tried to reason with him, but it's no good.' She looked up at him appealingly. 'If I'm going to be seeing you, John. I'd like it to be out in the open.'

John gave her shoulders a squeeze. 'Don't worry,' he said. 'If I have to ask his permission, then that's what I'll do.'

On the drive home they were both quiet, each occupied with their own thoughts. Rachel felt triumphant. She'd accomplished what she came out to do and she'd been pleasantly surprised by John's hungry passion. That had been a bonus. He wasn't as skilled or as adventurous as Peter, but not bad. And certainly more than adequate. She wondered who Peter was treating to his not inconsiderable sexual techniques now and felt a pang of jealousy which she quickly thrust aside. Got to be practical and think of herself now, she told herself. No good mooning over what was past. And anyway, there'd be nothing to stop her seeing Peter when he came home on leave.

John was silent, wondering if he'd been quite wise in allowing himself to be seduced by Rachel, because he recognized it now for what it was. They'd had a very enjoyable day together but did he really want to have to go round and ask the formidable Herbert Sands's permission to see her again? It was too archaic to be true! Perhaps he could somehow ease out of it. If his guess was correct Rachel was not without admirers and he really couldn't believe that she felt anything especially deep for him.

Theresa sat in the drawing-room at Cedar Lodge, the local paper spread out on her knees and her reading glasses on her nose. She'd been scanning the classified advertisements page. She felt sure that she'd seen the kind of advert she was looking for in this paper in the past. Her finger moved down the 'Personal' column. Then she spotted it near the bottom.

Kendal Private Detective Agency. Investigations carried out in strictest confidence. J.D. Kendal. Late Metropolitan Police. Telephone Queensgrove 9187.

Strictest confidence. That was the important part. With her embroidery scissors, Theresa carefully snipped out the advertisement and slipped it into her spectacles' case. First thing tomorrow morning she'd ring and see if this man could help her.

CHAPTER SEVEN

IT WAS THREE WEEKS now since the disastrous weekend. Cathy had heard nothing from John since. She was angry and miserable. He'd been the one who'd walked out. Surely he should apologize. During the first week she'd watched every post for a letter, but there had been nothing.

She threw herself into her work at college and at the Marine Bay. They were busy now, fully booked almost every week and during the hours that she was on duty Cathy worked very hard.

She hadn't spoken to Harry for three days after the débâcle with John, but he'd been so apologetic, so comically remorseful that in the end she'd had to relent. Besides, she didn't have so many friends that she could afford to throw them away.

On the day she'd finally given in he'd found her in the canteen at the evening coffee break and planted himself firmly in the chair opposite, leaning towards her with such a pleading, hangdog expression on his face that she had been hard put to it not to laugh.

'Go away, Harry,' she said, hiding her face in her coffee cup. 'I've got nothing to say to you.'

'I hope you realize that I'm totally devastated,' he said tragically. 'Ask anyone.'

'I don't believe you.'

'All right then. I hope you won't blame yourself when they find my broken body at the foot of the cliffs in the morning.'

'Shut up.'

'Look, I really am sorry,' he said. 'I don't know how many more times you want me to say it. Christ! I can't even remember what kind of clanger I dropped now. You know me. Dropping clangers is part of my nature.'

'You don't have to tell *me* that.'

'OK then. So you forgive me?' He looked at her like a hopeful puppy.

'I didn't say that either.'

'Are you really that fed up about it, Cathy? I mean, he didn't look all *that* exciting to me. A bit stuffy if you ask me, all togged up in his Sunday suit. And if he doesn't trust you not to run around . . .'

'*Ah!*' Her eyes met his across the table. 'So you *do* remember what you said!'

Harry held up both hands. 'OK, it's a fair cop. I'll come quietly. What do I get, life?'

'Idiot.'

'Tell you what; I'll treat you to a film on Saturday evening to make up. Is it a deal?'

'I don't know.'

He frowned at her. 'It's a real sacrifice, you know. I only get fourpence a week pocket money and I'm willing to spend it all on you! I'll have to starve for the rest of the week. You might be a bit more appreciative.'

In the end they settled for two cheap seats at the cinema and a fish and chip supper which they took back to Harry's attic room to eat.

'Are you going to tell me what really happened between you and his lordship?' Harry asked as he plugged in the kettle. 'I mean, it wasn't all my fault, was it? You didn't look exactly ecstatic when you arrived.' He peered at her. 'In complete confidence. That goes without saying.'

'I don't really know,' Cathy said, shaking her head. 'It was more what didn't happen. I was looking forward to seeing him so much and then everything went wrong.'

'Why did it? And what do you mean by "what didn't happen"?'

'He just – expected too much of me.'

Harry sat down beside her. 'How come?'

She shrugged. 'Well – I think I – I disappointed him.'

'How could *you* disappoint anyone?'

'Oh! You don't understand,' she said crossly.

.He regarded her as she took a sip of her coffee. He said: 'At the moment you're talking in riddles.'

She sighed. She had to talk to someone about it and Harry was the only person she knew well enough.

'If you really want to know I'm beginning to suspect that there might be something wrong with me,' she said.

'In what way?'

She put down her mug. 'Promise you won't breathe a word of this to anyone.'

'Cross me 'eart and 'ope to die!'

'Oh, be serious, Harry. This is something I'm really worried about.'

He reached out and took her hand, holding it firmly in both of his. 'Cathy, look, I know I talk a lot of old guff at times but I'm your friend. For ever and ever, till death et cetera. If you tell me something private wild horses won't tear it from me. And that's a solemn promise.'

She bit her lip hard. 'Harry – I think I'm frigid.'

For a moment he stared at her, then he burst out laughing. Blushing furiously she snatched her hand away and stood up. 'There! I *knew* you'd laugh! You're a pig, Harry. I hate you!'

Instantly he was on his feet, all contrition. 'I'm sorry love. I wasn't laughing *at* you. It's just that I can't imagine anyone less likely to be frigid than you. You're so warm and sweet and natural. Anyway, what on earth gives you that idea? Did *he* say so?'

'No.'

'Then it can only mean one thing – that you couldn't fancy him. *God*! Now I know why he was in such a foul mood. Poor sod!' He smiled at her. 'Come on, love. Talking about it will help. Come and sit down again.'

She sighed and allowed him to draw her down again. 'He was expecting us to . . . I couldn't, Harry. Oh, not because I didn't want to. I don't *know* why. I've thought and thought about it. It's just . . .' She lifted her shoulders helplessly.

'So?' He raised his eyebrows. 'It's not the end of the world, is it?'

'It seems to be – for him. He hasn't written or been in touch with me since that night.'

'Then if that's all he wants he isn't worth agonizing over,' Harry said firmly. 'Look, I assume that you're a virgin?' She nodded,

86

avoiding his eyes. 'OK, so the first time is tricky. It has to be very special. There are so many things that could spoil it – spoil your whole outlook – the relationship – everything. You'll be fine when the right time comes. Just relax and stop being so uptight about it.'

She eyed him sceptically. 'Thank *you*, Doctor Flynn! You seem to know a lot about it, I must say.'

He assumed a nonchalant look. 'I've got two older brothers, remember. Anyway, I'm not exactly short of experience myself.'

'Oh yes?' She was smiling now. 'How *much* experience?'

'Enough!' He stood up and picked up the mugs. 'Right, so now we've got that cleared up, do you want another coffee?'

'OK.'

He switched on the kettle and looked at her. 'I've been meaning to talk to you about the rag.'

'Rag?'

'The college rag. It's only a few weeks away and they rely heavily on the art department to design a lot of the stuff; floats, costumes and so on. I'm on the committee. Can we rope you in?'

She smiled. 'Yes, it sounds like fun.'

He poured water into their mugs. 'Oh, it is,' he said. 'I can definitely promise you that!'

Theresa came downstairs and looked at herself in the hall mirror. Dressed in her best black suit and carrying her silver-fox fur, she considered herself suitably attired, but her stomach was full of butterflies. A fortnight he'd said. 'Come and see me again in a fortnight, Mrs King. I should have some information by then.'

After her initial telephone call she'd found the office of J.D. Kendal easily enough, although it was in a part of the town she never normally visited. This she considered an advantage. She had no wish to be seen entering the building by anyone she knew. At the top of a flight of dusty stairs she found a door marked KENDAL DETECTIVE AGENCY. Her knock was answered by a voice calling out to her to 'Come in.'

Inside she found a small, sparsely furnished office. Behind the desk sat a grey-haired man who introduced himself as Jim Kendal.

'How do you do, Mrs King,' he said, holding out his hand. 'I hope I'll be able to be of service.' He indicated the chair opposite. 'Do have a seat and tell me how I can help.'

Theresa sat nervously on the edge of the chair. It felt all wrong now that she was here. Now that she came to think about it, she didn't know why it bothered her so much, seeing someone putting flowers on Albert's grave. She eyed the man surreptitiously. He wore a crumpled tweed suit and a polka-dotted bow tie. There was a stain of some sort on the front of his shirt too. He looked faintly sleazy – until he smiled.

'Don't look so apprehensive, Mrs King,' he said. 'I promise you that anything you say will go no further than these four walls. If I believe I can help you I shall do my best, but if I feel that your problem is beyond me I shall say so.'

Briefly he outlined his fees and expenses, which seemed reasonable. What he said was fair enough, she supposed. Despite his appearance he had a pleasant voice and honest brown eyes. She felt reassured.

'Well – you'll probably think it's silly,' she began.

He shook his head. 'Believe me, Mrs King, when you have sat in this chair as long as I have nothing seems silly any more.'

Theresa bit her lip. 'My husband has been dead for four years,' she began. 'Ours was not a happy marriage, but he was a good provider and he loved our two sons. It was soon after my elder boy was killed in the war that Albert died – from the shock.'

The man nodded. 'I understand.'

'I go to the churchyard each week, to put flowers on the memorial to my son. Recently I've seen a woman there. Last week I saw her putting flowers on my husband's grave.'

'And you'd like to know who she is?'

'Yes.'

'Well, that shouldn't present too many problems.' He made a note on his pad. 'Can you tell me on which days she visits the churchyard, or does it vary?'

'I don't think so. At least, it has always been a Wednesday when I've seen her.'

'Any particular time?' He glanced up at her, his pencil poised. 'And could you perhaps give me a brief description?'

Theresa described the woman as best she could and came away from the office feeling confident and relieved, though what she would do with the knowledge J.D. Kendal might obtain for her, she wasn't altogether clear.

In the meantime she had pushed her visit to the detective from her mind, but now that the two weeks had passed and she was on her way to find out what he had discovered she was feeling apprehensive.

'You look very nice, Mrs King, if I might be so bold.' Clarice Harvey had come into the hall, a duster in her hand, and caught Theresa studying her reflection.

Theresa flushed. 'Thank you.'

'Going somewhere nice?'

Theresa bit back the retort that it was none of her business. Clarice persisted in being familiar and no matter how much Theresa tried to freeze her out she failed to take the hint. 'A business call,' she said stiffly.

'Aah, that's a shame,' Clarice said, leaning against the banisters. 'You really should get out more, Mrs K. Enjoy yourself. Why don't you go to the pictures now and again? It'd take you out of yourself.'

'I've never been a cinema enthusiast I'm afraid,' Theresa said, adjusting her fox fur and pulling on her gloves.

'Oh, but you should be,' Clarice persisted. 'There are some lovely films on nowadays. I go every Wednesday evening, regular as clockwork. Last week I saw *The Man In Grey*. That James Mason fair makes your toes curl, and as for Stewart Granger!' She rolled her eyes ceilingwards. 'Oh, he's *so* handsome. You know just for a couple of hours you can forget all your worries.'

Theresa opened the front door and turned. 'I shall be about an hour, Mrs Harvey. I'll see you before you go home.'

'Oh, right. Tell you what, I'll have the kettle on for a nice cuppa when you get in, shall I? You'll be spittin' feathers after all that business talk.'

Walking down the drive Theresa suddenly realized that it would indeed be pleasant not to return to a silent, empty house. She might even welcome Clarice Harvey's chatter after what she suspected she was about to discover.

This afternoon Jim Kendal looked, if anything, even more crumpled than before. The suit and the bow tie were the same, but Theresa was relieved to see that he was wearing a clean shirt. He waved her to a chair.

'You have news?' She looked at him expectantly.

'I have, though I don't know whether it will be of any use to you.'

'The woman – you know who she is?'

'I have discovered that the woman you have seen tending your husband's grave is a Mrs Jane Linford. Does the name mean anything to you?'

'No. Do you know any more?'

'The lady in question is aged forty-eight. She is a widow. It appears that her husband was once a foreman in your husband's factory. He was killed in an accident before the war, in 1925. I assume that was how she and your late husband became acquainted.'

'Are you saying she was his mistress?' Theresa felt the blood rush to her cheeks. 1925. If the woman was only forty-eight now she couldn't have been much more than a girl when she and Albert began their affair. She'd always suspected that he hadn't gone without his carnal pleasures after she locked him out of the bedroom; not with a sexual appetite like his. But to think he had been deceiving her all that time.

'According to my sources they were good friends,' Jim Kendal said discreetly. 'I think he helped her financially when she was tragically widowed. I suppose he felt responsible, the man being his employee.'

Theresa was barely listening. Inwardly she seethed, trying to shut out the images of them in bed together. She recalled Albert's demands, the language he used and his coarseness. It was too disgusting for words.

She opened her handbag. 'Thank you. How much do I owe you, Mr Kendal?'

The detective looked up in surprise. 'Don't you want to know any more? Her address . . .'

Theresa shook her head. 'No! Just tell me what I owe you.' He named his fee and she passed him a handful of notes, then made hastily for the door.

'Mrs King, there is something else I feel you should know.'

She turned. 'I told you. I don't want to . . .'

'There was a child,' he put in quickly. 'Born around 1927. I don't know what sex or where he or she is now. Only that at present Mrs Linford lives alone. But I believe you should be aware of this in case any demands are ever made on your late husband's estate.'

Theresa's eyes glittered with fury. 'You – you mean that Albert was openly named as the father? His name was on the birth certificate?'

He shook his head. 'That I cannot tell you,' he said. 'I just felt that you should know. Forewarned is forearmed as they say.'

At the bottom of the stairs Theresa leaned against the wall for support. She felt sick and faint. If only she had never set eyes on the woman. If only her curiosity hadn't got the better of her. She felt dirty somehow, almost as though by seeking out the truth she was reviving Albert's infidelity. To think that he had been living this lie, this double life behind her back. She *hated* him. She hated Jim Kendal for telling her, even though he was only doing her bidding. But most of all she hated herself for ever having been Albert King's wife.

Travelling home on the bus she thought of Ian; dear, sweet Ian, killed in all that hell of fire and blood. They had loved each other so much. If it hadn't been for the war she would have been happily married to him, lived a useful, rewarding life as a doctor's wife just as her mother had done. Now the fact that had always comforted her – that she had married Albert to save her father from ruin was of no comfort at all. She even hated *him* for expecting it of her. Bitter tears of anger and regret coursed down her face, their sourness making her stomach churn.

Clarice heard the front door slam and put her head round the kitchen door.

'Tea up, Mrs K!' she called cheerfully. When there was no reply she went through to the hall in time to see Theresa wearily climbing the stairs. She looked ten years older than when she had gone out this afternoon. And Clarice was shocked to see that her eyes and face were blotched and swollen with tears.

'I've made the tea,' she said more gently. 'Why don't you come down to the kitchen and have a cup with me?'

Theresa paused to look down into the woman's homely face and suddenly the tears began afresh. Kind words had been the last thing she expected. Sinking down half-way up the stairs she covered her face with her hands and gave in to the sobs that racked her body.

Clarice stared at her, then she did what she would have done for anyone, man, woman or child. She went up to her and put an arm round her shoulders.

'Come on then dear,' she said gently. 'Don't take on so. It can't be as bad as all that.' She watched as Theresa struggled for control. 'There, that's better. Come on down and have that tea. It'll do you the world of good.'

Theresa could not remember ever sitting at her own kitchen table, drinking tea, but now, with the Aga throwing out warmth and the willow-pattern plates on the dresser reflecting the sunlight from the window, she found it oddly comforting. Clarice, her face creased with concern, refilled her cup.

'How about if I put a drop of brandy in it for you?' she suggested. 'Buck you up a bit.'

Theresa nodded and watched passively as the woman brought the bottle of medicinal brandy from the pantry and slopped a generous measure into the teacup. She raised it to her lips and found it warm and calming. She'd expected Clarice to start asking questions but the woman remained uncharacteristically silent. She looked up and their eyes met across the table.

'You must be wondering what's happened,' she said.

Clarice shrugged. 'It's not for me to ask why.'

Clarice's discretion had the effect of making Theresa want to talk. She badly needed to talk – to tell someone of her shattering discovery.

'I've had a shock,' she said slowly.

'Well, I'd gathered that,' Clarice said.

'It's to do with my late husband. It's shaken me dreadfully.'

'I can see it has.' Clarice poured more brandy into Theresa's third cup of tea and leaned her elbow on the table. 'My hubby gave me a few shocks while he was alive, bless him,' she said reminiscently. 'A devil, he was. Horses – women – barmy schemes that lost us money, he had them all.'

'But you loved him?' Theresa asked.

Clarice's face softened. 'Oh yes. You couldn't help but love my Reg. He had a sort of talent for making folks love him. Mostly it was their undoing, mind. Many's the time I've had my bags packed and my Dennis dressed ready to leave him, but he'd only to say "sorry love" with that look in his eyes, and kiss me and I'd just sort of melt.'

'I didn't love mine,' Theresa confessed, pouring more brandy into her empty cup. 'I never wanted to marry him. The man I loved was killed in the first war. Ian was a doctor. He was clever, handsome and educated with a useful life and a good career before him – till a German shell put an end to it all.' Her voice hardened. 'Albert King was an ignorant pig. And now I find he was a lying, cheating one too.'

Theresa looked up at Clarice with brimming eyes. The brandy, coupled with the day's trauma had made her dizzy and reckless. Now that she'd started she didn't want to stop. 'Do you know, I found out today that he had a mistress and a child. He'd been living a double life for years without me knowing. I sacrificed my life for him and he betrayed me.'

Clarice bit her lip as she watched the tears well up in Theresa's eyes again. The poor woman didn't know what she was saying. The brandy must have gone to her head or she'd never be talking like this to her.

'Now, now,' she said soothingly. 'What you need is a nice lie down. Let me take you upstairs and turn the bed down for you. A nice sleep'll do you good, madam.'

Theresa allowed herself to be escorted up the stairs and helped out of her coat and skirt, then tucked up in bed like a child. As she sank into her comfortable bed she realized that Clarice had called her 'madam'. She looked up at her sleepily.

'Clarice – what I told you – what we talked about this afternoon . . .'

'Don't you worry, madam,' Clarice interrupted firmly. 'My lips are sealed and that's a promise.'

Theresa closed her eyes. She felt instinctively that she could trust Clarice Harvey. There was a lot more to the woman than she'd imagined. She had been a friend for her when she badly needed one and she wouldn't forget that.

Clarice tiptoed downstairs with a sense of importance. She'd been trusted with a secret. An intimate secret. By Mrs King too. *And* she'd called her Clarice at long last! Well, she can rely on me not to let her down, she told herself fiercely. Not after the talk they'd had this afternoon. If Mrs K didn't bring up the subject again, then neither would she, but it would always be there between them – a bond. Funny, she'd always thought that people with money had no worries. Just showed how wrong you could be. She washed up the teacups and tidied the kitchen, then she scribbled a note for John which she propped up on the hall table where he would be sure to see it when he came in from the factory.

Dear Mr John.

Your Mum's feeling a bit poorly so she's having a nice lie down. Let her have her sleep out. There's a casserole in the Aga for your supper. Hoping this finds you as it leaves me,

C Harvey. (Mrs)

CHAPTER EIGHT

THE FLYNN'S HOUSE WAS a hive of activity. Harry had designated it as the Rag headquarters and all the students who were involved with the event gathered in their spare time to work on the designs and organization of the great occasion. Cathy spent as much time as she could helping. She had put in her own ideas and some sketches, but the summer season at the Marine Bay was well under way now and her time off was at a premium.

One morning in July Clare Tanner called her into the office. She closed the door and invited her to take a seat. She said: 'Cathy, I wonder if I could ask a huge favour of you?'

'Of course,' Cathy said. 'You've been so good to me. If I can help out in any way I'll be glad to.'

'It's just that unfortunately we find we have to have a new boiler,' Clare said. 'As you know this is only our second season here. During the war nothing was done to the place and there have been difficulties lately with the hot-water system. The plumber said there was no more he could do. The boiler and the whole heating system has to be replaced.' She sighed. 'Obviously. it's going to be terrifically expensive.'

Cathy nodded sympathetically. 'What a nuisance. So – what can I do?'

'We've been trying to think of ways to make some extra money,' Clare said. 'If we could get the central heating working efficiently we could open for Christmas.'

'Oh – I see.' Cathy's heart began to sink. Was Clare trying to tell her that they were letting her go? What would she do if she had to give up her course and go home now?

Reading her crestfallen expression Clare put in hurriedly. 'Oh – please don't worry. We're not going to dispense with your services – far from it. We'd hate to lose you. It's just that we've been think- ing of letting the three staff rooms on the top floor. 'The thing is – would you mind living out?'

Cathy was relieved – until she thought how difficult finding somewhere else to stay might be. 'Well, I'll certainly try and find somewhere,' she said.

'Obviously we'll pay you a little more to make up,' Clare added hurriedly. 'And you'd still take all your meals here with us as you do now.'

'I was wondering if perhaps some of the student accommodation in the town might soon be vacant,' Clare suggested. 'A lot of the students will be going home for the summer holidays shortly. Or maybe a friend. . . ?' She looked enquiringly at Cathy.

Suddenly Cathy thought of the Flynns. She would have to ask Harry about it. 'Leave it with me,' she said. 'I'm sure I can sort out something.'

She mentioned it to Harry that same evening over their coffee break at college. He shook his head.

'We're absolutely stuffed at the moment,' he said. 'Though of course you could always bunk down with me.'

'I don't think so somehow, do you?'

'The folks wouldn't mind,' he assured her. 'They're very broad- minded.'

'I would though.'

'Oh! Thanks very much!' He assumed an injured expression.

'Don't be silly, Harry. Look, I seriously need a place to stay. Otherwise I'll probably have to go home and give up the course. Clare thought that maybe some of the students would be going home soon.'

'That's a point. It could well be, though I think that most of our present crop of boarders are working folks. But leave it with me. I'll see what Faith thinks.' His eyes twinkled at her wickedly. 'Failing that, surely even sharing a room with me would be better than going home. I promise I don't snore.' He raised an eyebrow at her. 'The only thing is – do you?'

She laughed in spite of herself. 'Yes!' she said. 'Deafeningly! Nice try, Harry. I appreciate the sacrifice, but no thanks.'

The following day he rang her at the hotel.

'Harry! What's wrong?'

'Wrong? You're such a pessimist, Cathy. No, it's good news. One of the boarders has just given Faith his notice. Been offered a better job up north. Couldn't have been more opportune, could it? It's a nice room on the first floor. There's a really romantic view of the railway if you lean out far enough. She won't charge you much either as you and I are practically engaged. What do you say?'

'About the room or the engagement?' she asked him wryly.

'Either – both!'

'Yes to the room. No to the engagement,' she told him.

'OK. Fair enough. Can't win 'em all. See you at coll' this evening. I'll tell Faith the room's booked then, shall I?' And he rang off without waiting for her confirmation.

Harry helped her move her things over to the Flynn's a few days later. As they carried the cases upstairs he remarked that now she was here on a permanent basis she could help more with the rag. As she put down the pile of boxes she was carrying she gave him a wry look.

'I might have known you'd have an ulterior motive, Harry Flynn.'

The room was larger than the one she had occupied at the hotel and she was delighted to see that there was a desk as well as all the normal furniture. It stood under the window, which, as Harry had said, overlooked the railway bridge. Although most of the furnishings had seen better days, they were of good quality and comfortable. Cathy was well satisfied with her move. To save her a long walk in the mornings Clare had lent her a bicycle. All in all Cathy knew she should be happy here. She liked her work – loved her course and now she would be close to her friends too. If it wasn't for the fact that she still hadn't heard from John she would have been completely happy, as she told Harry late one night when they were working on costumes for the rag in his room after evening class.

'I can't think why you're still bothering about him when you've got a handsome devil like me to squire you around,' Harry said. He looked up and caught her wistful expression. 'When are you going home?' he asked.

'September, when things start to ease off at the Bay.'

'So write to him. Tell him you miss him and that you're looking forward to seeing him again. Give him an excuse to unbend.'

She shrugged. 'Maybe I will. It's just that there doesn't seem to be much point. If he still cared anything for me he'd have written.'

Harry nodded. 'Well, if you're both going to be stubborn you might never get back together again.' He shrugged. 'He's barking mad if you ask me. Who in his right mind would let a girl like you slip through his fingers over some silly misunderstanding?'

'He didn't see it that way though, did he?'

'Then write. Tell him you still love him.' He glanced up at her sideways. 'If you *have* to. That ought to do it.' Suddenly he threw down the length of muslin on to which he was sticking sequins. 'What am I *saying*? I must be mad – chucking you into the arms of another man when here I am lusting after you like mad!'

Cathy laughed. 'No you're not.'

'Want to bet? Is that a challenge?' He threw himself back, arms outstretched in a gesture of abandonment. 'Go on then, try seducing me and see how easily I give in!' He raised his head and looked at her. 'No? Oh well. How about a coffee instead?'

She watched as he got to his feet and picked up the kettle. 'I don't know what I'd do without you, Harry,' she said affectionately. 'You save my sanity.'

He pulled an ironic face at her. 'Gee, *thanks*!' he said in his best Humphrey Bogart accent. 'You sure know how to make a guy feel good. Here's me wanting you to leap on me and tear my clothes off in a rampant frenzy and all you can say is that *I save your sanity*.'

She collapsed with laughter. 'Well, you do.'

As they sat drinking their coffee she asked him suddenly, 'Harry have you already done your National Service?'

He made a dejected face. 'I reckon they've forgotten all about poor old me. Story of my life.'

'No, really. You've never actually said how old you are but you must be at least as old as me – twenty.'

'Yeah,' he said noncommittally.

'So – did you get a deferment, or what?'

'What.'

'I said . . .'

'I know. I *heard* you!' Harry jumped to his feet and began to pour more coffee. 'And the answer is, *what*!'

'Mind my own business, you mean?'

'If you like.'

'I'm sorry. I didn't mean to be nosy.' She peered at his closed expression. It was so unlike Harry to clam up like his. What could she have said to upset him?

He sat down beside her again, then, into the silence that followed he said, 'I didn't pass the medical if you must know.'

'Oh, is that all? Why didn't you just say?'

He turned and looked at her. 'I thought you were the sensitive type. Don't you realize that blokes just don't go around telling girls that they're seven-stone weaklings that even the army doesn't want? Types like that get sand kicked in their faces.'

'Not by me, they don't.'

'Really?'

'Of course not. You have to be a hundred per cent fit to be in the services. I expect it's just . . .'

'Just a dicky ticker?' He sighed. 'There's something a bit dodgy about my heart. Seems it's something I was born with and nothing can be done. Funny, no one knew till this sadistic army quack put me through the paces.' He looked at her. 'Oh, for God's sake don't look at me like that! It's not life threatening. Nothing so bloody romantic. The damned thing just beats too fast or too slow or something.'

'Do you have to have treatment?'

'No. I told you, there is no treatment. Look, can we talk about something else. I feel like one of those old women in a bus queue, nattering on about her operation.' He held up the length of cloth he'd been working on. 'I reckon that will do. What do you think?'

Cathy nodded. 'It looks fine to me.'

'There's something else, Cathy.'

'Yes?'

'Something I've been trying to pluck up the nerve to ask you for ages. And now that you know about me . . .'

'Harry – what is it?'

'It's just . . .' He looked into her eyes pleadingly. 'It's just – God, how do I put this?' He bit his lip. 'How would you feel about being a mermaid on the Neptune float?'

She reached for a cushion and threw it at him. 'Harry Flynn, you're a devious pig!'

★

The college rag took place on the Saturday before the end of term and Clare gave Cathy the day off so that she could take part.

In the evening there was a ball at the college. Cathy, glad to be rid of her mermaid tail, which was hot and restricting and made her legs go to sleep, wore a white dress that Faith had helped her to make. She danced with all her fellow students, including Harry who seemed to be in great form. Towards the end of the evening Paul Samuels asked her to dance and as they circled the floor he said,

'I've been meaning to have a talk with you, Cathy. Maybe this isn't the ideal time but I might as well say what's in my mind.'

She looked at him enquiringly. 'Are you going to tell me – that my work isn't up to standard?'

He shook his head. 'Far from it, though your confidence has every right to be better. I've been impressed by the work that you and Harry Flynn and his crowd have put in these last weeks with the rag. I don't know how you've managed it with your job too. But I worry that getting your diploma is going to take for ever if you can't give more time to your studies.'

'I haven't neglected my college work,' she told him earnestly.

'I know you haven't. That's not what I was getting at,' Paul said. 'I just wondered if there was some way you could manage a full-time course?'

She sighed. 'Not without earning money.'

'Why don't you try applying for a government grant?' Paul suggested. 'Anyone who qualifies for a place at university or college is entitled to one as from last May. Why don't you give it a go?'

Cathy felt her cheeks grow warm with excitement. 'A grant? Do you really think I'd get one?'

'I certainly do. I don't know if there's any kind of test, but I'll help if you need a reference. If you're going home for the holidays why don't you talk to your parents about it?'

After the dance they all went back to the Flynns' house where the party went on far into the small hours. Dawn was already lightening the sky by the time an exhausted Cathy fell into bed. But it was not to sleep. She lay thinking of the grant Paul had told her about, and wondering if she would be lucky enough to get one. By next term she could be at college full time. And she could be taking her final exams in a year and a half.

She turned over and punched her pillow. Soon she'd be going home. She longed to see her parents again, and her sister and little nephews.

With luck she'd see John too and make up their quarrel. She hadn't written, afraid of making things even worse. She found it so hard to put her true feelings on to paper. If she left it till they met they would be able to talk things through face to face.

During the week after the memorable trip to the coast Rachel saw John almost every evening. Although he had encountered her only occasionally in the past he now found himself running into her round almost every corner. And the subject she always brought up was the prospective meeting between him and her parents.

'I don't think it's a very good idea, Rachel,' John told her uncomfortably. 'We went out the once and we had a nice time. Maybe we should leave it at that.'

He'd had a prickly feeling about Rachel ever since their Sunday outing. He knew he'd been a fool to allow her to seduce him. Clearly she was not inexperienced, and now she seemed to think she had some kind of claim on him. He looked at her in dismay as she affected her little girl pout.

'You like me, don't you, John?'

'Of course I like you, Rachel. I like a lot of people though but . . .'

She tucked her arm through his. 'You have to admit that I'm a bit special,' she said.

'Well . . .'

'Look, I've told Mum and Dad that I've seen you on the way home from work a lot lately – sort of paving the way – and now I've said that you've asked me out. They're expecting you to call round tomorrow evening after supper.' She turned her eyes up to his. 'You will come, won't you? Just for me?'

The Sandses received John in their hallowed Front Room. It was the room they normally used only at Christmas and for special days and when John arrived he was somewhat taken aback to be ushered into the sacred sanctum by an excited Rachel.

101

The moment she opened the door and pushed him gently forward into the musty-smelling gloom he could see that the whole room shrieked *Special Occasion.* Everything from the three-piece suite with its fawn loose covers to the potted palm standing on a lace-covered whatnot in the bay window spoke to him of burning boats and he wondered how he was going to get out of the situation he found himself involved in.

Herbert and Mary Sands stood to receive him, Herbert wore the suit he wore for chapel and funerals; teamed with a white shirt and high starched collar; Mary twittered nervously in her 'best blue'.

'Rachel tells us you wish to speak to us,' Herbert said formally.

John cleared his throat. 'Well, yes,' he said, running a finger round his collar, which suddenly seemed to have shrunk several sizes. 'I would like to take Rachel out – with your permission.'

'I see.' Herbert nodded gravely. 'I'm sure you understand that she is still very young,' he said. 'Therefore we would expect you to observe our rule that she be in by ten at the latest.'

John swallowed. 'Of course.'

'And we would prefer it if you did not take her into public houses. Her mother and I do not hold with alcohol.'

'No. I see.'

'And on the occasions when you accompany her we would expect to be informed of your destination.'

'Yes.'

'Are you a churchgoer, Mr King?'

'I – er – go sometimes – on occasions.'

Herbert's mouth turned down at the corners. 'Well, I suppose that is better than nothing.' He cleared his throat. 'I take it that would be the Anglican church?'

'St Mary's, yes.' John glanced at Rachel.

'Very well.' Herbert took out his pocket watch and studied it. 'I suggest that on this first occasion you take Rachel for a walk. Shall we say for one hour?'

'Thank you.'

Once outside and out of sight of the house Rachel burst out laughing. 'If he only *knew!*' she giggled. 'I told you what he was like. *Paralysed!*'

This time John did not correct her. He considered she'd probably got it just about right!

How had he got himself into this? And how in the world had the Sandses managed to produce a daughter as uninhibited as Rachel? He knew that she wasn't their flesh and blood of course, but they had brought her up from infancy. She must have an extremely rebellious spirit to have survived with her individuality intact. He looked down at her as she walked at his side, and reflected with some misgivings that Rachel knew exactly what she wanted and meant to get it, whatever the opposition.

In the three weeks that followed John had reluctantly taken Rachel out twice, unhappily aware that her father now considered them to be formally 'walking out'. He knew that he must find a way of breaking it gently to Rachel that the arrangement must end.

He called for her the following Wednesday evening and they got off to a bad start because Rachel wanted to go to the cinema but John had insisted on a walk in the park. It was a beautiful summer evening, warm and mellow. They walked round the lake for a while in silence then John drew Rachel towards a bench.

Rachel sat down beside him. Her sulkiness concealed the feeling of panic that had been growing over the past two weeks. John was not as amorous and attentive as she had hoped. Once they had made love that Sunday she had expected him to be ensnared, to fall deeply in love and under her spell. Now she knew she'd overestimated her effect on him. It had become clear since that he regretted what had happened between them. He had agreed to see her father and to continue seeing her out of – what? Pity? Certainly not love. He'd been cool and distant with her most of the time and she knew that it was now essential for her to play her trump card – the sooner, the better.

'I want to talk to you,' John said. 'As I said before, Rachel, I like you; like you very much – as a friend. But I feel that we should stop . . .'

'I'm having a baby!'

John's carefully rehearsed words died in his throat and the silence between them was almost tangible. It was as if the ripples on the lake froze and the air became a vacuum. He felt his heart miss a beat and his brain turn into solid ice.

'What?' Slowly he turned to look at her.

'I'm going to have a baby. I'm *pregnant*.'

'Are you sure?'

'Of course I'm sure.'

'You've – been to a doctor?'

'In this town? Don't make me laugh. If I went to our doctor Dad would be told right away. Dr Harris is a strict chapelgoer.'

'There are other doctors. I'll find you one and make an appointment.'

'There's no need. Look, it's my body and I know. I've missed and I've been sick every morning. There are other signs too. Do you want me to go on?'

He shook his head. 'No, no, I believe you.' He looked at her. 'Rachel – look, I have to ask you . . .'

Her eyes widened. 'You're going to ask if it's yours! You *are*, aren't you?'

'No – I . . .'

'Look, we went all the way on that beach – without taking any precautions. Didn't it ever cross your mind, John, that this might happen?'

He looked stunned – shocked even, but not solicitous or concerned, at least, not for her. To press her point she burst into noisy tears. 'Oh God! What am I going to *do*? When Dad finds out he'll kill me! He'll send me away – chuck me out! I'll be on the streets with nowhere to go!'

'Oh, come on, Rachel, surely not.'

'He will! You've seen what he's like – how strict and narrow-minded.'

Shocked and embarrassed by her outburst he put an arm awkwardly round her shoulders. 'Look, don't cry. There must be something you can do.'

Something you can do! She didn't like the way this was going – didn't like it at all. She'd imagined that even if he didn't fall in love with her, meeting her father would have prompted him into offering to do the right thing by her.

'It's our baby, John,' she whispered with all the pathos she could manage. 'Do you want me to kill it?'

'*No!* I just meant . . . Look, it's very early, isn't it? You could be mistaken.'

'You want proof?'

'I didn't mean that.'

'OK. You make me an appointment and I'll see a doctor if that's what you want. But what then, John?'

He swallowed hard. In his mind he saw Cathy – his lovely Cathy and the end of all his dreams. He saw his mother. If she had disapproved of Cathy what would she think of Rachel as a daughter-in-law? She still owned the factory. She was capable of doing anything – selling up – disinheriting him. He sighed. Worst of all, he saw his lifetime ahead of him, shared with a girl with whom he had nothing in common. It looked as bleak as a life sentence. He'd been a fool and now he had to pay the price. There was no escape.

CHAPTER NINE

THERESA STOOD AT THE foot of the stairs and rang the little brass bell. It was Clarice's signal that her elevenses were ready. Back in the kitchen she opened the new packet of chocolate biscuits she'd begged from the grocer yesterday. They were by way of a treat because she'd discovered that it was Clarice's birthday. She tipped the contents on to a plate and fetched the milk jug, adding it to the tea tray.

'Oh my goodness, madam?' Clarice stood in the doorway. 'Where did you get those?'

'From Williamson and Gregson's,' Theresa told her proudly. 'I happened to be in the shop when they came in. I reminded Mr Snedgar that I'd been a good customer all through the war – always been registered there for our rations. I think regular customers are entitled to expect a few little privileges, don't you?'

'All your precious points coupons though,' Clarice said, sitting herself down at the table. 'Chocolate biscuits take so many.'

Theresa blushed. 'I thought you deserved a little treat,' she said. 'I believe it's your birthday.'

Clarice gasped. 'How did you find that out?'

'Never mind.' Theresa poured the tea and seated herself opposite.

Ever since the day of her visit to the private detective the relationship between herself and Clarice Harvey had relaxed. Although the dramatic events of that afternoon had never been mentioned since, Clarice's kindness and understanding on that afternoon as well as her own revelations had opened Theresa's eyes.

106

She'd slept soundly that afternoon; a sleep induced by exhaustion and the brandy. She was wakened eventually late in the evening by John who brought her a cup of tea and asked how she felt. Sitting up in bed and sipping her tea Theresa suddenly saw life entirely differently. For the first time in her life she saw that beneath the skin all women were the same, no matter what their race, creed or social standing. Although she had been less than kind to Clarice Harvey the other woman had listened sympathetically and exchanged confidences. Theresa knew instinctively that Clarice would keep her secret. After all, she had suffered herself and knew how it felt to be betrayed. Apparently when Clarice was widowed she too had become reclusive, but feeling needed by her son had been her salvation. Theresa was so lucky. She had a beautiful home, no financial worries and an attentive son to whom she had given little affection. From now on, she told herself, things would be different. Clarice had made a new life for herself. Surely she, with all her advantages, could do the same.

Since that afternoon Theresa had gone out of her way to make herself agreeable to Clarice. She made the elevenses without complaint, even sharing it at the kitchen table. Now she found herself looking forward eagerly to their chats – to the scraps of gossip and family news the other woman would impart along with the tea and Osborne biscuits.

Two weeks after the new rapport had sprung up between them Clarice had tentatively suggested that Theresa might like to accompany her to the cinema on her weekly Wednesday jaunt.

'Why don't you come, madam? It'd take you out of yourself,' she said. 'They've got that new film with Ingrid Bergman on at the Roxy. It's called *Notorious* and it's a thriller. Cary Grant's in it too.' She sighed. 'You know, it's funny but Cary Grant always reminds me of my Reg.'

'Well, I don't know,' Theresa said doubtfully.

Clarice pressed her. 'Oh, do come, madam. If you don't mind me saying so you ought to get out more. It'd cheer you up – give you something to think about.' Clarice looked at her employer thoughtfully. 'Though of course if you're afraid of being seen with me by some of your friends I'd quite understand.'

'No – no, it's not that.' Theresa did not add that she had no friends; that in fact she'd kept herself to herself for so long that she had no longer had any acquaintances either. There was no one to know or care where she went, or with whom. She realized now that she no longer wished to remain a prisoner in her own home. In fact she suddenly glimpsed a kind of freedom in the situation that she found positively exciting.

'Very well, Clarice,' she said with a smile. 'Thank you for asking me. I think I would like to go.'

So Theresa had gone along to the cinema with Clarice the following Wednesday afternoon, sitting happily in the front row of the circle and becoming quite absorbed in the film. And although she had declined Clarice's invitation to join her in an ice cream when the lights came up for the interval, she had found herself enjoying the selection of musical comedy hits played by the mighty Wurlitzer organ that rose up majestically from somewhere in the basement. She enjoyed her afternoon enormously.

The following week she embarked on another daring adventure. She took the bus to Peterborough to buy herself a new summer outfit. Afterwards, feeling cheered and light-hearted she went into a hairdressing salon on a sudden impulse and recklessly instructed the hairdresser to cut and restyle her hair.

Sitting before the mirror she watched, holding her breath as the girl removed the pins from the plaited 'earphones' she had worn ever since she was married and began to snip away. Soon skeins of iron-grey hair lay all around her on the floor and the reflection that looked back at her through the mirror was transformed. Allowed its own natural inclination and relieved of years of restriction, her hair sprang into the newly cut shape, curling flatteringly to frame her face in a way that quite astonished her. When the girl suggested a blue rinse Theresa had hesitated at first, then nodded her agreement. Why not?

John had been astonished at the transformation. 'Mother! You look at least twenty years younger,' he'd remarked.

Theresa felt almost light-headed. It was as though a hated part of her old life had been cut away along with her hair. The bitterness she'd felt at first on discovering Albert's deception lessened. She reminded herself that she may have wasted the years of her marriage, but, as Clarice had pointed out, life was far from over so why shouldn't she enjoy the years that were left?

'You are going to have a chocolate biscuit too, aren't you,

madam?' Clarice pushed the plate towards her and Theresa took one and bit into it with relish,

'Have you heard from your grandson?' she asked Clarice.

The other woman laughed. 'My Peter's not exactly Charles Dickens when it comes to writing,' she said. 'But give him his due, he does send me the odd postcard. He tells me he's finished his – what do they call it – square-bashing. And he's in line for a stripe. Lance-Corporal Harvey. Sounds all right, eh? Of course, him being a skilled mechanic helps.'

'So he likes the army?'

'Oh yes. But then he's always been a good boy, has my Peter. Never had much of a chance of a proper family life with his dad away in the army and his mum God knows where. I've done my best, but it's not the same, is it?'

'I'm sure you've tried to make up to him for what he's missed,' Theresa said. She sighed. 'I'm a little worried about John to tell you the truth. He hasn't been at all himself lately. It's as though he has something on his mind.'

Clarice said nothing. She had seen John King once or twice with the Sands girl and been surprised. That little baggage wasn't his sort. Not at all. She was grateful that Peter had gone to do his National Service in some ways. It would give him a chance to get the girl out of his system. Much too thick, those two had always been, ever since childhood. Always leading one another into trouble.

Helping herself to another chocolate biscuit she said, 'I daresay the young ones have problems of their own. Best not to interfere, I always think. They know we're here if they want us.' She smiled wryly. 'Mark my words, they'll come running fast enough when things go wrong.'

Theresa was silent, wondering if John felt free to 'come running' to her. She doubted it. She had never encouraged him to confide in her; never even tried to understand how he felt. She only hoped she hadn't left it too late. After all, he was her only son now.

She sighed. 'I hope you're right.'

John lay in bed and listened to the church clock strike the hour. Two o'clock. This was the third night he'd lain awake, wondering what the future held for him. He'd seen Rachel again this evening. She told him she'd been to a doctor on the other side of town – privately and at the cost of a week's wages, she said pointedly, prompting him to take out his wallet. The result was not reassuring. He'd confirmed her pregnancy and also told her she should be having regular antenatal checks and applying for her free vitamins and orange juice. It had all sounded horribly official and irreversible. Closing his eyes now he could still see her pleading look as she gave him the news.

'So what do I do, John? I've got three choices. Get rid of it; tell Dad and get chucked out – or . . .'

John knew what was coming. 'You're saying that we should get married?'

Rachel sighed and looked at him like a wounded puppy. 'It wouldn't be that bad, would it, Johnny? I mean, we do like each other, don't we? We had a great time that Sunday. If we were married it could be like that all the time.'

'There's more to marriage than sex, Rachel,' he'd said more sharply than he'd intended.

'Well, it's all right you saying that now,' she snapped back. 'It's not what you were thinking at the time, is it?'

'What I thought – or what I think now is irrelevant, isn't it?' He looked at her crushed expression and felt a sudden rush of guilt and compassion. What she was saying was true. He had looked on that afternoon on the beach in an opportunist way if he were honest with himself. He'd been a stupid, weak fool. But he could not run away from his responsibilities.

'Look,' he said turning to her. 'You could have the baby adopted. I'd give you the money to go away somewhere until after it's born and . . .'

'I thought you were different, but you're not!' Her eyes brimmed with tears again. They spilled over, coursing down her cheeks in rivulets, carrying streaks of mascara with them. 'I've always thought you were good and decent, but now all you want is to run away from it. *I* can't run away, can I? I've got to go through with this; carry it and have it – risk my life having an abortion or hand over my baby to a complete stranger after I've been through it all; while all *you* think you need do is hand over a bit of cash and forget all about it!'

110

Put like that it made him look like a prize rat. He sighed. 'All right, Rachel. If you think it's best, we'll get married.'

Her eyes lit up. 'Oh Johnny! *Really?* You mean it? Oh, I'm so happy.' She threw her arms around his neck and kissed him soundly on the mouth. 'I do love you, really I do. When will you come and see Dad then? We'd better name the day as soon as we can. We don't want people thinking we had to get married, do we?'

'Oh no,' he said ironically. 'Anything but that.'

He still couldn't quite believe it was happening to him. Now he had to face Rachel's father and ask for 'her hand' That was a joke. Although he wasn't looking forward to the ordeal he wasn't expecting any objections from that quarter. What really worried him was breaking the news to his mother. Just when she seemed to be having some kind of renaissance too. The change in her over the past weeks had been mystifying. He didn't know what could have brought about the transformation but he put it down to Clarice Harvey's influence. The cheery little cleaning woman had taken some stick from his mother when she first arrived. She had put up with his mother's arrogant high-handedness as few others would have done. But ever since the day when Clarice had put her to bed with a bad migraine headache the two of them seemed to have become firm friends. He wished he knew Clarice's secret. Whatever it was he hoped he wasn't about to reverse its effect.

'What do you mean, you're getting married?'

John's heart sank as he saw his mother's jaw drop with dismay.

'What I say, Mother.' He'd thought about it and decided that the best course of action was the ultimatum. 'Rachel and I will be getting married the week after next.'

'*Rachel?* Rachel who? How long have you known this girl?'

'I've known her – slightly – since we were children. Her name is Rachel Sands and she lives in King's Walk.'

'The Baptist minister's daughter?' Theresa stared at him incredulously. 'But – I thought it was Catherine Ladgrove that you . . .'

'*Mother!*' John's strident tone brought Theresa's eyes up sharply to meet his. He took a deep breath to calm his nerves. 'Mother, listen, Cathy and I decided to part some time ago, soon after she went away.'

'I see.'

'Let's not pretend you were in favour of that, Mother. You weren't exactly welcoming when I brought her to meet you, were you? Anyway, not long afterwards I met Rachel.'

'I thought you said you'd known her since your childhood.'

He sighed. 'You know what I mean. It was only recently that we got to know one another – as adults.'

Theresa's eyebrows rose. 'And now you're going to *marry* her? Just like that?'

'That's what I said.'

There was more than a hint of defiance in John's reply and Theresa began to suspect the worst.

'So, where is this – this *charade* to take place?' she asked.

'At the Baptist chapel,' John swallowed hard. He'd tried to persuade Hebert Sands to agree to a register office wedding but the man had been scandalized; adamant that his daughter would not be properly married unless it was in his chapel.

'The Baptist *chapel*?' Theresa repeated. 'I see. Well, I hope you won't expect me to set foot in that place!'

John sighed. It was what he'd expected. The old look of disdain was back on his mother's face. It was there in the tightening of her lips and the imperious arch of her eyebrows.

'Obviously I would like you to be there, Mother,' he said patiently. 'But if you feel that you . . .'

Suddenly she was looking at him with concern. 'John – there's something odd about all this. I hope she's not . . . in the family way, is she?'

Shocked into speechlessness by his mother's outspokenness John gaped at her.

She shook her head. 'Please, tell me the truth. It's bound to come out sooner or later after all. If the answer is no, then I apologize for asking.'

'I'm not sure I know what you mean.'

'Oh, for heaven's sake do let's have plain speaking, John.' Theresa was beginning to be irritated. 'Of course you know what I mean. Have you got the girl into trouble? If you have there are other ways,' she went on. 'You don't have to marry her if you don't want to.'

John looked up at his mother in astonishment. '*Mother!*'

'John! Listen to me. Being married to the wrong person can bring a lifetime of misery. Believe me, I know what I'm talking about. I think I can see what probably happened. You were hurt by Catherine leaving. You missed her and you let yourself get carried away when the Sands girl threw herself at you.' She held up her hand. 'Oh yes, I've heard what kind of girl she is.'

'That's not fair. You don't even know her,' he said. 'Anyway I have to do what's right.'

'Don't be a fool, John. It's the oldest trap in the world. The girl is looking for a better life and she's picked you. It wouldn't surprise me if she'd planned the whole thing. So if it's not what you want, for goodness sake don't let yourself be caught by it.'

John shook his head. 'I have to marry her, Mother. It's all been decided.'

'Decided by whom? Her father?'

'No! He doesn't know about the baby. And he mustn't. He's a very strict man. Rachel is afraid of him.'

Theresa leaned forward earnestly. 'Don't let yourself be emotionally blackmailed into this. It's you I'm thinking of. I don't want to see you ruin your life.'

John reached out and took his mother's hand. He was touched. He had never known her be so concerned for him. This reaction was the last one he'd expected. Anger, scorn, threats even, but not this.

'We'll be all right,' he said softly. 'Don't worry about it. We'll be all right. And this child will be your grandchild, remember. You wouldn't want me not to acknowledge that, would you?'

Theresa bit her lip. It seemed his mind was made up and nothing she could say would change it. Suddenly she thought of John's leaving. Just when she had begun to think of having the business legally made over to him he was going to leave her. The thought of living alone in this great house filled her with dismay. 'So – where will you live?' she asked.

'We'll have to look for something. It won't be easy with the housing shortage.' With a sinking heart John remembered Mary Sands's suggestion. 'As a matter of fact Rachel's mother has offered us their spare room—'

'*Oh!*' Theresa's look of horror stopped him in mid-sentence. 'You surely cannot seriously contemplate that?' she said. She paused to consider for a moment. Suddenly it seemed ridiculous, having so much space when people were overcrowded.

'We have more than enough room here,' she said at last. 'You could have your bedroom, and use the morning room for a sitting room – just until you find a place of your own.'

Relief almost swamped him. 'Thank you, Mother. That's extremely generous.'

'But, John . . .' she said as he got up to leave. 'I meant what I said. You really don't have to make this lifetime commitment if it's not what you truly want. I advise you to think very carefully about it. It's not too late.'

He smiled at her from the doorway. 'I know. Please trust me to do what I think best.'

When the door closed behind him Theresa allowed her face to crumple. Much of this was probably her fault. She'd been less than kind to the Ladgrove girl and now John had got himself into this unholy mess. A mixture of anger and exasperation filled her. She hated to see her only son sacrificing his life for the outcome of a few moments' recklessness. And what had she let herself in for, sharing her house with the Sands girl?

But of one thing she was decided; she would not be making the business over to John now. From what she had heard the Sands girl would run through the money in no time. If only darling Laurence hadn't been killed . . . Her eyes filled with tears as they fell on the cherished photograph of her elder son. Laurence would never have made a fool of himself over some common little slut. She only hoped the wretched girl appreciated the sacrifices they were all about to make on her behalf.

'Two rooms at Cedar Lodge? Well, I suppose it's better than sharing a house with my dad.' Rachel pulled a face. 'A pigsty would be better than that!'

Rachel's reaction to his news about his mother's offer was hardly what John had expected, but nevertheless he could not disagree with her.

'I thought it was very generous of her to offer,' he said.

'Mmm – as long as she doesn't expect me to be a free skivvy for her.'

'Of course she won't. She has Clarice Harvey in to clean every day.'

Rachel smiled to herself. She quite liked the notion of Peter's grandmother cleaning up after her. The old bitch had never made any pretence of liking her. 'And it won't be for long, will it?' she added. 'We'll soon be getting a place of our own. I've always fancied one of those houses in Meadow Grove,' she said dreamily. 'They were only built just before the war and they've got ever so many modern features and lovely gardens.'

'And they're all firmly occupied,' John told her. 'There's absolutely nothing on the market at the moment, and hardly any building going on either. Anyway, you still need a building permit.'

She pouted. 'Oh? I should have thought with your influence . . .' She took his arm and hugged it. 'Maybe one of those lovely flats in Sylvan Mansions will be vacant soon, eh? Someone told me they have an underground garage in the basement and a man to wash your car.'

'And rents to match,' John said ironically.

'Don't be an old meanie.' She gave him a push. 'You're the owner of King's Footwear. You can afford it. And you should live somewhere suitable.'

'Correction. My *mother* is the owner of King's Footwear,' he told her. 'I'm only the manager.'

Rachel stared at him, aghast. 'You're joking!'

'Not at all. I do my job and get paid a salary, just like everyone else.'

'But it will be yours, won't it – when she – you know, one day?'

'I suppose so. Meantime I'm just a hard-up worker like so many others. Even the car belongs to the firm. I'm afraid we won't be rich, Rachel.'

Rachel was silent as she took in this latest bombshell. She had imagined herself living in the lap of luxury once she was married to John. Not for her the struggle to make ends meet that her mother had suffered all her married life. Still, she told herself, what John thought of as poor was surely a far cry from the way she'd been brought up.

'Well, if we have to live at Cedar Lodge could we furnish our own rooms then?' she asked. 'I hate old-fashioned furniture, don't you?'

'Well, I don't know . . .'

'Johnny,' She gave his arm a squeeze. 'I've seen a lovely dress that'd be perfect for the wedding,' she said. 'Can we go and get it on Saturday? We could meet in my lunch-hour. It wouldn't take long.'

'Isn't it at the shop where you work?'

She pulled a face. 'Glenda's? I'm not getting married in a dress from Glenda's. It's all cheap rubbish in there.'

'I see.'

'And can we go to Blackpool for our honeymoon? I've always wanted to go to Blackpool.'

When Clarice heard about John's impending marriage to Rachel Sands over the mid-morning tea at Cedar Lodge next day she guessed the rest for herself. Madam clearly wasn't happy about it, she could see that. There was only one reason why a young chap of John's standing would go out with a girl like Rachel Sands, and clearly it had rebounded on him in the age-old fashion. The problem was, what could she do about it? She could say plenty, but it wasn't her place to speak her mind, especially on a delicate matter like this.

Mrs King had made it clear that she was worried about the situation. She hadn't exactly said that Rachel was pregnant, it could be that she didn't even know. But with the wedding taking place in such a rush what else could it be?

Clarice had passed the girl several times in the street lately and been treated to one of the little madam's mocking smiles. She might have known she was up to something. Rachel had always known that Clarice neither liked nor trusted her and now she clearly felt she had the upper hand. Clarice's fingers itched to smack her common little face. That poor silly young fool, John King, getting taken in by the likes of her!

Passing the time of day in Ladgrove's corner shop with Mary Sands a couple of days later it was clear that the girl's parents were delighted with their daughter's engagement. Clarice wasn't surprised. If she had a girl like that she'd be glad to get her off her hands too, especially to a catch like John King. And it was plain from the look on Mrs Ladgrove's face that she was shocked by the news.

It was only later, when she had her feet up at home with a cup of tea that Clarice began to remember things.

Just before Peter went off to do his National Service he'd taken Rachel out for the evening. She remembered it well because he'd borrowed a car from his employer without asking first and they'd had words about it.

'You want to have a job to come back to after serving your country, don't you?' she'd reminded him. 'What can be so important that you need to nick a car? I do hope you're not into anything crooked.'

Peter had given her that cheeky grin of his. 'Keep your hair on, Gran. I'm not nickin' it, only borrowin' – and I'm not gonna use it for a getaway car or nothing like that. Been seeing too many of them James Cagney flicks, that's your trouble.'

'All right, what do you need it for then?' she challenged.

'I'm taking Rachel out, if you must know. Might be the last time we see each other for a while. I want to give her a good time.'

'And what are you doing for petrol, pray?' she asked him suspiciously. 'Black market coupons, is it? Or are you using that pink stuff from the garage? You know what'll happen if you get caught with that stuff in the tank, don't you? You'll even get your boss in trouble as well!'

'Oh Gran, do leave off can't you?' He waved her fears away. 'I know what I'm doing.'

'Well I just hope you do, my lad!'

They'd been very late back that night. Although he'd crept in Clarice had heard him and looked at her alarm clock. Well after midnight, it had been. She'd heard next day from Mrs Briggs, the woman who lived in the house adjoining the Sands that there had been a terrible row when Rachel got in. Screaming and yelling fit to wake the dead. Mrs B had confided to all and sundry in Ladgrove's shop the following day that she suspected Herbert Sands of hitting the girl too. Remembering all these things, a terrible suspicion crept into Clarice's mind. She longed to get it off her chest, but she felt bound to keep it to herself.

It was still on her mind a week later when she got home from Cedar Lodge at lunch-time. She was taking off her coat in the hall when there was a ring at the front doorbell. Through the frosted glass panel in the top half of the door she could see a shape and she knew instantly whose it was. Running to the door she threw it open.

'*Peter*! Why didn't you let me know you were coming home? How long've you got, love?'

He laughed. 'Hang on! Let's get in first, Gran!' Stepping over the threshold he threw down his kit-bag and hugged her hard. 'Good to see you! Got a cuppa, have you? I'm spitting feathers.'

'Come through and I'll get the kettle on.' She looked up at her tall grandson. He'd grown. She was sure of it. He'd filled out too. He was truly a man now. And so much like his granddad. He looked every inch a soldier, as she told him. He laughed, pulling off his cap and bending to kiss her cheek.

'You look well too, Gran. Working at Cedar Lodge for the old witch suits you, I reckon.'

'Just you watch your tongue young man,' she said. 'Mrs King's all right when you get to know her. We rub along just fine.' She poured boiling water into the teapot. 'Might surprise you to know we've even been to the pictures together.'

He laughed. 'Get away! You're pulling my leg!'

'No I'm not. True as I'm standing here. We went to see *Notorious*. She loved it!'

'Trust you, Gran,' he said. 'You could sell ice to Eskimos. I've always said so!'

They laughed together as she poured two large mugs of tea almost as though he'd never been away. Sitting opposite each other at the kitchen table they exchanged their news. Peter displayed his new stripe and explained what it meant. He seemed so proud and pleased with himself that she put off breaking the news about Rachel's imminent marriage.

It was the end of the week and the rations were short, but she made him his favourite meal of egg and chips. It was as they were finishing it that she said, 'There's something you should know, son.'

He looked up from wiping his plate with a piece of bread. 'Oh yeah, what's that then?'

'It's about Rachel.'

'Rach?'

'She's getting married.'

She saw his face drop.

'Who to?'

'John King.'

'King? I don't get it, Gran. When?'

'A week next Saturday.'

'You're joking!'

'It's true, Peter.'

He frowned. 'She don't even know John King.'

'She does now.'

He pushed his plate away. 'What's it all about, Gran? Rach and me, we love each other. We've always said we'd get married one day. Ever since we was kids.' She saw the hurt in his eyes. '*Bloody hell*! The minute my back was turned she had to go off and get herself engaged to some bloke she hardly knows. What's the matter with her?'

'Look, Peter – maybe I shouldn't say this to you because I can't know for sure but I've an idea it might be a case of having to.'

'You what?'

'I think – only *think*, mind, she might be expecting.'

'*Christ*! It gets worse! I've only been gone three months! John King! I'll break his bloody neck for him, I'll go round there right now and give him a bloody good hiding. Just because he lives in a posh house and owns a factory he thinks he can take my girl from under my nose and . . .'

'*Peter*!' Clarice got up and went to him, laying a restraining hand on his shoulder. 'Peter – look, I *said* I wasn't sure. I might be wrong. Don't go doing something that'll get you into trouble.'

He looked up at her. 'I know you, Gran. You wouldn't have said that if you weren't pretty sure.' He leaned back in the chair, clearly trying to get his emotions under control. Clarice poured him a cup of tea but he waved it away. 'I've got to see her,' he said. 'I've got to see her now.'

'Please don't go doing anything rash,' Clarice begged. 'See her if you want, but don't make a scene in public. Wait till she's finished work. And don't let that temper of yours run away with you. No girl is worth that. Look, why don't you go upstairs and have a wash. Unpack that kit-bag, and if you've got any washing I'll nip out to the wash house and light the copper.'

'What time does she leave off work? Half-five, isn't it?'

'I think so. Wouldn't do to go rushing in while she's still working, would it? Only get you off on the wrong foot.'

To her relief he agreed and went upstairs to unpack. He had a

forty-eight hour pass, he'd told her. Two days was a long time for a
man in turmoil and she just hoped they'd get through it without
him doing anything he'd regret. At 5.15 he came downstairs in
civvies, washed and shaved and looking calmer.

'I'm off then, Gran,' he said. 'I'll meet Rach out of work and
have it out with her. See you later.'

She stood at the front-room window and watched him go, her
heart aching for the wounded look in his eyes. 'He'll get over it,'
she told herself aloud. Better like this in the long run. She knew
that Rachel was wrong for him. That girl was wrong for anyone.
She was greedy and common and downright devious. Whoever she
got her hooks into she'd make them pay. She was sorry for John
King – even sorrier for poor madam.

He stood in the doorway of the ironmonger's shop two doors down
from Glenda Gowns and as he saw the girls come out he stepped
back out of sight. Mrs Gifford and the other two girls who worked
at the shop said goodnight and dispersed, then Rachel began to
walk in his direction. As she came level with the doorway he
stepped out.

'Hello, Rachel.'

'*Pete*!' There was a look of panic on her face and just for a
moment he thought she was going to turn and run. His hand shot
out to grasp her arm. Her mouth dropped open in surprise. 'I
didn't know you were coming home on leave.'

'Didn't know myself till last night. It's like that in the army – all
last-minute surprises,' he said. 'But you'd know all about surprises,
wouldn't you?'

'I – don't know what you mean.'

'No? Pity I didn't know about the wedding. I think my invitation must've got lost in the post. What a shame.'

'Who told you?'

He laughed. 'Who d'you reckon? My gran works for your ma-
in-law to be, remember?'

'Oh – yes.'

He grasped her arm more firmly and began to walk. 'I reckon
you'n me have got some talking to do, Rach.'

'Not now, Pete. You know what Dad's like if I'm late home.' She
tried to pull her arm away but he held it fast.

120

'Later then. I'll meet you in the park – about seven.'

'No. I can't.'

'I think you'd better, Rachel.' His eyes were dark with anger and hurt as they looked into hers. 'If you're not there I'll come and get you.'

'*No*! I'm engaged. Dad won't let you in.'

'Oh yes he will when he hears what I have to say!'

'What do you mean?'

'Does your dad know you're expecting?

The colour drained from her face. 'No!'

'I think he might be interested to know that, don't you, Rachel? 'Specially when I tell him that it's *my* kid you're having!'

'You wouldn't!'

He laughed. 'You reckon? Better be in the park at seven unless you want to try me then, hadn't you?'

She stared at him, her face white. 'I'm getting married. There's nothing you or anyone else – including Dad – can do about it now.'

'No? We'll see about that!'

Stunned into silence she stared at him, then suddenly she became aware that people were looking at them. Any moment now someone who knew them might come along and Peter was in the kind of mood where he'd blurt anything out.

'Look – OK then,' she said. 'I'll meet you. I can't promise seven though. It might be nearer eight.'

'OK, eight then, but no later.' His grip on her wrist tightened painfully. 'I won't be messed about, Rachel. You know what'll happen if you're not there.'

'I've said I'll be there, haven't I?' she said, her voice shrill with fear. 'But you've got to promise you won't come near the house.'

'I haven't got to promise you anything!' He stood looking down at her, his eyes blazing; then he let her go abruptly.

'Eight o'clock then, near the bandstand. I want to hear it all. And I mean the truth, Rachel.'

It was almost half past eight when he saw her hurrying across the park towards the bandstand.

'I thought you weren't gonna show up,' he said gruffly as she came up. He grabbed her arm. 'Come on, we'll sit on that bench over there.'

'I can't stay long,' she told him breathlessly. 'I told Dad I was going out to post a letter.'

'In that case you'd better get straight to the point, hadn't you? I'm waiting.'

'I missed you, Pete,' she said as they sat side by side on the bench. 'I was lonely. And when I saw John one afternoon on the way home from work and he asked me out for the day . . .'

'Wait a minute,' he interrupted. 'King's factory isn't on your way home from work.'

She shrugged. 'I had to do an errand – for Mum.'

'OK. So he asked you out.'

'Yes. We went to the seaside.'

'Yeah – *and*. . . ?'

She bit her lip. 'It was a really hot day and we wanted to go swimming.'

His lip curled. 'You're gonna tell me in a minute that salt water makes you pregnant.'

She shook her head. 'We didn't have any costumes. There was no one about, so we went in – without.' She glanced at him. 'It was my idea.'

'I can imagine,' he said drily.

'Afterwards – well . . . It just happened.' She turned to him, her eyes brimming. 'I told you, Pete. I missed you. I – I kept on wishing it was you and not him.'

'When was this?' he asked. 'As soon as I went away? Didn't take you long, did it?' He turned and grasped her shoulders. 'Might amuse you to know that there's been no one else for me since I left here. That gives you a bloody good laugh, I bet!'

'Don't, Pete – please.' She choked on a sob and the tears spilled over. 'I just wish it could be different. Really I do.'

'It can!'

She looked at him, her mouth agape. 'What? What do you mean?'

'Easy. Marry me instead.' He felt her stiffen and his grip on her arm tightened. 'Look, chances are, it's my kid anyway. I don't care. I want you, Rach. We'll forget about King. I forgive you. So – what d'you say, eh?'

She was shaking her head, panic gripping her stomach muscles so hard that she felt sick. '*No*! I can't. It wouldn't work.'

' 'Course it'd work, Rach. You could move in with Gran till I've done my stint in the army, then we'd set up together somewhere.'

'Share with your gran? We'd have no money. How would we manage? We can't, Pete.'

'Yes, we *can!*' He pulled her to him and kissed her hard. 'I've been thinking of signing on for the regulars. We'd get married quarters then; a place of our own. We love each other, don't we? We always have. You can't marry John King. I won't let you!'

'You've *got* to! Look, I'm engaged. It's all fixed. What would I say to Dad and Mum? They'd never allow it.'

'Then we'll run off.'

'*No!* I said no and I meant it.'

'You're just after his money, aren't you?'

She pulled away from him and stood up, dashing away the tears that ran down her cheeks. 'You don't know what I've been through all these years, Pete. Dad's been horrible. He stands up there in that pulpit every Sunday and makes out he's a good man when all the time he's hard and wicked. He hasn't got a kind bone in his body. He used to hit me when I was little – unmercifully on the bare bottom with a cane – till I bled sometimes. He'd shut me up in my room for hours on end for the slightest little thing. I've had it dinned into me that I'm a wicked girl just like my mother and that it's his duty to knock it out of me. I know he'd like to beat me now if he thought he could get away with it. He smacked me in the face that night before you left 'cause I was late home.'

'I could make all that up to you, Rachel.' Peter was on his feet too now, his eyes moist.

'It's not just that. I've never had anything other kids have,' she said. 'No toys or pretty dresses, no outings. But worst of all, no *love*, Pete; no hugs and kisses; no bedtime stories or Christmas trees. No one to make me feel I was special.' She shook her head, 'I know your mum walked out on you, but at least you still had your dad and gran.'

'But *I* love you, Rachel. *I* make you feel special – don't I?'

She shook her head. 'It's too late. Look, Pete, I don't want to hurt you but if we got married we'd be hard up. Life would be a struggle and I can't be poor any more. I want nice things. I want people to look up to me. I want to *be* somebody!' She looked at his uncomprehending face and sobbed with exasperation. 'Oh, why can't you *see*? I need these things, Pete. I *need* them!'

'OK, I'll get them for you – somehow.' He reached out for her but she backed away.

'I can't marry you, Pete. It's not what I want. Please don't make it hard for me. Just go. Leave me alone – *please*.'

'You bloody little slut!' His eyes flashed with tears of pain and his hands clenched into fists at his sides. 'Your dad was right when he said you were wicked. You don't give a shit for anyone but yourself. You're rotten to the core. I pity that poor bastard you're marrying. I hope you both rot in . . .' She stopped his words by throwing her arms around his neck and fastening her mouth on his. Her kiss was hard and fierce and it took his breath away, but as his arms closed around her she shrugged them off.

'Goodbye, Pete,' she said, backing away. 'I hope you have a happy life. I hope you meet someone who deserves you. Someone nice – nicer than me.'

He made no reply but stood watching helplessly as she turned and ran away from him into the gathering dusk.

CHAPTER TEN

ONCE THE COLLEGE TERM ended the holiday season really began.

The municipal orchestra was on a month's break and the Flynn family had gone away. An uncle of Faith's had a villa in Provence which he had bought cheaply just after the war ended. It was in a neglected state and he had been busy restoring it all summer. He had invited the Flynns to join him there for three weeks on condition that they helped him with the redecorating. They had all gone, Faith, Mike and Philip, Andrew and his friend, Finn and of course Harry.

Harry had gone under protest. He was disappointed that Cathy couldn't go too. He'd wanted to stay behind, but she'd urged him to go with his family, pointing out that she'd be working most of the time anyway. But once they'd left she rather wished she'd let him stay. The house in Penrith Avenue seemed so deathly quiet without the family. Most of the boarders had either gone home or away on holiday and the house had a cavernous emptiness which Cathy found depressing. Each night she climbed the stairs to her room, dog-tired and missing the happy chatter and the buzz of life that normally filled the place.

Each morning she looked hopefully among the post for an envelope with John's handwriting. Although there were regular letters from her mother and from Pauline with news from home, neither of them ever mentioned John. Several times she began a letter to him, trying to explain that although she had a new life here and had made new friends, he would always be the important person in her life. But somehow the words never seemed to come out right.

The letters always read like an apology and she knew she had nothing to apologize for. Most of her efforts ended up in the waste-paper basket. In the end she decided it was better to wait and talk to John face to face. After all, she hadn't long to wait now.

August came to an end and the bookings at the Marine Bay began to ease off. The Tanners had had a good season and were pleased with their profits. Cathy was to have the first two weeks in September off so that she could go home before the new term began.

The Flynns returned from their holiday at the end of August. It was as though the house came back to life again as they piled nois-ily in through the front door with their heaped-up luggage and various cascading parcels. Cathy was delighted to see them. Harry looked tanned and relaxed, but he insisted that the holiday had been a bore without her. He'd brought her a sketchbook full of exquisite watercolour sketches that he'd done to while away the long days.

'I thought they were better than photographs,' he told her. 'And you can tell just by looking at them how much I was missing you,' he added wistfully.

Leafing through the book, Cathy was touched and enchanted by the delicately painted pictures. 'I'll treasure them,' she told Harry. 'It's the nicest present I've ever had.'

He shrugged off her delight, but couldn't disguise his pleasure. It was short-lived however when he learned that she was to spend the first two weeks of September in Queensgrove.

'I've only just got home and now you're going,' he wailed. 'And I bet you don't come back.'

'It depends whether I get this government grant thing. If I don't get it I couldn't afford college without a job to support it.' She smiled ruefully at him. 'I'd love you to come home with me, Harry,' she said. 'I'd love my family to meet you too. It's just . . .'

'I know. You don't want to throw another spanner in the works with that boring bloke of yours.'

'I do need to talk to him,' Cathy said.

'And I'd be in the way – yes I know. Well, if it's any comfort I'll be here waiting when you get back,' he told her stoically. 'And I'll make sure that Faith doesn't let your room, so don't worry about that.'

On the day she left he went with her to the station and bought her an armful of magazines at the bookstall. Leaning in at the train window he assumed his little-boy-lost look. 'Is it too much to hope you'll try not to forget me?' he asked sadly.

She ruffled his hair. 'How could anyone ever forget you?' she laughed. 'And I'm determined to come back next term if I can. If I get that grant I'll be studying full-time in the autumn.'

The train pulled out and Harry walked along with it until he reached the end of the platform. Cathy waved until she couldn't see him any more, then settled back in her seat and opened one of the magazines. She reminded herself that she would soon be seeing John and the thought made her stomach lurch with excitement. She was sure she could put things right between them once they were together again.

Her father was there to meet her at the station. Cathy was shocked by his appearance. It was only five months since she had seen him but he had lost weight and looked ten years older. However, his delighted smile as she stepped off the train was reassuring. He hugged her and insisted on carrying her case.

'Your mother has been counting the days till you came home,' he told her.

At King's Walk Phyllis had the table set for tea. Pauline had taken over for her downstairs while she prepared a special meal; ham and salad, tinned peaches she'd been saving from the last delivery they'd had at the shop and a chocolate cake she'd made the previous evening. She'd changed into her best dress, shampooed her hair and put on a little of the lipstick Pauline had bought her last Christmas. When her elder daughter saw her she whistled.

'Wow, Mum! Anyone would think we were expecting royalty,' she teased. 'It's only our Cathy, you know.'

But Phyllis shook her head. She was proud of her daughter and longed to have her home again, but not only that; if what she had heard in the shop lately were true, Cathy was in for a cruel shock. She only hoped that they as a family would be able to cushion the blow for her.

'Will you break the news about John to her, Pauline?' she asked her elder daughter. 'I don't think I could find the right words to tell her.'

'I will if I have to,' Pauline agreed. 'But surely John will have written. She must surely know.'

But Cathy's light-heartedness over tea gave no indication that she was aware of John's impending marriage. She made them laugh with stories about the college rag and her part as a mermaid. She told them about Harry Flynn and his unconventional family and the house in Penrith Avenue, filled with interesting characters. Later she explained what she had learned of the new government grant and showed them the application form that Paul Samuels had already obtained for her. Her father was quite excited about it and insisted that they must apply as soon as possible, promising to help Cathy fill it in. He in his turn was full of the latest happenings in the news: the Nuremberg trials of Nazi war criminals and the fearsome atomic bomb recently set off in the Pacific. Phyllis shuddered.

'Robert! What subjects for the tea table,' she chided him. 'Cathy doesn't want to hear about nasty things like that. Let's talk about something cheerful.'

Pauline remained silent, wondering how her sister would take the news of John's forthcoming marriage. Cathy seemed so happy and she dreaded seeing all that radiance dashed. But, glancing at her mother's face, Pauline knew that the unenviable task of breaking the news would fall to her.

Later, as Cathy helped her sister to bath the twins, she marvelled at how much Paul and Michael had grown.

'I know. Proper little devils they can be at times too,' Pauline said. 'I managed to get them a place at a day-nursery, thank goodness. They go from nine till four every weekday. It makes life easier. Dad just couldn't cope with them any more.'

'I noticed how much weight he'd lost,' Cathy said. 'Is he all right?'

Pauline shook her head. 'He caught a cold soon after you left and it turned to pneumonia. It really pulled him down. Ever since then his chest has been really bad. First thing in the morning he can hardly get his breath and when he's having a bad day it's all he can do to get out of his chair. That was why I had to get Paul and Michael fixed up.'

'Why didn't you write and tell me?' Cathy asked.

'You couldn't have done anything. And we didn't want you

coming home and losing your place at college.'

'And what about you?' Cathy looked at her sister.

Pauline shook her head. 'The divorce is going through. I've had the papers and everything.' She sighed. 'I suppose I should think about getting a place of my own with the boys getting bigger. I feel it's a strain on Mum and Dad.'

Cathy sighed. 'It must be horrible for you. Does it still hurt as much, Pauline?'

'Not as much as it did. After all, if he doesn't love me any more it wouldn't have worked, would it?' She shook her head. 'Since the war ended there have been so many divorces. Sometimes I wonder if love ever lasts, and just what marriage really is. Mum says people should work at it, but does that just mean putting up with a situation you hate?'

'Surely not,' Cathy said. 'Surely real love has to be strong enough to survive a few problems.'

'I thought what you and John had was strong – and now look . . .' Pauline paused to haul one of her protesting sons out of the bath. She wrapped him in a towel and began to dry him vigorously.

Cathy frowned as she followed suit with the other little boy, glancing at her sister over his head. 'What do you mean – now look?'

Pauline flushed. 'Oh, nothing.'

Cathy frowned. 'Is there something I should know?'

'I'm sorry. That just slipped out. I didn't mean to say anything till later.'

'Anything about what?'

Pauline bit her lip as Michael scrambled down from her lap and ran giggling round the bathroom. She grabbed him and began to bundle him into his pyjamas. 'We can't talk now,' she said. 'Wait till we've got these two settled, then we can have a heart to heart.'

When the boys were safely in their cots Cathy looked at her sister.

'Are you going to keep me waiting for ever?' she asked.

'Let's go out for a walk,' Pauline suggested.

They walked across the park and found a seat near the lake.

'For heaven's sake, Pauline – are you going to tell me?' Cathy said impatiently.

Pauline drew a long breath. 'This isn't easy. I quite thought you would have had a letter.'

'A letter? What *about*?'

'From John. Did you and he have a row?' Pauline asked.

'Yes, when he came down to see me for the weekend. He got the wrong idea – thought I was seeing someone else. But it wasn't serious. I tried to write, but then I thought it would be better to wait till I came home and talked to him face to . . .' She looked at her sister's anguished face. 'Pauline – what's happened?'

'There's no easy way to say this, Cath.' Pauline paused. 'John's getting married.'

Cathy stared at her. 'Married?' she said at last. 'No. That can't be right. You must have got it wrong.'

'It's true, love. I'm sorry.'

'But – I don't understand. Who to?'

'Rachel Sands.'

'*Rachel*? But I thought that she and Peter Harvey . . .'

'I'm not sure that was ever serious, just a boy and girl thing. Anyway, Peter's doing his National Service.' Pauline looked at her sister's stunned face and laid a hand on her arm. 'I'm really sorry, love. I know it seems unbelievable. Maybe it was a rebound thing.'

'Perhaps you're right.' Cathy shivered. Suddenly the balmy summer evening had turned wintry. The sky had clouded over and a chill wind sprang up. 'It's getting cold,' she said. 'Shall we go home?'

Cathy lay awake for most of that night. It seemed inconceivable that John would simply go and marry someone else – without even writing to tell her. How could he be so cruel as to let her come home and find out like this? She alternated between anger and misery, her tears scalding her cheeks and dampening the pillow. In the morning she looked so hollow-eyed that her mother suggested she went back to bed again.

'What's the matter, love? Have you got a headache?' she asked.

'Pauline told me last night about John,' Cathy said. 'It was a shock. I didn't sleep very well.'

'I'm not surprised.' Phyllis dried her hands. 'We weren't sure if you knew about it. I just can't understand him. A girl like Rachel Sands. And not writing to let you know, even.' She put her arms round her daughter and hugged her. 'If he can treat you like that love, he's not worth upsetting yourself over. Look, if you don't want to go back to bed why don't you take the bus into Peterborough and have a look round the shops?' she suggested. 'Pauline could go with you once she's taken the boys to the nursery. I can easily manage by myself. Things are always quiet on a Monday.'

But Cathy shook her head. 'I've got a better idea. You take Dad out for the day. Pauline and I will manage the shop. It'll take my mind off things. If anyone deserves a day off it's you.'

Cathy would have enjoyed helping Pauline in the shop if it hadn't been for the looks of sympathy she received from some of the customers. By now everyone in King's Walk knew about the forthcoming wedding. Nothing was said but looks said all. Cathy tried valiantly to make a joke of it.

'Anyone would think I'd grown another head or a set of horns,' she remarked to Pauline.

'Take no notice, they mean well.'

At four o'clock Pauline made a pot of tea and then put on her coat to go and fetch the boys. 'You'll be OK on your own?' she asked.

'Of course. In fact why not do some shopping afterwards if you want to. I'll be fine.'

Teatime was a quiet period in the shop and Cathy busied herself tidying the shelves in the back room. It was just after five when the shop bell rang and she hurried into the shop.

'What can I get. . . ?' She broke off, the colour flooding her cheeks as she came face to face with an equally startled John.

'Oh – Cathy! I just came in for an evening paper and . . .' He trailed off, his eyes troubled. 'I'd no idea you were home.'

'Obviously. If you'd known you wouldn't have come within a mile of the shop, would you?' She couldn't keep the bitterness out of her voice. 'I understand congratulations are in order.'

'Cathy – it's hard to explain . . .'

'I suppose that's why you didn't even try!'

'I didn't know where to begin. It's not straightforward. There are – reasons.'

'Well, there would be, wouldn't there?'

'You never wrote, Cathy – after that weekend.'

'Neither did you.'

131

'Because I thought . . .'

'Because you jumped to conclusions, you mean. You never gave me a chance to explain and I couldn't do it in a letter. I tried.' She took an evening paper from the pile on the counter, folded it and passed it to him. 'So you came home and found someone else. Someone who suited you better. All right. That's fine!'

'It wasn't like that. Rachel and I . . .'

She held up her hand. 'I don't want to hear about it, thank you. So – is there anything else you want?'

'Cathy – please . . .'

'There's nothing more to be said. Now – do you want anything *else*?' Her voice trembled, perilously close to tears.

'No.' He handed her the money for the paper and she put it into the till.

'Thank you. Goodbye.'

For a long moment he looked at her, then he picked up the paper and left.

A few moments later Pauline came in with the boys.

'I thought I saw John coming out of here as I turned the corner,' she said. One look at her sister's face answered her question. 'Oh, love, are you all right?'

'I'm fine,' Cathy said, swallowing hard at the thickness in her throat.

'What happened? What did he say?'

'He asked for an evening paper,' Cathy said. 'I took his money and he left. That's what happened.'

'Nothing else? He didn't – explain?'

'What is there to explain? He's marrying Rachel Sands. I knew that.' Cathy came out from behind the counter and took her nephews' hands. 'Come on you two,' she said brightly. 'Auntie Cathy is going to give you your tea. And you can tell me all about what you've been doing while Mummy minds the shop.' And the look she gave her sister as she passed warned her that the subject was closed.

John slept fitfully on Friday night and when he wakened on Saturday morning and remembered what day it was his heart sank. This was his wedding day – for most people the most important day of their life. As for John, he would have moved heaven and earth for it not to be happening. At half past seven he got up and went downstairs.

In the kitchen Clarice Harvey was busy preparing breakfast. She glanced up when he came in. Unshaven, he looked haggard, as though he hadn't slept much. She felt sorry for him and slightly guilty. Knowing what she did, perhaps she should have spoken out. But what could she prove? Even Peter had refused to be drawn on the subject. On the evening that he came home on leave he'd been out, she suspected, to meet Rachel. On his return he'd been abrupt and reticent and he'd stayed that way throughout his brief leave. He had refused to answer her questions, insisting that he was perfectly all right. All he did say was that he would probably sign on for the regular army like his father, once his National Service came to an end.

'I've always wanted to see the world,' he told her. 'Maybe there'll be another war somewhere and I'll get the chance to get into a real fight.'

His words saddened her. She could see the bitterness in his eyes despite his flippant words and she guessed that she'd been right in her fears. But they were unconfirmed and she knew she must remain silent about them.

She looked at John. ' 'Morning, Mr John. Kettle's on. Fancy a cuppa?'

'Thanks, Clarice.' He sat down at the kitchen table, his head in his hands.

'Looks as if you're going to have a fine day for it,' she said as she poured water into the teapot.

John looked up, 'Fine day?'

'For the wedding.'

'Oh – yes.' He drank the tea she poured for him, then got up suddenly from the table, as though he'd suddenly remembered something. 'Thanks, Clarice,' he said. 'Look, I have to go out for a while. If Mother asks will you tell her I've gone for a walk?'

'Yes – 'course.' She watched him go with a shake of her head. Poor devil. The last thing he looked like was an eager bridegroom.

The corner shop opened at half past seven and when John opened the door and saw Pauline behind the counter his courage almost failed him. He had passed Cathy's elder sister several times in the street over the past weeks and she'd given him a look that said it all. It was likely she would refuse his request point blank. All the same, he had to try.

'Pauline, I need your help,' he said. 'I have to see Cathy.'

Her expression was stony. 'Haven't you hurt her enough?'

He ran his fingers through his hair. 'Please – I must see her. Can you just ask her? If she says no, I'll understand. But it is important.'

She was about to tell him to go to hell, then something about his haggard expression and exhausted eyes made her soften.

'I'll ask her,' she conceded. 'But if she says no, I'm not going to persuade her.'

'Thanks. I'll wait round the corner.'

He waited anxiously in the shadow of Cedar Lodge's garden wall as the minutes ticked by. After a while he looked at his watch and decided she wasn't coming. He was about to turn away when she appeared round the corner.

'Cathy!'

'Pauline said you wanted to see me.'

'I couldn't let it go like this,' he said. 'I want you to know why I'm marrying Rachel.'

She drew a deep breath. 'All right.'

'I went out with Rachel just once.' He paused to lick his lips. 'Even then it was her idea. It was just after that weekend when everything went wrong between us. We went to the coast – the first time I'd really relaxed for weeks. One thing . . .' His eyes slid away from hers. 'Well, one thing led to another and . . .'

'*Stop!*' She shook her head. 'I can't take this, John. I don't want to hear any more.'

As she turned away he reached out and grasped her arm. 'Please – I *need* to tell you. This isn't easy for me either, Cathy.'

'What you're trying to say is that you made love to her,' she said, the words knifing through her heart. 'I wouldn't – but she did. Right?'

He winced. 'It was just the once.'

'And once was enough to make you fall in love with her.'

'*No!* What I'm trying to tell you is that because of that one indiscretion Rachel is expecting my child. *That's* why I'm marrying her.'

For a long moment she stood staring at him. 'Rachel is pregnant?'

'It's the last thing I intended or wanted. It's one hell of a mess. But there's nothing I can do.' He grasped her shoulders. 'If only things had been different. If only you'd . . .'

She shook herself free and backed away from him, shaking her head. 'You're trying to put the blame for this on *me*!' she said. 'What you're saying is that if I'd slept with you that weekend this would never have happened!' Angrily she brushed away the tears that spilled down her cheeks. 'I *hate* you, John! I hope I never see you again.' She turned and ran from him.

Theresa sat at the back of the chapel with Clarice beside her. She thought it quite the worst day of her life. It brought back echoes of her own wedding day to Albert with all the accompanying misery. After the ceremony the Sands had arranged a small reception at the Co-operative Luncheon Rooms in the High Street. Throughout the whole proceedings John had looked white-faced and gaunt, whilst Rachel by contrast looked happy and triumphant in her rose-pink dress and picture-hat.

Theresa sat at the back of the room, as far away as she could from the Sands and their assorted relatives. Clarice brought her a plate of ham and lettuce which she picked at disconsolately. Later there was a sliver of wedding cake and a glass of alcohol-free wine with which to toast the bride and groom. When it was time for the couple to leave for their honeymoon she was infinitely grateful that the whole sorry business was coming to an end.

Clarice looked with some concern at her employer's pale face as they stood on the pavement, waving the newlyweds off in the Rover.

'Why don't we go back to Cedar Lodge, madam?' she suggested. 'You can put your feet up while I make you a nice omelette with some brown bread and butter, and then later on you could listen to Saturday Night Theatre on the wireless. You know you always enjoy that.'

Theresa allowed herself to be taken home and pampered by Clarice, but only on condition that Clarice remain to share her supper. The thought of being alone depressed her. Over the omelettes she said suddenly:

'You realize of course that she's pregnant.'

Clarice's heart missed a beat. 'Rachel?' She laid down her fork, her blood turning to ice as she avoided her employer's eyes. 'Well, I must admit I did wonder.'

'I daresay half the neighbourhood *wondered* too,' Theresa said bitterly. 'A girl like that! And John. I can't think what possessed him. It's my fault of course.'

Clarice frowned. 'Your fault? How can it be?'

'He was going out with Catherine Ladgrove, but I thought she wasn't good enough. He brought her to tea and I was horrible to her. I did everything I could think of to put her off.' She looked up at Clarice. 'It serves me right, doesn't it? Snob that I am! Now, instead of Catherine, a nice, well-brought-up girl with a reasonable education I've got Rachel Sands for a daughter-in-law. I expect the whole of King's Walk is laughing at me.'

'Oh no, madam,' Clarice said, trying to sound convincing.

'And Blackpool!' Theresa cried plaintively. 'Of all places to go for their honeymoon!'

But Blackpool was the last thing on Clarice's mind. Rachel Sands was now Rachel King yet the baby she was expecting would be her great-grandchild in truth, no relation to Theresa at all. Now she was sure of it. But there wasn't a single thing she could say or do about it.

CHAPTER ELEVEN

CATHY DECIDED TO RETURN to Bournemouth two days before her fortnight was up. Her parents were disappointed, especially as she had not yet heard whether she would qualify for the government grant she had applied for.

'What will you do if you don't get it?' Phyllis asked anxiously.

'I'll get a job like I did before,' Cathy said. 'The Tanners still need me at the hotel for a few weeks yet and when the season's over there's sure to be something else.'

Robert, however, was more positive as he waited with her on the station platform. 'You'll get your grant all right, love. If they turn you down they'll have me to contend with!' he said bravely. 'All that time I spent as a prisoner of war – I reckon they owe me something. Too late for me now, but you and other youngsters like you are this country's future.'

After that they became tongue-tied but in spite of Cathy's pleas for Robert not to wait with her until the train arrived he stayed on resolutely, looking at his watch every few seconds. In all the time she'd been at home her father had said nothing about John's marriage, now suddenly he brought the subject up.

'You're not too upset about young King, are you love?' he asked, his eyes searching hers.

Cathy shook her head. 'No, Dad,' she lied. 'If he likes Rachel better than me it's up to him, isn't it?' She hadn't mentioned the other girl's pregnancy to anyone, not even Pauline.

'Must be off his head if you ask me,' Robert said angrily. 'Mind you, they always used to reckon that his father had an eye for the

137

common type of woman, if you know what I mean. And they say the apple never falls far from the tree.'

Cathy blushed. 'Oh well, it's done now.' She tried her hardest to sound dismissive. 'Pauline says there are plenty more fish in the sea.' She forced a dry little laugh. 'But as I told her, who wants to marry a fish?'

Her attempt at humour failed feebly and to her relief the clatter of the signal announced the train's imminent arrival. A few moments later it steamed into the station. Robert hugged her hard.

'Well, this is it, love. Take care of yourself,' he said gruffly. 'I'll post your letter on. I know you'll be anxious to hear about the grant.' He patted her shoulder. 'And you know where we are if you need us.'

'Of course I do, Dad. And thanks – for everything.' Cathy swallowed hard at the lump in her throat as her father held her away from him and looked into her eyes.

'You are all right, aren't you, Cathy, love?' he asked.

'Yes, Dad. I'm fine. Look after yourself – and Mum. I'll write soon. And the minute I hear anything about the grant I'll let you know.'

She climbed on to the train. Leaning out of the window she waved, watching the tall, stooped figure as he walked towards the barrier. The thought crossed her mind that her beloved dad seemed to be slipping away before her eyes. Neither he nor her mother had said much about his health, but she'd heard him coughing in the night and noticed how breathless he was after the slightest exertion. As she sat down in her corner seat her heart was heavy. If only Mum and Dad could move away from the Midlands to somewhere where the climate was kinder. They should be the ones going to Bournemouth and not her. And she reflected that if it were not for them she'd never come back to Queensgrove again. These past two weeks she'd come to hate the place.

Briefly she allowed her mind to dwell on John, due home from his honeymoon tomorrow – the main reason for her early departure, and the lump in her throat expanded until she thought she would choke. As she stared unseeing out of the window tears misted the view of passing fields and houses. In her heart she made a solemn vow – to work hard and get her diploma. Once qualified she would find a good job that would make her independent.

Maybe she could even earn enough to help her parents to an easier life. From now on she would concentrate on that. Nothing else mattered.

The journey to Bournemouth seemed endless. Crossing from King's Cross to Waterloo Cathy was caught in the lunchtime rush and consequently missed her train. When at last she arrived at Bournemouth Central she was glad for once that Penrith Avenue was close to the railway and by the time she had walked the short distance, let herself in and climbed the stairs, all she wanted was to lie down and go to sleep. However it wasn't to be allowed, as she might have known in the Flynn household.

She was unpacking when there was a knock on her door. She sighed and called, 'Come in.' A moment later Harry's head came round the door.

'Cath! Someone said they'd seen you come in. You're not due back till the weekend.'

She shrugged wearily. 'I know. Sorry about that.'

'Hey! Don't be. I can't tell you what a treat it is to see you. This old place hasn't been the same without your smiling phizzog.' He bent down to peer into her face. 'Not so smiling now though. You OK?'

She nodded. 'Just tired. Pig of a journey. Lost my connection. I had to wait an hour at Waterloo.'

'Oh, bad luck. Have you eaten?'

She shook her head. 'It's all right though. I'm not hungry.'

He stood regarding her for a moment, then closed the door behind him and put his hands on her shoulders, gently turning her towards him.

'What's happened?' he asked softly.

'Nothing. It was wonderful, seeing Mum and Dad again. And the twins have grown so much I hardly – hardly . . .' She couldn't finish the sentence. His genuine concern and sweet familiarity overwhelmed her. Her throat closed and tears welled up in her eyes.

'Damn!' she said between clenched teeth. 'Damn, damn, *damn*!'

He pulled her close and held her, resting his chin on top of her head.

'Don't worry. Let it all out, Cathy. Have a good howl – tell me about it when you're ready if you want to. Plenty of time.'

'He's married, Harry,' she whispered at last, swallowing hard. 'John's married. He didn't write to tell me or anything. Just let me find out. The wedding was last Saturday. I couldn't stay on – till they got home from the – the . . .'

He swore softly in her ear. 'Bloody hell, Cathy! I'm so sorry. He wants a good kicking if you ask me. Well, you know I never liked him. Too bloody smooth by half.' He fumbled in his pocket for a handkerchief and gently dabbed at her cheeks. 'Here, sit down and tell me about it. Then I'm going to take you out for something to eat. We'll pop down to The Rendezvous and have a piece and three penn'orth.'

'I told you, I'm not hungry.'

He shook his head at her. 'Hey, don't you know what happens to girls who don't eat?' he asked. 'They turn into little paper dolls and blow away.' He drew her down on to the edge of the bed beside him. 'Come on, Cath. Talk about it. Get it off your chest.'

Suddenly she knew that more than anything in the world she wanted to do just that. Slowly and painfully she unfolded the story to him; beginning with Pauline's revelation and ending with the part she hadn't been able to bring herself to mention at home.

'He blames me for it all, Harry,' she said. 'I was angry and resentful at first but now I see that he's probably right. If things had been as he wanted that weekend. If I hadn't been so stupidly repressed about it, none of this would have happened.'

'Stop it!' He took her hand and squeezed it tightly. 'You're not to say that, Cath. You're not to even think it. He's been a fool and it's caught up with him. Sure, he'll probably live to regret it, but it's not your problem. And it's certainly not your fault. Don't let it spoil your life. You've got to think of yourself now – get on with your own plans.'

'I know.'

He looked at her stricken face and smiled ruefully. 'But you still love him in spite of everything – is that it?' He tipped up her chin and looked into her eyes. 'OK, right now you think you do. But you'll get over him, Cath, I promise you. Once you get back to college and start studying again things will start to work out for you. Did you apply for that government grant?'

'Yes, but I haven't heard yet whether I'll qualify.'

'You will,' he said positively. 'I know it!' His mouth curved into a smile. 'How do you fancy hearing some good news? Matter of fact, I've got some.'

Her eyes widened. 'Oh, Harry, I forgot. Your exam results?'

He nodded. 'Managed to scrape through this time. *And* I've got an interview for a job next week.'

'A job? Where?'

'Not far away. A private school at Wallisdown. Boys' prep. It's about three miles out of town. I'd have to teach the little horrors football as well, mind. But I can stand on a touchline bellowing and blowing a whistle with the best of 'em. Just have to dig out the old shorts I had when I was in the Scouts and I'm in business.' He grinned at her. 'I just hope the moths haven't been at them. So – wish me luck, eh?'

'Of course I do, Harry. You deserve the best.'

'That's not all either, I've got a holiday job, taking snaps of the sunburnt holidaymakers on the prom.'

She laughed. 'I didn't know you were a photographer.'

'I'm not, but it doesn't matter, half of them never pick the finished product up from the kiosk anyway. I had one bloke last week who paid me a fiver for the film – confided that he was on a dirty weekend with his secretary.'

Cathy was really laughing now. 'Harry Flynn, I don't believe a word of it!'

'Never mind. It made you laugh so what's the difference?'

She leaned across and kissed him. 'You're a real gem, Harry,' she said softly. 'And I'm going to miss you at college next term. You're the best friend a girl could have.'

He winced. 'Ouch! I thought that title was reserved for mothers and cocker spaniels.' He gave her a wistful smile. 'Never mind. First things first. How about some grub? All your old mates will be down at The Rendezvous. Cheer you up.'

'Well – perhaps I should eat something after all,' she said. 'Just give me a few minutes to freshen up and I'll be with you.'

Rachel stood in the middle of the large front bedroom at Cedar Lodge and looked around her.

'Christ! It stinks in here,' she announced. 'What is it – moth-balls or what?'

John closed the door hurriedly, hoping his mother hadn't over-heard the loudly expressed opinion.

'Rachel! Keep your voice down. I'm sure Mother has gone to a lot of trouble to make the room nice for us. Those are new curtains if I'm not mistaken and by the way, the smell is beeswax polish. It looks as though Clarice has really gone to town in here.'

'This furniture though! It must have come out of the ark! So dark and gloomy. You said we could go and buy some of our own,' Rachel reminded him.

'No. *You* said that,' John corrected her. 'What's the point of buying furniture before we know what sort of house we'll be living in? Besides, where would all this go?'

'For all I care it could go on a dump somewhere,' Rachel said with a sniff. 'Seems to me, John, that a lot of the things you promised aren't going to happen now that we're married.'

'This room has been good enough for me ever since I moved out of the nursery and I'm quite happy with it for the time being.' John sighed wearily and turned away. He began to unpack. The honeymoon had been a disaster. The weather had been dismal, it had rained every day. Rachel had complained about the food at the hotel, saying that it made her morning sickness return. But worst of all had been John's reluctance to make love to his bride. Rachel had teased him about it at first, then the teasing had turned to reproaches and finally to tearful accusations.

'What's *wrong* with me, then?' she had demanded, sitting up in bed and staring down accusingly at him. 'You wanted me before all right so why not now? What do we have to do, go down to the beach?'

He got out of bed and went to stand by the window, his back towards her so that she would not see the guilt and misery in his eyes. When he did not reply she challenged him.

'It's her, isn't it – Cathy Ladgrove? Miss high-and-mighty college student. You're still hankering after *her*! Well, I'm your wife now and you better not forget it.'

That remark finally goaded him into anger.

'All right, Rachel,' he swung round to face her. 'There's no need to rub my nose in it. I made a mistake, but I've tried to do the right thing. Are you going to go on making me pay for it for the rest of my life? Because I'll tell you now, I won't stand for it.'

His white face and wounded, angry eyes pulled her up sharply. She saw that she had overstepped the mark. She might have succeeded in snaring John King but she was wise enough to know that she could just as easily lose him again and finish up worse off than before. Divorce was not the disgrace it had been before the war. The taboos seemed to have vanished since the war had ended and the servicemen had started to come home. She did not intend this marriage she had worked so hard to achieve to end up as a statistic.

She bit the inside of her lip, the trick she had learned to induce the tears to well up in her eyes, then she slipped out of bed and went to him.

'Please, Johnny, don't be cross with me,' she wheedled. 'You don't know what it's like, expecting a baby. I get all nervy and strung-up. I do try not to but I can't help it. They say it gets better half-way through.' She simpered up at him through damp lashes. 'It makes a big difference knowing you're loved and wanted. That's why it hurts so much when you turn your back on me.' Standing on tiptoe she slid her arms round his neck and kissed him, insinuating her pointed tongue between his lips and pressing herself close to him.

'Come on – undress me,' she whispered, tugging at his pyjama cord. 'I still look nice, don't I? I'm not fat yet. We should be having the time of our lives, not quarrelling.' Shrugging the straps of her nightdress from her shoulders she let it slide to the floor and, taking his hand she cupped it round one breast. 'There, that's nice isn't it? You know you like it. Come back to bed, Johnny. I'll make you smile again. Let me – please.'

Later as he lay beside her, wide awake in the thin light of dawn, he cursed himself again for his frailty. Rachel knew how to find the weak spot in his armour and twist him round her little finger. And every time he allowed her to do it he hated himself a little more. It was what had landed him in this mess in the first place and lost him the girl he truly loved. At this rate he would soon have no self-respect left. But they were man and wife now. She carried his child and there was no going back. He thought of Cathy. She'd been so hurt. The stricken look on her face that morning haunted him. He would carry it deep inside his heart for ever.

Cathy – his lovely Cathy. It would surely not be long before someone else came into her life, he told himself. He tortured himself, imagining her giving her love to some faceless stranger – marrying, writing him off as a teenage crush; dismissing him with a laugh.

Rachel stirred sleepily beside him, reaching out her arms and murmuring his name. He slid away from her and got out of bed, going into the bathroom and running himself a bath. If she had her way she would start and end each day with sex as well as wanting to spend the long wet afternoons of their honeymoon in bed as well. He only hoped that as her pregnancy progressed her voracious appetite would lessen.

Now they were home and already Rachel was already expressing her dissatisfaction with Cedar Lodge. John wondered where it would all end.

'I hope everything is all right for you.' Theresa stood in the doorway. 'Clarice made the curtains for me. They're silk brocade. The material is pre-war and I've had it tucked away for a long time.'

'Yeah, looks like it,' Rachel muttered under her breath.

'There's a nice casserole in the oven,' Theresa went on. 'Clarice queued up at the butcher's this morning and managed to get some best end of neck of mutton. She made it before she went home. We can eat in about half an hour. I thought that would give you time to . . .'

'John and me'll be eating out, thanks.' Rachel interrupted.

John stared at her. 'No, we won't. I'm tired after the drive. Thank you, Mother, we'll be down in half an hour.'

When his mother had gone downstairs John rounded on Rachel. 'Why do you have to be so rude? Mother has opened her home to us. She's trying her best. Why can't you co-operate?'

Rachel opened her case and began to unpack, pouting sulkily. 'I'm not eating anything that old Harvey bitch has made,' she said. 'She hates me – wouldn't put it past her to poison the stuff!'

'Don't be ridiculous!'

'Is it ridiculous to want a home of my own, so that I can cook meals for you? Isn't that what being married is about?'

John grasped her arm and turned her round to face him. 'Listen, Rachel, as soon as I can I'll find us somewhere of our own. In the meantime please try to get along with Mother. She's a very private person. I happen to know it's hard for her to share her home.'

'It's hard for me too.'

'It's harder for her though. Mother has been used to being in control, she . . .'

'Go on,' she challenged. 'Why don't you just come right out and say it!'

'Say what?'

'That a common girl like me is more the sort of person she'd have in her house as a servant than as a daughter-in-law. It's what you're thinking, isn't it?' She laughed. 'God! She must have nearly dropped dead when you said you were marrying me!'

John turned away. 'Just try – for my sake,' he said quietly, his heart full of foreboding. 'That's all I ask, Rachel. For the time being just try and be patient.'

'Mother, I think it's time I had full control of King's.'

John faced his mother across the desk in the study that had once been his father's. Theresa sat in her late husband's chair.

'No, John,' she said firmly.

'But why? I'm a married man now.'

'Precisely!'

John winced. He knew better than to ask her to clarify her one-word statement. 'The salary you pay me isn't enough,' he said. 'It was all right before I was married, but not now. I can see that sharing the house is difficult for you. Surely you can understand that it would be better for us to have a home of our own, preferably before the baby comes. There isn't much building going on at the moment, but I've been talking to a builder I know and if I could get a permit and put down a deposit now we could be in by Christmas.'

'I don't think you would get a building permit when there is plenty of room here,' Theresa said. 'You can hardly plead over-crowding, can you? But there is nothing to stop you from renting a flat somewhere.'

'Decent flats are very hard to find,' John pointed out. 'Landlords can charge whatever they like and rents are sky-high. It would be wasting money. I'm sure I'd get a permit with the baby coming and I need the money for that deposit, Mother.'

She sighed. 'All right. We'll go through the books this evening

145

and see what can be done about an interest-free loan for you, out of the business. I think that's more than generous under the circumstances.'

John ran an exasperated hand through his hair. 'The business will be mine eventually. I run it now so why not just sign it over? I would have thought you'd be glad to be free of the responsibility. What is it, Mother? Don't you trust me?'

Theresa shook her head. 'Of course I trust *you*, John. As a matter of fact it was my intention to hand over to you just before you announced that you were getting married.'

'So why. . . ?'

'But when you told me who it was you intended to marry I was obliged to change my mind.' She looked at him with her sharp grey eyes. 'She's put you up to this, hasn't she?'

'No. I told you. There will be three of us soon. We need more money. There are things to buy for the baby and . . .'

'I'll arrange with the bank for you to have what you need for the child. It can be paid into your account.'

'Mother, really! I'm not a child asking for more pocket money.'

'Since you mention it, John, I sometimes wonder about your maturity,' Theresa said. 'You've already been foolish enough to open a joint account with her. You let her have all her own way. Surely you can see just as I do that the moment she realizes you have sole control of the business she'll start spending money like water.'

'She won't. I'll . . .'

'Why should I feel you are fit to have control of King's when I can see very clearly that you have no control whatsoever over your wife?'

John was silent. His mother's remark had touched a raw nerve. Without another word he got up and left the study.

Theresa sighed. She did not relish having to deny John what he asked for. It was true he worked very hard and deserved to have control of the business. In fact she had been looking forward to handing the reins of King's to John. But she had made her decision and she was determined to stick to it.

Since his marriage to Rachel two months ago John seemed to have aged ten years. She felt sorry for him, but his problems were all of his own making and she knew it would be folly to give in.

Even though the walls of the old house were thick she had heard the rows and arguments that went on late into the night – often about money and Rachel's demands for more and more of the kind of luxuries she'd never been used to. There were other sounds too, penetrating the bedroom walls at night. Lying in the dark Theresa shuddered, remembering the horrors she had had to endure in her own early marriage. But for Rachel it was clearly not displeasure that made her groan and cry out. Theresa felt it was nothing short of disgusting under the circumstances. She thought that a girl in Rachel's condition would have had more decency.

At any rate she was determined that a daughter-in-law who could barely bring herself to be civil and treated her with contempt in her own house, should not get the better of her. Or of her easy-going son.

She had confided some of her worries to Clarice over their elevenses. The other woman had been guardedly sympathetic.

'Well, I must admit that I was never over-fond of the girl as a little thing,' she said. 'But I made allowances because I couldn't see her having much of a time of it with those parents of hers – narrow-nosed lot. Always Bible-punching and dead against anyone having a good time. Discipline's one thing, but keep a child tied down and you'll regret it later, I always say. I did think perhaps Mr John would bring out the best in her once they were wed.'

What Clarice had actually thought was that once Rachel had managed to get her own way she'd thank her lucky stars and behave herself. She'd been wrong. She looked at her mistress's anxious face and added,

'Maybe it's her condition. After all, it's only natural to want to make a home for the baby.'

'It's not her condition that made her spend all her own clothing coupons and John's as well on clothes that won't fit her in a few weeks' time,' Theresa said. 'And to get John to buy that wretched radiogram. Those records nearly drive me mad; that horrible cheap music played for hours on end.'

Clarice nodded sympathetically. 'I often think that if I hear that song about "a gal in calico" one more time I'll scream.'

Theresa shook her head. 'She hasn't been to see her parents once since the wedding, you know.'

147

Clarice nodded. 'I did hear something about that in the shop the other day. The Sandses are quite upset about it by all accounts.'

'I'm not surprised. Then there's the matter of her confinement,' Theresa went on. 'Did you know that she's refused to go into the local hospital?'

'No! So where? Is she having it here?'

'Not a bit of it. She insisted on being booked into the Sarah Lilley nursing home. She'll be there for two weeks at the most exorbitant fees. And then, as though that isn't enough, she's insisting on having a private nurse at home for a month afterwards.'

'Well I never!' Clarice Harvey's mouth folded itself into a determined line. Inwardly she decided it was time to exercise a little firm pressure on that young lady before she got too big for her boots.

Clarice's chance came unexpectedly soon. Rachel happened to be in the kitchen, when Clarice arrived back at Cedar Lodge later that afternoon to prepare the evening meal. She knew that Theresa had gone into town to visit the chiropodist and John was at work so they were alone in the house.

As she dumped her heavy shopping-bag on the kitchen table she eyed the girl speculatively, noticing that she was already beginning to show. The skirt she wore was straining at the waistband and there was quite a bulge below it. For a woman who was only supposed to be four months pregnant she was quite a size.

As usual Rachel had not deigned to acknowledge her presence, but this time Clarice did not intend to be ignored.

'Not gone off tea then?' she observed as she unloaded her shopping-bag. Rachel glanced at her insolently and shrugged.

'Not really.'

'Couldn't abide it when I first fell for my Dennis,' Clarice went on. 'But by the time I got half-way through I could eat and drink anything.' She paused, looking pointedly at Rachel's expanding waistline. 'Let's see, when's yours due?'

Rachel turned to stare at her defiantly. 'March.'

'March, eh?' Clarice continued to suck her teeth thoughtfully. 'Mmm. That means you're only – what, *four* months?' She shook her head doubtfully. 'Have you seen your doctor lately? Looks to me as though you might be having twins!' Without replying Rachel picked up her cup and began to walk towards the door, but

Clarice hadn't done with her yet. She let her open the door and get half-way through it before she said, 'Except of course that you and I both know that you're at least *five* months gone.'

Rachel stopped in her tracks and turned to look at Clarice. 'What are you talking about?'

Clarice noticed with satisfaction that the colour had drained from her face. 'Come off it. You know what I'm talking about as well as I do.' She took a step towards Rachel and looked straight into her eyes. 'That child you're expecting is my Peter's.' As Rachel opened her mouth to protest Clarice held up her hand. 'Don't bother to deny it. Save your breath to cool your porridge, my girl. That boy thought the world of you and you broke his heart, though if you ask me he's had a lucky escape. Nothing but a lying little slut, that's all you are, getting Mr John to marry you. You should be ashamed of yourself.'

'Shut your mouth, you old cow, or I'll see you get the sack.' Rachel's eyes were flashing and hot colour had flooded her face.

Clarice saw with satisfaction that her shot had clearly found its mark. She shook her head.

'Mrs King won't sack me, miss high and mighty. I'm too valued in this house. More valued than you are by a long chalk. And don't you dare threaten me. Just you remember what I know and think on.'

'There's nothing you can do,' Rachel said defiantly.

'No?' Clarice smiled 'I wouldn't bet on it if I was you.'

Rachel tossed her head. 'Say what you like,' she blustered. 'Anyway, you can't prove anything.'

'And when your baby is born two months too soon – what then?' Clarice shook her head. 'Better pray it comes late and doesn't weigh too much, that's all I can say!' She stepped up to Rachel and wagged an accusing finger in her face. 'Dumping your mum and dad too. What kind of behaviour is that? Or are they in on this deception too?'

'Why should I bother with them? They're not my real mum and dad.'

'All the more reason to be ashamed then. I daresay they made sacrifices for you and everyone knows you haven't been to see them once since you got wed.'

'No, and I'm not going to either!' Rachel said defiantly. 'Nobody

149

knows what I had to go through in that house. All the time I was growing up that man made my life a hell on earth! And it never stopped when I was grown up either. Ask your Pete if you don't believe me. They made me a scapegoat for their self-righteousness, for ever rubbing it in how I was born in sin and how they took me in when no one else wanted me. Well, I reckon they've had their money's worth out of me and now I don't give a bloody toss if I never see either of them ever again!'

Clarice was slightly taken aback by the vehemence of Rachel's outburst. Her face was pale again now and there was bitterness in her eyes. She had no idea things had been that bad for the child at the Sandses'.

'Well,' she said, softening a little. 'all the more reason why you should behave proper now. You treat Mrs King with the respect she deserves and stop behaving like a slut and you'n me'll get on better. Mr John has married you and you should count yourself lucky. Just you toe the line, miss, or you'll find yourself back where you came from double quick!'

Rachel stared at her for a moment, then turned and barged her way through the kitchen door, letting it slam shut behind her. Clarice smiled to herself. Maybe her few well-chosen words would have some effect. She hoped so. Whatever Rachel had suffered in her childhood she didn't have to be a lying little trollop. In spite of what she'd just heard she'd shop the girl if she had to, if only for the hurt she'd caused Peter.

There was a big celebration in the Flynn household when Harry announced that he had got the job. It coincided with the letter forwarded on to Cathy from home, agreeing that she qualified for the educational grant.

They all sat up till the small hours, drinking champagne and dancing to records in the back yard, Faith having carefully invited all the neighbours to join them so that there would be no complaints.

At one o'clock Cathy announced that she was tired and said goodnight. Harry walked up to her room with her.

'Are you going to offer me a nightcap?' he said when they arrived at her door.

'One cup of coffee and then I'm throwing you out.' She looked at him. 'As a matter of fact I think you could do with it. You look decidedly tipsy to me.'

He laughed. 'Look who's talking. Let's face it, we're all going to have hangovers in the morning. What the holiday snaps I take tomorrow will look like heaven only knows.'

'Will anyone know the difference?' Cathy asked.

'Probably not. It's a good job next week is my last. I'd never make my fortune at photography.' Harry threw himself full length on the bed. 'Oh, to hell with it. Forget the coffee. Come here and give me a cuddle. I'm in need of some feminine reassurance.'

'I can't think why.' Cathy lay down companionably beside him. 'I'm really pleased about the job, Harry,' she said. 'Coming today when I've heard about the grant it's just about perfect.'

He smiled. 'You know, I still can't quite believe that someone actually wants to employ me. It's going to be wonderful, earning money of my own and not having to rely on Faith and Mike.' He turned his head to study her face. 'Cath – anyone ever tell you you're beautiful?' he said suddenly.

She laughed. 'I'm not.'

He raised himself on one elbow and kissed her. 'Shut up arguing, woman. If I say you're beautiful then you are.' He kissed her again, and when he looked into her eyes again he saw that they had a dreamy look and wondered wistfully just how much credit went to him and how much to the champagne.

For her part, Cathy was experiencing a mixture of sensations; the sudden shock of pleasure that took her completely by surprise; the kind of arousal she had only felt before with John. She stared up at Harry. They had kissed before, friendly pecks that meant nothing. Suddenly now it was different.

'What?' he asked, his eyes puzzled as they searched hers.

'Nothing. It's just . . .' Lifting her arms she drew his head down to hers again. Her lips parted for him and for a long time neither of them spoke. The mixture of champagne and kisses was heady and intoxicating. In a haze of uninhibited delight their hands caressed and explored, finding intense pleasure in flesh and muscle – in hardness and softness. Mouth explored mouth in sensuous pleasure.

Cathy's heart drummed dizzily as clothes were shed and skin melted into skin with the sizzling impact of electricity. All she was

really aware of was the rising excitement in her that became more
and more urgent with every tantalizing touch.

Harry's breath was warm and moist in her ear as he whispered
her name – asked her if she was sure – if this was really what she
wanted. Then they were making love and it was as though the
world had dissolved into billowing clouds, erupted into sparkling
stars.

Afterwards they slept, each of them falling deep into the luxurious warmth of the other's embrace.

It was getting light when they woke. Cathy opened her eyes to
find Harry looking down at her.

'Hello.'

She smiled hesitantly, wondering how much of what was in her
head was a dream. 'Good morning.'

'I've got a confession to make,' he said gravely.

'Really?'

'Last night I took advantage of your drunken state.'

Her eyes opened wide in mock reproach. 'How dare you! I've
never been drunk in my life. And I remember everything that
happened.'

He grinned. 'In that case forget the apology.' He bent and kissed
her. 'And by the way, for the record, you are definitely *not* frigid.'
He lay back, his arm around her shoulders. 'God! It was wonderful, Cath. Know what? Even if it never happened again it wouldn't
matter. Last night was perfect.'

'Oh! So – you don't want to repeat the experience, then?'

He laughed. 'Can't you see that I'm doing my best to be romantic and poetic?' He brushed his cheek against hers. 'Of course I
want to repeat it,' he said softly. 'Again and again. For ever and
ever. What I'm really trying to say is that I think I'm in love with
you.'

'Oh, Harry.' She turned to look at him. 'You don't think you're
getting a little bit carried away?'

'No. I definitely do *not* think I'm getting carried away,' he said.
'I've been in love with you for a long time if you really want to
know. I just didn't think I had a cat in hell's chance till last night.'
He looked at her. 'Even now I'm not sure. Well – have I?'

With one finger she traced the line of his forehead, nose and
chin. 'Harry Flynn,' she said softly. 'I think you're the loveliest

person in the whole world and, yes, of course I love you.'

He frowned. 'Yes, but what *kind* of love? I mean – the sort you feel for your faithful old labrador or the sort you feel for a lover?'

She laughed. 'Do you have to ask after last night.'

'Yes, but – would you marry me?'

She stared at him, too shocked for words.

He looked down at her. 'I'm not fooling, Cath. I'm dead serious. I've got prospects now. And in a couple of years you'll be qualified too. Together we'd be a force to be reckoned with.' He shook her gently. 'Oh, for Christ's sake – come *on*! Put me out of my misery. Is it yes, or no?'

'Don't you think we should wait till we're older?' she asked cautiously. 'Till we've saved up some money and all that. Getting married is a terribly big step.'

'Who wants to wait?' he said. 'Who wants to waste time? How does any of us know how much of it we have? I think you should grab a good thing when you can. And they don't come much better than this! So what do you think?'

Suddenly light-hearted she threw her arms around him. 'Oh Harry, I *do* love you. And yes, I'll marry you if that's what you really want.'

His face lit up. 'You *will*? Right. Only one more question then – when?'

'She laughed with him. 'Whenever you like!'

CHAPTER TWELVE

CLARICE HATED THE AUTUMN. She dreaded the long winter nights ahead, alone in the back room at Number 20 with the curtains drawn, isolating her from the outside world.

She was getting old, she told herself. She'd got to face it, she was getting to the age when nobody needed her any more. Peter had had another leave since his first forty-eight hours. He'd mentioned it in one of the scrappy letters he occasionally wrote. He'd spent it in London. London! He'd hardly known the place existed till he went into the army. Now it seemed he couldn't get enough of it! Well, she could thank that young madam Rachel for that, she told herself. He wouldn't want to risk running into her – seeing her body expanding with his child – knowing she was John King's wife. She'd got a lot to answer for, that little bitch. But at least she knew now that Clarice had got her measure.

Dennis never came home nowadays either. He hadn't been home to see her for almost a year. His letters were hardly more satisfactory than Peter's. They told her very little about his life. Until the one she'd received yesterday, that was. It was the contents of that that was responsible for her feelings of insecurity and depression.

If it weren't for her job at Cedar Lodge life would be pretty dreary, she told herself as she reached the park gates. At least the Kings still needed her, each in their different ways. She paused to shift her laden bag from one hand to the other and wondered as she did so how much longer she'd be up to her job at Cedar Lodge. And, even more frightening, what she would do when she had to give it up.

Letting herself in at the back door Clarice put the kettle on for a cuppa. The kitchen at Cedar Lodge felt like her own now. After they'd come to terms with each other Mrs King had given her free rein and allowed her to reorganize the domestic regions of the house, the wash-house, the dresser cupboards and the big walk-in larder. Until she came here she'd never used a refrigerator and she loved the Aga with its two ovens and constant supply of hot water. On this chilly autumn afternoon its warmth was especially comforting as Clarice sat at the big pine table with her pot of tea and custard creams. Her own little scullery at Number 20 with its stone sink and meat safe seemed quite primitive by comparison.

She opened her handbag and took out Dennis's latest letter again. She'd read it a dozen times so that she knew it almost by heart, but she still couldn't make out what he was trying to tell her. It was clear that he'd met a woman. Sylvia, he said, a war widow. He sounded pretty keen on her. But Dennis had never been divorced so he couldn't marry again. Peter's mother had run off with a sailor whose ship had been torpedoed during the war. After that she'd disappeared and Dennis had never tried to find her – till now.

He said in his letter that he intended to retire from the army very soon and that he'd been trying to trace his wife. Tracing lost relatives was very difficult since the war ended, he explained. Bombing in all the big cities had taken so many lives and records had been lost. As far as Clarice could see there could only be one reason for Dennis going to so much trouble. He was serious about this Sylvia. If he did find he was free to marry again – what then? Presumably he'd want to bring his new wife home to King's Walk. And where would Clarice stand then? She'd given up her own home to come to Queensgrove and look after young Peter. Number 20 King's Walk was the only home she'd known for the past fifteen years.

She glanced up at the clock. Almost four. Better get the shopping unpacked. Mrs King had gone to the hairdresser's and Mr John would be home as usual at 5.30 so she had plenty of time to prepare the evening meal and get it started. She folded the letter and put it away. No point in speculating, she'd better just wait and see.

She was peeling the potatoes when the sound reached her ears, faint at first, then louder. She paused and listened, her head on one side. Sometimes after school the children got quite noisy, playing football in the park. But this sounded as though it was coming from inside the house. She heard it again, a sort of wailing noise and this time she was sure it came from upstairs.

She dried her hands and went into the hall. Standing at the foot of the stairs she called, 'All right up there?'

There was no reply but a moment later a scream made her jump. 'Oh Lord!' She hurried up the stairs. 'Hang on. I'm coming.'

The door of the large front bedroom stood open and there, kneeling on the floor, clutching at the bedpost with both hands was Rachel. The girl's face was white with pain as she looked up at Clarice appealingly.

'Please help me,' she ground out between clenched teeth. 'I – I think it's the baby.'

'How long have you been like this?' Clarice asked. 'Here, give me your arm. Let me help you on to the bed.'

'No.' Rachel shook her head. 'Leave me,' she said. 'I can't . . .' Her face contorted with another spasm of pain and her cry echoed harrowingly round the room.

Clarice stared helplessly at her. If the cries she had heard downstairs had come with each pain they must be pretty frequent. Far too frequent! The girl must be well into labour, and yet it wasn't time yet – even if her own calculations were correct it was too early. She waited for the pain to subside then fetched a damp flannel from the bathroom and sponged Rachel's forehead.

'What happened? Just start, did they?'

The girl shook her head. 'I was walking home through the park and I slipped on some wet leaves. I fell. I thought I was all right. Then just after I got home the pains started.'

'Let's get you up on the bed,' Clarice said. 'You try and rest. I'm going to get help.'

'Don't go,' Rachel pleaded. 'Don't leave me alone again – *please*.'

Clarice stood in the doorway, biting her lip with indecision. 'All right. I'll try and use the telephone,' she said. She went down into the hall. Unfamiliar with the instrument she picked up the receiver as if it were red hot and held it gingerly to her ear.

A voice at the other end made her jump as it said, 'Number please.'

Clarice shouted: 'There's someone here having a baby and I've got to get help.'

'Do you require an ambulance, police or fire service?' the voice asked.

Clarice snapped. 'Ambulance of course!' Her pains are coming – coming fast!' Another cry came from above and she began to panic. 'I've gotta get help – and *quick*!'

'Give me your address.'

Clarice gabbled the address, then slammed down the receiver and hurried back upstairs. Rachel was curled up into a tight ball on the bed. She looked very frightened. Reaching out to Clarice she clutched at her sleeve. 'Don't leave me again,' she begged. 'I think I'm going to die. Don't go, Mrs Harvey – please.'

'I'm not going nowhere.' Clarice took the small tense hand and held it tightly. 'Try not to worry,' she said. 'It's just the baby. It's always like this. Help's on its way.'

'I never thought it'd be this bad,' Rachel's teeth were chattering now and Clarice squeezed her hand reassuringly.

'You'll soon forget the pain once you're holding that little baby in your arms,' she said.

When the next pain had released her from its grip Rachel looked up. 'I'm sorry, Mrs Harvey,' she said. 'I'm sorry about Peter. I did love him. I always loved him. It was just that I had to get away from home – couldn't stand it any longer.'

'If only you'd told him,' Clarice said. 'About the baby I mean. He would have married you.'

'I know. I did tell him.'

'You did! Then why. . . ?'

'Because I'd have had to stay at home. Dad would have made my life a misery, knowing I'd had to get married. You don't know what he's like. I'd had it drummed into me day and night since I was little that I'd come to no good.' She swallowed a sob and tears ran down her cheeks. 'I should never have lied to John, should I? Everyone hates me, don't they? Dad would say I deserve this. And he'd be right.'

'Don't talk so daft,' Clarice said stoutly. 'This pain won't last. It's just the baby coming.'

'I've been wicked though. I don't want to die, Mrs Harvey.'

'Now, now. Don't talk like that. 'Course you're not going to die.

I'm not saying what you did wasn't wrong,' Clarice said. 'But you can make it all up to Mr John if you've a mind to. You can turn over a new leaf and make him happy if you try.'

'I will try. I promise. You won't *tell*, will you?' Rachel's eyes were dark with fear and anguish. 'You wouldn't really tell them that the baby's Peter's – would you?'

Clarice sighed. 'No, I've never been one to make mischief. What's done is done and you're married now. I won't tell – not if you try to be a good girl.'

'Did my real mother go through this?' Rachel whispered. 'Is that why she didn't want me?'

' 'Course it wasn't. No doubt it broke her heart to have to part with you, but I expect she had no one to stand by her,' Clarice said soothingly. 'You've struck lucky. You've got good people to take care of you.'

Downstairs there was a hammering on the door and a voice calling out, 'Anyone in there need an ambulance?'

Clarice extricated her fingers from Rachel's iron-like grip. 'They're here, she said. 'I'll go down and let them in. You'll soon be in good hands.'

John sat in the stuffy little waiting-room at the hospital where he had been for the best part of six hours, thumbing unseeingly through the dog-eared magazines and staring at the walls.

The ambulance had brought Rachel here to Queensgrove General and when he'd arrived he'd been allowed to see her only briefly before they wheeled her off to theatre. Since then he'd been along to the ward several times to enquire about her but the last time he was told stiffly by the ward sister that he'd be told as soon as there was any news.

He'd just read the same article for the fourth time without taking in a word of it when the door opened and a young man in a white coat came in. John hadn't seen Gerald Bailey for some years, but he recognized him immediately as a boyhood friend with whom he'd been at school. After matric Gerald had gone off to medical school and had qualified the previous year. Now he was a houseman at Queensgrove General. They exchanged smiles of recognition and Gerald took a chair, inviting John to do the same.

'I told my chief that you and I were at school together,' he said. 'So he thought I should be the one to come and talk to you.'

'Yes?' John searched his face anxiously. 'Rachel. . . ?'

'I only wish I had something good to tell you,' Gerald said. 'As it is I'm afraid I'm the bearer of bad news. I'm sorry, John, but in spite of all we tried to do your wife has lost the baby.'

John's heart sank. Rachel's news that she was pregnant had dismayed him at first but he'd had time to get used to the idea and he had begun to look forward to having a child.

'I see,' he said flatly. 'And Rachel – is she all right?'

'She will be. She's had a difficult time and of course having no baby at the end of it all is a devastating blow for her. But she'll make a full recovery. She should be able to conceive again without any problems in time. Say six months.'

John swallowed hard. 'Are miscarriages always as bad as this?' he asked.

'Miscarriage?' Gerald looked at him curiously. 'It was a premature birth, John. Not a miscarriage.'

John frowned. 'But – she was only – only five months pregnant.'

'No, seven,' Gerald told him. 'At least seven.'

John shook his head. 'Are you sure?'

'Positive. The child would have had a good chance of survival if only we'd got her in sooner. We could have performed a Caesarean section. Labour was too far advanced by the time she got here and the baby was too weak to withstand the trauma of birth. I really am very sorry.' He laid a comforting hand on John's arm. 'You'll be wanting to see her,' he said. 'I'll take you along to the ward. Just five minutes. She's still very tired.

John's footsteps echoed along the polished corridor. *Seven months. He was too small to withstand the birth,* the words seemed to drum in his ears. The child had been a boy. A son. But not *his* son. It wasn't possible. Seven months ago he had been convinced that his future was with Cathy.

There were screens around her bed. He stepped inside. Her face on the pillow was pale and when she saw him her eyes filled with tears.

'I'm sorry, Johnny,' she whispered. 'You won't leave me, will you? You won't send me away?'

John looked up and caught the expression in the eyes of the

nurse who stood at the foot of the bed. Her thoughts were all too clear. He reached out and took Rachel's hand.

'Just sleep,' he said. 'Get some rest now. And don't worry – about anything.'

The nurse jiggled the screen impatiently. 'I think you should go now,' she said sharply. 'She's been through a lot – obviously,' she added pointedly.

'I'll come again tomorrow,' John said. 'Goodnight.' The nurse's steely eyes still on him, he bent and kissed Rachel's cheek.

At Cedar Lodge Clarice had been sitting with Theresa ever since she had arrived home from the hairdresser's to find an ambulance in the driveway.

'What is happening?' she'd asked Clarice who stood in the doorway.

'Rachel,' Clarice explained. 'She slipped on some wet leaves. It brought things on.'

It was now almost 1 a.m. and she was just carrying in the fourth pot of tea she had made when John's car was heard drawing up outside. Theresa stood up.

'Perhaps you would leave us alone, Clarice,' she said. 'John will not have had any dinner so perhaps you could make him something.'

'Of course, madam. I'll be in the kitchen if you need me.' She passed a white-faced John in the hall. 'Your mother's in the drawing-room,' she said. 'I'm just going to get you something to eat.'

He tried to summon a smile for her. 'Thanks, Clarice.'

In the drawing-room he faced his mother. 'You shouldn't have waited up.' He had hoped he would not have to face her until morning. As it was she made it easy for him.

'Has she lost the child?' she asked. He nodded.

'So! All the anguish has been for nothing.' Theresa said bitterly.

'She seemed to be in a great deal of pain,' John said, sinking wearily into a chair. 'It's tragic that it was all for nothing.'

'I was thinking of *you*!' Theresa said sharply. 'It's damnable to think that you have thrown your life away on that girl, and all for nothing.'

'Please, Mother . . .' He rubbed a hand over his aching eyes. 'I've had enough for one day.'

Clarice knocked on the door and came in with a plate of sandwiches and another cup. 'Just you tuck in to those,' she said. 'And there's fresh tea in the pot. You'll feel better when you've got something inside you.' She paused, looking from Theresa's grim expression to John's haggard face. 'May I ask, sir. . . ?'

Theresa looked up. 'Rachel has lost the child,' she said crisply.

'Oh, I'm so sorry.' Clarice bit her lip, wondering just how much of the truth had come out. Neither of them gave anything away. 'Now – I'll put a hot bottle in your bed for you, Mr John. You look so tired.'

John glanced up with a smile. 'It's good of you.'

'If there's anything else I can do . . .' She hesitated in the doorway. 'Would you like me to call and tell Mr and Mrs Sands that their daughter is in hospital?'

John winced. He'd forgotten all about the Sands. Rachel might have rejected her parents but, nevertheless, they had every right to be informed. 'No,' he said. 'I'll go and see them first thing in the morning.' He smiled at Clarice. 'But thank you for offering.'

'That will be all, Clarice,' Theresa said. 'Please go home now. You must be very tired. And thank you for staying.'

'Very well, madam.' Clarice withdrew thoughtfully, knowing that however grateful Theresa was she would still expect her to arrive on time in the morning.

The following morning John rang in to say that he would not be in to the office until later. His secretary promised to rearrange his appointments.

Clarice made him eat what she called a 'man's' breakfast at the kitchen table after taking Theresa a tray in her room. For once she had taken the initiative into her own hands and cooked them both the bacon and egg rations normally reserved for Sundays.

'You've got to keep your strength up,' she said as she put the plate down in front of John. 'That missis of yours is going to need a lot of looking after when she gets home.'

161

John did his best to do justice to the food, although it stuck in his throat.

His first visit was to Number 12. Mary Sands answered the door to him in a print overall, her sparse hair tucked into a hairnet and a duster in her hand. When she saw John she twittered nervously.

'Oh! Mr King – er – John. I'm terribly sorry but Herbert is out . . .'

'May I come in, Mrs Sands,' John interrupted. 'I need to talk to you. It's about Rachel.'

Mary paled visibly and her jaw dropped. 'Oh! Of course.' She led the way into the musty front room. 'Perhaps it would be better if you came back when Herbert is here,' she began doubtfully.

'Rachel is in hospital,' John put in. 'She had a slight accident yesterday afternoon. Nothing serious but it – caused her to lose the baby we – she was expecting.'

Mary's mouth gaped. 'Baby? We had no idea. Oh dear. How awful.'

John reassured her. 'She isn't seriously ill. I just thought you should know.'

'Yes, yes, thank you.' Mary waved her duster in the direction of the front door. 'Thank you for calling, Mr – er . . . I'll tell Herbert as soon as he comes in. I'd better not keep you. . . .' She trailed off as John passed her on his way to the door. 'Well, goodbye then Mr – er – John.'

Standing outside on the pavement John thanked heaven that Herbert Sands had been out when he called.

But his relief was to be short-lived. Later that afternoon, when he was busy at his desk, his secretary rushed in, looking upset.

'Mr John, there's a man here called Mr Sands who says he must see you at once. I told him you were busy but he just won't take no for an answer.'

John's heart sank. 'It's all right, Doris, show him in. And don't put any calls through while he's here.'

Herbert Sands burst into the office a few minutes later. He wore a baggy grey suit and a starched collar and his face was grim with fury. John stood up.

'Good afternoon, Mr Sands. Will you have a seat?'

'What I have to say is better said standing,' Herbert glowered at him, his spectacles glinting menacingly. 'My wife and I have just visited the hospital,' he went on. I have spoken to the doctor and I gather that Rachel gave birth to a premature stillborn child last night.'

John sighed. 'Sadly, I'm afraid that is so.'

'*Sadly*! You call it sad? I call it sinful deception. A premature – birth when you have been married a mere two months and you calmly stand there and tell me it is *sad* that the child you and she conceived in mortal sin is dead. Judgement!' he roared. '*Judgement*! That's what I call it.' He pointed an accusing finger at John. 'You took advantage of my daughter!' he shouted. 'Corrupted her with depraved and vile fornication. And now she is quite rightly reaping the rewards of that evil sin. And I intend to see to it that you also get your just deserts.'

'Do I need to remind you that I married Rachel?' John asked calmly.

'You married her because you could do nothing else,' Herbert thundered. 'You corrupted a young woman, brought up in a devout and respectable home. And if you think that marrying her will absolve you from the abomination you have visited on my family you are very much mistaken.'

'Mr Sands. I have no . . .'

'You can tell Rachel that she is no longer our daughter,' Herbert hissed, leaning forwards, his hands flat on the desk between them. 'Her mother and I know now that we have nursed a viper in our bosoms. I always suspected that something of the kind would happen. The girl was born to sin and she will never, *never* sully our house again. And as for you – this town shall certainly hear about the kind of man you are. I intend to go to the local paper and . . .'

John sprang up from his desk. 'Mr Sands. Will you please be quiet and listen to me!' His commanding tone made Herbert straighten up and take a sudden step backwards, the hot colour sliding from his angry face like water down a plughole.

John drew himself up to his full six feet and stepped out from behind his desk to tower over his father-in-law.

'Mr Sands. Rachel has described to me the kind of life she experienced with you. The repression and cruelty she suffered at your hands. She no longer wishes to associate with you and that goes for me too. I called this morning to tell you she was in hospital purely out of common decency; something of which you seem to have a twisted view.' He strode to the door. 'And if you even *attempt* to blacken my name you will be hearing from my solicitor. There is such a thing as the law of slander.' He threw open the door. 'Good afternoon!'

After his irate father-in-law had left John found it impossible to concentrate. At four o'clock, when Doris, her face creased with silent sympathy, bustled in with his tea and biscuits he decided to call it a day.

'There's nothing else pressing this afternoon, is there?' he asked.

The secretary shook her head. 'Just the letters for you to sign. Oh, and there was a call from Mason's of Northampton when your – er –visitor was here. They want a delivery date for their latest order. I said I'd ask you . . .'

'Deal with it, will you, Doris? Go down to the shop floor and ask the foreman in charge, then get back to them. I'll sign the letters, then I'm going home.'

'I don't blame you, sir. You look all in if you don't mind me saying so. I'll see to everything.' She hesitated, biting her lip. 'I'm really sorry about the . . . intrusion. I did try to stop the man from coming in but he just barged past me.'

'Don't worry. It wasn't your fault, Doris.' He began to clear his desk. 'But if Mr Sands comes here again you have my permission to call the police.'

He didn't go straight home but took a walk in the park to try to calm the turmoil in his mind. It was a mellow afternoon and after a turn round the lake he felt slightly better. He was heading for home when he looked up to see Cathy's sister Pauline sitting on a bench whilst her twin sons were playing on the grass. There was no avoiding her and by the look on her face when she glanced up and saw him she had no wish to. As he drew level with her she stood up.

'I was sorry to hear about Rachel's baby,' she said.

'Thank you.'

'Rachel's mother says it was a premature birth. Seven months. That means you were seeing her at the same time you were seeing Cathy!' Her face was pink with rage.

John stared at her, speechless with the injustice of it all. 'It's not the way you think. There's a lot you don't understand,' he said.

'Oh no?' she said, with a shake of her head. 'Not that it matters any more. Our Cathy is well rid of you and she knows it. You might be interested to know that she got engaged last week. She's really happy – getting married soon. Thank God she got away from you before you could hurt her any more.'

She called to the little boys and bundled them into their pushchair, then, with a disdainful look at John, she walked quickly away in the direction of King's Walk.

Ten days later John collected Rachel from the hospital. She still looked pale, but she seemed to have recovered her spirits. It was market day and as they drove through the busy streets she looked eagerly into the shop windows.

'I was thinking, she said. 'Nothing I've got will fit me now. I think I'll go up to London when I feel better and get myself some new clothes.'

John drove in through the park gates and parked under the trees. Rachel looked at him enquiringly.

'Whose was it, Rachel?'

Her eyes widened innocently. 'What do you mean?'

'You know very well what I mean; the child. It wasn't mine, was it? It couldn't have been. I think I have a right to know whose it was.'

'It *was* yours. It *was!*'

He sighed wearily. 'No, it wasn't, Rachel. It couldn't possibly have been and you know it. What do you take me for? I won't tolerate any more lies. Let's have the truth for once in your life.'

She burst into noisy tears. 'I was so ashamed. I didn't want anyone to know. . . .'

'Rachel? What are you talking about?'

'It – it was an accident,' she sobbed.

'An accident! What fairystory are you asking me to believe now?'

'No. It's true. I – I was attacked,' she said, turning swimming eyes on him. 'When I was walking home through the park one night. I'd been to the pictures with Sally from work. I was later than Dad had said I was to be, and I was scared, so I cut through the park. This man jumped out of the bushes on me. I struggled with him but he was too strong.' She took a handkerchief from her handbag and snuffled into it. 'It was horrible – *rape*! I'll never forget it. Then, when I got home it was really late and Dad was furious. He hit me – blacked my eye. I didn't dare tell him what this man did to me. He wouldn't have believed me – always said I was a wicked girl. And then – when I found out I was expecting – I was *desperate*! He'd have killed me!'

'You should have gone to the police.'

She peered at him over the handkerchief she held to her face. 'They wouldn't have believed me any more than Dad would have.' She laid a tentative hand on his arm. 'You've got no idea what I went through, Johnny. I felt so ashamed – so dirty. I couldn't tell anyone. I turned to you because you're such a decent man. You've always been so kind. But I daren't even tell *you* the truth.'

'So you let me think the baby was mine,' he said bitterly.

'Only because I wished to God it could be.' She took his hand. 'I always used to dream that we'd be together one day, you'n me. I've always loved you, Johnny, ever since I can remember. Maybe it's just as well the baby was stillborn, eh? Maybe it's a sign. We're good together, aren't we, Johnny? It's all over now. No more secrets between us. We can look forward to the rest of our lives together, can't we?'

'I don't know.' He was disturbed by what she'd told him; even more disturbed by the fact that she seemed to feel no grief for the child. Even though he'd known it wasn't his he had felt a deep sadness for the tiny snuffed-out life lying in the hospital mortuary. He stared out through the windscreen. 'I'm not sure that I believe you, Rachel. I'm not sure I can ever trust you again.'

'You really think I'd make a thing like that up?' she said reproachfully. 'No one else knows about it. Just you and me and that – that *swine*. After it happened I thought I'd never want another man to touch me, ever again.' She took his face between her hands and turned it towards her. 'Till you, Johnny. You're the only man I'll ever want to touch me and love me. You have to believe that because it's true.'

'If you say so.' He was thinking of that day on the deserted beach when she had deliberately seduced him. Now he knew why.

Could a woman that devious ever be trusted again? He pressed the starter and the car began to move forward.

'You're going to kick me out, aren't you?' Rachel said, panic making her voice gratingly shrill. 'You never wanted me, did you – not really? It's still *her*, isn't it?' she said accusingly. 'You can't forget Cathy. You only married me because of the baby and now you know you didn't need to after all.'

'Rachel! Please, keep your voice down.'

'You think I tricked you – let you down. You hate me, don't you? You wish I'd died as well as the baby.'

She was crying almost hysterically now and John stopped the car again.

'Stop being so melodramatic. Of course I don't hate you or wish you dead. That's just plain silly. You've been through a very bad time. I've been through a bad time too. But we're married now, for better or worse, and we'll have to make the best of it, so try to cheer up and dry your tears before we get home.'

'Does she know?' Rachel asked fearfully, blowing her nose. 'Your mum?'

He shook his head. 'Only that you lost the baby.'

She heaved a sigh of relief, 'What about Mum and Dad?'

'Unfortunately your father went to the hospital on the morning after you were admitted. Naturally they told him the truth, that you'd given birth to a near full-term baby. He came to the office and threatened me.'

'Oh God! Poor Johnny. I'm so sorry.'

'It's all right. I don't think there'll be any more trouble from that quarter.'

'I've finished with them,' she said. 'I'm never going near them again.'

'I can't say I blame you.'

She peered up at him through damp lashes. 'So – are we all right, Johnny? I'll try hard to make you happy. I promise.'

He sighed, trying to ignore the weight of his sinking heart, trying not to think of Cathy, happy in the arms of another man. 'Yes, we're all right,' he said bleakly.

She tucked her arm through his and laid her head on his shoulder. 'Oh, Johnny, I'm so happy,' she sighed. 'And we can soon get a place of our own can't we?'

'If we can find one, yes.'

'And Johnny, I've been thinking. Could I have a fur coat this winter?'

CHAPTER THIRTEEN

CATHY AND HARRY WERE to be married quietly the Saturday before Christmas at the local register office with Harry's family and her own parents present. Afterwards Faith had arranged a buffet lunch for family and friends at Penrith Avenue.

An excited Cathy met her parents at the station late on Friday afternoon and took them for tea at the tiny flat she and Harry had taken in Woodhurst Road over the Rendezvous Café.

As they sat at the table in the window she filled them in on her news.

'Harry's been at St Gregory's School since September and he absolutely loves it,' she told them. 'He even seems to enjoy the football.' She opened the door with a flourish. 'There, how do you like our flat? Faith gave us most of the furniture and helped me make the curtains out of some old ones she had packed away,' Cathy explained. 'They were huge curtains so we cut out the best bits. They look good, don't they? You'd never be able to buy velvet like that nowadays, even if it wasn't on coupons. You'll like her and Mike, and Harry of course. Now, shall I take you on a conducted tour while we wait for the kettle to boil?'

The flat consisted of a living-room, one bedroom and a tiny kitchen and bathroom. Cathy was clearly proud of what she and Harry had achieved in the short time they had been engaged.

'We had to snap it up while it was vacant. Flats are so hard to find. We've had it for just over a month and we've worked so hard. Don't you think we've worked miracles?'

'You certainly have,' Robert said with a smile.

Phyllis exchanged a glance with her husband. Cathy looked so excited. She certainly looked like a young woman in love on the eve of her wedding and that at least was a relief to Phyllis. When she had received the letter saying that Cathy and Harry were engaged she'd had grave doubts.

'It's too soon,' she told Robert. 'It's on the rebound after John. She never said much. I had to get most of it out of Pauline. But it must have hurt her dreadfully.'

Robert had shaken his head. 'Leave it to Cathy, love,' he said. 'She's got her head screwed on the right way. And she's far too sincere a lass to risk hurting anyone else. If she says she loves Harry I think you can rest assured that she does.'

Pauline had quietly agreed with her mother however. 'It certainly is quick,' she said. 'Just a few months. I think I'm the only one who really knows how cut up she was over what John did.'

Phyllis sighed. 'I do want her to be happy,' she said. 'She's been such a good girl. She deserves better than that John King.'

Pauline sniffed. 'Well, now that we know the full story I'd say she was well rid of him,' she said. 'I wouldn't want her to go through what I've been through.'

But now that Phyllis had seen her daughter for herself she felt reassured. It had been a long journey from Queensgrove to Bournemouth and she could see that Robert was tired. Although he had tried to disguise his breathlessness, climbing the three flights of stairs to the little flat had exhausted him. She could see the tell-tale line of grey around his mouth and she knew that he badly needed to rest. She smiled at Cathy.

'Would you mind if we went round to Penrith Avenue now, love? I think your dad could do with a lie down.'

Cathy's face fell. 'Oh, I'm sorry. I should have thought. We'll go round there at once.' She looked anxiously at Robert. 'Are you all right to walk round there, Dad. You could have a lie down on the bed here first if you want.'

Robert shrugged off his wife's and daughter's concern. 'How you two do fuss! A little walk in the fresh air will do me good.'

Faith had organized a meal for the Ladgroves, though, as she explained, she and Mike would be playing in a carol concert at the Pavilion that evening, so they wouldn't be able to join them.

'Just help yourselves,' she said. 'Cathy will tell you, we don't stand on ceremony. Just treat the place as your own.' She looked at her watch. 'Where can Harry have got to? It's really too bad of him not to be here.'

Cathy too had been wondering where Harry could have got to. He'd promised to be back in time to go with her to the station, but he'd failed to turn up.

'He said he had an appointment,' she said. 'He wouldn't tell me what for, but I thought he'd have been back before now.'

'Well, I'll have to go now,' Faith said. 'Just make yourselves at home. I'll see you all later, if you're still up. If not, first thing in the morning.'

Phyllis went upstairs with Robert and settled him down for a rest, then she came down to the basement and joined Cathy in the kitchen. They were chatting when the front door was heard slamming above. Then Harry called out:

'Cath! Where are you? I've got something to show you.'

Cathy shot her mother an apologetic look. 'We'd better go and see what he's been up to.'

They climbed the basement stairs and found Harry standing in the hall, his striped college scarf wound round his neck and his hair tousled. There was an air of excitement about him, but when he caught sight of Phyllis his jaw dropped and he clapped a hand to his head.

'Oh *no*! You're Cathy's mum. And I was supposed to meet you at the station.'

'You certainly were!' Cathy turned to her mother. 'This, as you'll have gathered, is your scatty son-in-law to be. Harry, this is Mum.'

Much to Phyllis's astonishment, Harry enveloped her in a bear hug.

'Lovely to meet you at last, Phyllis' he said, surprising her with his informality. 'And I'm so sorry I forgot to meet you. I've heard so much about you and I've . . .' He looked round. 'Where's your father, Cath?'

'Robert is tired after the journey,' Phyllis said. 'He's having a rest.'

'So – did you have a good journey? Have you seen the flat?'

'*Harry*!' Cathy broke in. 'Are you going to tell us what all the excitement is about? Where on earth have you been? You said you had something to show me.'

'Oh! I almost forgot. I can't wait for you to see it.' He took her hand and led her to the door. 'It's my wedding present – to both of us. Now, close your eyes.' When he was quite sure her eyes were firmly closed he threw the front door open. 'OK. Now you can look.'

Cathy opened her eyes and her mouth fell open with surprise. There, standing at the kerbside was the smallest and oldest car she had ever seen. 'What is it?' she asked.

Harry looked hurt. 'What *is* it! It's our new car! I've christened her Gertie. She's an Austin seven. It's going to be wonderful, having our own transport. No more hanging around for buses on chilly mornings. And she's very economical on petrol,' he added earnestly.

'Does it actually go?'

'Of course she goes!'

'How old is it though?' Cathy asked.

'She, not *it*!' he corrected. 'She was made in nineteen twenty-eight, so that makes her eighteen by my reckoning, a mere stripling! She was laid up all through the war but she's been well looked after.' He grinned. 'And the best bit is that I only paid twenty quid for her.'

Cathy was about to say that she could think of more essential things on which to spend twenty pounds, but the look of elation on Harry's face stopped her. Instead she laughed and hugged him. 'I think she's beautiful,' she said.

His grin broadened. 'I knew you'd love her. This is going to be our wedding carriage,' he announced. 'I'm going to deck her out in white ribbons tomorrow and drive you to the register office in style.'

Cathy couldn't sleep that night. When Harry had first asked her to marry him she had been surprised – shocked even. She had said yes on impulse and then worried about it afterwards. When Harry had broken the news to his parents the troubled expression in Faith's eyes had not escaped her notice. Later Cathy had asked her if she disapproved of the engagement. Faith had smiled gently.

'Sit down, Cathy. I think we should have a talk.' Closing the door against any possible intrusions she had faced Cathy across the kitchen table.

'I wonder if Harry has told you about his heart condition,' she said quietly.

Cathy nodded. 'Oh yes. I know all about that.'

'It's a congenital thing,' Faith went on. 'Apparently he was born with it but it was never picked up when he was a baby. We knew nothing about it until he went for his National Service medical.'

'But it's not serious, is it?' Cathy said. 'Just a slight abnormality – too many beats per minute or something.'

Faith paused, frowning slightly. 'Well, yes. At least that's it basically. We – Mike and I talked to our own doctor as soon as we knew. He told us that Harry had nothing to worry about and could easily live to be an old man. On the other hand . . .' She paused, taking a deep breath. 'On the other hand, with this kind of condition the heart can give out quite suddenly, at any time.' She looked at Cathy. 'We were faced with the agonizing decision, whether to tell Harry or not. In the end we decided that he must never know,' she said. 'As we saw it, he was a naturally happy person who loved life and we couldn't bear to have him changed in any way. As he had no responsibilities we decided not to tell him.'

Cathy shook her head. 'But – you said he could live to old age.'

'That's true, and we all hope that he will, of course. When Mike and I made the decision to keep it to ourselves no one else was involved. Now things are different. I felt it only right and fair that you should be aware of the facts,' Faith said. 'So that if you feel unable to go through with the marriage you still have time to let him down gently.'

There was a lump in Cathy's throat. 'I'm glad you've told me, Faith. And I won't tell him either. I believe you were right about that. But as for marrying him, I'm even more determined to go through with it now.'

Faith reached out to squeeze her hand. 'I had a feeling that would be your reaction. I told Mike so,' she said. 'I know he loves you very much.'

Cathy had thought about what Faith had told her many times, mostly during the small hours when sleep wouldn't come. Although it had been a shock she saw it as something fate had guided her towards. She felt destined to marry Harry. Everything that had happened in her life so far – good and bad, seemed to

173

make sense now. She vowed to enjoy their life together in the joyful way that Harry himself had taught her.

She was just beginning to fall asleep when her door opened quietly and Harry crept in.

'Couldn't sleep,' he said, sitting on the edge of her bed. 'Something told me you couldn't either.'

'Something told you right.' She moved over and drew the covers aside. Here, get in. It's freezing. You'll catch cold.'

He slipped in and snuggled down beside her. 'Just think, Cath, this time tomorrow we'll be tucked up together in our own little flat.'

'I know. Better get some sleep now.'

He slid his arms around her and held her close. 'I still can't believe it's happening, Cath. Mr and Mrs Harry Flynn.' He sighed. 'Sounds good, eh?'

'Very good,' she said sleepily, her head against his shoulder.

'Cathy – look, you are still sure, aren't you? I mean, you don't still think about John whatsisface, do you?' He looked down at her. 'Cath. . . ?' Her eyes were closed and her breathing had deepened. 'Are you asleep?' he whispered.

She stirred a little in his arms, murmuring something incomprehensible as she settled more comfortably against him. She felt so good – so warm, so *right* in his arms. He sighed and drew her closer. He couldn't remember ever feeling happier.

The day passed in a flurry of emotions. Everyone agreed that Cathy looked lovely in a dress of lavender blue towards which everyone had contributed coupons. Faith's buffet was a delight and they were surrounded by family and friends from college. Clare and Martin Tanner came to wish them well too, taking time off from the preparations for the first Christmas opening of the Marine Bay Hotel. Informal speeches were made, telegrams read, including one from Pauline and the twins; toasts were drunk.

It was late evening and they were all in a mellow mood when Harry got to his feet and cleared his throat.

'Shut up all of you. I want to say something!' He stood smiling round at the wedding guests, looking uncomfortable in his unaccustomed suit and tie, now slightly askew. 'I just want to say thanks to everyone for making this such a special day for Cath and me. Thanks to Faith for the smashing eats and Mike for the drinks. Thanks to Phyllis and Robert for letting me marry their beautiful daughter and thanks to the rest of you for – well, you know, just turning up – oh, and the presents.' He looked down at Cathy and reached for her hand. 'But if you've got any bloody imagination at all you'll have guessed by now that I can't wait to get her all to myself, so, if you'll all excuse us – or even if you won't, we're clearing off now.'

There was a round of applause, mingled with cat-calls and ribald remarks from Harry's brothers and ex-college friends. Laughing, he took Cathy's hand and together they escaped down the hall and out through the front door where Gertie stood at the kerb.

As they drove away Harry looked at her.

'Think I handled that rather well, don't you?'

'You didn't ask *me* if I wanted to leave,' she said. 'What makes you think I can't wait to be alone with *you*, Harry Flynn?'

He turned the corner into Woodhurst Road, stopped the car and turned to her, his face grave. 'I've done it already, haven't I? I've taken you for granted.'

She laughed. 'I'm only teasing, silly. But you're right; neither of us should ever take the other for granted. Let's make a promise here and now that we won't.'

They linked little fingers and vowed solemnly.

Unknown to them, Faith had left a cold supper in the kitchen at the flat and Mike's contribution was a bottle of champagne. A note attached to it said,

Sleep well. Laugh a lot. Love each other and be happy!

As Harry popped the cork and poured two bubbling glasses he said. 'We'll do all that.' He raised his glass. 'And much, *much* more. And that's another promise, my darling Mrs Flynn. Here's to us.'

Cathy touched her glass to his. 'To us!'

'Somehow, madam, Christmas isn't the same as it used to be before the war.' Clarice was in the kitchen at Cedar Lodge, putting the finishing touches to the Christmas cake she had made a month earlier.

175

'I know what you mean, Clarice.' Theresa was fishing the ancient pre-war cake decorations out of the dresser cupboard and dusting them off. 'I used to love marzipan but this mock stuff made with soya flour just isn't the same, though I must say that yours is the best I've tasted yet,' she added.

'Good job neither you nor Mr John takes sugar,' Clarice said. 'Means you can save some of the ration for things like icing – when you can get the icing sugar, that is.' She sighed. 'I was saying to Mrs Ladgrove in the shop the other day; we all thought when the war ended we'd get back to normal right away, but no such luck. I read in the *Daily Herald* the other day that there's talk of the meat ration being cut again next year.' She sniffed. 'Sometimes makes you wonder just who it was won the flippin' war, doesn't it?'

'What are you doing for Christmas, Clarice?' Theresa asked.

'I'm hoping Peter will get leave and come home,' Clarice said. 'Dennis too. It'd be really nice. Seems ages since we were all together.'

'Well, if they don't you know you'd be very welcome to join us here,' Theresa said.

'Thank you, madam.' Clarice smiled to herself, knowing that what Theresa really meant was that she'd be welcome to come and cook the Christmas dinner, and wash up after. Mrs King might have loosened up as far as their personal relationship went, and she meant well, right enough, but she was still the boss and now and then she let Clarice know it. And that little madam, Rachel, never lifted as much as a finger.

Since she had come out of hospital Rachel had reverted to type. She seemed to have forgotten Clarice's kindness to her on the day she'd gone into labour and if she was grieving for the child she'd lost – all Clarice could say was that she had a funny way of show-ing it. In the room she and Mr John shared the wardrobe was full of new clothes, bought with her husband's money and clothing coupons that Clarice suspected had been acquired on the black market. The girl made no secret of the fact that she hated living at Cedar Lodge and nagged poor Mr John day and night to find them a place of their own. Clarice sniffed, wondering what kind of housewife she'd make when they did find one. She was no home-body and she was obviously a stranger to anything in the kitchen except perhaps a frying-pan.

When she arrived home that evening Clarice found two letters waiting for her on the doormat. One bore Peter's smudgy writing. She opened that first.

Aldershot. Tuesday Dec. 17th
Dear Gran,
   Sorry I won't be with you for Christmas. Spending it with a mate in London. But I'll come home for a flying visit on my way. Expect me sometime next Monday morning.
                    Love Peter.

She sighed. London again. Still, she told herself, folding the letter and slipping it into her overall pocket, he's young. Couldn't expect him to want to spend all his free time in a small town like Queensgrove with an old woman like her. She was just glad he wasn't still fretting over that blasted girl.

The other letter was from Dennis and she opened it with a feeling of apprehension.

Dear Mum,
   I'll be popping in over the holiday on my way up north to meet Sylvia's family. (Clarice sighed. Another one on a flying visit) *I've had confirmation that Doreen died in one of the buzz-bomb raids in London about two years ago. That means I'm a free man now and I've asked Sylvia to marry me. When I get my discharge next April we'll be coming back to Queensgrove to live and I'd like her to see the house before then. I daresay she might want to make some changes. See you soon.*
                    Your affectionate son, Dennis

Clarice sighed. Reading between the lines it was clear that she would be expected to find somewhere else to live before they married. It wouldn't be easy. If a young couple like Mr John and Rachel couldn't find anywhere, what chance had she got? It was all very worrying. She knew that Dennis wouldn't see her out in the street, but all the same, sharing a house with him and his new wife was not a prospect she relished.

She confided all this to Theresa next morning over the elevenses which had now become a regular ritual.

'S'pose I'll have to go and see the council,' she said. 'Throw myself on their mercy, though from what I hear young couples have to go on a waiting list and they don't get a house till they've got kids. Same goes for them prefab places they're putting up on what used to be the allotments.' She took a sip of her tea and voiced the fear that had been keeping her awake at nights. 'I reckon all I'll be considered fit for is one of them homes.'

Theresa looked up, frowning. 'Homes?'

'Old people's homes. Used to be called the workhouse,' Clarice said glumly. 'Not much better now from all you hear.'

'Oh dear! Where would that be?' Theresa asked, clearly more afraid of losing her domestic help than concerned for Clarice's threatened homelessness.

'Nearest one to here is St Norbert's, about five miles away, on the Peterborough road,' Clarice told her. 'Everyone grumbles about how far out it is – those who bother to visit, that is. It's always the same,' she went on, her normally cheerful face sagging with dismay. 'When you're young and able they want you – keep house, look after the kids. Jump in when ever there's a crisis. But it's a different story when you're old and no more use.'

'What do you mean, no more use?' Theresa protested. 'You're not old, Clarice. And as for being able, look at the work you get through.'

'Not for much longer,' Clarice said. 'Once they chuck me on the scrap-heap I'll be too far away to come to you every day,' she added glumly.

Theresa considered for a moment, then looked up. 'Of course! Why didn't I think of it before. The answer is staring us in the face! I'll be alone again myself soon. You must come and live here as resident housekeeper.'

Clarice looked up. 'Oh! Do you really mean it, madam?'

'Of course I do. You can have a bed-sitting room of your own so you can have your privacy – whenever you want it.'

Clarice guessed that what Theresa really meant was that she'd be expected to keep to her own quarters when she was off duty, except when invited to do otherwise. But she didn't mind that. A room and her keep and maybe some pocket money to augment her pension, in exchange for what she did now on a daily basis. It sounded good to her.

★

After Clarice had cleaned John and Rachel's room that morning Rachel found the letter. She'd been out all morning, looking round the town. Bored out of her mind as usual. Taking her coat off in the bedroom she caught sight of a piece of paper sticking out from under the wardrobe. That Clarice Harvey was a nosy old cow, always poking round to see what she'd got. She must have dropped it. It certainly wasn't there this morning. But when she bent down to pick it up she saw that it was a letter. Unfolding it she recognized Peter's handwriting. It was very short and she read it at a glance. So, he was coming home? She felt a frisson of excitement shimmer up her spine. It seemed ages since she'd seen him. Pete. The very name conjured up the thrill of illicit meetings – snatched kisses and sex. *Oh*, the exquisite sex! Nothing could compare with what she and Pete had enjoyed together. She'd missed him, especially on those nights when John turned his back on her in bed, leaving her numb and edgy with frustration. She looked again at the note. Monday. Only two days away. She had to see him.

Making sure she was alone in the house that afternoon, Rachel telephoned the railway station and asked for the times of trains arriving from Aldershot on Monday morning. There were three. She replaced the receiver with a smile, making a note of the times. She'd be sure to meet all of them.

Rachel had breakfasted early and dressed in her new red winter coat. She'd had her hair done on Saturday, bleached to silver-blonde, cut and set in a mass of glinting curls. She bought a platform ticket and waited by the barrier so as not to miss him.

The first train came in and her heart quickened as her eyes raked the crowd of alighting passengers. But the familiar figure was nowhere to be seen. The platform emptied and she waited, growing colder by the minute as the icy wind swept relentlessly down the platform. She watched the big round station clock as the minutes ticked slowly by, turning up the collar of her coat and stamping her feet in the new high-heeled shoes that were beginning to pinch.

The next train was late but it arrived at last, drawing in at the platform with much hissing of steam and clanging of doors. As passengers poured off the train Rachel looked eagerly for the familiar figure. The passengers thinned and then, when she'd almost given up, she saw him, hefting his kit-bag on to his shoulder as he walked down the platform. Tentatively she raised her hand in a wave.

When he saw her he stopped, dropping the kit-bag to the platform and staring as though he couldn't believe his eyes. She walked quickly towards him, eager for his arms to open and enfold her. Instead he stared at her unsmilingly.

'What are you doing here?' he asked. 'How did you know I was coming?'

Her face fell. 'I thought you'd be pleased to see me, Pete. Your gran happened to drop your letter and I couldn't help seeing what it said.'

He shouldered his kit-bag again and began to walk – so quickly that she had to run to keep up with him. 'Huh! Trust Gran,' he muttered.

'Pete – can we go somewhere?' she asked, 'I need to talk to you.'

He walked out on to the forecourt, Rachel following. There he put his kit-bag down again and turned to her.

'Look, Rach, I want to see Gran. I've only got a few hours. I think we said everything the last time we met.'

'But a lot's happened since then.' She reached out to touch his arm. 'Pete. Please, we need to talk. Can't we just have a drink? For old times' sake?'

'Oh – all right then,' he conceded. 'Just one, mind.'

In the lounge bar of the Railway Hotel Rachel studied the tall figure buying drinks at the bar. He'd grown; broadened out. His face had altered too. He looked tougher, more manly. She found it irresistibly attractive. He brought the drinks over to the table and sat down.

'You look wonderful, Pete,' she said. 'You're bigger and stronger. Army life obviously suits you.'

He looked at her.

'Yeah. So what d'you want to talk about?'

'I had the baby, Pete,' she said quietly.

'I can see that.'

'It was a little boy. But he died.'

180

'Oh – I'm sorry,' he said dispassionately. 'These things happen, don't they. Is that it, then?'

'Don't be like that, Pete,' she said. 'I know now that I made a mistake. I'm unhappy. I think about you all the time.'

'No kidding?' he said sarcastically. 'I'd have thought all that money would have given you a short memory.'

'It doesn't. Pete – do you think you and I could see each other? I could meet you if you like – perhaps I could go up to London and we could . . .'

'*Rachel!*' He held up his hand. 'Listen, anything we had is finished. Over and done with. You made your choice, now you must live with it.'

'I see. You never made a mistake, did you?' she asked bitterly.

'Oh yes. I made mistakes all right,' he said. 'But *I* always knew what I wanted. And I've learned from mine.'

She ignored the implication. 'Say you haven't missed me too,' she challenged. 'Go on. I dare you.'

'OK, if you want the truth, I haven't missed you,' he said brutally. 'Maybe I did at first, but now it's different. I got over you, Rach. I've grown up I've got a new life and new friends, in London where I'm going for Christmas. There's going to be a job for me there when I get out of the army. And, yes, there's a new girl too. She's my mate's sister and she's called Lorna. She loves me for what I *am*, not what I've got!'

Rachel was unprepared for the hurt that pierced her to the heart. 'I don't believe you!' she snapped. 'You're just saying all that to pay me back.'

'I'm not interested in paying you back, Rachel,' he said, draining his glass. 'I reckon you're making a pretty good job of that by yourself. I've got plans. Great plans that don't include you. If there'd been a kid and I'd been sure it was mine it might have been different. I'd have wanted to see him – make sure he was all right. As it is I know now I'm really free of you once and for all. And I'm glad.' He stood up and picked up his kit-bag again. 'I've got to go now,' he said. 'I don't suppose I'll see you again. Goodbye, Rachel.'

She caught the bus back to King's Walk, hardly able to see for the tears that stung her eyes. At Cedar Lodge she sneaked in through the tradesmens entrance and ran up the back stairs to lock herself in the bedroom. Throwing herself across the bed she sobbed till her eyes were red and swollen and her chest ached.

In the little lobby just off the kitchen Clarice had been putting on her coat to go home. Madam had given her the rest of the day off to spend with Peter. She heard Rachel's hurried entry, her stifled sobs and the clatter of her heels as she ran up the back stairs. She sniffed as she tied on her headscarf. Something had upset young Mrs King and no mistake. She raised an eyebrow at her reflection in the mirror as she speculated what it might be. Maybe she was getting her come-uppance at last. And not before time.

CHAPTER FOURTEEN

'**Y**OU'RE SO LUCKY, CATHY.'
    Pauline sat by the window sipping her tea and looking down on to the busy street below. 'I think Bournemouth is gorgeous. Not to mention Harry. He adores you. Anyone can see that.'

Cathy smiled. It was lovely to see her sister. It was almost a year since she'd been home. College had just broken for the summer recess and Mum had engaged some temporary help so that Pauline and the twins could come down for a week's holiday. They were staying in a nearby guest house and spent most of their days on the beach. But today was Faith's day off and she and Mike had taken the two little boys out for a picnic so that the two girls could spend some time together. In a few days' time Cathy would be starting her summer job with the Tanners at the Marine Bay Hotel so the timing was perfect.

'And you passed your driving test too,' Pauline added with a sigh. 'I just love that crazy little car.' She sighed. 'You're racing so far ahead of me, Cath. I can't see me ever achieving anything. At least, not until the twins are grown up.'

'That's nonsense,' Cathy said. 'You were so clever at school and you had a good job before you were married. I'm sure they'd have you back like a shot.'

Pauline shook her head. 'My secretarial skills are rusty. Besides, I couldn't leave Mum to cope with the shop alone.'

'You make me feel guilty,' Cathy said. But her sister smiled.

'No. You mustn't feel that. I did what I wanted to do at the time.'

'I think being the twins' mother is achievement enough,' Cathy told her. 'You're a really good mother.'

'Haven't much choice at the moment, have I?'

'Would you marry again?'

Pauline smiled. 'Chance'd be a fine thing! It'd be a brave man who'd take on my two. Not that I'd ever trust another man after what Jack did. Mind you, if I could find someone like your Harry I might just think again.' She peered at her sister. 'You are happy, aren't you?'

'Of course. I couldn't want a better husband than Harry.'

'No sign of any little Harrys yet?' Pauline asked, her head on one side.

Cathy laughed. 'You sound just like Mum. No. We both decided that I should finish my course first. After all, I am on a government grant and it's what I came here for. Then I want to work for at least a year.'

'Well – I do see the point of course, but don't leave it too long.'

Cathy hesitated. 'Pauline – no one's ever mentioned it, but did Rachel have her baby?'

'Rachel gave birth to a stillborn child.'

'Oh. I'm sorry.'

'I was hoping you wouldn't ask, Cathy,' Pauline went on. 'But now that you have you might as well know the truth. It happened last autumn and everyone thought it was a miscarriage. It leaked out later that it wasn't. It was a seven-month premature birth; which means . . .'

'Yes.' Cathy shook her head. 'I can see what you're saying.'

'I'm sorry, love, but you'd have found out sooner or later.' Pauline laid a hand on her sister's arm. 'You were well out of it there. Anyway, it doesn't matter any more, does it?'

'Of course not!' Cathy picked up the teapot and headed for the kitchen. 'I'd better make some more tea. This is stone-cold.'

She stood staring out of the window as she waited for the kettle to boil. So John had been seeing Rachel while he was going out with her? More than just *seeing*. She shuddered. It was hard to believe that he could have betrayed her so despicably. He had made her believe he loved her. And surely he had known how much she loved him'

'Cathy – are you all right?' Pauline asked from the doorway.

'I'm fine. I won't be a minute.'

'Cath! Look at me!' Pauline took her sister's shoulders and forced her round to face her. Seeing her tears she pulled her close. 'Oh, Cath. I'm so sorry, love. I wouldn't have told you if I'd thought it would still hurt.' She looked into her eyes. 'Cath – you do love Harry, don't you? You are happy?'

'Of course I am.' Cathy dashed at her wet cheeks with the back of her hand. 'Harry is the best person in the whole world and I love him very much.'

Pauline held her eyes. 'But you're not *in* love as you were with John. Is that it?'

Cathy shrugged. 'It sounds really adolescent put like that.'

Pauline held her firmly. 'Just listen to me, Cath. For what it's worth, I think that if you're lucky enough to find a man like Harry – who loves you and wants to be with you, you should stick to him like glue. That's my advice. I've had the head-in-the-clouds, *in love* thing and believe me it's an illusion. It's – some sort of temporary mental aberration. And when it dies it just causes disillusionment and heartache.'

Cathy laughed in spite of herself. 'Pauline! I never knew you could be so cynical.'

'I'm serious, Cath, you're really lucky. All I got out of marrying the man I fell madly in love with was heartbreak.'

'I know. I am lucky.'

'You certainly are. So no more hankering after something that was never real?'

Cathy nodded. 'No, I promise.'

'Good!'

Footsteps on the stairs outside heralded Harry's arrival. Although school had broken up he'd been helping the headmaster to organize a new art syllabus for the coming year. It had been his own idea and he was quite excited by it. He opened the door and stood regarding his wife and sister-in-law, an expression of mock dismay on his face.

'Oh my Gawd! You two look solemn. What's up?'

Pauline laughed. 'We've been gossiping. It's a good job you came home while there was still someone in Queensgrove with an unstained character.'

Harry pulled a face. 'Why is it these small towns are so full of

goings-on? Or is it that down here we're more broad-minded?'
Without waiting for a reply he went on, 'Now, get your glad-rags
on girls. I'm taking you both out to dinner.'

'Not me,' Pauline protested. 'You're forgetting the boys.'

'No I'm not,' Harry said. 'I've just looked in on Faith and Mike
and they're perfectly happy to keep the twins all evening. Faith
will put them to bed in my old room and you can collect them in
the morning.'

'Oh no. I couldn't impose—'

'Yes, you could.' Harry cut her off in mid-sentence. 'In fact it
was Mike's suggestion to keep them. He and Faith haven't had any
kids to play with for years. The four of them have had a whale of a
time. If you like I'll run you round to the hotel in Gertie and pick
you up in about an hour.'

When he got back Cathy was in the bedroom, changing. Harry
came up behind her and slid his arms around her waist, pulling
her back against him.

'Mmm, you smell gorgeous,' he said, burying his nose in her
hair. He met her eyes in the mirror. 'You are all right, aren't you?'

'Of course.'

'It's just the way you looked when I came in earlier. Your
father's not ill again?'

She turned and slipped her arms around his neck. 'You worry
too much. Dad's fine, I'm fine. And you – you're more than fine.'
She kissed him. 'I love you, Harry Flynn.'

He drew her close. 'I suppose you realize that you're asking for
trouble, Mrs Flynn,' he said, his lips against hers. 'You're going the
right way to missing that dinner I promised you. Poor Pauline will
be left standing there in her posh frock and wondering where we are.'

'Oh no she won't.' She wriggled out of his arms and gave him a
little push. 'Off with you and put on something that doesn't have
paint and charcoal all down the front or I shall pretend I don't
know you!'

They drove out to a little restaurant on the edge of the New
Forest and ate dinner by an open window with the scent of pine
and bracken drifting in on the summer breeze. The evening was a
great success, with Harry in fine form, making them laugh with
his stories about the little boys he taught and some of the funny
things they said.

Much later after they had fallen into bed and made love, Cathy lay staring into the darkness, her mind going back over what Pauline had told her that afternoon. So, Rachel had lost the baby. It must have been a blow to them both. She wondered how their marriage was standing up to the strain. It couldn't be easy. Perhaps you got what you deserved in this life, she told herself.

She turned to look at Harry's sleeping face, the curly hair falling over his forehead and the curve of his mouth, soft in repose. And knew that however hurt she had been, she had the best part of the bargain.

Dennis Harvey and his fiancée, Sylvia, had been married three months and already Sylvia was pregnant.

Clarice had been surprised and slightly shocked when they had told her. At his age, forty-five, she'd have thought her Dennis was past that lark. However, she kept her mouth closed on the subject and secretly looked forward to a belated second grandchild.

She'd had a surprise when Dennis had brought his intended home at Christmas. She didn't really know what she'd expected but it certainly wasn't the bespectacled, mouse-like girl in her mid twenties who stood behind him on the doorstep, looking for all the world like a scared rabbit.

From the first it was obvious that Sylvia adored Dennis, which Clarice conceded must have been extremely flattering for him at his age. But she was slightly disconcerted at the way the girl leapt to his every whim, trying to anticipate his needs even before he expressed them. Clarice found her dog-like devotion frankly embarrassing.

She was to stay on at Number 20 until the wedding, of course – to act as chaperon and stop the neighbours gossiping. Theoretically Sylvia was supposed to be sleeping in Peter's old room, but Clarice knew that it wasn't mice that made the floorboards creak in the middle of the night!

When she told them she was moving out to take the resident housekeeping job at Cedar Lodge neither of them bothered to conceal their relief. Not that Clarice minded. She thought herself lucky to have found an acceptable alternative. Life under the same roof as the servile Sylvia would have driven her barmy.

Peter was already aware of his father's impending marriage

when he came home on his Christmas visit. Madam had given Clarice time off that day to see him. But he was very withdrawn when he arrived at King's Walk. He seemed upset, though when she asked if everything was all right he insisted that he was fine. Clarice wondered if it had anything to do with Rachel's distressed dash up the back stairs that same morning. Though how she would have known Peter was due home was a mystery.

She told him about the flat she was to occupy at Cedar Lodge and explained that Mrs King had said he'd be welcome to visit her there. He had shrugged noncommittally and she guessed that he'd never visit while Rachel was there. Besides, he mentioned that there was the chance of a job in London after he had served his time in the army. Clarice was trying to come to terms with the fact that Peter, the affectionate little grandson she had brought up and loved dearly, was growing away from her.

Clarice moved into Cedar Lodge the first week in April, while Dennis and Sylvia were on their honeymoon in Clacton. From the first, she knew she'd be very snug in her quarters at the top of the house, which had once been the nursery. There were two quite large rooms, one to sleep in and one to use as a sitting room. She had brought her own wireless and her favourite chair and Theresa had had a wash-hand basin fitted up in the bedroom so that she was almost self-contained. It was really quite luxurious. It also meant that she didn't have to risk running into anyone on the landing first thing in the morning on her way to the bathroom, before she'd put her dentures in.

Since Christmas things had gone from bad to worse as far as the younger Kings were concerned. 'The onlooker sees most of the game' was one of Clarice's favourite maxims and she'd had much to muse over during the winter months. The younger Kings hardly seemed to speak to each other these days but Rachel's demands and her airs and graces grew worse by the week. Since Dior's celebrated New Look had come in she'd had a whole lot more new clothes. But although Rachel swaggered about looking like a film star there was an atmosphere of gloom in the house. They seemed no nearer moving into a home of their own either, but although she tried tactfully to elicit a reason for this from Theresa no plausible answer was forthcoming.

Right on top of the Royal Family's visit to South Africa came the news of Princess Elizabeth's engagement to the handsome Philip Mountbatten. That had caused a stir and no mistake. Like Theresa, Clarice had always been a staunch royalist and they were both thrilled at the prospect of a royal wedding to look forward to. Every day it was the main topic of conversation over their elevenses.

Clarice wondered where all the clothing coupons would come from for the outfits, not to mention the points for the wedding breakfast, especially as the rations had been cut again. Would they have a slap-up sit-down meal, she wondered, or a buffet? And who would organize it all? The Queen? Or old Queen Mary? But Theresa, who was knowledgeable about such matters, pointed out that the Duke of Norfolk would take care of everything. Anyway, whoever was doing all the work it made a lovely change to have something to look forward to.

In the early spring Clarice had made a new friend, though the acquaintance she struck up quite by chance was to cause her some disquiet in the months to come.

In late February Theresa had been struck down with a nasty attack of influenza. She recovered slowly with a chesty cough that stubbornly refused to clear up. The doctor advised her to stay indoors until the weather improved, but she worried about her weekly visits to the cemetery and asked Clarice to buy flowers and go in her place.

It was bitterly cold in the churchyard. Clarice found the two memorials easily enough; one to Laurence King, missing in action, and the other to Theresa's brother. She threw away the dead flowers and laid the bunch of bronze and white chrysanthemums on the frosty grass while she went across to the tap.

'I think you'll find it's frozen.'

Clarice looked up to see a tall, handsome woman with greying hair.

'I guessed it might be, so I brought some water in a bottle,' the woman went on with a smile. 'There's some left over if you'd like it.'

'Oh, that is kind of you,' Clarice replied. She followed the woman to where she'd been arranging some out-of-season roses on a grave. Seeing Clarice's surprise the woman smiled.

'It's his birthday,' she explained. 'I always like to get him something a bit special.'

But Clarice's surprise was not just for the roses, it was for the name on the headstone. *Albert John King.* She looked at the woman. 'Is he your. . . ?'

The woman smiled and shook her head. 'A friend,' she said. 'A very dear friend from a long time ago.' She held out her hand. 'I'm Jane Linford, by the way.'

Clarice took the hand, noticing that it was white and soft. Jane Linford was obviously not a working woman in spite of her local accent. She instinctively liked this softly spoken woman, but she guessed that she was the mistress whose existence had upset Theresa so much a few months ago. She realized that Mrs Linford was looking expectantly at her and said hurriedly, 'I'm Clarice Harvey.'

Jane smiled. 'Pleased to meet you, Mrs Harvey. Goodness how cold your hands are. I only live on the other side of the park. Will you come and have a cup of tea with me when you've done your flowers?'

Clarice felt she should refuse. It would be disloyal of her to drink tea with Theresa's late husband's mistress. But her natural curiosity got the better of her. After all that she'd heard about Albert King she wondered what kind of woman had found him lovable enough to want to keep his memory alive all these years, even celebrating his birthday with roses. It might be interesting to hear the other side of the story.

Jane Linford lived in a neat little terraced house in Picardy Terrace, a small cul-de-sac on the far side of the park. It was comfortably furnished, warm and welcoming. In a cosy living-room at the back a fire burned, protected by a fire-guard. Jane removed it, prodding the fire to brightness.

'That's better,' she said. 'Take off your coat, Mrs Harvey and I'll put the kettle on.'

Over the tea and home-made biscuits Clarice learned that Jane had been widowed in 1925.

'I was only twenty-five,' she said sadly. 'Tom and I had only been married a year. We met at King's Footwear where we both worked. I was just a machinist, but Tom was a foreman. He was ten years older than me.'

'So what happened to him?' Clarice asked.

'In those days they used horse-drawn wagons,' Jane said. 'One day a horse went berserk in the yard as it was being harnessed up. Poor Tom fell under its hoofs and it trampled him. He was terribly injured. He died in hospital before I could get to him.'

'That's dreadful.' Clarice shook her head sympathetically. 'So young to be widowed.'

'We'd just managed to get this house to rent,' Jane said. 'These houses were built by King's for their workers. So proud of it, Tom was. I didn't know which way to turn after it happened. I've no family, you see. I was brought up in an orphanage – never knew who my parents were. Before Tom and I started walking out I lived with foster-parents. They used to take all my wages off me and half-starved me. I couldn't go back there, but I couldn't keep this house on on a machinist's wage.'

'What about your in-laws?' Clarice asked.

Jane poured Clarice another cup of tea. 'They weren't interested. Never wanted Tom to marry me in the first place.'

'So – what happened? Did you get compensation for the accident?'

'No. They said Tom shouldn't really have been there so it was his fault. I thought I'd have to go into cheap lodgings.'

'But you didn't.'

'No. It was like a miracle,' Jane told her. 'After my claim had been turned down Albert – Mr King – came to see me – promised he'd see I was all right. This house belonged to his family as I said, and he arranged for me to stay on rent free. It was such a relief.'

'I can imagine,' Clarice said drily, guessing what Albert King had expected in return.

That afternoon was the first of many visits to Jane Linford's house. She could tell that Jane was lonely and in need of a friend to talk to, and over the weeks Clarice discovered that she had no friends and the neighbours shunned her.

'They look on me as a fallen woman,' she told Clarice. 'Even after all these years. Folks round here have got long memories. They soon got to know that I wasn't paying any rent, you see, and they didn't like it. You know what some people are like, forever squinting through the net curtains, putting two and two together.'

'And making five?' Clarice asked.

191

'Well – not exactly, to be fair. Most of them worked at King's too, you see. And soon after Tom's accident I was promoted at work,' Jane told her. 'I learned how to type at evening classes. Albert arranged it all. And then I got a good job in the office.' She looked up defensively. 'But I wouldn't have been given the job if I couldn't do it, would I?'

' 'Course not,' Clarice agreed.

'Then he took to dropping in in the evenings to make sure I was all right.'

'Oh yes?' Clarice muttered, her face hidden in her teacup.

Jane sighed. 'You know, he had a name for being coarse. I don't know why. I can honestly say that he was never anything but gentlemanly and kind with me.'

'Was he?'

'He was dreadfully unhappy,' Jane said. 'Just between ourselves, he married for convenience and his wife didn't love him at all. Seems she'd been engaged to a young doctor who was killed in the first war and she'd never got over it.'

'Well, that's understandable, isn't it?' Clarice said, beginning to feel slightly uncomfortable. If Jane knew who she was confiding in she wouldn't be saying all this.

'Oh yes. But then you shouldn't marry a man you can't love, should you?' Jane said. 'It only leads to unhappiness.'

'So – he was good to you?' Clarice prompted.

Jane nodded, sipping from her cup. 'I grew to love Albert. I know he loved me too, though of course we had to be discreet. He bought this house for me in the end, put it in my name. He invested money for me too, so that I'd be all right if anything happened to him. He was so thoughtful. Twice a week regular, he used to come, Mondays and Thursdays. I could never see that it was wrong in spite of what folks said. He felt rejected in spite of his wealth. And I was young and alone in the world. We were two of a kind really.' She smiled reminiscently. 'Orphans of the storm of life, Albert used to call us. His wife never suspected a thing, so we weren't hurting anyone either.' Jane's mouth hardened. 'Not that she'd have cared anyway. Wouldn't even share a bedroom with him after their two sons were born. And Albert such a passionate man too.' She looked up at Clarice. 'Do you know, she never even tends his grave. If it wasn't for me it'd be overgrown with weeds by now. No one would even know where it was.'

Clarice nodded. 'So now you're like me – just your memories to keep you going. Though of course I've got my Dennis, and Peter, my grandson.'

Jane was silent as she looked into the fire. 'That's my one sadness,' she said softly. 'That I've no child.'

Clarice looked up at her. Theresa had told her that the detective had said there was a child. Had he been wrong, then?

'That's a shame,' she said. 'I know they're often a worry but it's a comfort when you're getting on, knowing there's someone to remember you after you've gone.'

Jane was silent for a moment, then she looked at Clarice. 'I did have a baby,' she said, in a voice so soft that Clarice had to lean forward to hear her. 'A little girl. No one knew, except Albert of course. I couldn't keep her. Well, there was enough gossip as it was and everyone would have known at once whose it was. There would have been hell to pay. Albert arranged for me to go away for my confinement. Then afterwards for the baby to be – taken away.'

'Away?'

'For adoption.'

'Oh, I see. That must have been hard.'

'It was – very hard. At the time I thought I'd never get over it. I couldn't stop crying. Albert never left me alone for longer than he could help – tried to be with me as much as he could.' She shuddered. 'It's a time of my life I try not to think about.'

'I'm not surprised,' Clarice said. 'Not knowing where your child is – that must be terrible.'

'I have a vague idea,' Jane said. 'She went to a good couple who had no children. I know that – somewhere nearby. It was one of the things I made Albert promise. It helped, knowing she wasn't too far away.'

'I see. So, she's here? In Queensgrove?'

'Yes. Albert promised. In return I had to promise not to try and find her. If I had I would have lost all this.' She spread her hands. 'And Albert too, of course.'

Thinking about it later Clarice thought Albert King was a selfish, philanderer who'd had things all his own way. The best of both worlds. A pretty and grateful young mistress who was gullible and besotted enough to give up her child to let him off the hook. And all this going on behind poor Madam's back. She felt so sorry for both women, but especially Jane. At least Theresa had her sons. How could Jane bear it, knowing that she could run into her own child any day and not know her?

As the winter turned to spring and then to summer Clarice gradually cut down her visits to Jane's house, afraid that if Theresa found out she'd be angry. She couldn't afford to upset her employer and maybe lose her home. She didn't want Jane to know that she worked for Albert King's widow either. Once she knew that she'd feel betrayed. And even though Clarice had vowed to herself that she'd never breathe a word of what Jane had told her she knew she'd feel like a Judas.

But as August melted into September and the leaves began to fall something happened that was to put that and all other worries out of Clarice's mind and turn the lives of everyone at Cedar Lodge upside down.

CHAPTER FIFTEEN

'**M**OTHER, I SIMPLY HAVE to have more money.'

John and his mother were closeted in the study, with Theresa as usual on the business side of the desk.

She stared at him. 'I've already given you a rise, John. Why do you need more?' She held up her hand. 'No, don't tell me, it's Rachel, isn't it? I've never known such extravagance. If it isn't new clothes it's permanent waves or make-up. You should put your foot down. King's wasn't created just to keep her in a style to which she has never been accustomed.'

'We *need* to have a home of our own,' John said as patiently as he could. His mother wasn't listening.

'And she's so rude,' she went on. 'I've tried to ignore her atrocious manners, John, for your sake. But now that you've brought the subject up yourself I really must speak. She's insolent, not only to me in my own home, if you please, but to poor Clarice too. I've always said that being rude to servants is the height of ignorance. The poor souls can't answer back and I simply won't have it.'

John swallowed hard, sorely tempted to remind his mother of her own attitude to Clarice Harvey when she first started work at Cedar Lodge. Not to mention Clarice's supreme ability to stand up for herself. Arguing with his mother was a luxury he could not afford at the moment.

'All the more reason for you to see that we need to move out,' he said quietly. 'Surely it would be more comfortable for all of us.'

Theresa looked at her younger son thoughtfully. 'John, I'm disappointed in you,' she said. 'I haven't mentioned it before. In fact I've tried hard not to think about it. You married Rachel and did the decent thing, if it can be called that. But when I discovered that you were actually seeing her at the same time you were seeing the Ladgrove's girl I was shocked.'

'Mother – that has nothing to do with . . .'

'It has everything to do with it,' Theresa persisted. 'How could you have deceived a nicely brought-up girl like Catherine? You even brought her to tea here and all the time you and Rachel were . . .' She shuddered delicately. 'I really cannot bring myself to say it.'

John cringed. It was so unfair. His mother had behaved appallingly to Cathy on the one occasion he had brought her to tea. Yet now . . . He was in an impossible position, totally unable to defend himself without betraying Rachel's confidence. Although he refused to admit it to himself he had grave doubts about Rachel's claim of being attacked. Under the circumstances he had no choice but to give her the benefit of the doubt and try to make the best of things, but in spite of his forbearance things had gone from bad to worse since last Christmas. After the loss of the child he had done his best to comfort Rachel. She had seemed so vulnerable, especially when she had poured out the tale of the alleged attack. For weeks afterwards she had been subdued and compliant. Then, at Christmas for some unexplained reason, she had changed overnight. Suddenly he could do nothing right. She was tearful and discontented, always demanding this or that. Never losing an opportunity to taunt him with what she saw as his shortcomings.

A couple of months ago he had been delighted to see a flat advertised on the other side of town and he had hoped that the prospect of a home of her own might cheer Rachel up. The rent was reasonable and it was in a pleasant neighbourhood. But when he had taken her to see it she had turned it down.

'I want my own house,' she had insisted petulantly. 'When we were married you let me believe that King's was yours. What will folks think if we live in a place like this?' She swept an arm round the empty living-room of the flat. 'It's not much better than a slum.'

Hardly a day went by that John didn't think of Cathy and wonder if she was happy. Since Pauline had told him that she was getting married he had tried hard to put her out of his mind, yet if anything his longing for her was worse. He reminded himself that they'd both married different people and that must be the end of it. Cathy had a new life now and deserved to be happy. He tortured himself with the thought that by now Pauline would have told her that he had been seeing Rachel at the same time as her. Would she believe it? Why wouldn't she? After all, he had behaved pretty badly. Her opinion of him now must have hit rock bottom.

'So you are refusing to increase my present salary?' he said, dragging his thoughts back to the question in hand.

'I didn't say that, John,' Theresa said patiently. 'You know I don't like to refuse you anything. I know how hard you work for us and I appreciate it. I just don't like to see you being led by the nose by that – that *spendthrift!*'

'She's my wife, Mother.'

'Then put her straight!' Theresa said. 'Tell her you won't tolerate it any longer. When I see that you're putting your foot down perhaps I'll reconsider.'

John walked out of the house and across the road to the park. He was almost at the end of his tether. He could hardly tell his mother about the rows – about Rachel's tantrums and threats. On one occasion in sheer desperation he had even offered her a divorce, thinking it must be what she wanted.

'Rachel – look, I don't seem to have anything you want,' he said. 'I don't please you physically. You're disappointed that I don't own King's outright. If you want your freedom I'll give it to you.'

But the suggestion had thrown her into a fury of angry tears. 'Oh yes! You want to be rid of me,' she'd wailed. 'Throw me out like a piece of rubbish, just because you're a failure as husband – because you can't provide for me properly. Well, you don't get rid of me as easily as that. Just tell that old cow of a mother of yours that you deserve to have that business in your name. Doling out shillings and pence to you like you were some snotty-nosed errand boy. I don't know why you put up with it. Be a man and stand up to her! And get us out of his bloody awful hole before it drives me mad. It's all right for you, at work all day. I have to put up with your mother and that old bitch Clarice Harvey watching every move I make and criticizing me. I can't stand it much longer!'

It went on and on. No matter what he said or did it was impossible to please both Rachel and his mother. He was trapped. Without more money there was no way he could move out.

197

A possible solution to John's problem came unexpectedly the following Friday. Doris, his secretary, came into his office just after lunch to remind him that there was to be a presentation after work for Bill Jackson, one of the long-serving foremen, who was about to retire. It was always her job to organize these occasions and she enjoyed it immensely.

'I've got his watch all wrapped up for you,' she said, her homely face alight with anticipation. 'And I thought we'd have it in the canteen as so many people want to join in. The girls are making a few sandwiches and they've put up some balloons and a banner that Freda has made. It says, "Good Luck Bill".' She smiled. 'It looks really nice in there. I hope he'll be pleased.'

'I'm sure he will.' John took out his wallet and handed Doris some notes. 'If we're drinking his health you'd better send out for some champagne, or at least the nearest you can find.'

John remembered now the collection that the men had made for Bill Jackson some weeks ago. He was a very popular member of the workforce and he knew that they had all given generously. 'What did you decide to get him?' he asked.

'A set of gardening tools,' Doris said. 'Bill and his wife Mary are moving into a bungalow down at Hunstanton – with a garden. Those little houses in Picardy Terrace only have a yard at the back, as you know. As a matter of fact they've already moved in. Mary went down there last weekend and this evening Bill will be off too.'

John looked up. 'I'd forgotten they lived in one of our houses,' he said.

'Yes. I was going to ask you about that. Do you want me to put a notice on the board in the canteen – advertise that it's vacant?'

'No, leave it for now,' John said thoughtfully. 'Has he handed the keys in?'

'Yes. Do you want them?'

'Yes please. I might pop round there this evening and inspect the place.'

The little ceremony went off well. John presented the man with the statutory gold watch and made a speech wishing him well and thanking him for his hard work and loyalty. Doris gave him the set of tools on behalf of his colleagues, and an embarrassed Bill responded by making a stumbling speech of thanks.

When it was over John drove over to Picardy Terrace. The little row of eight houses had been built by his grandfather after the First World War. They were designed to house King's valued skilled workers, foremen and mechanics newly returned from the war. It had been considered something of a privilege to qualify for one of them. Only loyal workers with a good record were allowed to rent one.

Although they were just two up and two down they had been well maintained and shortly before the war John's father had extended the primitive little sculleries at the back into more modern kitchens and had bathrooms and electricity installed. Whatever else Albert King had been he was a considerate employer who valued his workers' loyalty and was prepared to reward it.

Number 1, vacated by the Johnsons, was the first house in the terrace. John pulled up in front of it and sat for a moment, looking at the red brick façade and yellow-painted front door. It would be the answer to all his problems if only Rachel would agree to move in. He got out of the car and let himself in.

Bill had decorated the rooms tastefully, fitting shelves and cupboards in the kitchen and John looked round with approval at the spotless state in which Mary Jackson had left everything. He climbed the stairs and found the two bedrooms equally well maintained. The front room was quite spacious, stretching the width of the house, whilst the back bedroom was smaller to make room for the stairs. Between them was a tiny landing and being the end-of-terrace house it was the only one with a window lighting the staircase and giving a view of the park.

It was ideal, but would Rachel consider it good enough? He decided to go home and pick her up right away, before dinner.

Rachel refused even to get out of the car. 'You honestly think I'd live in that?' she asked him scathingly. 'It's even scruffier than King's Walk! I thought when I married you you'd want to give me something better.'

'Just come inside and see it,' John said. 'We could make it snug and cosy.'

'*Snug and cosy!*' she mimicked. 'Couldn't swing a cat in there! Your mother never lived in a house that was *snug and cosy* so why should I?'

Clarice was about to dish up the evening meal when the front doorbell rang.

'Drat it!' she muttered, as she put the four chops into the Aga's warming oven. Bad enough Mr John suddenly wanting to take Rachel off somewhere, putting the meal back half an hour. She'd set her heart on listening to a play on the Home Service tonight and it started at eight. At this rate she'd hardly have started the washing-up by then.

Theresa opened the kitchen door. 'Clarice, could you answer the door, please?' she said.

'All right, madam. But I've only got the one pair of hands,' Clarice retorted, her face red with heat and annoyance. 'I was just dishing up. And what with Mr John going out and everything . . .'

'All right. I'll go.' Theresa disappeared and Clarice sighed. *Really!* Now that she lived in at Cedar Lodge she seemed to be at everyone's beck and call. There was a danger of getting taken for granted if she wasn't careful! Who could be calling anyway, at this time of an evening? Downright inconsiderate, she called it.

She opened the kitchen door a crack to listen and as she did so she heard a man's voice – then a sudden cry and a crash.

Alarmed, Clarice hurried into the hall, the teacloth still in her hand. At the front door a disturbing sight met her eyes. Theresa lay crumpled on the floor in a dead faint. Bending over her was a tall man with fair hair.

'Here! What d'you think you're doing? Get out of my way.' Clarice elbowed him aside and sank to her knees beside Theresa. '*Madam!*' She picked up one of Theresa's hands and began to chafe it. 'Madam – are you all right.' She glared up accusingly at the man. 'What have you done to her?' she began. Then she stopped. There was something familiar about the man. As she stared disbelievingly up at him he smiled.

'Good evening. It's Mrs Harvey, isn't it?' he said. 'Perhaps you'll help me get her on to a chair.'

'Yes – but . . .'

The Rover turned in at the gate at that moment, drawing to a halt on the drive. John got out of the car to stare at the tall stranger who smiled calmly at him.

'Hello, John.'
John's face drained of colour. 'My God! *Laurence.*'

Clarice was irritated almost beyond belief. If Laurence King had tried he couldn't have timed it worse – choosing to come back from the dead on an evening when it was chops for dinner. She'd have to go without hers now and have an egg instead. And precious little thanks she'd get for her sacrifice either. Well, if he was staying she'd have to make sure she got his ration-book off him tomorrow, either that or he'd have to go down the Food Office for emergency coupons. She did not intend to go without for the likes of him.

'Never did like him, even as a kid,' she muttered to herself. 'Stuck up, snooty little sod.' More than once he'd given her Peter a bloody nose. Just 'cause he could stick up for himself. Never stopped to consider that he was older and bigger than Pete. Not him. *Bully!* She slapped the plates on to a tray and kicked open the kitchen door. And to think she'd have to miss her play just for him!

Seated round the dining-table the Kings listened to Laurence's astonishing story. He'd been wounded, he told them, at Anzio; the battle for Monte Casino. A severe head injury. When he came round in hospital he had no memory of who he was or anything about his past life.

'What about your dog-tags?' John asked. 'Surely they'd have identified you by those.'

Laurence shook his head. 'God knows where they went. As most of my clothing seemed to have been shredded in the explosion they must have been lost too.'

'And you weren't taken prisoner?'

Laurence shook his head. 'I don't think anyone knew whether I was British or German at that stage. I was in hospital for months and after that they put me into a mental asylum.'

Theresa gave a distressed little whimper. Laurence reached to cover her hand with his and went on: 'I suppose they didn't know what else to do with me. I had to learn everything again, just like a baby, walking, reading and writing – how to feed and wash myself. Anyway, after some time – the war was over by now of

201

course – they got me back on my feet and eventually released me. The authorities gave me a new name and papers and I wandered round Italy and through France, working where I could and sleeping rough most of the time. Then one day, a couple of months ago, I got a job helping to clear a minefield the Germans had laid. One day a mine exploded very close to me and suddenly it all came back.' He shrugged. 'The shock triggered my memory again. I remembered everything as clear as day. Even my own language, because when they taught me to speak again at the hospital it was Italian they taught me. Suddenly I remembered everything – Queensgrove, King's Walk, but most of all my home and my dearest mother.' He raised her hand to his lips and kissed the fingertips. 'I saved till I had the money for the fare to England, then I got a job in London and saved again.' He smiled. 'I didn't want to come home in rags. So . . . That's the story.'

'But why didn't you write and let us know you were alive?' Theresa asked. 'You know I would have sent you the money to come home at once.' She dabbed at her eyes with her handkerchief. 'Oh, thank God you're safe, Laurence. I've prayed for this moment every night since that terrible telegram came,' she said. 'And now my prayers have been answered. I can hardly believe it.'

Across the table Laurence and John exchanged looks. Laurence was smiling confidently, but John's eyes held doubt and distrust.

Coffee was served in the drawing room by a tight-lipped Clarice. Theresa smiled sweetly at her.

'Will you prepare Mr Laurence's room for him? Make up the bed and put some hot-water bottles in to air it, please.' She turned to Laurence. 'It's exactly as you left it, darling. Nothing has been touched.'

Clarice withdrew without comment. So – he was staying. And if Mr John's face was anything to go by he wasn't happy. She withdrew, all hopes of hearing her radio play finally dissolving.

When they had finished coffee Laurence got to his feet.

'I'll take a turn in the garden, Mother,' he said. 'I'd like a smoke and I know you don't like it in the house.' He bent as he passed her, dropping a kiss on the top of her head. 'After that I think I'll turn in.' He smiled. 'I can't tell you how wonderful it is to be home again.'

John found his brother leaning against the corner of the

potting-shed, smoking a cigarette. 'Are you going to tell me the real story?' he asked.

Laurence looked at him with an expression of mock surprise. 'You've just *heard* the real story.'

'Please don't insult my intelligence, Laurence. You might have got Mother to swallow that stuff about losing your memory, but it won't wash with me.' He looked at his brother. 'What did you do? Are the Military Police after you? Are you using this as a bolt-hole? And what the hell possessed you to turn up out of the blue like that? You could have given Mother a heart attack.'

Laurence laughed. 'You always had an overdeveloped sense of the dramatic.'

'All right, tell me the truth. I'm entitled to that at least if I'm going to have to share a house with you. If you've been back in this country all this time why didn't you get in touch?'

'Are you saying you wish I'd come back sooner?' Laurence raised an indolent eyebrow. 'If the looks you've been giving me are anything to go by, my return now is far from welcome.'

'I'm not going to pretend we haven't managed pretty well without you,' John said pithily.

Laurence threw down the stub of his cigarette and ground it under his heel. 'I dare say! But things are about to change now that I'm home. You might do well to remember that this is *my* house now that father is dead,' he said, his voice hard. 'I know what was in his will and as the elder son I have certain rights. So I'd be careful if I were you. As for being entitled to the truth, you've heard it, and if it doesn't suit you to believe it, that's your problem, not mine. Goodnight, John.' He strode off through the darkness, leaving John gasping at the sheer effrontery of it. It was only later that it occurred to him to wonder just how Laurence knew of his father's death. Albert King had died some months after his elder son had been reported missing.

Laurence had just reached the landing when a door opened and Rachel stepped out. She gave a little gasp, hastily wrapping her filmy blue negligée around her, but the gesture did not deceive him. Although her smile was shy and innocent he recognized the unmistakable boldness in her eyes.

'Oh, I'm sorry,' she said. 'I thought you were still in the garden.'

'Don't apologize. It's Rachel, isn't it? We haven't had time to get acquainted yet, but I hope we soon will.' He held out his hand and she put her own into it.

'Me too, Laurence. I've heard so much about you.' She met his eyes full on. 'You coming home like this has knocked everyone for six. Nothing this exciting has happened in Queensgrove for years.'

He laughed. 'How flattering! We'll have to have a long chat.'

'I'll look forward to that.'

Laurence squeezed the hand that lay so submissively in his, and felt the strength of the bones through the soft flesh as she held his eyes with her challenging gaze.

'So will I, Rachel,' he said, his lips curving in anticipation of the challenge he instantly recognized. 'So will I.'

CHAPTER SIXTEEN

HARRY WAS PROMOTED TO housemaster in the new school year. His sudden promotion came about because the middle-aged PE master had a serious car accident and injured his legs. When it was clear that he would be spending several months in hospital and would not be fit to carry on at the school the headmaster offered his job to Harry. With the job went living-accommodation, which consisted of a small cottage in the school grounds.

When Cathy first heard about the job she had misgivings. 'It's a long way from college.'

'That's OK,' Harry assured her. 'You can drive into Bournemouth in Gertie each day.'

'But it's going to mean a lot more work for you, isn't it?' she asked.

He shrugged off her concern. 'I already take the boys for most games,' he said. 'And since poor old Frank had his accident I've been taking them for PE too. I quite enjoy it as a matter of fact. Might as well carry on and get the perks as well.'

'Don't you think you should ask the doctor?'

Harry stared at her. 'What for?'

'You know what for, Harry. Does anyone at the school know about your heart condition?'

'For heaven's sake, Cath. You make me sound like some feeble invalid!'

He was always touchy about his health and she let the subject drop. After all, it was right enough what he said. He had been required to take a medical before he could take the job in the first place and he had been passed fit.

The cottage was delightful. A little apart from the main school building, it was built of rosy brick with a slate roof and a pretty little porch set in the angle of its L-shape. It had two rooms and a kitchen downstairs and two bedrooms upstairs, with a further room in the attic. It meant that for the first time Cathy's parents or Pauline and the twins could come and stay.

Cathy made curtains, borrowing Faith's sewing-machine and by the time they moved in, at the beginning of October, they were both delighted with their first real home.

It was a golden autumn and at half-term Cathy's parents came to stay. Robert's health seemed better than it had for some time. Phyllis told her that the doctor had started him on a new drug and an inhaler for his breathing, which seemed to suit him well. He even volunteered to lick the small garden at the back into shape.

During the evenings Phyllis sewed cushion covers for the sofa, regaling them with all the latest news from King's Walk as she worked.

'The biggest shock we'd all had since the war was when Laurence King suddenly came home,' she said.

'Why was he missing for so long?' Cathy asked. 'After all, the war has been over for two and a half years now.'

'Seems he was badly injured and lost his memory,' Phyllis told her.

'So how did he get it back?' Cathy asked.

'Seems he was helping to clear a minefield when there was an explosion and all of a sudden he remembered everything!'

Harry laughed. 'I saw that film too,' he said scathingly. 'Robert Taylor played the hero, I think. Who does he think he's kidding?'

'Stranger things have happened,' Cathy said.

'Yes, but only in fiction.'

'As a matter of fact I thought the same,' Robert spoke for the first time. 'The lad doesn't look to me as though he's gone through all that suffering and hardship. I saw more than enough of that kind of thing during the war and the blokes who came through it didn't look as hale and hearty as young King.'

'I don't trust him either.' Phyllis sighed. 'He's been sniffing round our Pauline.' 'He was always sweet on her when you were all youngsters. I don't mind telling you, it's had me worried.'

'What does Pauline say?' Cathy asked.

206

Robert laughed. 'No need to worry about our Pauline. Her head is not to be turned by the likes of him,' he said. 'Last I heard she'd sent him packing.'

'Well, I hope you're right,' Phyllis said, screwing up her eyes to thread her needle.

Cathy wanted to ask about John, but didn't know how. Then as though reading her mind her mother said suddenly,

'Of course, say what you will, it's young John I feel sorry for.'

Robert gave her a warning look. 'Now, Mother.'

'No. Credit where it's due,' Phyllis persisted. 'I know his behaviour left a lot to be desired, but he has worked hard since the end of the war, getting King's back to working commercially again. It doesn't seem fair that his brother should come back out of the blue and reap all the benefits.'

'Is Laurence working at King's too, then?' Cathy asked.

'Working? Not on your life!' Phyllis said with a sniff. 'He's living like a lord. Somehow or other he's managed to get a new car for himself when no one else can. And Clarice Harvey says he's got his mother wrapped round his little finger. She can't refuse him anything.' She frowned. 'I can't remember whether I told you that Clarice lives in at Cedar Lodge now.'

'Yes, you did, Mum. Her son Dennis got married again.'

'Yes. Well she says that Laurence King treats her like some kind of skivvy,' Phyllis went on. 'Even expects her to clean his shoes for him!'

'The house must be crowded now with all of them living there,' Cathy observed.

'Oh, but they don't now,' Phyllis said. 'John and that Rachel have moved into one of those little houses in Picardy Terrace. You know, the ones old man King built for his workers.' She sat back, folding her arms. 'And not before time, if you ask me. It was common knowledge that Rachel and Laurence were carrying on. I reckon that was why John moved out.'

Robert clicked his tongue. 'Mother! That that's only gossip. You really shouldn't repeat it.'

'Doesn't matter,' she protested. 'It's not as if Cathy lives in Queensgrove any more.'

Later Harry brought up the subject again. 'Sounds as though Queensgrove is positively heaving with intrigue and passion,' he said. 'I reckon you're missing out, living out here in the wilds of Hampshire.'

Cathy snuggled up to him. 'Being in the shop Mum hears all the latest gossip,' she said. 'And what she doesn't hear she makes up.'

'Only a few more months to go now before your exams,' Harry said. 'I bet you pass first time with honours.'

Cathy sighed. 'Don't! I hardly dare think about it.'

'While we're living here it'd be nice to start a family,' Harry said dreamily. 'It'd be a lovely place for a kid to grow up.'

Cathy looked at him. 'We agreed I should work for a couple of years first. It seems only fair when I'm studying on a government grant.'

'Don't you want kids, Cath?'

She kissed him. 'Of course I do, silly. But not just yet.'

'It might not happen right away. Some people try for ages.'

'On the other hand it might happen right away. No, Harry. The time's not right yet.'

John had been surprised when Rachel suddenly changed her mind and agreed to move into Number One Picardy Terrace. Theresa had been doubtful when he suggested it, but having refused to give him money for the deposit on a house she could hardly complain.

He and Rachel agreed on a day for moving and Rachel had a field-day choosing furniture and soft furnishings.

Her first visitor, albeit in secret, was Laurence. He had been home for almost a month now and had wasted no time at all in seducing his brother's wife. Not that she had taken much seducing.

He arrived soon after lunch by the back door and wandered round the little house, nodding his approval.

'Clever of you to persuade old John to move into this little place,' he said. 'A veritable little love nest if ever I saw one.' Privately he thought it typical of his loser brother to settle on a house meant for a labourer.

They spent the afternoon in bed and as they lay together after an energetic session of lovemaking Rachel asked:

'Are you going to settle here for good now, Larry?'

'Christ! What an idea!' He laughed.

'So what will you do? You said you had a job in London. Have you chucked it in or will you go back to it?'

He shrugged. 'I might. I haven't worked out what I'll do yet.'

'If you go will you take me with you?'

Laurence laughed. 'Give me a chance. I need time to settle down again and sort my life out before I make any plans for the future.'

She looked thoughtful. 'All that stuff about the war – you losing your memory and that – was it true?'

'What do you *mean?*' he said indignantly. 'Of course it's true.' He drew her to him. 'But right now I've only one plan that you need concern yourself with and I think you can guess what that is.'

She giggled. '*Larry!* We can't. John will be home soon.'

He rolled over to pin her down with his weight, a hand on either side of her head. 'That's the fun of it. A bit of danger gives it an edge, don't you think?'

'I don't know. I . . . *Ow!*'

He bit her shoulder painfully. 'Shut up, woman. You talk too much. The day you're satisfied with just the once I'll be drawing my old-age pension!'

Half an hour later she saw him out through the back door. Into the lane at the back she waved until he turned the corner. Larry was the most exciting lover she had ever had, even more exciting than Peter. True, he could be rough. Sometimes she had to hide the bruises and love-bites from John so that he wouldn't suspect, though she was becoming increasingly careless. Deep down she knew she would half-welcome his finding out. He had offered her a divorce once. If he offered again she would probably accept. After all, Larry was the elder of the King brothers. It would be to him the factory and the house passed when Theresa died. He'd already hinted as much. He was by far the better bet.

'Good afternoon, dear.'

The woman's voice startled her out of her reverie. 'Oh – hello.'

The woman had stepped out into the lane to put out her dust-bin. Tall and middle-aged, she had a pleasant face and a welcoming manner. But Rachel had no wish to hob-nob with neighbours. She was about to step back into the yard, cutting off the woman's attempt to draw her into conversation when she said:

'Seeing off a friend?'

So the nosy old so-and-so had been watching. Rachel hesitated, a sharp retort on her tongue. Then she swallowed it, reasoning that it would be a bad move to make enemies. She smiled. 'My brother-in-law,' she said. 'He came to collect something of my husband's.' The unintended irony of the remark made her smile.

'That's nice.'

'Yes.'

The woman took a step towards Rachel. 'I'm Jane Linford. I used to work for King's some years ago. That's why I live here,' she said. 'My husband was killed in an accident at the factory.'

'I see, well if you don't mind . . .'

'It's lovely having young people like you living next door. Don't be lonely, will you dear? Come round and have a cup of tea with me sometime.'

'Well, I don't really get lonely,' Rachel said truthfully.

'Well, you know where I am.'

'Yes.'

Rachel escaped indoors and swore under her breath. 'Just her luck to have some nosy old biddy living next door, watching everything she did.

The next time Laurence came she told him about the over-friendly woman next door. 'I don't know what to do about her,' she said. 'If we're not careful she'll find out about us and tell someone.'

'It's easy', Laurence said, his hands behind his head. 'Just get her on your side.'

Rachel stared at him askance. 'You mean *tell* her – about us?'

'No. Spin her a line. Say we're planning a surprise for your husband's birthday. Make her feel she's important and you'll have her eating out of your hand.'

Laurence was feeling positive. He was doing well – even better than he had expected. Everyone seemed to have swallowed the story about the amnesia – with the exception of John of course. But then what did he matter? He couldn't prove anything anyway. Laurence knew he had always been his mother's favourite. And coming back from the dead had done him no harm at all.

It had been so easy to point out to her subtly that he had waited too long for his inheritance and that it was time King's and the deeds of the house were transferred to him. She was giving the matter some thought but he was confident that the outcome would be in his favour. One visit to the solicitor and it would be done. He

couldn't wait to see John's face when he realized that he was working for his brother. All he had to do was bide his time. Theresa had
already arranged a generous monthly allowance for him. And
bought him the car. Now all he had to do was to spend a little time
here, convincing everyone of what a dutiful son he was. Once the
papers were signed and King's was in his name it would then be a
simple matter to secure a substantial loan against his assets. After
that he'd lose no time in making his exit, paying off the gambling
debts that had driven him out of London and setting the wheels of
his latest scheme rolling.

Meanwhile Rachel was providing him with some first-class
amusement. The fact that she was married to his brother was a
bonus.

Rachel had just seen John off to work a few days later when
there was a knock on the door. Thinking that Laurence was
becoming bolder she hurried to open it and instead of her lover
found Jane Linford waiting outside.

'Good morning dear. I'm sorry to disturb you but I wondered if
you'd like to come round and have a cup of tea with me this afternoon.'

Rachel ground her teeth with irritation. Why couldn't the
stupid woman take the hint and leave her alone? She forced a
smile. 'Not really,' she said. 'My afternoons are pretty busy really
and . . .'

'Why not this morning then,' Jane said quickly. 'Now if you
like.'

'Well . . .'

'Of course. It's early and you'll have your jobs to do. Shall we say
half-ten?'

Rachel remembered what Laurence had said. Get her on your
side. Make her feel she's important. 'All right, then,' she said. 'But
I mustn't be too long.'

Jane beamed with delight. 'Oh good! See you later then.'

Rachel closed the door with a sigh. Damn the woman.

At half-past ten she presented herself at the door of Number 2.
Jane ushered her in and sat her down in the best chair, chattering
animatedly all the time. She poured tea and passed Rachel a plate
of chocolate biscuits.

'Do take one, dear. I haven't got a sweet tooth myself and I never

211

use up all my points coupons.' She looked at Rachel over the rim of her cup. 'So. I take it your hubby works at King's?'

'Not *for* King's exactly,' Rachel said. 'John King is my husband.'

'Really?' Jane's eyes widened as she put down her cup. 'And you're living here – in Picardy Terrace . . .'

'It's only temporary,' Rachel said quickly. 'Flats and houses are so hard to find. We're staying here for the time being. Till something else turns up.'

'Of course. So – how long have you been married?'

'Just over a year. We got married last September, the day after John's birthday.'

'How nice. And no little ones yet?'

'No. I had a baby but he died.'

'Oh my dear, I'm so sorry.' Jane paused to pour more tea, looking at Rachel as she did so. 'I do know what you must have gone through,' she said. 'Between you and me I had a baby years ago.'

'And yours died too?' Rachel asked.

'Well, no dear. I had to give her up for adoption.' She shook her head sadly. 'I wonder sometimes if that doesn't hurt even more.'

'Why couldn't you keep her?' Rachel asked, growing interested in spite of herself.

'Between you and me, I wasn't married,' Jane confided. 'It was after my Tom was killed. I had a man-friend and he was married.'

Rachel sighed. 'Men, eh?'

'Oh, he wasn't unkind to me,' Jane went on. 'But it would have caused so much trouble.' She looked at Rachel. 'The people round here aren't very friendly; there was gossip. They've never really forgotten.' She cleared her throat. 'I'm telling you this, dear, because of your brother-in-law calling so often. I'd be careful if I were you. People are so spiteful and they have such long memories.'

'Really?' Rachel felt the hair on the back of her neck begin to prickle. She longed to tell the old bitch to mind her own business, but she remembered Laurence's advice to keep cool and said, 'Laurence and I are arranging a special treat for John – for his birthday.'

Jane frowned. 'But you've just said that was in September, so surely it's over?'

Rachel bit her tongue hard. 'I meant *my* birthday,' she said quickly. 'On November the nineteenth.' In a sudden spurt of inspiration she added, 'We're trying to work something round the royal wedding.'

Jane was staring at her. 'November the nineteenth?'

'I'll be twenty-one,' Rachel went on. 'It's a special birthday, you see. All the more reason for celebration.' She was rather pleased with herself. It was all fitting in very well. 'So that's why Laurence has been coming round. You won't give the game away and spoil the surprise, will you?'

'What?' Jane was looking slightly abstracted. 'Oh no, of course not. It's really none of my business anyway.' She passed Rachel the plate of biscuits again. 'I daresay your parents will be planning a celebration for you too, won't they?'

Rachel shook her head. 'I don't have anything to do with them any more,' she said. 'They're not my real parents anyway and we never got along.'

'Not your real parents?'

'No. They adopted me when I was a baby. Never let me forget it either. Kept telling me I was wicked. I was glad to get away from them.'

Rachel left Jane Linford's house feeling rather pleased with herself. And when Laurence came round that afternoon she told him what she had said.

'I've been thinking,' she said. 'It would be nice to go up to London for the royal wedding, wouldn't it? Nothing exciting ever happens in Queensgrove. Do you think we could go?'

He pulled a face. 'All those crowds? Anyone with any sense will be keeping away.'

'Oh, go on, Larry. You know London. You'd know where to stand so's to see everything. Say you'll take me.'

'Well, we'll see,' he said reluctantly. 'You'll have to be very, very nice to me.'

'That's easy,' she said, sliding her hand down the length of his body. 'I'll be nice to you anyway.'

Ever since John and Rachel moved to Picardy Terrace Clarice had been meeting her friend Jane Linford in the town. Sometimes they met in a café for tea and buttered teacakes and occasionally at the cinema.

Clarice was afraid she might run into Rachel on one of her visits, but she was rapidly running out of excuses. Jane was no fool and she was clearly curious about Clarice's reluctance to visit her at home, so this afternoon Clarice had decided that it was time she told her friend the truth.

'I've got something to tell you, Jane,' she said over tea. 'I should have told you before. I've always been one for having things open and above board, especially between friends.' She glanced anxiously at Jane as she passed her the sugar basin. 'I do hope we'll still be friends when you know.'

Jane looked up at her from the other side of the table. 'I'm quite sure we will,' she said. 'Why don't you just get it off your chest?'

'Well – you know I work as a housekeeper?'

'Yes.'

'It's *where* I work – and who I work for.'

'Oh? So who is it then?'

Clarice took a deep breath. 'I work for Mrs King. At Cedar Lodge.' With dismay she watched as the colour drained from Jane's face. 'There's no need for you to worry though,' she said hurriedly. 'I'd never give away your secret or tell anyone what you've told me. I'd rather die, Jane. Honest I would.' She watched anxiously to see what reaction she would get.

Jane looked up. 'There's just one thing I have to ask – that day in the churchyard – when you and I first met. Did she send you to find out who I was?'

'Oh *no!*' Clarice said, appalled at the very idea. 'It was like I said. She was ill with the flu.' She did not add that Theresa had already tracked down her identity through a private detective. That was nothing to do with her after all. 'I just wanted you to know once and for all. I don't want us to stop being friends and there should-n't be secrets between friends, should there?'

'No.' Jane smiled. 'I think I know you well enough to trust you, Clarice. And I certainly wouldn't like us to fall out. I haven't that many friends that I can afford to lose one.'

Clarice smiled and sighed with relief. 'I can't tell you what a load that is off my mind,' she said. 'I think that calls for a fresh pot of tea, don't you? I've got time.'

They chatted for a while, about Dennis's new job at the canning-factory and Sylvia's pregnancy, which was proving problematic, but Jane hardly seemed to be listening, her eyes were preoccupied and far away until suddenly she said:

'Clarice, what you've told me about who you work for puts a whole new outlook on something I'd decided to tell you this afternoon.'

'Why? What is it?'

'It's been on my mind for days now. I can't sleep for worrying about it.'

'Oh dear. It must be bad.'

Jane looked up. 'Living at Cedar Lodge, you must know that John King and his wife have moved to Picardy Terrace. Next door to me in fact.'

'Yes, I know.'

'I tried to be friendly with Rachel, but I got the impression she thought I was just being nosy.'

Clarice pulled a face. 'Between you and me she's a flighty little piece.'

'Well, I rather suspected she might be. You see, the thing is, her brother-in-law visits, almost every afternoon. He's there for hours and sometimes I can – *hear* them through the wall. It's awful. Quite shameless they are.'

Clarice nodded. 'I'm not a bit surprised. I could see the way things were going between those two before they moved. If you ask me that was why she agreed to move out. And that Mr Laurence – wouldn't trust him within yards of any woman.'

'The problem is though . . .' Jane looked agitated. 'Oh dear, you see, the thing is – I think she's my daughter!'

Clarice stared at her. '*No!* She can't be.'

'Everything fits,' Jane said. 'Her age – the fact that she's adopted. Even her birthday. It's too much of a coincidence not to be true. The only thing different is her name. I called my baby Janet. But then they could have changed that, couldn't they?' She leaned towards Clarice. 'Who are they? Who are her parents? You must know.'

Clarice shook her head. 'I can't tell you. It wouldn't be right.'

'If you don't tell me I'll think up some excuse to ask her.'

Clarice shook her head. 'You promised never to try and find out, didn't you?'

'I know I did, but can't you see?' Jane's face was intense as she

grasped Clarice's hand. 'I have to know. I have to do something –
tell someone. It's not just for me any more. Because, without knowing it, Rachel has married her half-brother, hasn't she?'

It was late on Friday afternoon and Cathy was hard at work in the
life class at college. The model was a beautiful young Chinese girl
and Cathy was engrossed in her work, finding the soft shadows
and the girl's glossy dark hair and beautiful skin texture fascinating. She barely looked up when the studio door opened and Paul
Samuels came in. After a word with the tutor he came across to
Cathy and touched her arm. She looked up.

'Oh, hello.'

'Cathy, can you come with me to the office, please?' he said.

'Can't it wait till the end of this class?' she asked.

'No. Now please.'

She looked up and saw the grave look in his eyes, then without
a word she put down her brush and followed him out of the room
and along the corridor, a cold feeling of foreboding in the pit of her
stomach.

Inside his office he closed the door. 'Sit down, Cathy.'

She frowned. 'What is it? Is it bad news? It's not my father, is
it?'

'No.' He sat down behind his desk. 'Cathy, I don't know how to
tell you this, but it seems that this afternoon Harry had some kind
of attack and collapsed on the playing-field at school.'

'Harry!' She leapt to her feet, her heart thudding. 'Where is he?
I must go . . .'

'No!' Paul was on his feet too, his hand on her shoulder, his eyes
dark with compassion. 'Cathy. Oh my dear, I'm so sorry to have to
tell you – I'm afraid there's nothing anyone can do. It was instan-
taneous. He's dead.'

For a long breathless moment there was silence. Cathy stared at
him. At last she said, 'His parents – do they know?'

Paul nodded.

'I must go to them,' Cathy said, half-way to the door.

Paul put a hand on her arm. 'Not now, Cathy. Not for a moment.
Sit down again. Let me get you a brandy and then I'll drive you
there myself.'

As she sipped the brandy the stark reality of Harry's death

began to sink in like pain returning after an anaesthetic. To hold back the tears she began to explain breathlessly to Paul about Harry's heart condition.

'We knew it might happen,' she said. 'We tried not to think about it. It could have happened at any time – or not at all. He could have lived to be an old man, or . . .' She put the glass down and stood up, the pain inside her twisting like a knife. 'Oh *God*! Why did it have to be like this?' she demanded, her fists tightly clenched. 'He was such a good person. Why is God so cruel? Why couldn't we have had more time?'

At Penrith Avenue Faith was alone. Mike had gone to the hospital where they'd taken Harry to make a formal identification. They held each other helplessly.

'Everything was going so well,' Cathy said numbly. 'We were so happy. He loved his new job and the cottage so much.' Suddenly she looked at Faith's drawn white face and the tears she had suppressed so far erupted like a volcano. 'Oh, *Faith*,' she sobbed. 'He wanted us to start a family. And I wouldn't! I said we should wait. He wanted a baby so much. Oh my God, if only I'd known. It was such a little thing and now I'll never be able to forgive myself.'

CHAPTER SEVENTEEN

CATHY HAD ALWAYS KNOWN that she would have to move out of the cottage, yet it came as a blow when the headmaster gave her notice. He was apologetic.

'It's just that the new housemaster needs somewhere to live,' he told her. 'He's married man and he wants to bring his wife and child here next term. There's no hurry. You can remain until Christmas if you need to.'

But Cathy couldn't bear to stay. Everywhere she looked she saw Harry. His books, his paints and easel, still set up in a corner of the spare bedroom. His clothes still hanging in the wardrobe. Each sighting was a sharp pain to her heart and yet she could part with nothing.

Her mother had urged her to go home, but she was determined now more than ever to stay on at college and get her diploma. Harry would have wanted that. Besides, she needed qualifications to earn a living now because she had already decided that she would never marry again.

As soon as Faith knew her situation she came up with the solution.

'You must move back into your old room here,' she said. 'You know Mike and I would love to have you. After your exams it will be up to you of course, but under the circumstances it's the least we can do.'

So Cathy moved back to Penrith Avenue the second week in November. She sold the furniture she and Harry had bought for the cottage, but kept Gertie because she knew how much the old car had meant to Harry.

After the funeral she threw herself almost frenziedly into her work, studying late into the night when she couldn't sleep; driving herself harder and harder until at last Paul Samuel took her aside one afternoon as she was coming out of the canteen after lunch.

'You must ease up, Cathy. You're working far too hard,' he warned. 'You're well on course. There's no need for all this.'

'I'd rather be working,' she said.

'It's as if you're punishing yourself,' he said. 'You look so tired. Are you getting enough sleep?'

She sighed. 'I can't sleep so I might as well get up and work. Don't worry about me,' she said tetchily with an impatient wave of her hand.

He put his hands on her shoulders and made her look at him. 'Cathy! This has nothing to do with me, I know. But Harry wouldn't have wanted you to work yourself into the ground like this. If you don't mind me saying so, you look terrible and you've lost so much weight.'

'Thanks,' she said sharply. 'That really cheers me up. Look, I'm going home for Christmas. I expect my mother will stuff me full of food. She won't take no for an answer. I'll probably come back four stone overweight. Will that satisfy you?'

He smiled in spite of himself. 'Only if you look more relaxed as well.'

'All right, I'll try.'

'Come and have a coffee,' he said suddenly.

'I can't now. I've got a class.'

'To hell with the class. Skip it for once. No, not in the canteen. Come down the road to the Bluebird Café. You need to talk – get things off your chest.'

As they sat opposite each other in the steamy little café Cathy stared into the cup of coffee she was stirring.

'Faith and Mike are wonderful,' she said. 'They've been so kind to me, but Harry was their son and I feel that if I talk about him it might hurt them.'

'I doubt that,' Paul said, 'but I do know what you mean.'

She looked up at him. 'I feel so strange, Paul – like only half a person. There are things I can't do or say any more. It's as though I've had some vital part of myself removed.'

He nodded. 'It's always like that when you lose someone close.

You can never be quite the same person with anyone else as you were with them, so a little bit of you dies too.'

She nodded, tears filling her eyes. 'That's it exactly. How did you know, Paul?'

'I had a twin brother,' he told her. 'He was drowned in a boating accident when we were sixteen.'

'How awful. I'm sorry.'

'So I do know what you mean about Harry's parents. I could never talk to my parents about my brother for the same reason.'

'He's everywhere,' Cathy whispered. 'In everything I see. In my art and the books I read. In my *head*. It's torture and yet I can't let him go because if I ever feel better it will mean I've started to forget him and I couldn't bear that.'

The tears were streaming down her cheeks now. He touched her hand and she swallowed hard, fumbling for a handkerchief.

'Oh God. I'm sorry.'

'No, let the tears come,' he said softly. 'They're what you needed. To let go. And as for forgetting him, you won't do that. The memories will just be different; softer and comforting even – eventually.'

She looked up at him. 'Will they, Paul? *Will* they?'

'Yes, they will. I promise you. Look, I'm going to take you home now and I want you to rest. But if you want someone to talk to – any time – my door is always open. Promise me you won't bottle it all up again?'

'I promise.'

'And that you'll take it easier in future? You don't want to make yourself ill before the exams next spring. That would defeat the whole object.'

'I know. I'll be sensible. And thank you, Paul.'

He shook his head. 'Nothing to thank me for. You're the best student I've had for years. I want some of the credit too, you know!'

'I can't believe you're serious about this.'

John sat opposite his mother in the study at Cedar Lodge where she had summoned him on Sunday afternoon. 'Laurence knows nothing about the business. He hasn't the least interest in it. Are you seriously asking me to step down and let him run the firm – work for him as an employee?'

'King's was always meant to go to Laurence,' Theresa said. 'It was in your father's will, John. I can't go against his wishes, can I?'

'When did you ever worry about Father's wishes?' John asked bitterly. 'This is what *you* want. Isn't it?'

'Please do not speak to me in that tone, John.'

'What have I done to be treated like this?' He was on his feet, his face flushed with anger. 'I've kept the business going ever since Father died. Even when I was doing my National Service I kept an eye on things when I could get home. Is this all the thanks I get?'

'Laurence is your father's heir, John,' Theresa said. 'I appreciate all that you've done. And I shall see that you're properly rewarded.'

'Rewarded. In what way?'

'Please don't be sharp with me, John. What I suggest is that you and Laurence work together as partners until Laurence is fully conversant with the business. After that you can assume the position of managing director.'

'With Laurence as owner?'

'King's is to be in his name, that's right. Although you and I will still be directors. We'll both have a vote on any decisions that are made. It's only a matter of practice.'

'And what about the profits?'

'You and Laurence will each draw a salary. The profits will be utilized exactly as they are now, to improve and build the business. It isn't a question of either of you having the larger share.' She paused. 'And I thought that as compensation for all your hard work you and Laurence should share the proceeds of the house after I am gone. In your father's will Cedar Lodge was left solely to Laurence, but I shall adjust my own will accordingly.' Seeing that John was far from appeased she went on quickly, 'I am seeing my solicitor tomorrow. He will have the papers ready for me to sign.'

'I see. So it's all settled then?' John said. 'A *fait accompli* I don't really have any say in it. I wonder you even bothered to inform me!'

'I'm giving you fair notice so that you can't say I'm imposing it on you.'

He laughed. 'What do you call it then? What you are actually doing is showing a complete lack of faith in me,' he said. 'In spite of all my work. All my loyalty and . . .'

'If you were really loyal to me, John, if you had any real judgement you would not have done the foolish things you have done,' Theresa interrupted.

John stared at her. 'What foolish things?'

'I did not intend to bring it up, John, but as you insist – marrying Rachel for a start. The girl is a disaster as a wife. You allowed yourself to be hoodwinked by her. You forced me to share my home with her. It has been extremely difficult.'

John opened his mouth to protest, then closed it again. What was the point in arguing? His mother had already set things in motion. He stood up. 'Is that all then, Mother? Or have you any more shocks for me?'

'I think you are being most uncharitable,' Theresa said. 'Poor Laurence has been through so much. It's nothing short of a miracle that he's alive at all. But now that we have him back with us, surely the least we can do is to assure him of the future he deserves.'

John turned on his heel, passing Clarice as he strode through the hall and out of the front door, slamming it hard behind him.

She stared after him. It was the first time she had ever seen Mr John in a temper. Something must have happened to upset him badly and she reckoned that his brother was at the bottom of it somewhere. Pushing at the half-open study door she looked in. Theresa was sitting at the desk, her face troubled and preoccupied. Clarice cleared her throat.

'I'm just off now, madam? Would you like a cup of tea or anything before I go?'

Sunday afternoons and evening were her own to do as she liked. Today she was going across to Number Twenty to see Peter, who was home on leave.

Theresa looked up with a start. 'Oh, Clarice. No, you go.'

'Are you all right, madam?' Clarice closed the door. 'You look upset if you don't mind me saying so.'

'I've just had to give John some rather unwelcome news.' Theresa sighed. 'You should be thankful that you only had the one son, Clarice,' she said. 'I owe John so much. And yet Laurence is the elder son. It's only fair . . .' She pulled herself up sharply. 'That poor boy has suffered so much. You'd think his only brother would have more feeling for him, wouldn't you?'

Clarice didn't know what to say. She wondered what Mrs King

would think of her darling boy if she knew what he'd been up to with Rachel every afternoon while John was at the factory.

The thought of Rachel reminded her of what Jane had told her a few days ago. She didn't believe for one minute that it could possibly be true. And yet the details certainly did point that way. And if it *were* true then someone should definitely be told. But who? She felt it was not her place to interfere. Yet who else was there? The knowledge was a heavy burden for her, especially as Jane was growing more anxious about it every day.

At Number 20 Peter greeted her in the hall, hugging her so hard he lifted her off her feet.

'Gran! It's so good to see you.'

'Good to see you too, love. You're looking well too.'

'Be home for good soon,' he told her. 'And there's a job waiting for me, too.'

'Yes, and I want to hear all about it.'

They went through to the living-room where Clarice noticed the changes that Sylvia had made. There was a new carpet on the floor and two new easy-chairs. Dennis sat in one of them and the heavily pregnant Sylvia in the other. When Clarice came in she rose awkwardly to her feet, one hand in the small of her back.

'You sit here, Mother,' she said. 'I'm going up for my rest now. My blood pressure was high again this week. In fact the doctor says I might have to go into hospital until after the baby's born.'

Dennis rose and took her arm. 'I'll help you up the stairs, love.' He glanced at his mother. 'I'll see you in a while.'

When they had gone Clarice pulled a face at Peter. 'What a fuss! I hope your little brother or sister gets born without your dad having a nervous breakdown!'

They laughed together, then Clarice said. 'I expect you heard about Laurence King coming back from the dead.'

Peter nodded. 'Yes. Dad said he'd finally turned up. I was a bit surprised. He's been back in this country for some time now.'

Clarice frowned. 'Back in England? How do you know that?'

Peter settled himself in the chair his father had vacated. 'My mate worked as a trainee barman in a club in Soho before he was called up. The boss is his uncle and I've been staying with his family in London on leave. The owner of the club, Max Leyton,

has offered me a job as his driver when I'm demobbed. A smashing motor he's got. A Jaguar, real class. I'm to have the
maintenance of it and . . .'

'What's all this got to do with Laurence King?' Clarice asked.

'Yeah, all right. I was coming to that. It's just that I've seen him
at the club lots of times.'

'No.' Clarice shook her head. 'It must have been someone who
looked like him.'

'Nah, it was him all right,' Peter said. 'He calls himself by
another name now – Larry Hill or something. But I recognized
him right off. Used to make my life a misery when we were kids. I
wouldn't forget a sadistic bastard like him in a hurry!'

'Peter! Language!'

'There was no mistake. I even made a few enquiries. There are
various stories going round about him.'

'What sort of stories?'

'None of them good. One theory is that he deserted from the
army, but no one really knows anything definite about him. He's a
bit of a mystery. I was surprised to hear he was back here, though.'

'Wasn't till a few weeks ago he turned up,' Clarice said. 'Says he
was injured at Anzio, lost his memory and was in hospital for
months. Then he wandered round Europe, getting work where he
could till one day an explosion in some minefield suddenly
brought his memory back.'

'That's a laugh!' Peter snorted. 'And they swallowed it? Look,
Gran, I've been going up to London ever since I was called up and
he was around there then, already a regular at the club.'

'What kind of club is it?' Clarice asked suspiciously.

Peter shrugged. 'The usual kind – drinking, bit of dancing . . .'

Clarice frowned. 'Nothing illegal going on there I hope?'

'A bit of gambling in the back room,' Peter confessed. 'Poker
and roulette mostly. That's what King was interested in. If you ask
me he ran up some hefty debts and had to do a disappearing trick.
Some people can get very nasty if you don't pay up.'

'That's not the kind of place I want to see you working in,'
Clarice said.

Peter waved her fears away. 'I don't have anything to do with
that side of things,' he said. 'All I do is drive the boss.'

'And you say that Laurence King has been around all that time?'

'No mistake about it.' He paused to look at her. 'Gran – how's Rachel?'

But Clarice was busy with her own thoughts. There was more to this than met the eye. If Laurence had been living in London and used to leading that kind of racy life why had he suddenly come back to sleepy little Queensgrove? There was only one answer. Peter was right. Laurence owed money and he'd come home to get some off his mother. Once he got it he'd be off again, leaving them all in the lurch. Suddenly she remembered Theresa's words this afternoon. *I owe John so much and yet Laurence is the elder son.* Had he persuaded his mother to settle everything on him? She bit her lip. Poor Mr John. He didn't deserve that.

'Gran! I asked you about Rachel.'

Clarice looked up angrily. '*Her?* You don't want to bother yourself about that little slut. She got poor Mr John to marry her and now she's carrying on with his brother behind his back.'

'Carrying on?'

'Yes. Large as life. Her and Mr John live in Picardy Terrace now. In one of them houses that King's built for their workers. I know the woman who lives next door. She says Laurence goes there every afternoon.'

'She's having it off with him! Is that what you're saying?'

Clarice bridled. 'I wouldn't soil my lips with what that little bitch gets up to,' she said. 'If Madam knew I don't know what she'd say, let alone poor Mr John.'

'Then why don't you tell them?' Peter's face was red.

'It's not my place. I'm not paid to tell tales,' Clarice said.

'Could you prove it?'

'It wouldn't be difficult,' Clarice said. 'They don't try all that hard to keep it dark by all accounts. But I don't intend to get involved.'

'Somebody should.' Peter stood up and began to pace the room. 'We can't let this go, Gran. We've got to do something about it.'

Clarice felt stirrings of apprehension. She wished now she hadn't said anything about Rachel. She had no idea Peter still felt so strongly about her. 'Let it be, Peter,' she said. 'It's none of our business.'

He stopped pacing and looked down at her. 'I never told you,

Gran, but the kid she was expecting was mine. I begged her to marry me but she wouldn't. She wanted more than I could give her, she said. A better life. More money. Now it seems she's not content with that. I thought she loved me, Gran. I'd loved her ever since we were kids and I was so sure we'd be married one day.'

'Well, I reckon you've had a lucky escape, love,' Clarice said.

He rounded on her. 'Lucky escape! If you only knew how it tortured me, knowing she was marrying someone else – someone who'd give her all things I couldn't – who'd even give my kid his name. Then I saw her last Christmas. She was waiting at the station when my train got in. She was bored and looking for a bit of excitement. She told me the baby had died. She didn't give a damn about it, Gran. I was so mad! I wanted to hurt her back, as much as she'd hurt me, so I gave her the brush-off – told her I'd got someone else – that I didn't want to see her again.'

Clarice recalled the day last Christmas-time when she'd heard Rachel rushing up the back stairs. Now it all fell into place.

'That must be why she's taken up with Laurence King.' Peter mused. 'She was fed up again and looking for someone new. He's taken advantage of her, hasn't he?'

'Well, I don't know about that.'

Peter sat down again, nodding to himself. 'That'll be it. He saw how lonely she was and he pounced. Well, maybe there's something I can do about it.'

Rachel was expecting Laurence on Tuesday afternoon. She was waiting in the kitchen to let him in at the back door when there was a knock at the front. Thinking he was growing even bolder she rushed to open the door, a rebuke on her lips. It froze on her lips when she found herself looking at Peter Harvey.

'Pete! How did you know I lived here?' Her eyes narrowed. 'That nosy grandmother of yours! I might have guessed. *Here*! What do you think you're doing?'

He had pushed past her into the house. 'What I've got to say isn't for the neighbours' ears.'

'What have you got to say that I could ever be interested in?'

'You've been carrying on with Laurence King, haven't you?'

Her mouth dropped open with shock. 'No!'

'Come off it, Rachel.'

226

'What the hell has it got to do with you, anyway?'

'Everything!' He stood squarely in front of her. 'And there's no point in denying it. I saw him leaving here yesterday afternoon.'

'You've been spying on me?'

'Yes, if you want to call it that.'

'You've got a bloody nerve! Well – what of it then?' she said defiantly.

'He's no good, Rachel. He's a cheat and a liar and God knows what else.'

She laughed. 'You're a fine one to talk! Anyway, I don't believe you.'

'No? Well, you'd better, because I know a thing or two about him. All that stuff he told you all about losing his memory. It's a pack of lies. He's been back in this country a year and a half to my knowledge, and some say he deserted. That on its own carries a prison sentence. He owes money too, Rachel; a hell of a lot of money. He's a gambler and the people he owes are already on to him.' He looked at her. 'Has he told you he's leaving yet?'

'Of course he's not leaving!'

'He will be.'

She flushed. 'He did say he might go back to London – sometime.'

He grasped her by the shoulders. 'Wake up, Rachel! Look, you wanted to be married to John King. You wanted the money. It was important to you. So important you didn't care who you hurt to get it. Well if he finds out about Laurence he'll chuck you out and then where will you be? Laurence King won't want you tagging along. He's in enough trouble as it is!'

'You're just saying all this because I turned you down,' she said.

He threw up his hands. 'For God's sake grow up, Rachel. Look, I was hard on you at Christmas. I expect you were upset and you let that slimy bugger take advantage of you. I just thought that for old times' sake I should come and put you wise about him before you get hurt.'

She laughed in his face. 'You've got a big opinion of yourself, Pete Harvey! Don't flatter yourself that I was upset by anything *you* ever had to say! I'll tell you something, shall I? Larry King is a better lover than you ever knew how to be!'

Peter flushed with anger. 'Right! Please yourself, Rachel. I've

227

told you the truth. Now it's up to you.' He turned and opened the door. 'He's big trouble, so don't say I didn't warn you.'

Although Rachel would not admit it, Peter's warning had upset her. What he had said awoke fears she already had about Laurence's cavalier manner and some of the lies she'd already caught him out on. But when he arrived her fears were forgotten. He seemed so relaxed. She followed him eagerly upstairs where they made love as enthusiastically as ever. It was only later, as he lay on his back smoking a leisurely cigarette, that he said suddenly, 'There's something I have to tell you, Rachel. I'm leaving.'

She sat up and looked down at him, her heart plummeting. 'Leaving? When?'

'Tonight.'

Dismay swamped her. 'How long for?'

'Could be for some time sweetheart,' he told her. 'In fact I might not be back at all.'

She frowned. 'You never said anything about leaving for good. Anyway – why wait till now – after we'd . . .'

He pulled her down to him, kissing her hard. 'I thought you might get annoyed with me and I wanted our goodbye to be something special that we'd both remember.'

She pushed him away. 'You wanted to make sure you got what you wanted first, you mean.' She glanced at him. 'You haven't said yet where you're going.'

He shrugged. 'London first. After that – who knows?'

'But why? I thought you were all set up here.'

'Here?' he sneered. 'In this one-horse town? When you've seen the world and lived as I have you don't settle for a lifetime of boredom.'

'Oh – thanks!'

'Not you, sweetheart,' he said. 'You're the one thing that's made it bearable.'

'Do you really have to go?'

'Yes. It's all arranged. I've even sold the car. I'm taking it round to Carson's at five o'clock.'

'Take me with you. Please, Larry.'

'I can't.' He turned to stub out his cigarette with an air of finality.

'Why not? I hate it here too. John's boring – everything's boring. I'm sick and tired of being watched. In London we could be free. We could be happy. We're good together.' She clung to him not caring whether what Peter said was true or not. She had never wanted anyone as much as she wanted Laurence. 'Oh, Larry, please don't go without me,' she implored. 'I don't think I could bear this bloody awful place without you now.'

He took her arms from around his neck. 'Listen, Rachel, I can't take you with me.'

'Yes you *can*. I won't be any trouble to you. I've even got some money I've saved from the housekeeping. You can have it all. Oh, *please.*'

'John would come and find you.'

'I don't care. I want to be with you, Larry.'

'Well – maybe when I'm ready I'll send for you,' he said awkwardly. He was regretting now that he'd told her he was going. He hadn't anticipated her reaction, thinking that their affair meant as little to her as it did to him.

Her eyes brightened. 'Will you?'

'Yeah – yeah, sure I will.'

'When?'

'I don't know. Soon as I can.'

'Promise?'

'Oh for God's sake! I *said* so, didn't I?' He was uneasy and on edge. For Christ's sake! If there was one thing he despised it was a woman who didn't know when to say goodbye. He had enough problems without a clinging woman.

His plans had had to be rescheduled. His mother had only just signed the papers, handing King's over to him and he'd have preferred to have waited a few weeks for the dust to settle before going to the bank for a loan. What he hadn't bargained for was the phone call.

It had come on Sunday evening just as he was going to bed. He'd been passing the telephone in the hall when it rang and he had picked it up without thinking.

'Hello. Cedar Lodge.'

'Larry Hill?'

The blood turned to ice in his veins. He'd covered his tracks so carefully and he could have sworn no one knew he was here.

229

'Who is this?' he asked quietly.

'I'm calling for Max Leyton.'

Laurence's heart almost stopped. 'There's no one here of that name,' he said abruptly.

The voice at the other end of the line laughed softly. 'Nice try. Perhaps I should be asking for Laurence King. I heard he lost his memory. Sad, isn't it.'

Laurence paused, his mouth suddenly dry with fear. 'You must have the wrong number.'

'Don't hang up! Just listen.' The voice was harder now, with an edge like a razor. 'Have it your way – for now. But if you happen to run into Larry Hill, give him this message, will you? Tell him we know where he is and if he doesn't settle his debts by the end of this week someone will be along to collect in person.'

Laurence was in no doubt that the caller knew perfectly well who he was speaking to. Also that it was no idle threat he was making.

'If I don't hear I'll ring you again in a few days' time.' The caller hung up.

He hadn't slept a wink and first thing this morning he was outside the bank at ten o'clock, waiting for it to open. His first setback was finding out that Harold Barker, an old friend of his father was still manager. He'd been hoping the old fool would have been replaced by some new bloke who didn't know the family at all. Barker looked surprised by his request.

'A loan, Mr King? As far as I can tell King's finances are in pretty good shape. Why do you need to borrow?'

'We're planning to expand,' Laurence told him. 'And to do so we'll need to buy more land.'

'Is the land in question available?' Barker asked.

Laurence was ready for this question. 'I believe so,' he said. 'The land at the rear of the building is for sale and I understand that a local builder is applying for planning permission to build six houses on it. It seems doubtful that permission will be granted, though, because the access would be partly through our premises.'

'Seems you hold the trump card then, Mr King.'

'Yes.'

'As I'm sure you know, Mr King, the bank needs to be assured that this expansion would be profitable.'

'But you know King's.'

'I'm sure it need not be a problem,' Barker said mildly. 'I would need to see some kind of business projection. Figures, prospective orders and the names of new customers. That kind of thing.'

Laurence cringed inwardly. It was going to be more difficult than he'd thought. 'Perhaps a better idea would be to mortgage Cedar Lodge,' he suggested.

Barker's eyebrows rose. 'I suppose that is a feasible alternative.' He picked up a pencil and made some notes on a pad. 'Though of course your mother still hold the deeds so we would need her permission.'

'Is that absolutely necessary?'

'I'm afraid so.'

Laurence's face fell. 'But – I was hoping to have cash transferred to King's account by the morning.'

Barker looked faintly amused. 'That's rather naïve of you, if you don't mind me saying so, Mr King. Large sums of money are not lent without thorough scrutiny.'

'But surely . . .'

'The rules are for everyone,' Barker said. 'I am sure that the vendors of the land in question can wait a few days for your offer.'

'So how long *will* it take?' Laurence asked, struggling to keep his temper.

Barker shrugged. 'You can come in – let's see – around the middle of next week,' he said. 'Or if I hear anything before then I'll telephone you at the office.'

'No. Don't do that,' Laurence said quickly. 'I'll come in.' He walked to the door.

'Good morning, Mr King,' Barker said politely.

Now he was in trouble. He had to have some cash – and soon. As he was getting into the car a possible solution hit him. He'd sell it. What he'd get would not be enough, but it might sweeten Leyton enough to buy him some time. He drove straight round to a dealer he knew would pay him in cash, no questions asked.

The price the man offered was ludicrous. Far less than the car was worth. Used cars, especially almost new ones, were in demand and fetching high prices, but the dealer had taken one look at Laurence and known instinctively that he was desperate. He made his offer and Laurence was obliged to take it. He needed the money now – today. He fumed with frustration. If only he could slip away down to Folkstone and on to a ferry, but that was out. There were red-caps at every port these days. He accepted, promising to deliver the car that evening.

As he saw it, he had two options. He could offer Leyton what money he had and hope for the best. Or he could go into hiding again. If only he knew who had shopped him to Leyton. Someone here in Queensgrove knew where he was. It was a disturbing thought.

In spite of Rachel's wheedling he dressed hurriedly and left, anxious not to pursue the question of taking her with him any further. When he had gone she wandered around the house, distraught. Laurence was the only man she had ever truly loved. And now he was leaving. She knew he would not be back, and if she didn't go with him she would never see him again. There had to be something she could do.

The idea of going to Jane Linford was one of sheer despera- tion. There was no one else. Besides, Jane would not judge her. She had had a lover once, hadn't she? She made up her mind and went next door.

'Rachel! How nice.' Seeing Rachel's agitated state Jane drew her inside. 'What's wrong dear?'

'It's Laurence,' Rachel blurted. 'He's leaving. Oh, Jane. I don't know what to do.'

Jane took her hand and led her gently to the living-room. 'You just sit there while I get you a cup of tea.'

'I don't want any tea!' Rachel said. 'I want Laurence!'

Jane cleared her throat. 'Why is he leaving?' she asked.

Rachel shook her head. 'I expect he feels it's wrong for us to be together. Because I'm married to John. But it's *not*! It should always have been Laurence and me. I love him.'

Jane sighed. 'Rachel. Listen dear. There's something I need to tell you. You being with Laurence isn't right. Nor with John either. You shouldn't really be with either of them.'

'Why?' Rachel frowned impatiently. 'What are you talking about?'

'I've been trying so hard to think of a way to tell you,' Jane said. 'The fact is – you are my daughter.' Rachel stared at her blankly. Jane went on, 'Don't you see? You are the baby I gave up for adoption.'

232

'I can't be.' Rachel shook her head. 'Anyway what does that have to do with anything?'

'It has everything. You see, my – my lover – your father – was Albert King. John and Laurence's father. That makes you their . . .'

'*No!*' Rachel was on her feet. This was the last thing she wanted to hear. 'It's not true!' she shouted. 'I don't believe you.'

'It *is*, Rachel. There are too many coincidences for it not to be.'

But Rachel had no intention of waiting to hear more. She was out of the house and in through her own front door, locking it behind her. If that crazy old woman started telling people what she'd just told her it would be the finish of her. She'd be ruined – out on the street. Even her parents would not take her back once they knew this. A thought struck her. Had they always known? Had they allowed her to marry John to get her off their hands – all the time – knowing. . . ?

She paced up and down, racking her brain for a solution. No one must ever know. If only Laurence would take her with him. But he wouldn't. She'd tried hard enough. There was no way she could make him.

Or was there? Suddenly she stopped pacing, remembering what Peter had told her. If he was right there was a way. Without meaning to, Peter had armed her with just the power she needed.

It was already dusk when she arrived at Carson's garage. It was a down-at-heel place in a rough area down by the river. Some people said that Jim Carson dealt in stolen cars, took the plates off crashed ones and changed them. So far no one had ever proved it but everyone knew he sailed close to the outer fringes of the law.

Rachel could see Laurence's grey Vauxhall parked on the fore-court and knew he must be inside, collecting his money. She waited, hiding herself as best she could in the shadow of the petrol pumps.

It was about five minutes before he emerged from the hut Carson used as an office. She waited until he was level with her, then stepped out.

'Larry.'

He started. 'My God! You gave me a fright. What the hell are you doing here?'

'I'm coming with you,' she told him firmly.

'No, you're not. I've told you.'

'I know about you, Larry,' she said quietly. 'I know you owe money. That's why you came back, isn't it? To get round your mother. I know the story about losing your memory was a lie too.' She smiled at him defiantly. 'You can't afford to leave me behind, Larry. If you do I'll see that you're arrested the minute you step off the train.' It was sheer bluff but she could see that it had found its mark.

For a long moment he stared at her, then he grasped her arm and hurried her away from the prying eyes of Jim Carson. In a little café a few doors along he pushed her into a seat near the window and went to collect two coffees. When he came back his face was bleak.

'Who's been filling your head with all this junk?' he asked.

She shook her head. 'Never you mind. It's true, isn't it, Larry?'

'Why should I tell you anything?'

'I'd never tell. I don't care what you've done – just as long as I can come with you.'

'And if I say no?'

'I'll go straight to the police. I mean it, Larry. I'll tell your mother too.' She smiled. 'I'd enjoy seeing the look on her face when she heard the truth about her precious boy.'

He looked at her with grudging admiration. 'You bloody well would too, wouldn't you?'

'Put it to the test if you want,' she challenged. 'I wouldn't advise it though.' She opened the hold-all she'd brought with her. 'I've got something for you.' She dangled a bunch of keys in front of him. 'Spare keys to John's Rover,' she explained. 'And the keys to the garage at the factory where he keeps it. He always walks home so all we have to do is wait till he leaves at half-five.' She looked at her watch. 'That's in about twenty minutes.'

His eyes brightened. 'You said something about some money this afternoon.'

She smiled and patted the bag. 'In here. I'm packed and ready to go. So what do you reckon, Larry? Are we on?'

He downed the last of his coffee and pulled a face. 'Doesn't look as though I've got much choice, does it?'

When the telephone rang at Cedar Lodge just before dinner that evening it was Clarice who answered it. She was used to the instrument by now.

'Hello! Cedar Lodge!' She shouted.

'Clarice, it's John. Is Rachel there?'

Clarice frowned. Why should he think that his wife was here? She never came to Cedar Lodge unless she was forced.

'No,' she said. 'Isn't she at home?'

There was a pause, then John said, 'No. I went home to find the house empty. There must be a perfectly simple explanation. I just thought I'd ask.'

'Well, if she does turn up I'll tell her you were asking,' Clarice said. 'I'll get her to ring you. Are you at home?'

'No. I'm ringing from the office. I thought I might as well come back and do some work.' There was a pause, then John said, 'Clarice. . . ?'

'Yes, Mr John.'

'Do you know if Peter has taken the car?'

'My Peter? Why would he do that?'

'I asked him to have a look at it for me this morning and he said he would. It isn't in the garage here at the factory where I keep it and I thought he might have taken it to the place where he used to work – to use their inspection pit, maybe.'

'Oh, I see. Well I suppose he might have. Tell you what, Mr John, I'll pop across the road as soon as I've served dinner and ask him to give you a call. Though I'm sure he wouldn't take it away without asking you first.'

'That's what I thought. But if you could just make sure.'

Clarice put down the receiver thoughtfully. They'd been waiting dinner this half-hour because Mr Laurence hadn't come in. Odd that he should be missing too. Putting her head round the drawing-room door she said, 'That was Mr John, madam. He's a bit worried because his car is missing, but we reckon that my Peter might have taken it to repair. Is it all right if I pop over the road to ask if he's got it?'

Theresa looked at her watch. 'No sign of Mr Laurence yet?'

'No, madam.'

'Then you had better start serving dinner. It will be ruined at this rate. Really, it's most inconsiderate of him not to telephone

235

when he's going to be late.'

'Yes, madam. I'll bring in your soup now. Then can I go and ask Peter about the car?'

'Yes, yes. Do what you have to,' Theresa said abstractedly.

Peter had not taken the car. He was concerned about it though.

'John asked me to go round to the factory and have a look at it,' he told his grandmother. 'I told him right off not to drive it. I could see at a glance that the brake cable was almost worn through. I've been trying to get a new one for him but they're not easy to find. I did track one down in the end and I was going to fit it for him tomorrow. But now you say the car is missing?'

'Yes. Mr John says it's not there. You're sure you put it back in the right garage?'

'Of course I did.' He frowned. 'This is serious. If someone has borrowed it without asking they could be in for a nasty surprise!'

Theresa was asleep when a loud knocking on the front door awakened her. Clarice had heard it too and the two women almost collided on the landing.

'What time is it?' Theresa asked sleepily.

'It's three o'clock,' Clarice told her. 'Who can it be at this hour?'

The knocking came again, accompanied by the doorbell ringing as though someone was leaning on it.

'I expect it's Mr Laurence. He'll have forgotten his key again.' Theresa said. 'Will you go down and let him in, Clarice? I'm going back to bed. I'll speak to him in the morning.'

Tutting loudly Clarice hurried down the stairs. 'I'll give him a piece of my mind too while I'm at it!' she muttered under her breath.

In the hall she opened the door an inch.

'I'm sure there's no need to make all that noise!' she said. 'Enough to wake the dead!'

'Mrs King?'

The voice was not Laurence's and as Clarice peered through the darkness she was startled to see a policeman standing there.

'No. Mrs King's in bed. I'm her housekeeper.'

'Could you waken her, please? It's urgent'

Clarice's heart quickened. 'Whatever's wrong?' she asked as he stepped inside. 'Is it bad news?'

The policeman's face was grave but uncommunicative as he removed his helmet. 'If you wouldn't mind fetching Mrs King.'

In the drawing-room a pale-faced Theresa faced the policeman. 'What can I do for you, officer?' She looked at Clarice. 'Would you mind making us some tea?'

The man cleared his throat. 'It might be better if your house-keeper stayed for the moment, Mrs King.'

Theresa shook her head. 'What is it you've come to tell me?'

'Can you tell, me, madam, if your son is the owner of a Rover car, registration number NV 144?'

'Yes, that's the number of John's car.'

The policeman took a deep breath. 'In that case I'm very sorry to have to tell you that there has been an accident. Your son and his wife ran off the road in their car late last night.'

Theresa reached for the back of a chair and swayed dizzily. '*John*. Oh my God. What happened?'

'It seems the car failed to negotiate a bend in the road. It rolled down an incline, overturned and hit a tree.'

'Where is he?' Theresa was heading for the door, but the police-man reached out a hand to stop her. 'I'm afraid there was nothing anyone could do for them, Mrs King. They must both have died instantly.'

Theresa let out a strangled sob and Clarice's arm went out instinctively to help her to a chair. It was terrible news, but in the confused traumatic moments that followed Clarice remembered the telephone conversation she had had earlier with John and she knew for certain that Rachel's companion and the car's driver must have been Laurence.

CHAPTER EIGHTEEN

O NCE THE POLICEMAN HAD left, a hurried call from Clarice to Picardy Terrace brought John quickly to Cedar Lodge. When Theresa saw that he was alive and well her relief was almost overwhelming, but she was still upset and John was concerned enough to send for the doctor. He came and gave her a sedative for the shock.

Once Clarice had seen her safely to bed she made tea for herself and John and they sat facing each other at the kitchen table. From his grey face and crumpled clothes she guessed he had not been to bed.

'I'm really sorry, Mr John,' she said. 'About your brother and Rachel. It's a terrible thing to have happened. I hope I did the right thing in phoning you before I said anything to that policeman.'

'Of course you did. Don't worry, I'll go along to the police station in the morning and try to get the whole wretched business sorted out.' He sighed. 'Ever since Laurence came home there's been trouble. It's as though he was determined to wreck all our lives. He had Mother wrapped round his little finger, and as for Rachel . . .' He sighed wearily. 'You knew they'd been seeing each other?'

'I had my suspicions.'

'It wasn't hard to guess what was going on,' he said. 'Rachel made little effort to conceal it. There didn't seem to be anything I could do about it.' He looked at her resignedly. 'To be perfectly frank, Clarice, I was past caring, although if I'd known it would end as disastrously as this . . .'

'I think there's something I should tell you about your brother,' Clarice said. 'My Peter has been spending his leaves working for a man who owns a club in London. He says he's seen Mr Laurence there lots of times over the past eighteen months. He was gambling heavily and owed a lot of money. Those kind of people can get nasty with those who don't pay up.'

John nodded. 'Obviously that was his only reason for coming home – to get money out of Mother to pay his gambling debts.' He looked at her. 'Between you and me, Clarice, I had a call from the bank manager a couple of days ago. Laurence had been trying to raise a loan. He'd even suggested mortgaging Cedar Lodge. The manager is an old friend of Father's and he called to warn me.'

'And why was he driving your car?' Clarice asked. 'When he had one of his own.'

'Of course!' John suddenly saw why. 'When the bank refused to advance him any money he'd have to sell it. And Rachel knew where to lay her hands on a spare set of keys to my car. That's why Laurence had to take her. She made sure of it.' He looked at Clarice. 'I'll tell the police that Laurence and Rachel were running away together and maybe they'll leave it at that. It'll save Mother any more anguish. Anything that's passed between us tonight is between you and me, Clarice.'

'You needn't worry, Mr John,' Clarice said firmly. 'Wild horses wouldn't drag anything out of me.'

By morning the whole of King's Walk had heard about the tragedy. In the shop Phyllis Ladgrove had heard so many different accounts of it by nine o'clock that she hardly knew which one to believe.

At Number Twelve, Mary Sands wept over the breakfast table. 'She was such a dear little baby. If only we hadn't quarrelled with her,' she said, dabbing her eyes. 'Now we'll never have the chance of making it right again.'

Herbert sat eating his porridge, the newspaper propped up against the marmalade as though nothing had happened.

'She had bad in her,' he said. 'Running away with her brother-in-law! God knows I tried to knock it out of her but I always knew she'd come to a bad end one day. Like mother, like daughter.'

Hot colour flooded Mary's face and she turned on him in a

239

sudden rage. 'How *dare* you say such a thing! Most women are what men make of them. You always want to twist and change us until you've made us into *nothing* creatures! You were always too hard on that girl!'

Herbert rose and threw down his napkin, his pale eyes glinting dangerously behind his glasses. 'You are upset, Mary, so I will make allowances,' he said.

He walked into the hall and up the stairs, his back ramrod-straight. But Mary's blood was up. For the first time in thirty years she'd found the courage to speak her mind. She ran after him, almost tripping over the carpet in her haste.

'All this is *your* fault, Herbert Sands!' she shouted up the stairs. 'If she was wicked, then you made her wicked, and shame on you for it!'

'Be quiet, woman,' Herbert thundered, turning to glare down at her. 'Do you want the whole street to hear your mad ramblings?'

'I don't care who hears me! The Bible says he who is without sin shall cast the first stone. Are *you* without sin?' She gave a dry bark of laughter. 'Huh! We both know the answer to *that*, don't we? All these years you made that girl pay for your sins. You denied her all the little things every child has a right to. You wouldn't let me cuddle her – wouldn't even let me read her a bedtime story. You took her in and then you made her pay for it – made me pay too just for wanting to love her. You're a swine, Herbert Sands!' Her voice rose to a shrill crescendo. 'A cruel, vicious, hypocritical *swine*!'

Herbert reached the foot of the stairs in seconds and struck his wife two stinging blows on either side of her face. Gasping, she collapsed on the bottom stair in a welter of angry tears as he slammed out of the front door.

At the police station John asked for the sergeant in charge of the accident.

'I am John King,' he explained. 'It was my brother, Laurence, who was driving my car when it crashed last night. He was with my wife.'

'I see, sir. So you're saying that you gave your brother permission to use the car?'

'No.' John gritted his teeth. 'I'm saying that he and my wife were running away together. I was told earlier yesterday by a mechanic that the car wasn't roadworthy.'

'And you didn't know that your wife was planning to leave you?'

'Of course not.' John looked at the policeman. 'And I certainly did not know they were planning to take my car. It seems my brother sold his own car yesterday.'

'I see.' The policeman made a note on his pad.

'I'd be grateful if this information could be kept out of the newspapers,' John said.

'I'll do my best, sir.' The man took a deep breath and looked at John speculatively. 'If you'll forgive me, sir, I think there was rather more to your brother's sudden departure than elopement,' he said. 'I should tell you that we have been informed by the Military Police that he was a deserter. They've been looking for him for some time and they'd recently received information that he was here in Queensgrove. You were unaware of this?'

John shook his head. 'All I know is that he arrived home suddenly a few weeks ago. My parents were informed that he was missing, believed killed in '44. The story he gave us was that he'd been wounded and had been suffering from amnesia ever since.'

'And you believed him?'

'We had no reason not to,' John said. 'And my mother was naturally overjoyed to have him home safe and well.'

The man nodded. 'I understand. I'm afraid that we shall have to ask you to identify the bodies, sir. They are being brought back to Queensgrove this morning.'

John nodded resignedly. 'Of course.'

'Meantime I shall inform the coroner. There will be an inquest of course. After that they can be released for burial.'

John walked out of the police station with a heavy heart, wondering how many more ordeals he must suffer. The policeman had been kind but impersonal. He realized that they must deal with incidents of this kind every day, but to him it felt like a living nightmare. And it wasn't over yet. He still had to tell his mother the full extent of Laurence's betrayal.

Clarice let Theresa sleep until eleven o'clock. Then she made a pot of strong tea and carried the tray up to her bedroom.

'I thought you might be ready for some elevenses, madam,' she said, setting down the tray.'

Theresa smiled drowsily. 'You always were one for your

elevenses, Clarice,' she said. 'I hope you've brought two cups as usual.'

Clarice smiled. 'Of course, madam. I've made you some toast too. And there's honey or marmalade if you fancy it.'

'I don't think I could eat anything.'

'Yes you can,' Clarice said firmly, spreading marmalade on a slice of toast. 'You'll feel better with something inside you.'

When Theresa had drunk a cup of tea and nibbled at the toast the colour began to return to her cheeks. Clarice waited for her to mention the accident and when she didn't she decided that she must broach the subject herself.

'Mr John has gone to the police station,' she said. 'He said he'd come back to see you later.'

Theresa's eyes clouded. 'When I first woke up I thought it was all a bad dream.' She sighed. 'Such a terrible thing to happen. Why did Laurence leave like that, without a word to anyone? And why did he have to take John's wife with him?'

'I daresay Mr John will have some answers for you when he comes back,' Clarice said.

Theresa sighed. 'Laurence was always my favourite,' she confessed. 'He was such a lovely child – always laughing and getting into mischief. One couldn't help but love him however naughty he was. I spoiled him dreadfully. He reminded me so much of my dear brother.'

'I know. I was the same with my Peter,' Clarice said. 'He was a lovely kiddie too with his red hair and freckles. My Dennis all over again, bless him. I reckon I spoiled him a bit too, because of his mother going off and leaving him. There was always something defenceless about him.' She smiled ruefully. 'Not that he was, of course. Always had the heart of a lion, my Peter.'

'You're lucky to have him,' Theresa said wistfully. 'And he doesn't lie to you either. Does he, Clarice?' Her eyes filled with tears. 'It wasn't true, was it – all that about Laurence being wounded and lying for years in hospital?'

'I'm afraid not, madam.'

Theresa shook her head. 'He only came home because he needed money, didn't he? I expect he was in trouble. He always told fibs when he was in trouble. He used to blame John when they were children. I'm afraid John took many a smacking for nothing,

242

poor child. Laurence always had to take what was John's too,' she said reminiscently. 'He never could bear him to have anything of his own.' She hesitated, biting her trembling lip. 'I'm going to tell you something terrible now, Clarice,' she said. 'Last night, when that policeman came and told us that John had died in the accident I was devastated. My John, so loyal and hard working. It was only then that I realized how much he meant to me. When I knew he was alive all I felt was relief.' She clutched Clarice's hand. 'I was so angry with Laurence for treating us so shabbily. I felt so let down.' Theresa sighed. 'But now that I've had time to think about it I realize that it was probably me who let *him* down.'

'You mustn't think like that,' Clarice said. 'What's done is done. You can't put back the clock. You're still upset, madam. Why not try to get some more sleep now? I'll send Mr John up as soon as he gets here.'

Clarice was in the kitchen peeling potatoes for lunch when there was a tap on the back door. She opened it and was surprised to see Peter.

'I'm sorry to call on you here, Gran,' he said. 'But my leave is up tomorrow and I had to see you.'

She opened the door. 'Come in. Mrs King is asleep. We won't be disturbed. I suppose you've heard the news,' she went on. 'Is that what you wanted to talk about?'

'I just can't take it in, Gran,' he said, shaking his head. 'Rachel – *dead*. It doesn't seem possible. And I can't help this awful feeling that it's all my fault.'

'Don't talk nonsense, boy!' said Clarice sternly. 'How can it possibly be your fault?'

'I went to see her,' he explained. 'I told her all I knew about – Laurence. I wanted to warn her. But she just laughed – wouldn't believe me. She taunted me, Gran. She made me so bloody fighting mad that I went straight out and shopped him.'

'You what?' Clarice stared at him.

'Laurence King. I grassed on him.'

'How did you do that?'

'Easy. I just rang the club – told Max where Laurence could be found. Then I rang the Military Police. I reckoned if one didn't get him the other would.' He looked at Clarice. 'I wasn't to know he'd take her with him though, was I? I wasn't to know they'd pinch John's car? Then I got to thinking that if I hadn't been so sodding lazy I could have fixed it yesterday afternoon. Then Rachel would still be alive.'

He raised his eyes to look at her and her heart lurched to see that his lip was trembling and tears were coursing down his cheeks. She hadn't seen him cry since he was eight years old. In a moment she was on her feet, her arms around him, pressing his russet head against her bosom.

'Now just you listen to me,' she said gruffly. 'They were two of a kind, them two. Bad right through, both of them. Nothing would ever have made that Rachel happy. And she'd have made you as unhappy as she made poor Mr John. All this what's happened – it might seem cruel to say so, but it's for the best.' She gave him a little shake. 'You'll see that some day. Just you learn a lesson from it. Treat people right and don't do no dirty tricks. Might not make you rich and famous, but it'll bring you something that's worth far more.'

'I don't know, Gran,' he said despairingly. 'In the army they've got a saying – Do unto others before they do it to you! Sometimes I wonder what doing the right thing gets you?'

'It gets you peace and self-respect. That's what,' she told him. 'And don't you never forget it.'

A few days after the funeral of Rachel and Laurence King Jane Linford walked down King's Walk and knocked on the door of Number 12. Mary Sands opened the door and stared at her.

'Yes?'

'Mrs Sands?'

'That's right. Who are you?'

'My name is Jane Linford. I've something important to tell you. Can I come in a minute?'

'I suppose so.' Grudgingly, Mary held the door open for Jane to step into the hallway. She stood facing her, arms folded. 'What is it?'

'It concerns your daughter, Rachel.'

'Rachel is dead.'

'I know. I was at the funeral.'

'You knew her?'

'Yes. I used to live next door. I like to think we became friends.
She told me that she was adopted. The fact is, Mrs Sands. I believe
– that I am Rachel's mother. And I wanted you to know that you
are not alone in your bereavement.'

Mary gave a snort of derision. 'That's rubbish!' she said
abruptly.

'No. It's true. I had a baby girl, you see. It was after I was
widowed and the father was married so I couldn't keep her. I
always knew she was here in Queensgrove somewhere. When
Rachel and I talked everything coincided. Her date of birth – her
looks and colouring. I'm *sure* Rachel was mine.'

'She couldn't have been,' Mary said.

Jane frowned. 'How can you be so sure. Do you know whose
child she was?'

'Yes.' Mary stared straight at her with a look of something close
to triumph in her eyes. 'Rachel was my husband's child,' she said.
'He seduced a young parishioner; a girl of fifteen. To hush things
up he offered to pay the parents and adopt the baby. I couldn't have
any of my own, you see. I was happy until I saw the way it was
going to be. He made both our lives a misery. He punished us both.
Me for not being able to have a child of my own, Rachel for being
born – just as though the whole sorry business was her fault. All
the time she was growing up he taunted her with what he said was
her mother's sin – told her she was born with bad in her – until
eventually the poor child believed him.'

Jane stepped back, shocked by the facts she was hearing. The
woman's bitterness was like a red-hot flame. 'Should you be telling
me all this?'

'Why not? I don't care who knows.'

'But – your husband. . . ?'

'He's gone,' Mary said shortly. 'Rachel's death was the last straw.
I told him that if he didn't go I'd tell everyone about him. I'll be
gone soon too. I've volunteered for church work. I'm going abroad
to be a missionary. I'm sure that even wild savages can't be as evil
and devious as some so-called civilized people.'

Jane was edging towards the door. 'You can rest assured that I
will tell no one what you've told me today,' she said.

Mary shrugged. 'I don't care who you tell. Shout it from the
rooftops if you like. I won't be here to hear it anyway. For the first

time in my life I'll be free to speak and do as I please and I'm never going to live a lie again.'

Jane stepped out through the Sands' front door and hurried down the road, her mind spinning. She crossed the road and went into the park. She found a quiet bench and sat down. So Rachel hadn't been her child after all? In a way it was a relief. It meant that her daughter, wherever she was, was still alive. On the other hand she knew now with a saddening certainty that she would never find her. As for Rachel, her heart went out to the girl. We're all what life makes of us, she told herself. And if what she had just heard was true Rachel had paid the ultimate price.

She sat for a while, until she began to shiver with cold, then she got up and made her way back to King's Walk. As she passed the rear entrance of Cedar Lodge she paused, wondering if she dared call in to see her friend Clarice. It would be such a relief to talk to someone. Creeping in through the tradesman's entrance she knocked on the back door.

Clarice was pleased to see her friend. It was some time since they'd last met. She assured Jane that Theresa was out at the solicitor's and not due back for some time. She put the kettle on and pulled a chair up close to the Aga for Jane to warm herself.

She listened with fascination to the tale Mary Sands had unfolded.

'Never did like that Herbert Sands,' she commented. 'His eyes are too close together.' She frowned. 'But how did you know they were Rachel's parents?'

'From the announcement in the paper,' Jane explained. 'It said, *daughter of Reverend and Mrs Herbert Sands of King's Walk.* I made up my mind then that I'd go and see them.' She took out her handkerchief again. 'If I'd known what I was going to hear I'd have left it alone.'

Clarice comforted her friend as best she could, then put on her coat and walked to the end of the road with her. Walking back alone, she mulled over what Jane had told her. Poor Jane. She had grieved for Rachel only to learn that she was not, after all, the daughter she had given away. Clarice knew just how it felt to grieve for a lost child – in her case a great-grandchild – that she was unable to claim as her own flesh and blood.

★

The shocking accident that had killed Rachel and Laurence was quickly submerged in people's minds as excitement over the royal wedding mounted. Most of the residents of King's Walk listened to the ceremony on their wireless sets. Phyllis Ladgrove even closed the shop for a couple of hours on the morning of 20 November so that she and Pauline could listen, sighing over the descriptions of the dresses and thrilling to the cheering of the crowds and the exciting rattle and clatter of carriages. If you closed your eyes you could almost see it all.

Christmas was a subdued affair that year in King's Walk. Cathy came home on a flying visit and was regaled with all the news. She was deeply shocked at the news of the accident and wished there were some way she could convey her sympathy to John and his mother. In the end she bought a card and sent it to John at the factory.

She had her old bedroom at the flat over the shop to herself this time. Pauline now had a little flat of her own. It was only two rooms, but, as she told Cathy, it wasn't fair to their parents for her to stay on at the shop with the twins growing bigger and noisier every day.

'Another year or so and they'll be going to school,' she said. 'Then maybe I'll go back to work. Mum and Dad are talking of selling the shop next year. There's a rumour that King's will be selling off the houses in King's Walk and I know Dad has his heart set on buying Number Four and moving back in. Now that his war pension has come through he and Mum could just about manage it.' She looked at Cathy. 'What about you? What will you do when you get your diploma? Can't be long now.'

'I take my final exam in May,' Cathy told her. 'Then I'll be looking for a job.'

'Will you come back here?'

Cathy shook her head. 'Too many memories.'

'You must miss Harry,' Pauline said.

Cathy was silent for a moment, then she looked up at her sister. 'I do miss him,' she said. 'In so many ways. He was my best friend and the best companion I could have had. There'll never be anyone quite like him.' She sighed. 'But I can't help feeling that I failed him.'

'Failed him? In what way?'

'For one thing, Harry wanted a child,' Cathy said. 'I insisted we must wait.'

'Well, that was sensible, seeing that you hadn't finished your course.'

'But that was only part of the reason,' Cathy said. 'I didn't love him as much as he deserved, Pauline.' Her eyes filled with tears. 'It haunts me. I'll never forgive myself.'

Pauline put her arms around her. 'You loved Harry in the only way you could,' she said gently. 'He was happy, Cath. Anyone could see that. You were the one he wanted and you made him very happy for the short time you had together. Just cling to that.'

Cathy dashed away her tears. 'I keep telling myself that, but the feeling just won't go away.'

She was in town the following day when she ran into her old friend and teacher, Jean Tanner. Eager to catch up on each other's news they went into a café for a cup of coffee. Cathy was delighted to hear that Jean was soon to marry again. Her husband, a young RAF pilot, had been killed in the Battle of Britain and she had always declared since that she would remain single. Now, it seemed, things had changed.

'Ken is older than me,' she told Cathy. 'Twenty years older in fact. He's a widower from London. His wife was killed in the blitz and he's been lonely since – like me. He's a talented artist and we met through the local art club. We get along so well that it seems silly not to share our lives.'

Cathy smiled. 'I'm really pleased for you.'

'What about you?' Jean asked. 'I know it's early days, but you're so young, Cathy. Don't do what I did. Don't waste the years cling-ing to a ghost.'

Cathy shrugged. 'We'll see.'

'There's only one thing that worries me a little,' Jean said with a sigh, 'Ken wants me to give up work. You see, his father died recently and left him quite well off. He' planning to give up his job and retire early. He wants to travel and paint. It's something we've both always wanted to do.'

'But that sounds really exciting.'

'Yes. I'm looking forward to it, of course, but it'll be such a wrench, giving up school.' She stopped speaking in mid-sentence. 'You wouldn't consider applying for my job, would you?'

Cathy was taken aback. 'Well. . . .'

'I'd give you a good testimonial. And I'm sure you'd stand a good chance as an old girl. Oh, please think about it, Cathy,' Jean said. 'I'd like to think of one of my ex-pupils taking over from me. It would give it a feeling of continuity.'

Cathy laughed. 'Thanks for your confidence in me, Jean. Yes, I'll certainly think about it.'

The only bit of excitement to happen over the festive season was the birth of Dennis and Sylvia Harvey's baby daughter who was born on New Year's Day.

Clarice was proud and pleased. To her the baby was a cherished reward, making up for the stillborn great-grandchild born to Rachel. She visited Sylvia and the baby in hospital and came home bursting with all the details which she conveyed to Theresa.

'Seven and a half pounds,' she exclaimed. 'And the bluest eyes you ever saw. Red hair just like Peter's, only Sylvia calls it auburn. She's going to be called Denise after her dad. A proper little smasher. And the first baby to be born in King's Walk since the end of the war. That's a good omen, isn't it, madam?'

Theresa nodded. 'I'm sure you're right, Clarice.'

She was worried about John. Since the accident that had taken his wife and brother he had been so quiet and subdued. Refusing to move back into Cedar Lodge, he had remained at Picardy Terrace. Unfortunately some of Laurence's exploits had got into the papers and consequently business at King's had fallen off. It was still close enough to the war for people to resent those they saw as traitors and John had inherited the stigma of his brother's desertion.

Each morning he went to work and every evening he came home, ate supper and worked on the books until bedtime. Clarice went round once a week, cleaned the little house through and did his washing. She usually made him a casserole and an apple pie too while she was there so that he had what she called 'something to go at' during the week. But she often found that he'd eaten only half of them when she returned the following week.

In Bournemouth Cathy worked hard. Winter melted into spring and the pressure increased as exam time drew near. At Penrith

Avenue the Sunday-morning parties carried on as usual, but Cathy mostly stayed in her room, working. Without Harry parties seemed like a mockery.

At last it was May and the week of the exams. Cathy sat each section, suddenly fearful for the future. Suppose she failed and had to stay on and re-take? She had already applied for Jean's post at Queensgrove Grammar School. At first she had been reluctant. Going home seemed like taking a backward step in her life. But the more she thought about teaching at her old school, the more the idea appealed to her. At Christmas she had realized how much of her family life she was missing too. Now that Harry was gone there was nothing for her in Bournemouth any more.

Once the exams were over Cathy felt as though she had been cut loose. Suddenly there was nothing to do. It would be weeks before the results came through. She thought about asking if there was any temporary work at the Marine Bay Hotel, then one morning she received a letter from the headmistress of Queensgrove Grammar School, inviting her to attend for an interview the following week. It was then that Cathy made up her mind. She would go home to Queensgrove for good. Her exam results could be sent on to her. Suddenly she had had enough as she told Paul Samuels in his office the following day.

'I'm homesick,' she said. 'I never expected to feel like this but at the moment all I want is to go home.'

'The past months must have been a terrible strain for you,' he said, 'losing Harry in the middle of your final year. Maybe a spell at home with your family is what you need to heal all the pain. I'm sure you'll do well and get a good diploma, but even if you don't we'll talk about it later, all right?'

Cathy packed and said a tearful goodbye to Faith and Mike Flynn, promising to keep in touch. The following morning she caught the train for Queensgrove.

It was the first week in June and already very warm. Cathy sat in the familiar corridor at Queensgrove Grammar School with the other candidates, awaiting her interview. As she sat there inhaling the familiar amalgam of smells she tried to separate and analyse them; chalk and beeswax; books, ink and cedar-wood pencils. It took her back to her schooldays. A time of daydreams, wishes and hopes. How sweet and easy life had been then.

Suddenly her name was called. It was her turn.

On the other side of the desk in the head's study were Miss Harrington, the head, Mrs Ray the deputy head and Jack Maybury, a local solicitor and chairman of governors. Miss Harrington smiled as Cathy sat down.

'How nice to see you again, Catherine,' she said. 'Let me put you at ease by telling you that Mrs Tanner has given you an excellent testimonial and so has your college tutor, Mr Samuels. He seems to think that the result of your diploma exam is very much a foregone conclusion.'

She was questioned closely by all three interviewers and almost before she had time to think about it, the ordeal was over and she was outside again.

At home her father asked her about it but all she could say was that she didn't really know. 'Some of the others have already got their diploma,' she said. 'One even had a degree. And they'd all had experience in other teaching posts. I don't really think I have an earthly.'

He smiled at her. 'Whatever happens love, it's going to be good to have you back at home again. I know how hard my girl has worked,' he said. 'You deserve to get that job.'

But we don't all get what we deserve, Cathy wanted to say, but she just smiled instead.

Pauline was looking tired. She'd had a bad bout of flu late in the winter and Cathy thought she seemed very run down.

'Why don't you take the boys away to the seaside for a week?' she suggested a few days after her interview. 'I'll take over from you in the shop while you're away. It'll take my mind off this awful waiting,' she added. 'And it'll be nice to see all the old customers again.'

Pauline argued at first, but once the boys had heard the word 'seaside' they gave her no peace until she agreed.

Late one afternoon, a few days later, the telephone rang. Cathy answered it to find Miss Harrington at the other end of the line.

'I'm ringing with some news, Catherine,' she said. 'You'll be getting a formal letter from me, but I wanted you to know right away that the job of arts teacher is yours. The appointment

251

depends on you getting your diploma of course, but I don't think there's much doubt about that. Details about salary and so on are in the letter. I'm looking forward very much to having you on the staff.'

Cathy swallowed hard. 'Thank you, Miss Harrington.'

'Not at all. Good luck and congratulations.'

It had been quiet in the shop all afternoon and Cathy had urged her mother to make a much needed appointment at the hair-dresser's. Her heart beating fast she ran upstairs to tell her father the news, only returning when she heard the shop bell ring down-stairs.

As she ran down the stairs she called out, 'Just coming!' Then she opened the door into the shop and came face to face with John.

'*Cathy*!' He was as startled as she. 'I had no idea you were home.'

'I've been home a couple of weeks now,' she said. There was a silence until she added, 'Sorry – what can I get you?'

'Oh. It's Mother's birthday and I'm on my way to have tea with her. I wondered – have you got a box of chocolates?'

'I think there are a couple left over from Easter,' Cathy said. 'They take so much of the sweet ration that there isn't much call for them.'

He smiled. 'I never use all my coupons. Rachel used to . . .' He stopped, looking at her uncertainly.

'I was so sorry to hear about the accident,' Cathy said. 'Your brother Laurence, too.'

'Thank you. It was . . .' He lifted his shoulders inadequately.

She found the chocolates and showed them to him.

'Would you like me to wrap them for you?'

'Thanks.' He was still looking at her. 'How are you, Cathy?'

'I'm all right, thank you.'

'Are you staying long?'

'It seems I'll be here for good. I've been offered a job at the grammar school.'

'I see. Congratulations.'

'There's nothing to keep me in Bournemouth now.'

'No. I heard about your husband,' he said. 'Your mother told Clarice Harvey and . . .' He smiled ruefully. 'You know how news travels in King's Walk. It must have been a terrible shock.'

'Yes,' she said without meeting his eyes. She passed the wrapped chocolates across the counter and took his money and coupons. 'If you can believe what you read in the newspapers we'll soon be dispensing with these,' she said lightly. 'Who would ever have thought that rationing would last this long after the ...'

'Cathy – could we meet some time?'

She looked up at him. 'Oh, I – don't know.'

'Please say yes. There's so much I want to tell you.'

She was searching her mind for a reason to refuse but the look in his eyes stopped her. 'All right,' she said quietly.

'We could drive somewhere – have a drink?'

'If you like.'

'I managed to get another car,' he went on unnecessarily. 'It's second hand, of course. A '39 Hillman. But it had a low mileage ...' He looked at her. 'When, Cathy?'

She shrugged. 'I don't know.'

'Is this evening too soon? I'm having tea with Mother but I could pick you up later.'

'All right.'

'Half past eight. Or is that too late?'

'No. It's fine.'

When he had gone she found herself trembling. It had been such a shock, suddenly seeing him again. He looked older, the traces of what he had been through etched on his face, but basically he was the same John. Suddenly she felt her heart lift for the first time in months, but she forced down the feeling of elation. A lot had happened since she and John had been together. Nothing could ever be quite the same.

The little country pub was quiet and they sat outside in the evening sunshine with their drinks.

'Did your mother like the chocolates?' Cathy asked.

John smiled. 'They always were her weakness. It's been a bad year for her. She's looking much older suddenly. I'd like to take her away on holiday but she won't hear of it. I'm just pleased that she's got Clarice living with her.'

'It must have been terrible for her, losing Laurence after she'd thought he was safe and well.'

'I believe his betrayal upset her even more than his death,' he said. 'He lied to us about why he'd been reported missing.' He

253

looked at her. 'You must have heard. The papers got hold of the story in the end.'

'You can't believe all that you read,' Cathy said.

'In this case it was true,' John said bitterly. 'He only came home because he was in trouble and owed money. He didn't give a damn about us. If he hadn't been up to his ears in debt we'd probably never have seen him again. What made me so angry was that he could have put Mother in danger too. As it was we had to pay off his gambling debts afterwards.' He looked at her. 'Then there was Rachel of course. They were running away together.'

'I'm so sorry, John.'

'I couldn't blame her really. She wasn't happy. I don't know what she wanted but I do know that it wasn't me.' He glanced at her. 'The baby – it wasn't mine, you know.'

'John – there's no need . . .'

'Not that it couldn't have been,' he added hurriedly. 'I'm not pretending I was entirely innocent.'

She laid a hand on his arm. 'John, don't. There's no need to put yourself through all this.'

'But I want to, don't you see? I need you to know, Cathy. It's important to me.' He paused. 'When the baby was born and the doctor told me it was a premature stillbirth. I knew then that it couldn't have been mine.'

'So – whose. . . ?'

'She told me some story about being attacked in the park one night.' John shook his head. 'It was all lies, of course, but what could I do? The baby had died anyway. I suppose I had some idea that we could patch things up – make the best of a bad job, but it never worked. It was King's she wanted, the money and status that went with it. When she knew that Mother still had control of the business she quickly lost interest.' He sighed. 'Then Laurence came home.'

'And he took her from you?'

He shook his head. 'She wasn't mine to take. The odd thing is that I'm pretty sure he never meant to take her with him. She was just a little diversion and a way of getting at me. I have a feeling that she forced his hand in the end.'

'And paid a terrible price for it.' She leaned forward to touch his arm. 'I'm so sorry, John. You didn't deserve all that.'

He looked at her. 'We never loved each other. It was all exactly as I told you – that morning. Clearly she needed a husband in a hurry and picked me.' He sighed. 'It was a rebound thing for me – after you. I behaved so badly, Cathy. I was such a fool.'

'No, no. It was partly me. I was – I don't know – young, scared, naïve.' She covered his hand with hers. 'I only know how much losing you hurt.'

'Did it?' He clasped her hand, lacing his fingers through hers. 'And you've had your tragedy too. What happened, Cathy? Or would you rather not talk about it?'

She shook her head. 'Harry had a heart condition, something he was born with. I always knew about it. It was something that might never have affected him.' She lifted her shoulders. 'As it was, it killed him in his twenties – just when he'd had promotion at work and we had our first real home.' She swallowed hard. 'You never really knew Harry, but he was such a lovely person – such fun to be with. Such a wonderful friend.'

John squeezed her hand. 'People like that are hard to find. Even harder to replace.'

'There'll never be another Harry,' she said.

He looked up and met her eyes. 'No. Of course not. So – what are your plans now, Cathy?'

'Well, I'm waiting for my exam results at the moment,' she told him. 'The job I've been offered depends on that.'

She asked about the business and he told her that things had been bad for a while.

'Mother made the business over to me after Laurence was killed. I think she felt it was time I had full control. I worked really hard, but at first we lost some orders. The story about Laurence hit the press and did King's no good at all. I decided then that it was time we branched out – sink or swim – so I engaged a designer and decided to go into fashion shoes.'

'Good for you.'

He smiled. 'I've been travelling, doing the salesman bit myself to see how it would go. It's doing so well that I'll have to take on a couple of reps soon.'

'That's marvellous. And you're selling the King's Walk houses?'

'Yes. I need some extra cash for expansion. I'll probably sell the ones on Picardy Terrace too. More people want to buy their own

255

homes now. The world is changing so fast, Cathy. At long last things are looking up. We'll soon have the new National Health Service too. It's all going to make such a difference to people's lives. Suddenly I can see light at the end of the tunnel.' He saw her shiver. 'You're cold. Shall we go?'

Both were quiet on the drive home. When they reached King's Walk John stopped the car and turned to her.

'I'd like to see you again, Cathy.'

'As we live in the same town again it would be difficult not to.'

'You know what I mean.' His eyes were grave. 'I missed you terribly, Cathy,' he said. 'There hasn't been a single day when I didn't think about you and regret the mess I made of things.'

'I missed you too.' She shook her head. 'But all that is over and done with, John. It's in the past. You and I – we're different people.'

'Does that mean you want nothing to do with the past – that you want to move on – without anything to remind you?'

'It means that we can't go back,' she said. 'But it doesn't mean we couldn't try to start again.'

Her eyes were almost luminous in the dim light from the street lamps and John felt his heart contract as he bent forward to kiss her. Just at first she held back, then her lips softened beneath his and she went into his arms.

His cheek against hers, she heard him whisper, 'I've never stopped loving you, Cathy. I never will.'

And suddenly her heart was filled with joy. Suddenly she knew why she'd come home.